AT SEA

Laurie Graham

Quercus

First published in Great Britain in 2010 by Quercus
This paperback edition published in 2011 by

Quercus
21 Bloomsbury Square
London
WC1A 2NS

A CIP catalogue record for this book is available
from the British Library

ISBN 978 0 85738 135 4

10 9 8 7 6 5 4 3 2 1

Printed and bound in Great Britain by Clays Ltd, St Ives plc

d contributing
med novels,
'in. Visit
her website at www.lauriegraham.com

AT SEA

'Delicious' *Scotland on Sunday*

'Laurie Graham, what a find! I was only about three sentences into *At Sea* when I knew I was going to savour every sentence and bitterly mourn the end . . . The kind of book you stay awake far later than you should do reading, only to wake bleary eyed the next day thinking of the time when you can pick it up again' Wendy Holden

'Laurie Graham's grip on the art of subversive comedy is as masterful as ever . . . Sailing along on a tide of joie de vivre, readers will cheer for Enid as she asserts her independence' Elizabeth Buchan, *Sunday Times*

LIFE ACCORDING TO LUBKA

'Graham wraps serious questions in glorious comedy . . . This scratchy, snappy heroine, a wonderful mixture of sass and solemnity, is a diverting addition to Graham's collection of highly original adventuresses'
Sunday Times

'Hugely entertaining clash-of-cultures novel from the razor-sharp Graham . . . a sunny book for sunny days' *Daily Mail*

'It embraces you with warmth and humour and makes the world a better place' Katie Fforde

Also by Laurie Graham

The Man for the Job
The Ten O'Clock Horses
Perfect Meringues
The Dress Circle
Dog Days, Glenn Miller Nights
The Future Homemakers of America
The Unfortunates
Mr. Starlight
Gone With the Windsors
The Importance of Being Kennedy
Life According to Lubka

To Mim, for safe haven in the mother of all storms

1

Twelve hours out from Istanbul and Jesus has just served us breakfast. Bernard feels we should have been allocated a balcony suite but an inside stateroom can be quite acceptable. Actually, I find it rather snug. After all, one hardly spends much time in one's quarters, except to sleep, and with my earplugs in I heard hardly any noise from the funnel uptake.

We sailed at seven yesterday evening from the Karakoy Pier, Bernard having cut things pretty fine. He'd been over Asia-side most of the day, in Uskudar, mugging up on Florence Nightingale ready for the Jewels of the Black Sea cruise in September. I'd passed my time having a good old solitary mooch, as per. I took the Beyazit tram up to the Grand Bazaar and bought Bernard an adorable letter opener with a rooster head carved from meerschaum. I lunched on the hoof, scrummy grilled sweetcorn followed by a salep rose petal ice cream, then collected our luggage from the hotel and took a taxi to the Dolmabahce Palace where we were supposed to rendezvous. Bernard, however, failed to materialize. As I later discovered he'd decided to make a mad dash along to the Phanar to drop off a bottle of single malt for Archimandrite Stefanos.

Bernard isn't at all a spiritual person but he seems always to have gravitated towards monastics and clergy, especially those of the more exotic persuasions. I once heard it suggested, rather uncharitably I thought, that it was because he admired their vestments and hung around in the hope of picking up some cast-offs. And though it's true he does own a modest collection of antique dalmatics and birettas I can personally vouch for the fact that he never actually tries them on, even behind closed doors.

I waited and waited for him until I dared wait no more, then proceeded to the passenger terminal without him, checked in and went aboard. When Bernard dices with sailing times I find the best thing to do is to keep myself occupied. But our bags had been delivered, I'd unpacked, laid out his clothes for dinner, read and reread the safety procedures and the evening's entertainment schedule and still there was no sign of him. I was on deck, pacing back and forth, when he came careering along the waterfront in a taxi with barely half an hour to spare. He can be so naughty about time. He said they wouldn't have dared sail without him but he hadn't had the Cruise Director berating him as I had. The dreaded Gavin Iles.

'If you'll pardon my spelling, Lady Enid,' he said, 'I don't give the slightest fuck about the Cultural Enrichment Programme. If Professor Finch doesn't turn up, it'll be no skin off my nose. His lectures will be cancelled and my clients will have all the more time for on-board shopping. Parting the passenger from his money, your ladyship, that's the name of the game.'

Mr Iles is a man who has sailed around the cradle of civilization for ten cruising seasons and managed to emerge quite untouched by culture. He reduces everything to pounds, shillings and pence and is fearfully ruthless, I'm sure. Not only would he have been willing to sail without Bernard last night, I believe he would have relished doing so. Then most probably I'd have been put ashore at Izmir and one would have had to make one's own way home.

It wasn't a good start. And I'd so looked forward to standing together at the rail, watching Istanbul recede with the sun going down behind the Topkapi and the Hagia Sofia. Aside from Venice it's my favourite view in the whole world. But Bernard refused to join me. He was in a massive sulk because the stewards had insisted on his attending muster drill along with everyone else. He always says that in the event of an emergency I must simply do as he instructs me because he has photographic recall of the layout of every ship he ever sailed on and is blessed with powerful survival instincts. But we've never sailed on the *Golden Memories* before, and though one has done lifeboat drill a million times one must see the stewards' point of view. There are three thousand passengers on board and at least another thousand crew members. If anything should go wrong, one shudders to think.

So he sat very resentfully in his lifejacket with his nose in an abstract on Homeric Troy while everyone else was being terribly jolly, and then his dark mood continued when he saw the seating plan for dinner. I really don't know why. It's only the first night of many, after all, and the Junior Assistant Accommodation Director is a perfectly agreeable young man to have as one's host. We're sure to have our turn at the Captain's table later in the voyage.

Of course Bernard is better suited to the more exclusive, *serious* cruises, where the guest lecturer is treated with reverential respect, but with stocks in the doldrums and a new roof to pay for one really has to take work where one can find it. Frankly, I'm not sorry he won't be presiding over his own table every evening. He collected an uncomfortable number of acolytes on the Treasures of Croatia voyage in April and as mere Wife of Guest Lecturer I can't say that ten nights of slavish adoration are always good for a man.

I was relieved to find we were dining with a pleasant group of English passengers last evening. The next table was all American and one husband and wife were making such an exhibition of themselves. They had apparently flown from the States to Paris and then travelled on to Istanbul by the wildly expensive Orient Express train.

'No air-conditioning,' he was yelling, 'no closet space, no

4

hot tub. Matter of fact, you don't even get a shower. They expect you to shave in the same basin you pee in. You know how much I paid for that? I'll tell you how much I paid.'

So vulgar, and the wife was no better. She's one of those bosomy frights with teased hair and scarlet nails.

'Don't listen to him,' she was screeching. 'He bellyaches about the price of everything. It was worth it. It was beautiful. Fresh table linens every meal. French soap. Anyhow, he can afford it, and I love a train ride. Frankie's not so keen. He reckons he feels cooped up. But he enjoyed it when we did the Royal Canadian Pacific out from Calgary. Every day they stopped some place different so the guys could fish. There wasn't much up there in the way of shopping but they put on an auction every day. Paintings and little antique doodads. We got a numbered Chagall. I don't really like his stuff. Kinda weird if you ask me. But we put it in the downstairs john so nobody has to look at it for long.'

Bernard imitated her perfectly as we were getting ready for bed.

'"Now what I want to know is, on that Orient Express train, how'd they ever get a grand piano through the door of the bar car?"'

He's a wonderful mimic. He really could have been an actor.

I said, 'Darling, you may mock them but they're *your* people.'

He said, 'They are, and I can only apologize. Another

reminder, though God knows I don't need one, why I fled the land of the deep-fried Twinkie.'

How we laughed.

A feature of the *Golden Memories* cruises that everyone seems to be talking about is the dance contests. Every day there's something called Ballroom Boot Camp, for those who feel a little rusty and would like to improve, and there are daily demonstrations by professional dancers who are also available for private lessons. The whole thing culminates in a Grand Dance-Off on Gala Night, The Ballroom Blitz. First prize is a ten-day Oyster Line cruise for two. Bernard jested that second prize might appropriately be a seventeen-day Oyster Line cruise. All very humorous but as I pointed out, every time he gives a lecture he's going to be vying with dance fever. Today, for instance, his opening lecture, Izmir, Three Thousand Years in Forty Minutes, clashes with the Rumba Showcase. It's jolly bad luck.

Jesus says this morning's forecast is for high winds and overcast skies, which will at least bring in people who might otherwise be out on the tennis courts.

2

Bernard was magnificent, as ever. His hair was looking particularly leonine this morning and he wore his charcoal seersucker with a canary-yellow bow tie. He gave them one of his masterly sweeps through history: Greek Smyrna, now the city of Izmir, the birthplace of Homer and once a vital presence on the great trade route from Anatolia to the Aegean. Sacked by the Lydians, rebuilt under Lysimachus, cultivated by the Romans, superceded by Constantinople, razed by the Mongols.

I'm afraid it was all quite over their heads. Bernard read to them from Tertullian and what did his first questioner ask? 'Where will be the best place to buy a leather jacket?'

Upon which an elderly blonde called out, 'Oh I can answer that. We've sailed this route before. Where we dock, at the Konak Pier, there's a very good mall. They have all the labels.'

Somebody else wanted to know whether there'd be a decent beach. The same blonde said, 'No, but if you're into scuba-diving and stuff like that you can easy get a cab to Dolphinland.'

Bernard and I have a little arrangement for these lectures. If things start to go awry during question time or he has a particular reason for wanting to wind things up quickly, he takes out his pocket silk and polishes his specs. That's the signal for me to raise my hand. Which I duly did, and asked about Chios's rival claim to be the birthplace of Homer, giving him the perfect cue to say a few words about the bardic guild of the Homeridae and then turn off the microphone.

The lounge emptied very quickly except for a couple I recognized as the loud Americans from the next-door table last evening. He, short and rotund and bald. She taller, with piled-up hair and an intrusive Easter lilies' scent.

She said, 'Hey, Professor, I have to tell you a funny thing. My hubby's middle name is Homer. Francis Homer Gleeson. Isn't that wild?'

As Bernard remarked, Homer isn't so very unusual a name in the United States but the woman was determined to make something of it. One has to be very guarded the first day of a cruise. There are people who will use anything to try and forge instant familiarity. Allow them an inch and they can then become pests for the duration.

She said, 'Frankie wasn't named after your guy, of course. Know why his folks gave him Homer? You'll love this. Because the day Frankie was born his brother hit a home run for Painted Post Little League. Isn't that cute? I'm Nola Gleeson, by the way. That was a very nice talk you gave. And I just adore your tie. It really makes you look the part.

Like one of those TV professors. And we hear your wife is an English Lady! That is so exciting! We never met a Lady before.'

One is so thrown together with strangers on a cruise. The boundaries of intimacy can be hard to maintain, particularly for a man as charismatic as Bernard, and when people fail to breach his defences they'll often try to get to him through me.

He began shuffling his papers. Bernard doesn't actually need them, of course. He can talk for hours without recourse to notes. But they can be a useful prop. When people close in on you, concentrating on one's papers can send out the message that you are a busy and serious man who doesn't have time for idle chit-chat. For me it signalled that the time had come to effect a swift exit. I know my role at such moments and I certainly didn't need Bernard to remind me by stepping on my toes so brutally. I can only think it was because Mr Gleeson was staring at him so rudely. He didn't say a word. He simply stared, as though Bernard were an exhibit in a glass case.

When we got back to the cabin Bernard was in such a peevish mood.

He said, 'Why did you linger? Why did you encourage those awful people?'

But I hadn't lingered. I'd returned at a normal pace, unlike Bernard who must have sprinted. And I'm quite sure I didn't encourage them. I never encourage people.

I said, 'I think Francis Homer Gleeson was bowled over by your lecture. Did you notice how he was studying you?'

'No,' he said, 'I didn't give the man a second glance.'

I said, 'I think he was rather taken with your dickie bow.'

'Please, Enid,' he said, 'don't call it a dickie. You know better than that.'

Bernard is such a perfectionist. I'm much more careful about what I say and how I say it since we've been together and I can understand how hard he finds it to face the day's work when the audience is clearly of limited education. One does feel for him. But it was either this or a three-night mini-cruise out of Harwich, and versatile though he is, the Hanseatic League is hardly Bernard's forte, so one must simply make the best of things and soldier on.

No port of call today. I love a day at sea. There are hundreds of things one might do to fill the hours but sometimes I rather enjoy doing nothing. I suggested we nab some deckchairs and snuggle under blankets, but Bernard said he needed to go through his lecture notes on Rhodes and the breeze would blow his papers about if he did it out of doors.

I said, 'Darling, you absolutely do not need to revise Rhodes. You could give that lecture in your sleep. Indeed I think I've heard you do so.'

A weak smile.

'Nevertheless,' he said, 'I *shall* revise Rhodes. One can always find something new to say.'

I said, 'I think you're avoiding the Francis Homer Gleesons.'

'Not at all,' he said. 'But I certainly don't intend to make myself an easy target, which I would be, lounging in a chair for all to see. Please bear that in mind, if you insist on going into public places. One can spend an entire voyage trying to undo the work of a few minutes of ill-considered familiarity on Day One. You must be on your guard. In fact I wish you'd run along and make sure we're not going to be stuck with them at dinner.'

This evening is the first of the Formals. We're at the Second Officer's table, eight-thirty seating.

I said, 'But what am I to do if they are at our table? I can hardly have them bumped.'

'Of course you can,' he said. 'Having them bumped is precisely what you can do. I won't sit with them, Enid, and that's all there is to it. And I pray to heaven they haven't signed up for my tour of Izmir.'

I said, 'On that point I think you can relax. Those kind of people are only interested in one thing. Shopping.'

He said, 'They came to my lecture.'

I said, 'Darling, some people will go to anything.'

Which didn't come out quite the way I meant it and was probably the cause of the ensuing sullenness. He refused to join me for a walk on deck and a spot of lunch.

'No,' he said. 'I'll have Jesus bring me a sandwich.'

There were plenty of reclining chairs available. I could

11

have had my pick. But an elderly lady caught my eye and beckoned me over.

She said, 'I'm Virginia. Come and sit with me a while. I've been talking to myself this past hour.'

Virginia is travelling with her daughter.

She said, 'Irene's at the dance class. It's a big day for her. If she doesn't find a partner she won't be able to go in for the contest. Then she'll spend the rest of the cruise feeling depressed.'

I said, 'It sounds rather hit and miss. Wouldn't it be a better plan to bring a dance partner with her?'

Virginia replied, 'Easier said than done.'

From what one could gather, Irene has had a long run of bad luck with men and is prone to attacks of the doldrums but is otherwise the perfect, considerate and attentive daughter.

Said daughter eventually arrived. Virginia just celebrated her eighty-fifth birthday, which by my reckoning must mean Irene is forty at the very least but she was dressed in a strikingly short, figure-hugging dress in mango yellow and she was chewing gum. It was apparent from her face that her morning hadn't gone well.

Virginia said, 'No luck, dear?'

It seemed there had been a tussle over the few available men.

Irene said, 'They should open it up. Let some of the crew come up and dance. Some of those Latin types. But no, the only extra guys we're allowed are the Gentlemen Hosts and half of them dance like stiffs. Don Harrington's the best of the bunch and he's kind of spoken for. There's this pushy hag called Dorcas got her claws into him. God knows how. You should see her figure. Tits like tennis balls in a sock. But I haven't given up yet. I reckon I can swing it with Don.'

Virginia said, 'This is Enid. She's been keeping me company. She's English.'

I said, 'I haven't danced in years. It must be such fun.'

Irene said, 'It's not fun. It's a competition. There's a ten-day cruise at stake.'

Quite cut-throat, Virginia said.

I said, 'Perhaps I'll come along and give it a try.'

Irene said, 'You got a partner?'

Sadly, Bernard never, ever dances. He won't even join in one of those wild circle dances with his Greek chums.

I said, 'No, but perhaps I could grab one of those spare Gentlemen Corpses. If no one else wants them?'

She said, 'You don't look like a dancer.'

What do I look like, Irene? A middle-aged wallflower, skin a little dry, hair not as thick as it once was, waistline not as slender? A woman whose only hope of a dance partner is someone who does it as a job of work?

She said, 'You bring your gear with you?'

I said, 'What is "gear"?'

'Costumes,' she said. 'Proper dresses and dance shoes. You can't do competition dancing in any old thing.'

She looked down at my feet, her scorn for my canvas deck pumps all too evident.

I said, 'No, I didn't bring anything.'

She relaxed.

'Not much you can do about it then, is there?' she said. 'See, experienced dancers, we come prepared for a contest like this.'

With everything except a partner, apparently. What a desperate creature. And her mother is so sweet.

I went up to the Sports' Deck. It was dry but the wind was still gusting and there were very few people about, just a few joggers and one determined soul out on the golf links. It was quite heavenly to be alone with the inky sea and the scudding clouds. I had a bowl of onion soup gratinée at the Sea Breezes Salad Bowl and then the sun began to break through so I decided to take another turn around the deck. It was quite by chance I looked up and noticed a figure on the Spinnaker Observation Deck training a pair of binoculars exactly in my direction. One instinctively looks away but then one has the strong compulsion to look back, and as I did so he lowered the binoculars and waved. It was the ridiculous Mr Gleeson, clearly identifiable by his white Bermuda shorts and garish Hawaiian shirt.

What to do? One hates to be impolite but Bernard is right, on a cruise ship, even one as capacious as the *Golden Memories*, it's as well to draw the line from the very beginning. I simply nodded, rather crisply, and walked quickly out of range.

Bernard was still hunkered down in the cabin, books and papers all over the bed and the remnants of a toasted sandwich on the night stand.

I said, 'You can relax. I checked the seating and Mr and Mrs Gleeson are at the Captain's table this evening.'

'Ha!' he said. 'Isn't that just bloody typical. We get Second Officer's table and they pull out the plum. They'll have paid, of course. They'll have slipped someone a little inducement. People like that always buy their way in.'

I really don't think it's anything to get upset about but Bernard has a very strong sense of entitlement and he's in a particularly testy mood today. Normally, on the first full day of a cruise he'd be out and about, holding court, encouraging his claque to assemble. The *Golden Memories* isn't that kind of cruise, though, as must have been brought home to him by his audience this morning. It's unsettled him and when anything unsettles Bernard he has a tendency to prowl.

I said, 'Dearest, do come and explore the ship. It's a beautiful fresh day and there are all kinds of activities we might try. How about deck quoits? Or there's a fashion show in the Verandah Lounge. We can get afternoon tea.'

'No,' he said, 'I don't think so.'

I said, 'I know these aren't our kind of people but we're here and there's no turning back so we may as well make the best of things.'

He said, 'I'll leave that to you. I'm afraid I lack your

English stoicism. I don't have your talent for getting along with the riff-raff.'

I said, 'Hardly riff-raff. Some of these people could buy and sell us many times over. Including, I imagine, Mr and Mrs Francis Gleeson who seem to have so rattled you. That was a considerable diamond ring she was wearing.'

'The nouveau riche!' he snorted. 'They're worst of all. But you're mistaken, Enid. I don't allow people like that to *rattle* me, as you put it. As a matter of fact, until you brought up their name I had quite forgotten them.'

I said, 'What a pity you didn't say. You might have saved me the trouble of poring over tonight's dinner seating plans.'

I do my very best to shield Bernard from life's irritations but he can be so thoughtless and sometimes he allows such silly little things to bother him. We've been together more than twenty years and yet there are times when I feel I hardly understand him at all.

Bernard and I met in 1980. At the time he was Clifford Dennis's companion and amanuensis, a role which kept him very busy. I'd just moved to Rome having taken every possible Tuscan cookery course and grown rather bored with Florence. I didn't know many people and so was glad to be invited into Clifford's little coterie. They were all such interesting and creative people, not at all the kind of friends one might expect of a retired English cleric.

Clifford Dennis wasn't universally popular. The Luxley-

Greenwoods, who had been in Rome for centuries and were practically rooted in the foundations of All Saints church, had great reservations about him, even going so far as to suggest that he might have obtained his certificate of ordination from a Christmas cracker. And when Roger Joad saw me enjoying an *aperitivo* with Bernard one evening he called me the next morning and was quite hateful about it.

He said, 'Enid, what can you be thinking, taking drink with that old fraud's catamite?'

I said, 'Bernard and Clifford are jolly decent friends to me.'

'Of course they are, dear,' he said. 'You're one of their obliging little smokescreens. Whenever Tommy Luxley-Greenwood cries "pederasts" Clifford tells Bernard to be seen with women. You're not the first, believe me. I don't know why they bother. As if anyone cares in this day and age. And Bernard is a positive chameleon. I remember when he first slithered across Clifford's threshold; he was as American as apple pie. To hear him now you'd think he was Eton and Oxford.'

I think Roger Joad must secretly have carried a torch for me because I'm sure Bernard had never done anything to deserve his hostility, nor that of the Luxley-Greenwood faction. For two years he was perfectly sweet to me, though it was all quite platonic. He cut such a romantic figure, particularly in the winter months when he'd wear a wonderful swirling, hooded cloak or a long raccoon coat and a black beaver hat. He had the kind of presence that opened doors and secured good restaurant tables, even if he didn't always have the jingle to pay for them. But poverty has never been a crime in my book and Bernard was clearly a treasure to Clifford, albeit an underpaid treasure. He did absolutely everything for him, from supervising two rather insolent houseboys to taming the torrent of dictation of Clifford's memoirs, which sadly have never found the publisher they deserve.

All of us who knew them assumed that Bernard's position was unassailable and though Clifford was quite elderly he was still very spry and an avid thrower of luncheon parties. It came as the greatest shock when he collapsed after a gentle game of mixed doubles and never regained consciousness. And poor Bernard, who had rather been given the impression that the house would one day be his, was disconcerted to discover a number of relatives, not least a sister Clifford had never mentioned, who flew in and landed with a vulturine thud on the roof of Villa Peruzzi. Which left him in a terrible fix. Both his home and his livelihood were gone, in the bursting of a capillary.

When I offered Bernard my couch for a week or two, I did no more than any friend might do, but we found ourselves thrown together, two single people, both a little lost. Then it so happened that around the same time Grandpa Lune visited on his way to Capri and Bernard, with his ever-enquiring mind, became fascinated by the whole history of the Lune marquessate, created, as I now understand, thanks to Bernard, in 1815 for my ancestor Guy Tallentine-Conyers, Earl of Sedbergh, in recognition of his services at the Battle of Waterloo. Bernard ferreted out a great deal more about my ancestors than I had ever known.

So Grandpa Lune stopped off in Rome and sprung for dinner at the Hassler and he and Bernard had a jolly good natter, with Bernard asking many penetrating questions that I myself would never have thought to ask. Then, that night, made audacious by drink, I invited Bernard to abandon his bachelor couch and join me in my bed. As he often jests, limoncello has a lot to answer for.

We were engaged soon after but we didn't marry for almost two years, first out of respect for Clifford and then because we were being harried this way and that by Mumsie's solicitor who had put the idea in her head that Bernard was a gold-digger, though heaven knows, I had nothing to interest a fortune-hunter and I never hid my circumstances from him. Apart from a small house in Eaton Mews and our little *pied a l'eau* in Venice I have nothing to my name. And when Mumsie dies Lowhope Fell Hall will go to Cousin Andrew, as I hope her friend Bobbie Snape fully understands.

No, Bernard and I have had twenty-three basically happy years. We travel the world because Bernard is so much in demand as a guest lecturer, but we live very modestly. We see little or nothing of my people and Bernard has no people for us to see, an only child with parents long dead. It suits us. We have each other. And one truly hardly misses lunches at Peter Jones and chatting to one's chums.

If Bernard snaps occasionally it's because his vibrant intellect chafes against the limited range of some of his audiences. He should really be teaching in one of our great universities but he insists it was never what he wanted. He's far too free a spirit to be tied down by academic term dates. Still, I do rather regret that his freedom of spirit doesn't extend to becoming a member of the Blockbuster video shop or going to the kind of parties where there's dancing.

3

Bernard's mood is always lifted by Formal Nights. He cuts such a fine figure in a dinner jacket and wing collar and he knows it. I joke with him that he was born a hundred years too late. Friends sometimes urge me to be a little more glamorous myself but I never quite got the hang of clothes. I suppose if one learns these things at all it's at one's mother's knee, but Mumsie's knee was always jodhpur-clad and I simply followed suit. When I was sent to board at Darnbrook it came as the greatest shock, being made to wear a serge gymslip. Apart from the annual torture of being squeezed into an ancient velveteen frock for a visit to Grandma and Grandpoppa Oakhanger, one had practically never worn a skirt.

Then in later years there was the whole nightmarish business of Coming Out which involved staying with the Aunt Oakhangers in Lennox Gardens and borrowing gowns from Cousin Tig. How much easier it must be nowadays with those marvellous charity shops. My faithful old evening skirt, only five pounds from Mencap, has seen me through hundreds of these Formal Nights. One can ring the changes with various little blouses and gay necklaces picked up cheaply on one's travels. The American women fight for hair and nail appointments and then they pile on everything they have in their jewellery case. It quite makes one shudder.

At our table this evening: Second Officer Scott Davenport; a couple from Delaware called Chip and Cricket McCuddy; the cruise chaplain, Reverend Tudor Griffiths from Swansea; and my new acquaintances from this morning, Virginia and her daughter Irene, now making a play to be my friend.

'Hey,' she said, 'Mom didn't realize you were a Lady, not till we looked at the dinner seating. You shudda said.'

Why, Irene? Would it have made you less pathetically territorial about spare men?

I smiled.

I said, 'I hope you found a dance partner.'

'Sure I did,' she said. 'I always get a partner.'

Virginia whispered, 'Don Harrington. There was another person hoping to get him but he chose Irene.'

Irene said, 'No need to whisper, Mom. Winner takes all.'

Virginia said, 'Don's English too. I expect you know him.'

Only by sight. He has that Gentleman Host look, English edition. Thick silver hair, a little toothbrush moustache, navy-blue blazer and a cravat.

Bernard was seated between Mrs McCuddy and Irene, décolletage to the left of him, décolletage to the right. He looked like a remote granite peak flanked by two deep, lush valleys. Cricket McCuddy was already quite pink, though whether it was down to the second cocktail she ordered before soup was served or to her enormous pleasure at having bagged what she described as 'a real live professor', one couldn't be sure.

'Honey,' she said, addressing Irene, 'we better watch what we say tonight. The Professor here's gonna be giving us marks outta ten.'

But Bernard's thoughts were far away, one could tell, and Irene's sights were firmly locked on Second Officer Davenport. One imagines she's the kind of woman who prefers scalps that come trimmed with a little gold braid.

I was partnered by Mr McCuddy and Fr. Griffiths. Chip McCuddy was very successful in burglar alarms and is now retired, apparently from society as well as from business because he spoke only when spoken to. Yes, the weather had turned out better than we'd feared. Yes, lobster tails are a great treat. Yes, he has sailed with Oyster Line before. The wife is the live wire in the marriage. One imagines there is an age difference.

Fr. Griffiths, on the other hand, doesn't stop talking even when he has a mouthful of bread.

'Thirty-three people for Morning Worship. Not bad for a Sunday. I mean, what can you do? People are on their holidays. They like to sleep in, particularly when it's a day at sea. And the liturgical duties – these days they're a bit of a sideline. I'm really more of a welfare officer. Think of me as a human iceberg. The bit you see, the dog collar, that's not the half of it. Most of me is below the waterline, if you see what I mean. I'm a roving social worker. Don't call me Tudor, by the way. Everyone knows me as Taff.'

Bernard said, 'Are you a Catholic priest?'

'I am indeed,' he said. 'But the minute a ship is under way I think of myself as non-denominational. The spirit calls, Taff delivers.'

Bernard said, 'But you say Mass?'

He began pronouncing it with the long 'a' after he met Mumsie. Around the same time he dropped the 'l' from golf.

Fr. Taff said, 'As required. Below decks mainly, for the Hispanics. The passengers, they tend to be looking for something a bit lighter. A couple of hymns, a prayer for world peace and a little sermonette. See, you have to keep it short because you're up against the lure of the other entertainments.'

'Entertainments!'

Bernard turned away with a smirk of disgust. He's not a church goer himself but his instincts are entirely traditional and he does prefer to see people taking their religion seriously.

Virginia said, 'Well I think it's wonderful. We're all God's children. The time me and Irene went to St Kitts they had a Seder two of the nights and anybody could go. They closed off the end of one of the dining rooms, white tablecloths,

24

candles, a roast-chicken dinner. It was beautiful. Even the wine was Jewish.'

'Kosher,' the Reverend said. 'Certified by the Chief Rabbi. I've tasted it myself. A most acceptable beverage.'

I said, 'Do tell me, what's it like below deck on one of these ships? I've always wondered.'

'Like a pressure cooker,' he said. 'Very noisy, very hot. Cramped quarters, long hours, too many boys and not enough girls. You can imagine the problems. But I do the best I can.'

To which Mr McCuddy added, 'You can't do more.'

His conversational style seems to be to grasp someone else's last remark and rework it.

I said, 'I should love to see down there some time. Could one get a guided tour, I wonder?'

Fr. Taff said, 'I wouldn't recommend it. It's a rough and ready old world. The language can get a bit colourful, if you know what I mean? It's not the place for a lady.'

Second Officer Davenport laughed.

He said, 'Come on now, Taff. You make it sound like the merchant marine.'

Taff said, 'Well, I speak as I find. Let's say I wouldn't want to take my mother down there.'

Bernard began to thaw. By dessert the morning's dark clouds seemed to have dispersed and he had the whole table in stitches with his Ancient Roman shipwreck joke. We were just starting on coffee and mints when Cricket McCuddy began waving her arms and called out, 'Frankie, Nola, come

25

on over and say hello. How'd you enjoy your dinner?' and I caught the distinctive musky scent of Mrs Gleeson approaching from behind.

It turns out that the McCuddys and the Gleesons are acquaintances from previous cruises.

Cricket said, 'We ran into this pair going from Fort Lauderdale to Cozumel and then gosh darn it if they didn't turn up on the *Empress of the Waves*, Rio to Buenos Aires and now here we are again. Once you know Nola and Frankie you'll never shake 'em off. I'm just kidding, of course.'

'She's just kidding,' confirmed Mr McC.

Bernard shot me a what-did-I-tell-you glance and both Gleesons moved into my field of vision. It appears they co-ordinate their outfits. This morning they were both wearing parakeets on a sky-blue background. Tonight their theme was green. She was entirely in dark aquamarine, from her high-heeled mules to her feathered hair ornament, he was in a mint-green dinner jacket and a strangely neat, brown, helmet-like wig.

Cricket McCuddy said, 'Don't look now, Frankie, but I think a seagull just dropped its nest on your head.'

She was in rather a merry condition.

Gleeson laughed. He said, 'I've heard it all before, Cricket. Heard it all before. The way I look at it, you ladies get dressed up for a party, stick-on nails, stick-on eyelashes. I don't see why a guy can't do the same. Hey, guess how many lobster tails Nola ate? Four.'

26

Mrs Gleeson said, 'Only because Frankie can't do shell-fish. Only because they'd have gone back to the kitchen untouched and I hate waste. Are you all coming up to see the show? The Silverados are playing tonight. We saw them in 2002 on the way to Grand Cayman. Best band we ever heard on a cruise ship.'

Cricket said, 'Not tonight, Nola. Only eight days left till the Dance-Off. We're working on our bossa nova.'

Something amused Irene. A sly little smile. Perhaps I was the only one to notice it.

Nola Gleeson said, 'How about you, Professor? You and Lady Enid coming to hear the Silverados?'

But Bernard, suddenly absorbed in the subject of weather systems with Scott Davenport, appeared not to have heard her.

I said, 'My husband's taste in music is strictly classical. Anyway, no entertainment for us tonight. I'm afraid he has work to do.'

Which wasn't a complete untruth because he has brought with him the essay he hopes to contribute to Gaetano Borin's *festschrift*. Though Bernard never had tenure at Pavia he and Gaetano did share rooms and they've always stayed in touch. Bernard has reading privileges at heaps of universities. Besides, we never go to these evening entertainments. They're not Bernard's kind of thing at all. He prefers us to find a quiet corner, have a little nightcap or two and chat about his day.

She said, 'Well I'm sure a night off would do him good. I know what these men are like. Frankie was just the same. I used to say, "Congratulations, any day now you're gonna be the richest man in the graveyard." Didn't make a lick of difference, not till they told him he needed a triple bypass. That made him think. Soon as they wheeled him out of surgery I booked our first cruise. I've been telling him ever since, I'm gonna make him relax if it kills me.'

I was about to point out that as on-board lecturer Bernard's not actually here to relax, but the Reverend Griffiths rather sabotaged my argument by offering to escort Virginia to the show.

She said, 'I'd just love to. If you're sure you can spare the time.'

'I don't see why not,' he said. 'I reckon I can be spared for an hour. All work and no play makes Taff a dull boy.'

Mrs Gleeson said, 'See? Father here's got the right attitude. So maybe we'll catch you guys in the ballroom later, or we might give the casino a whirl. We might go play the slots for an hour. I'm feeling lucky tonight. What did you think of the dessert, Cricket?'

Mrs C said, 'I don't remember. What was it like?'

The charlotte russe had evidently been eclipsed by the glass of sweet vermouth she'd ordered to wash it down.

Nola Gleeson said, 'I didn't like the look of it. I asked our waiter to check with the kitchen that it was made with a non-animal gelling agent but I don't think he understood.

So I got ice cream instead. And you know, they only had vanilla or chocolate. You'd think they'd give you more choice. Frankie says what's the odds, I cudda risked eating the mousse thing anyhow, seeing I'm a mad cow already. Did you catch CNN tonight? The Michael Jackson trial? They found him not guilty.'

The woman is a talking steamroller. I decided the only thing to do was to get out of her path. I stood up, but Bernard, infuriatingly, kept his face averted and failed to pick up my signal, leaving me to retrieve my wrap which had become tangled around the legs of my chair. Neither Chip McCuddy, who was busy reading the small print on a sugar sachet nor Fr. Griffiths who was tête-à-tête with Virginia stirred to help me. It was Don Harrington, approaching our table to speak to Irene, who noticed my difficulty and came to the rescue.

'Let me get that for you,' he said.

A Yorkshireman with a dark brown voice. I thanked him.

He said, 'It's that old boy-scout training kicking in.'

He jerked his head towards Bernard and Mr McCuddy.

'Modern men, eh?' he said. 'I blame it on those women's libbers.'

Irene said, 'All set, Don? I'm ready when you are.'

She was half out of her seat.

Don said, 'No, I just came to say, give me half an hour. I'll do the rounds, make sure everybody's happy, then I'm yours. Mustn't neglect the ladies, must we now, gents?'

It was only when Scott Davenport got to his feet that Bernard picked up his cue.

'Ah, yes,' he said. 'Quite right. Time to go. I must make my excuses, ladies and gentlemen, and get back to the grindstone.'

But Francis Homer Gleeson was blocking his exit.

'Professor,' he said, 'I gotta tell you a very funny thing. You remind me so much of an old pal of mine. I can't get over it. You could be his twin, only Willy didn't have a twin.'

I wasn't at all sure Bernard was even listening to him.

Gleeson said, 'Willy Fink. That was his name. You got any cousins called Fink at all? Fink, Finch, it's not a big stretch is it?'

Bernard towered over him, head and shoulders, but Mr Gleeson is so solid that getting past him was impossible.

He said, 'No. No cousins. The name means nothing to me.'

Mr Gleeson said, 'Only Nola was reading to me what it says about you in the cruise brochure, how you were born in the States, even though you sound like you're English. And you put me so much in mind of Willy, I can't tell you. Even the way you run your fingers through your hair when you were giving your little talk. After I'd watched you this morning, well, I'd have bet the farm you were Willy Fink.'

Bernard said very evenly, 'Then it's a good thing you didn't. Because I'm not.'

30

But still the Gleeson man wouldn't let him pass.

He said, 'And another interesting coincidence is, your name's Bernard and my friend Willy's middle name was Bernard. Wislaw Bernard Fink, only we always called him Willy. Lived on Brewster Street, Painted Post, Elmira, 1940 to 1958. That's in New York State, by the way. Whereabouts are you from?'

Bernard hesitated.

'New York,' he said, eventually. 'And now you really must excuse me.'

'New York!' Gleeson said. 'Same state, even! Well I'll be darned! You from the city?'

Bernard is from a town called Newburgh.

'No,' he murmured. 'Orange County.' He hardly opened his mouth wide enough for the words to escape.

Gleeson said, 'Well then maybe you had cousins in Painted Post and didn't even know it.'

I saw that little indentation that appears in Bernard's cheek whenever he's clenching his jaw. Always a sign that he's running out of his very limited supply of patience.

He said, 'New York is a very large state but I have no cousins there, nor indeed anywhere else. Good night.'

And still that awful little man barred his way. He just stood there, smiling at Bernard, until at last Mrs Gleeson said, 'Frankie, stand aside. The Professor doesn't know you.'

He moved, and Bernard hurried away, zigzagging between the tables. Gleeson called after him.

'Pity though,' he said. 'I'd have loved to run into Willy. I've often wondered what became of him. Wouldn't surprise me if he isn't a professor some place too. Willy was a real scholar.'

Bernard never looked back. He strode out of the dining room, leaving me to extricate myself from a rather awkward moment.

Taff Griffiths said, 'Well then. We'd best be getting up to the Show Room. Get a good seat for these Silverados.'

Mrs Gleeson said, 'Most cruises you find the guest speakers are very friendly, very approachable. But sometimes people think they're too important. They think they're too grand. Who is it pays the piper though? The passengers, that's who.'

'Oh yes,' Chip McCuddy said, 'it's the passenger pays the piper.'

Mrs Gleeson continued, 'And the passenger doesn't pay to be given the cold shoulder. I might just have a word to Gavin Iles.'

Chip McCuddy said, 'Frankie, I'll tell you where you should look up old friends. Your alumnus association. Did you ever think to get in touch with them?'

Gleeson said, 'No, Chip, I never did. I didn't feel the need. Most of us haven't gone far. There's some got businesses in Elmira and Binghamton, one I know of moved up to Utica, and few in the cemetery now too, and that's about it. Not many unaccounted for. Willy's the only one I can think of that's disappeared off the map. You know, I even remember his date of birth. January twelfth 1940. Ain't that something? Don't matter how hard I try I never forget a date.'

And I felt a horrid spasm in my tummy that I'm afraid I couldn't entirely attribute to the lobster tails.

Bernard was in the bathroom and he remained in there for so long that I felt compelled to tap on the door.

He said, 'I'm using the lavatory, Enid.'

I said, 'I know. But why are you taking so long in there?'

Silence.

I said, 'Are you unwell?'

More silence.

I said, 'I very much hope you're not hiding in there, because A: I rather need to do a tinkle myself and B: I have something rather remarkable to tell you.'

After an eternity I heard the flush and out he came, wearing his *noli me tangere* face.

I said, 'You left the dining room very abruptly. You might have waited for me.'

He said, 'I had to answer an urgent call of nature.'

I said, 'You gave a very churlish impression to the other people at our table. I wouldn't be surprised if Mrs Gleeson complains about you. I imagine she's a great complainer and she's already on first name terms with Gavin Iles.'

'First name terms with Iles!' he said. 'Then she's clearly a woman of enormous influence.'

I said, 'But the main thing is, you missed an extraordinary

revelation from Mr Gleeson. His long-lost friend Willy Fink had exactly the same birth date as you.'

He said, 'I thought you were in a great hurry to use the bathroom?'

I said, 'But don't you find it amazing that you apparently not only look very much alike but were born on the same day too?'

'No,' he said, 'I don't. And if you knew anything at all about probability theory, Enid, neither would you. It's a well-known party trick.'

I said, 'Then why are you so cross about it?'

'Cross?' he said. 'I'm not cross. I'm merely exhausted by having to perform for all those idiotic people. You don't realize how much it takes out of me.'

I said, 'This evening wasn't so very bad. We've had far worse. Scott Davenport is very pleasant and you had the bonus of gazing into the Grand Canyon of Mrs McCuddy's cleavage.'

'Ah!' he said. 'So *that's* why you're being so hostile. You're jealous of my attentions to another woman.'

Such a silly thing to say. I've never once, in all the years we've been together, felt he had the slightest interest in other women.

I said, 'I am not being hostile. I was just telling you about a remarkable coincidence.'

When Bernard has an important point to make he holds up his hand, to halt all other conversational traffic.

He said, 'If we *must* talk about this idiotic subject may I offer another suggestion that doesn't seem to have occurred to you: that this Gleeson chap has targeted me. He's one of those insane people who stalk celebrities. Have you forgotten Funchal?'

It's true we did have an alarming experience on a Gems of Iberia cruise in 2001, but that was a lonely woman who decided she and Bernard were destined to be lovers and took to lurking in corridors and popping out from behind pillars. It all came to a rather dramatic climax when she waited for me to attend a castanet demonstration and presented herself to Bernard at the door of our cabin wearing nothing but a pair of tights and a raincoat.

I said, 'I hardly think Mr Gleeson has designs on your body.'

He said, 'I'm not talking about my body. How obtuse you are, Enid. I'm talking about obsessive people with empty lives. The man has clearly researched my biography and decided to amuse himself by weaving this fantasy. If he approaches me again *I* shall be the one doing the complaining.'

I said, 'You must do no such thing. Gavin Iles is no great fan of yours and the Gleesons are avid cruisers. I'm sure they're the kind of favoured customers who get upgraded at the drop of a hat. And Mr Gleeson doesn't *look* like a madman.'

'They never do,' he said. 'Now I don't want to hear another word about it, not from that idiot and not from you. I warn you, Enid. I'm in no mood.'

I said, 'There's no need to be so unpleasant. Good gracious, the way you're behaving anyone would think that you actually *were* this Willy Bernard Fink. Anyone who didn't know you could be forgiven for thinking you're afraid of being unmasked by Mr Gleeson.'

He said, 'I refuse to dignify that with a reply.'

And he slammed a drawer shut and tied his dressing gown so savagely I thought he might injure himself. I left him with his head buried in Bamford's *Knights of Malta* while I tweezed a few chin whiskers and pottered for a while.

I don't know so awfully much about Bernard's background. He'd been in Rome for almost ten years by the time we met, and so many other wonderful places before that. Athens, Istanbul, Venice. I get in a fearful muddle about the dates. I sometimes wish I did know more but as Bernard says, our lives didn't really begin until we met each other. We did talk of visiting Newburgh, New York, not long after we were married. I thought I should like to see where Bernard grew up, but both the Finches senior were dead and the house had been demolished so, as Bernard said, there seemed little point. I could understand. I don't especially enjoy going back to Lowhope Fell Hall since Bobbie Snape brought her influence so very much to bear. It's no longer my home.

Lowhope struggles to look welcoming even when the sun shines. Its architecture somehow militates against cosiness. But I have some fond memories. My room under the eaves with a groaning floorboard just inside the door and my height measured and marked on the wall, twice a year. Mrs Capstick's damson jam that had to be poured onto one's toast because it never set. A Christmas tree put up in the Long Hall and a fire lit so Poppa could roast lemons for his special hot toddy. But since Mumsie became a Free Thinker they don't really keep Christmas any more and as for fires, Bobbie refuses to burn anything except the elms they've cut down, and elm is a hopeless, sulking kind of wood. Most of the year she and Mumsie huddle in the Yellow Breakfast Room with a paraffin stove and they make absolutely no effort vis-à-vis dog hair.

Bernard, though, is unusually forgiving of everything at Lowhope and nags me constantly for us to visit oftener. 'A bastion of English eccentricity' he calls it. I've even heard him refer to it as 'our place in the country' though not to anyone acquainted with the facts. Sometimes I think he's a tad embittered that it will never be in my gift to make him lord of the manor. He would certainly carry it off more stylishly than Cousin Andrew, who to my knowledge hasn't changed his pullover in years.

One can perfectly understand why Bernard left America directly after Cornell. He's altogether so European. Sophisticated, widely read, and such an accomplished linguist. He's quite lost his American accent and everyone mistakes him for an Englishman. Mr Gleeson is right on that point at least.

I begin to wonder about Mr Gleeson. He's a comical little

figure, with or without the bird's nest on his head. There's something almost childlike about him: the way he stared at Bernard after the lecture this morning; the way he barged up to our table this evening and made himself the centre of attention. Even when Bernard made it clear he had nothing to say, he still pressed on. And there was the lunch-time incident when he was looking at me through his binoculars. I haven't dared mention that to Bernard. With the Gems of Iberia incident one definitely sensed something deranged about Bernard's pursuer but Mr Gleeson seems so benign. I suppose he might be suffering from one of those diseases that make one revert to childish pranks, in which case, sad as these conditions are, he shouldn't be allowed to wander unsupervised. We discovered this to our cost with Granny Lune's forays into the Tesco supermarket wearing her poacher's coat.

Bernard's book was still open but he was snoring gently. I took his reading specs out of his hand and he opened his eyes.

I said, 'Izmir tomorrow.'

'Yes,' he said. 'Wonderful, tragic Izmir. *Smyrne est une princesse avec son beau chapel. L'heureux printemps sans cesse répond à son appel et, comme un riant de fleurs dans une coupe, dans ses mers se découpe plus d'un frais archipel.*'

I said, 'Darling, I'm so glad you're not Willy Fink from Painted Post. I bet he wouldn't be able to recite Victor Hugo in bed.'

He laughed and we snuggled up. Truce.

4

We docked just after eight and I could see our transport waiting for us at the pier. It promised to be a hot day but in Izmir you can usually depend on a breeze. Several members of the tour were in short shorts and skimpy tops. Seemingly however much one advises people to dress appropriately there are always a few who are determined to scandalize the locals and get sunburned into the bargain. As Bernard remarked, the inside of the bus looked like the meat slab in a pork butcher's window.

There was also a slight altercation with our driver who wanted to take us first to Kadifekale and then to his cousin's rug shop, but Bernard insisted that we stick to the agreed itinerary. First to the Agora, next to the markets and the caravanserai, then up to the Kadifekale. That's the way he always does Izmir. After they've seen the castle people have the rest of the day free, to wander back to the ship or to go to someone's cousin's rug shop should they so choose. There was much teeth-sucking from the driver but Bernard was extremely firm about it.

The ladies always admire Bernard's vanilla linen suit and his Montecristi panama and then when he starts bantering with the street urchins in Turkish they fall head over heels in love with him. Today one woman said to me, 'The Professor looks just like somebody in the movies.'

'Like Peter O'Toole,' someone else suggested. 'Any idea where us girls can find a few more like him?'

I said, 'I'm afraid he's a one-off.'

She said, 'I'll bet he is, dear. Well good for you. Look at the slowpokes we ended up with.'

It is true that no matter what the size of the group the women all stick close to Bernard, even if they're not listening to him with the closest attention, but the men straggle behind, talking about stock prices or comparing cameras.

Kadifekale makes the perfect climax to a tour, of course. It's a fabulous photo opportunity, looking down from the citadel walls, over the red rooftops to the harbour, and Bernard always tries to time it so that we're up there when the midday call to prayer begins. He has a marvellous sense of theatre.

He and I sat in a shady spot, drank mint tea and listened to the crickets. It's our usual routine once the shorts-clad chubbies have thanked him and pressed him with offers of lunch and finally lumbered off to buy their souvenirs. I think this was our fifth time in Izmir, though of course when

Bernard brought me here for the first time he already knew it intimately.

He said, 'I'm afraid I was in a rather hateful mood last night.'

I said, 'Don't let's talk about it. It's forgotten.'

He said, 'Nevertheless I think we should devise a strategy to deal with Mr Gleeson. If he makes another approach with this ludicrous Fink story I shall look into having him dealt with.'

I said, 'But what can you do? Put him in the scuppers with a hosepipe on him?'

He said, 'It's no joking matter.'

Of course I do agree that a nuisance on board ship is worse than a nuisance at large in the world because effectively one has no hiding place but still, having Mr Gleeson *dealt* with sounds rather draconian.

I said, 'I don't think for one moment he'll mention it again but if he should, surely the best thing would be to sit him down and simply acquaint him with the facts. Tell him your background. He can hardly argue that you don't know your own name.'

He took my hand.

'Enid,' he said, 'you're such an innocent.'

We strolled down through the Kemeralti, munched on some delicious sultanas and bought a little kilim for Bernard's study in London. We were heading back towards the ship along the Kordon Promenade when we heard excited voices calling 'Professor! Professor!' and one of those tourist phaetons went rattling past with the McCuddys and the Gleesons on board, the men waving and the wives squealing with laughter.

Bernard said, 'Do I need to say another word?'

I said, 'They only waved, darling. Hardly a hanging offence.'

He laughed, but there was no mirth in it.

I haven't seen Bernard this tense since just after Clifford's death, when those hordes of previously unheard of relatives began arriving and helping themselves to a lifetime's collection of antiquities. That Clifford hadn't thought to write a will was neither here nor there because it was widely known that he intended Bernard to be his major beneficiary. Instead of which, heaven knows what treasures were carted off to auction houses and poor Bernard ended up with a set of apostles' teaspoons and one week's notice to quit.

We went back on board and I took a swim in the salt-water pool while Bernard put the finishing touches to his lecture notes for Rhodes. It was such a pleasant afternoon I couldn't bear the thought of going back to our tiny quarters so after I'd dried off I slipped along to a demonstration of vegetable sculpture and then ordered finger sandwiches and a pot of Darjeeling in the Verandah Lounge. It was sheer self-indulgence, but I don't believe Bernard had even noticed how long I'd been gone. When he's working he gets so absorbed in his own thoughts and the Knights of St John are one of his particular passions.

'Strategy for this evening,' he said. 'You'll go ahead of me to the library, observe people coming in and meet me at the door if the Gleesons are in the audience. Best to be prepared. I intend to make a last-minute entrance, deliver my lecture and then make a prompt exit. We'll have dinner served in the cabin.'

I said, 'I do hope we're not going to spend this voyage hiding from Mr and Mrs Gleeson. It's terribly cramped in here for dining.'

'Nonsense,' he said. 'It'll be romantic. It'll be like the early days in Trastevere, remember?'

I had the tiniest apartment in Panfilo Castaldi and when Bernard had to vacate Villa Peruzzi he did bring with him an enormous quantity of clothes and books, but somehow we managed. Those were such happy days. I'd done a few courses – ceramics, watercolours – but frankly I was rather running out of steam, until I had Bernard to care for. I was rattling around in Rome, with no idea what to do next or where to go. One often wonders how differently one's life might have turned out. If Poppa hadn't gone away and left us I probably wouldn't have ended up in Rome and if I hadn't gone to Rome I would never have met Bernard. I might still be at Lowhope, borrowing thrillers from Carnforth lending library and hoping to win the National Lottery.

Lowhope Fell Hall was once described by a rather grudging architectural historian as 'a Gothic sandstone barracks glowering down upon the salt marshes of Morecambe Bay'. Poppa certainly never hid his dislike of the house. He'd get fearfully restless and drive into Barrow or Kendal three or four times a week for what he called his 'necessaries' and whatever they were he must have consumed them on the spot because he rarely brought home any packages. His people were from the gentler countryside of Hampshire which he found far more congenial than the wilds of Cumbria and Lancashire. He kept a place in town too, of course, in Eaton Mews, for when he had appointments with his gunsmith or his boot maker. But home is home and during the years I was sent away to board at Darnbrook I used to long for the school holidays and the sight of Mossop waiting for me in the station car park, seated at the wheel of our old boneshaker with the stub of a Woodbine cigarette hanging from his bottom lip.

Bobbie Snape, who was one of the Whernside Snapes, had been a neighbour simply for ever. She and Mumsie both hunted with the Vale of Lune and they shared an interest in the breeding of Dandie Dinmont terriers, so she was a frequent visitor to Lowhope. Nevertheless it came as something of a surprise when Bobbie moved in, lock, stock and Stak-o-Matik record player, less than a week after Poppa moved out. She said Mumsie was too distraught to be left alone, but Mumsie wasn't alone. She had me. At that time I was still in day school, when they remembered to send me. And neither was she distraught. She was soon laughing gaily and humming to gramophone records. Still, I had every expectation that Poppa would soon come back and in the meanwhile I saw no harm in Mumsie having a friend to stay. Actually, I should rather have liked to have a friend to stay myself.

Then Mrs Capstick, our housekeeper, gave her notice and no attempt was made to dissuade her or to replace her because Bobbie Snape said we didn't require an overpaid busybody to heat up our cans of soup, and soon after that Mossop, our Outdoors Man, began growling under his breath and threatening to follow Mrs Capstick's example. I begged Mumsie not to let Mossop go. He was the only one who consistently remembered which side of the road to drive on and sometimes he was kind enough to take me shrimping or to visit his sister in Flookborough for tea and fairy cakes. With Mossop gone we'd have been left with only Olive, the General Girl, and even she was considering her position. She said, 'If Mr Mossop goes, I'll not stay neither.'

As Mumsie pointed out to her, she wouldn't easily find anything else as convenient but that didn't deter Olive from saying very loudly, 'That's as maybe, but Mr Mossop told my mam there's things going on here that's queer as fook.'

I was only ten. I had no idea what was troubling all of them. Until I went into Mumsie's bedroom to report that Mercury had developed an inflamed fetlock and found Bobbie spanking Mumsie's bottom with a lunge whip. Immediately after that I was sent to board at Darnbrook. Then when I was eighteen Grandpoppa Oakhanger thought it would be a good idea if I went to St Gallen to be finished and afterwards

I worked for a year or so in a gallery in Cork Street, but I found London awfully lonely. Poppa was in Florida by then, with his new family, and Mumsie had fallen completely under the influence of Bobbie Snape and turned the West Lawn into a holiday caravan park.

Bernard was my salvation and frankly I was his, because he's not in the least domesticated and life with Clifford had made him accustomed to staff. After our marriage we elected to leave Rome, which had turned into such a back-biting gossip shop, and we began our wonderful new life, travelling and perching on any inexpensive twig we found. 'Cultural nomads,' as Bernard says.

We've camped out and muddled through, from Santiago di Compostela to St Petersburg and I think I can honestly say I've never complained, but the *Golden Memories* cruise ship has seven restaurants, quite apart from the main dining room, and I'm sure we could have found somewhere to eat, undiscovered by Francis Homer Gleeson. But Bernard rang for Jesus and asked him to have a bottle of wine chilled and ready for our return when the lecture is finished. Jesus is an obliging boy but I rather wish he hadn't winked at me in such an impudent way.

He said, 'We got a nice champagne on the list, Professor. Pommery. Pretty good price.'

Bernard said, 'No, the Jacob's Creek will do perfectly well.'

Jesus said, 'OK. Just thought I'd say. In case it was special occasion. In case it was Ladyship's birthday.'

Bernard said, 'It isn't.'

Jesus is like a little brown-eyed cherub. Thick black hair and deep dimples when he smiles. He was just leaving when Bernard said, 'Oh go on then, you wretched boy, placing temptation in my way! We'll have the Pommery.'

So extravagant. We both adore champagne but we agreed long ago that it tastes much better when someone else is paying for it.

I said, 'Darling, that's terribly lavish. I think you allowed Jesus to railroad you. I really don't mind drinking an Australian sparkler if you want to change your mind.'

He said, 'No, you're worth it, Enid. He's a cheeky little bugger though. Guatemalan, one imagines.'

Actually, Jesus is Honduran. I've noticed before that these boys have a way with Bernard. I suppose they're the sons he never had.

A sparse audience this evening and no wonder. Seven o'clock is a silly time for a lecture. People are dressing for dinner. Nevertheless the few who attended — all non-Gleesons I'm relieved to report — were treated to a scintillating introduction to Rhodes and the Hospitaller Knights. Bernard at his very best. He even overran his time, a sure sign he was enjoying himself, and his good spirits carried him through dinner in spite of there being no space under our tiny table for his long shanks and bony knees.

The champagne was delicious, as was the grilled salmon, though I'm not sure fish was the most prudent thing to have in such a poorly ventilated space and one's bedroom, to boot. Just before midnight we made our way up to the Observation Deck. The night was so balmy one hardly needed a cardigan, and we watched for the lights of Kos as we threaded our way between Cape Skandhari and the Turkish shore.

I felt it was the first time Bernard had been truly relaxed since this cruise began.

I said, 'Happy?'

'Mmm,' he said. 'Whatever happiness is.'

And tomorrow we have Rhodes to look forward to. First, Bernard's tour of the town, as much a pleasure as a duty, and then up into the hills to visit Tsampi. Bernard and Tsampikos Karagiannis have been friends for centuries, pre-Clifford Dennis even. His mother is now in her nineties and requires a good deal of nursing but that doesn't stop Tsampi being the most perfect host. I can think of few things more blissful than a leisurely lunch on his bougainvillea-draped terrace.

5

I'm sure the reason for such a low turnout for Bernard's tour of Rhodos Town was the early start. Cruise passengers do so hate to cut short any meal and the full breakfast menu isn't available before eight o'clock. But far better to grab a cup of coffee and a roll and get moving. No one feels like climbing to the Palace of the Grand Masters once the sun is high. There were just twenty takers for the tour, including Irene, the ferocious hunter of dance partners and her mother, Virginia. Irene seemed to have little interest in the Knights of St John. Her principal motive for joining the tour seemed to be to talk to me throughout Bernard's explanations and in the loudest of whispers.

'Those people,' she said. 'Those Gleesons? Mom and I felt so sorry for the Professor the other evening.'

'The Hospitaller Knights,' said Bernard, 'evicted from Jerusalem in the thirteenth century, came to Rhodes under the leadership of their Grand Master, Fulkes de Villaret.'

Irene continued hissing in my ear.

She said, 'I guess they thought they were having a bit of fun with him, pretending he was somebody else, pretending they knew him from way back, but it wasn't appropriate. And then barring his path like that when he'd told them he had to leave. It was disrespectful, and I told them so.'

I said, 'It was nothing. Truly. My husband hasn't given it another thought.'

She wasn't listening though.

She said, 'Any cruise, doesn't matter what its size, you're always going to get a couple of nuisances. But don't worry. I don't think you'll have any more trouble from them now.'

I said, 'I do hope there was no unpleasantness.'

Bernard glared at me.

'The walls you see now,' he said, 'are not original. They were rebuilt in the early twentieth century from the rubble of an explosion that largely demolished the palace in 1856.'

Irene said, 'You and the Professor, you're sitting ducks. Any head case can go along to his lectures or come on one of these tours. They could make your life hell.'

Virginia patted my hand.

'Leave it to Irene,' she said. 'Nobody crosses Irene.'

They both stuck by my side like glue until we reached the shops on Sokratous Street where other members of the group began to ask my advice on embroidered tablecloths and I managed to extricate myself. Irene's intentions were good, I'm sure, and she may have done Bernard a small favour, but she mustn't read encouragement into anything one says. One can't afford to become embroiled in factions, or to make enemies.

As the tour ended and people were dispersing she grabbed my arm again. 'Remember,' she said. 'Any more trouble, we're in J29.'

Tsampikos's driver was waiting for us by the Akandia Gate and he whisked us up through the pine forests to Villa Petaloudi. Mrs Karagiannis now has to be fed by her nurse and keeps to her rooms, so we were just three for lunch. Fried zucchini flowers, grilled lamb and cold rosé wine. From the terrace we could see the island of Khalki shimmering in the heat and the only sound was the cicadas and the braying of a donkey, out of sight somewhere below us. It was all too divine and my only complaint is that after the second glass of *souma* Bernard and Tsampi tend to reminisce about things that happened long, long ago, or worse yet, lapse into demotic Greek, leaving me to chat to the cats. Sometimes one feels quite invisible. Tsampi is very welcoming and very courtly, but I do realize *I'm* not the reason we were invited to luncheon.

He said, 'Enid, this guy looks younger every time I see him. I think you look after him very well.'

I flatter myself I do. Bernard is a performer. He has to focus on his moment in the spotlight and give his all and one can't do that if one is fretting about the price of butter.

At the time of our engagement several members of Bernard's circle remarked to me that they hadn't thought him the marrying kind but that only showed how little they really knew him. If ever a man needed a wife it's Bernard. He's most particular about his clothes and his surroundings, fastidious even, and becomes easily upset when things aren't as they should be. Keeping him happy is practically a full-time job.

I said, 'I do my best.'

Bernard said, 'Except this morning when you very nearly sabotaged my tour with your nattering. Why didn't you tell that woman to shut up?'

I said, 'Because *that woman* has appointed herself your avenging angel. She wanted to tell me that she confronted the Gleesons and warned them never to darken your door again. I think you have an admirer, Bernard.'

Tsampi laughed.

'Always he was the same,' he said. 'Everyone admires Bernard. But who is Gleesons?'

I said, 'They're passengers on the cruise. Mr and Mrs. The husband was convinced Bernard was his long-lost school friend. A funny little man, wasn't he, darling? And terribly disappointed when he found you weren't Willy Fink.'

'Was he?' he said. 'I really don't recall. Tsampi, I hear the Phidippides Award is going to someone from Princeton this year.'

★

We were driven back down the mountain at break-neck speed, Bernard having quite wilfully disregarded the time in spite of several reminders from me. One can't blame Tsampi. He's Greek. We made it back on board with less than an hour to spare, which is certainly not my idea of 'aeons of time' and Bernard was quite squiffy, weaving down the corridor, reciting Cavafy to a somewhat bemused Jesus. I was rather worried about Bernard's fitness to deliver his lecture, The Minoan Outpost of Thira, or, as Gavin Iles had very frivolously insisted on renaming it, Santorini and the Legend of Atlantis.

Jesus said, 'Oh Ladyship, Professor's in very good mood. I think you gonna be dining in your stateroom again tonight! Professor, you want me to put the Pommery on ice?'

Bernard snapped, 'No I do not! We have lunched extremely well and now we're going to take a little nap.'

At which point I'm afraid I had to put my foot down.

I said, 'Bernard, I refuse to be cooped up in here with the smell of last night's fish and anyway I don't need a nap. I haven't over-indulged. I'm going to stand by the rail for sail-away and then I'm going to sample some of the cultural activities.'

He was stretched out in his shirt and boxer shorts, looking overheated.

'Cultural activities!' he barked. 'Apart from my lectures there are no cultural activities! Don't tell me you're going to play Bingo?'

I said, 'Since I'm not asking you to accompany me I don't see it matters what I do.'

He said, 'Why are you always so irritable after we've visited one of my friends? I've noted it before. You were quite poisonous after we had dinner with Bog Stevovic.'

I said, 'Perhaps it's because you and your friends talk endlessly about people I don't know. And sometimes not even in English.'

He said, 'Bog is my only opportunity to keep up my Serbian and as for Tsampi, there's nothing preventing you from learning a little Greek. You have time enough on your hands.'

I said, 'I already know a little Greek, thank you. But you and Tsampi jabber away so fast, and quite unnecessarily. His English is perfect. I'm sure I wouldn't do such a thing to you if we were to see my friends.'

'Enid,' he said, 'you don't have any friends.'

I'd popped on my swimmer thinking I'd take a quiet dip but when I got to the pool a rather spirited game of water volleyball was in progress, ladies only. I sat down to watch and was very surprised to hear someone hailing me.

'Come and join us,' she said. 'We're one light.'

I said, 'I'm afraid I don't know the rules.'

'Neither do we,' she said. 'We're making them up as we go along.'

So in I plunged. And I must say, though it wasn't entirely

clear who won, it was the greatest lark. It was only after I'd accepted an invitation to join them for tea in the Verandah Lounge that I realized who one of my team-mates was. Mrs McCuddy. I hadn't recognized her in her flower-petal bathing cap.

'Cricket,' she said. 'You must call me Cricket. I know you're Lady Enid.'

I do so hate it when people make a fuss about titles. Especially when one is sitting in a damp bathing suit.

She said, 'Chip and I were only saying how we never see you and the Professor out and about. I guess there's a private lounge you go to?'

I said, 'No, we're very happy in our cabin. We find the public rooms rather rowdy.'

'Do you?' she said. 'I like things lively, myself. And they have some great activities on offer. Like last night, we went to a Murder Mystery dinner. It was very entertaining. You book it ahead of time, then they tell you who you're meant to be and what kind of costume to bring. Chip was supposed to be a retired navy admiral and I was an oil widow from Texas. We weren't neither of us the murderer but we had a great time.'

It did sound rather fun. But not Bernard's kind of thing at all.

The waiter had just brought us tea and cakes when a shadow fell across the table and the Francis Homer Gleesons arrived, in full aloha rig.

'Hi, Cricket,' Mrs G said. 'We ran into Chip. He said we'd probably find you here.'

Frankie Gleeson said, 'Chip thinks *he* ran into us. What he doesn't realize is, we just hang around in the atrium till we spot him. Then we jump out and surprise him. We know it makes his day.'

He chuckled at his own little joke.

Cricket said, 'You know we went to China last year? The Great Wall, Peking, you name it. And everywhere we went Chip kept saying "Any minute now Frankie and Nola are gonna show up."'

Frankie Gleeson said, 'And we did too. Remember those Terracotta Warriors? We were in Pit Three, Row Five. Only you didn't notice us.'

They plonked themselves down and one was rather trapped.

I said, 'I should be getting back.'

'No, no, no,' Cricket said. 'You haven't drunk your tea. Nola, Frankie, you remember Lady Enid?'

'Sure we do,' Nola said, rather coolly. 'So how'd the dancing go today?'

'Don't ask,' Cricket said. 'They won't accept a bossa nova. They say it has to be a rumba, a samba, a cha-cha-cha or a jitterbug. But jitterbug isn't Latin American so if they'll let you do that they oughta let you do the bossa nova. It makes no sense.'

I said, 'So what will you do?'

'The cha-cha-cha,' she said. 'It's not really our dance but we'll have to do the best we can.'

The Gleesons had just taken part in an activity called Team Trivia and done rather well.

Mrs G said, 'Not me. I'm just there for decoration. I'm just there to distract the competition with my earrings. Frankie's the one with the memory. Dates, names. All he has to do is read a thing once and he's got it, up there.' She tapped her forehead.

Cricket said, 'And what did you guys do this morning?'

Nola had spent her morning shopping and bought two coat collars in sheared Kastoria mink.

'One mandarin-style, one wing,' she said. 'Beautiful quality.'

Mr G said, 'Know what she said to me? She said, "Frankie, I've saved you hundreds of dollars this morning."'

She leaned across and planted a lipsticky kiss on his cheek. She said, 'Well what are you going to do, have your wife walk around catching a chill in her neck or order yourself a shroud with a money belt?'

While his wife was saving him money Mr G had visited the aquarium. Of all the things one might choose to do in the city of the Crusading Knights. Extraordinary. I didn't even know Rhodes had an aquarium.

'Oh yes,' he said. 'I always search out the aquarium, wherever we travel. And Rhodes wasn't bad, for a small town. They've got wrasse and stingrays, humpheads, goatfish, mullet, parrotfish, clownfish. Crustaceans too. You interested in fish at all?'

I said, 'My grandfather had a carp pond.'

He said, 'Never could see the attraction of carp, myself. There's no challenge to catching them. I'm a smallmouth bass man myself. I used to use a fly rod but nowadays I mainly use a light spinner. We had a cold spell just before we came on this trip and I was using spinner bait, a quarter ounce white rooster tail, cast against the rocks, then a slow retrieve. I caught a good number of fourteen-, fifteen-inch smallmouth.'

Below Lowhope, in Morecambe Bay, they fish with a rake, for cockles. And Mossop's family used to trawl for brown shrimp with a horse and cart. They use tractors now, of course.

He said, 'Does the Professor like to fish?'

A very comical notion, Bernard in waders. Bernard extricating a hook. He's terribly squeamish. When I prepare calamari, which is one of his favourite dishes, he insists on my doing so behind a closed kitchen door.

I said, 'My husband isn't an outdoors person.'

He said, 'I've been a fish man since I was knee high to a grasshopper. We all were in Painted Post.'

Mr Gleeson never looks away when he's telling you something. He concentrates on one's face most intently.

He said, 'Even Willy Fink. That was the friend I mentioned to the Professor? Yes, even Willy used to come fishing, and he was a real indoors kind of kid. Like the Professor would have been, I expect. More of a reader.'

'Frankie,' Mrs Gleeson said, very quietly, very firmly. 'We agreed. No more about that.'

Nola Gleeson is an interesting woman. Beneath that mahogany beehive she seems quite sensible. And she has such a jolly manner. She seems able to say anything to her husband and he doesn't get cross. How pleasant that must be, not to have to mind one's Ps and Qs.

Mr G picked up my book of crosswords.

He said, 'I see you're a puzzler, Lady Enid. I like a puzzle myself.'

Cricket McCuddy said, 'We're not to call her Lady Enid. She prefers just Enid. And we don't need to curtsey neither.'

'Good,' he said, 'I'm glad to hear it. Because when all's said and done, those titles are a load of hooey. Some guy hundreds of years ago grabbed himself a castle and we're supposed to go around bowing and scraping to his descendants. It goes against the grain with me. Course, I'm an American. We finished with all that in 1776. No offence intended.'

More tea was ordered.

He said, 'Now my sister Junie, she loves all that stuff. Lords and Ladies. She has the whole boxed set of *Upstairs, Downstairs*. And she always reckons these titles are very complicated. Dukes, earls, who gets called what. Is that right, Enid?'

I said, 'Well yes, there are certain rules.'

At which blessed juncture Chip McCuddy arrived, wearing a vaguely nautical blazer, and saved me from what I sensed might turn into a grilling.

He said, 'The Giants beat the Dodgers eleven–five. And Kayla's got the chicken pox.'

Kayla is apparently one of a vast tribe of McCuddy grandchildren.

Nola Gleeson said, 'Do you phone home every day, Chip?'

'Not on your life,' he said. 'You think I'm made of money? Email, Nola. Best thing since Wonderbread. You should try it.'

Mr Gleeson said, 'Save your breath, Chip. She won't. She reckons she's too old.'

Nola said, 'I do not. I'm not too old for anything. I just don't think these computers are good for you. They send out rays. They can give you tumours.'

Chip McCuddy said, 'I don't care. Something has to get you in the end. I wouldn't be without my computer.'

Gleeson said, 'Me either. Are you familiar with the World Wide Web, Enid?'

Obviously one has heard of it.

'Oh,' he said, 'you should give it a try. It's a wonderful thing. Information, at your fingertips. Here we are on this cruise ship, no land in sight, and yet I can go down to the computer centre and look up anything that interests me. Fishing conditions on Cayuga Lake. Result of the Pioneers' game against the Brockport Riverbats. Correct title for a duke. Anything at all. And then, with email you can keep in touch with people, anywhere in the world, any time of day. I'll give you an example. Yesterday I got a message from our neighbour to say our garden sprinkler wasn't working but he hoped to have it fixed by Monday. See? A quick email message and he'd put my mind at rest.'

Nola said, 'But if you didn't do all this emailing you'd never have known about the sprinkler and your mind wouldn't have needed putting at rest. You're supposed to be relaxing.'

Cricket said, 'I agree with Nola. Now I'm going to be worried about Kayla.'

I tried to pay for my share of tea but the McCuddys wouldn't hear of it.

Cricket said, 'We've loved talking with you. Your accent is just darling.'

One was clearly going to be discussed the very moment one left.

Cricket said, 'Y'all have a nice evening, Enid.'

Frankie said, 'And give our best regards to the Professor.'

Nola put her hand on his arm but her eyes were on me. Nothing said, just a look that said, 'Subject closed. Everything under control.'

Frankie Gleeson has a shiny, perpetually smiling face. He reminds me of a yellow labrador Poppa had many years ago, a dog with a good soft mouth but impossible to train to the gun because he believed the whole world was waiting to be his best friend.

He said, 'Lambada, by the way. Nineteen down. A Greek character enters the dance. Lambada.'

It was after six. I had completely missed Bernard's lecture.

I said, 'I fell asleep in the sun.'

A harmless fib.

He said, 'I'm disappointed in you, Enid. You go wandering around the ship, I have absolutely no way of locating you, and then you don't even take the trouble to attend my lecture.'

I said, 'If we had mobile telephones like everyone else you'd be able to locate me as often as you need.'

He said, 'We are *not* succumbing to mobile telephones. They're a blight on civilization.'

Actually, I'm quite happy to accept Bernard's ruling on this. I imagine there are many drawbacks to being too easily tracked down.

I said, 'I'm very sorry I missed your lecture. How was it?'

He said, 'My lecture was everything it should be. It was only dragged down to a level of stunning fatuity by the questions I was asked, for which I have to thank Gavin Iles and his meddling. The Legend of Atlantis indeed! First question: On Santorini do they sell any of those blue crystals, as shown in the Walt Disney movie? Second question: How does Santorini's claim stack up against the theory that the Bermuda Triangle is the most likely site of the lost city?'

I said, 'I hope you responded with good humour.'

'With the thinnest veneer thereof,' he said. 'I wouldn't want any remotely discerning member of my audience to think I encourage stupidity.'

I was safe from being asked to account for my lost hours. He was in full flood. They say it's caused by adrenalin.

He said, 'It was a perfect illustration of what happens if you allow idiots to get their hands on Plato. They completely miss the point of a good yarn.'

I said, 'Any thoughts about this evening?'

'Thoughts?' he said. 'Yes. To steer clear of the herd. I'm going to read.'

I said, 'Well then at least let's go to the Bridge Lounge where we can sit in comfort.'

He said, 'I'm comfortable here, thank you very much.'

As well he should have been, considering the way he'd monopolized the only armchair.

I said, 'Then you won't miss me if I go out for another hour.'

'More wandering?' he said. 'You're very restless today.'

I said, 'There's a demonstration of decorative napkin folding I thought I might look in on.'

'Sounds riveting,' he said.

I said, 'What do you want to do about dinner?'

He said, 'I had an ample sufficiency at lunch. I don't want even to think about food.'

I said, 'By the by, did you know, there's some kind of

computer on board this ship? Passengers can switch it on and use it to send messages anywhere in the world? And it will answer questions. You can ask it anything and it will give you the answer.'

'Yes,' he said. 'I also know that the moon is made of green cheese and Elvis Presley is alive and well.'

6

There is not one computer on this ship but ten. Every one of them was in use but Brady, the young man who takes care of them, said if I went back later, when people had gone to the evening entertainments, he'd have time to help me. He said it didn't in the least matter that I'd never worked a computer before. He said it's as easy as ABC and that getting people started made his job more interesting.

I went to the American-style diner on L Deck. It's called The Hash Sling and the waitresses all have ponytails and wear ankle socks. One has to be prepared for a certain amount of clatter because it's popular with young families, but it has the advantage of snug little alcoves where a person eating alone doesn't stick out. Nevertheless, before my All Day Breakfast arrived I was spotted by Irene and Virginia who slid into my booth without even waiting to be invited.

Irene said, 'We're just getting dessert for Mom. She doesn't care for a big meal at night.'

They ordered apple pie à la mode.

Virginia said, 'The Professor working again? Not much fun for you, is it?'

I said, 'I'm not here to have fun. It's more a working holiday.'

She said, 'He's the one supposed to be working, not you. He oughta have time to take his wife to dinner.'

Irene said, 'And how long does it take to think up one of those talks anyhow?'

People have no idea.

I said, 'We're an old married couple. I'm very happy to do my own thing.'

'Atta girl!' she said. 'That's the spirit. Doing your own thing!'

I caught a faint whiff of drink. And I do so hate it when people crowd my space.

'Everything OK?' she said. 'No more problems?'

I said, 'Problems?'

She said, 'You know? The pushy Gleesons?'

I said, 'No. Absolutely no problems.'

'Damn right,' she said. 'I took care of that. They'll be staying out of your hair from now on.'

The fact that I had tea with the Gleesons this afternoon is none of Irene's business. I had no obligation to tell her. And I only told an untruth to Bernard because I knew what a fuss he'd make. If people would only be pleasant and reasonable one wouldn't be pushed into deceitfulness.

I said, 'Did you enjoy Rhodes?'

Virginia said, 'We loved it. The Professor made it all come alive. He's marvellous. How does he remember it all?'

By not having to clutter his mind with anything else. By sitting with his nose in a book while the rain drips through the ceiling and the shutters rot on their hinges.

Virginia said, 'And then this afternoon I got a pedicure. So very relaxing.'

Irene said, 'I'll tell you the best thing, though. The hot stone massage. Did you ever try that? It's the best. They cover you with cocoa butter and open up your meridians. By the time they're done you'll feel like you don't have a care in the world.'

Brady said the best way to learn anything is by doing. He made me sit in the chair in front of the computer screen.

He said, 'Think of something you'd like to look up.'

He said it could be anything: an address, a recipe, facts and figures.

I said, 'I have a couple of crossword clues I'm stuck on.'

'OK,' he said. 'That'll do.'

It's like a very quiet typewriter. You type in *Madagascan primate*. You click with your mouse and almost immediately it finds 'lemur', which fitted exactly. You type *Vishnu*, you click, and you get pages of information, including the name of the eagle on which he flies. 17 Across. Garuda. Extraordinary. It only looks like a television screen but somehow it contains all the answers. Frankie Gleeson was right.

Brady said, 'I'll show you something else. This is something new, something pretty amazing. Tell me the address of a place. Where you live, maybe?'

On the screen there appeared a pattern of little grey rectangles with fuzzy patches of green. Brady clicked the mouse and the fuzzy green became little broccoli sprout trees.

He said, 'Now I'm zooming in.'

He clicked again, and I began to see it was a street, viewed from above. One could make out the water tank on the Biddulphs' roof and the Mercedes parked outside the Koutouzovs'. It was Eaton Mews North, SW1. Brady said it was an actual photograph, taken by a satellite far above the earth. Quite amazing. I asked him if we might look at Lowhope too.

First there appeared the purple and brown of Morecambe Bay then, as he zoomed in, the colours changed. The mud flats looked a kind of bilious yellow and the trees looked like moss. One could see Hest Bank and Cartmel Sands and Humphrey Head, and then one could make out the roads and houses of Silverdale and Arnside and the unmistakeable sprawling shape of Lowhope Fell Hall. Somewhere, under that patchwork of roofs Mumsie and Bobbie were sitting down to oxtail soup and *Coronation Street*.

Brady said, 'And that's all there is to it. You're up and surfing. Best thing now is if you just sit here and play around with it.'

I said, 'How do people send messages?'

'That's email,' he said. 'We'll have to set you up with an account.'

Which took no more than five minutes and cost absolutely nothing.

He said, 'Now, who are you going to write to? You'll need their email address.'

But I didn't think I knew anyone who has an email address. It's a rather different world.

He said, 'I'll bet you do. You'd be surprised. I get a lot of the older passengers in here.'

I just couldn't think of anyone. Cousin Andrew doesn't even have a telephone since he was cut off. He refuses to pay the charge for reconnection. Cousin Tig is slightly more *au courant* so she might conceivably be up to date about email, but then, as Brady explained, if one hasn't been given their address one has to use a little detective work. I'm eenymeeny@smallworld.com. Eeny Meeny was what Mossop and Mrs Capstick and Olive used to call me when I was very little.

He said, 'If you know somebody who owns a business, chances are they'll have email. We can do a search.'

I said, 'Well, I have a half brother in Florida who sells second-hand cars. And I have friend called Billa Thoresby. She finds antiques and suchlike for rich people who are too busy to find them for themselves.'

We found Ripley in absolutely no time. It's called a website. Ripley's Pre-Owned Autos, Gainesville, with an email address and a photograph of the staff, including Ripley who now looks shockingly like Poppa. It didn't mention that he's 6th Earl of Oakhanger. I suppose it wouldn't mean anything in Florida. Billa took longer to find. Her business is called Belinda Thoresby Interiors.

I sent a little hello to both of them.

I said, 'What happens next?'

'Now you wait,' he said. 'Come back in a few hours, or tomorrow morning might be better. Log on, like I showed you, look in your mailbox and who knows? Your first email might be sitting there waiting for you.'

Like putting a message in a bottle and casting it out to sea, but much, much more thrilling.

Brady said, 'I'll tell you another thing you could do. You ever hear of Friends Reunited?'

And that was the greatest surprise of all because not only did Darnbrook appear in the list of schools but so did two very familiar names from the year of 1966: Araminta Fellowes and Flissie Philpott. All one has to do is sign up, drop a line to people one remembers and Bob is one's uncle.

Brady said, 'I'll leave you to it. Have some fun.'

I said, 'I'm still worried I might break your computer.'

He laughed and said, 'You'd have to drop it on the floor to break it and maybe not even then.'

He said I was an extremely quick learner but it turns out to be so incredibly easy I don't think I achieved anything remarkable. For instance, one simply types in *Enid Cecilia*

Nellish Finch and up one pops. Born Carlisle, 2 February 1950, daughter of Bertram Cecil Nellish, Viscount Moyle (that's Poppa) and Lady Primrose Tallentyne-Conyers (that's Mumsie). Married 30 July 1982 in Rome to Bernard Finch (born US, 1940). Furthermore, one can then 'click' on another member of the family and reveal all their information. For instance, that Mumsie is the only daughter of Edward Guy Tallentine-Conyers, 6th Marquess of Lune and Blanche Spenser, and that Poppa was the only son of Mortimer Cecil Nellish, 5th Earl of Oakhanger and Clementine Teague. And one could go back and back through countless generations. It's really quite absorbing.

At eleven p.m. I dared to peek into my eenymeeny mailbox and miracle of miracles, there was a message.

hi enid, never thought to hear from you per email Id have expected
you were still writing with one of them quill pens hope your well
were pretty good cant complain all the best yr ½ bro ripley.

Bernard was watching television, an activity he affects to despise so very much, and tucking into a cheeseboard and half a bottle of tawny port.

He said, 'Where the dickens have you been?'

I said, 'Joining the twenty-first century. I've opened an account.'

He said, 'Not a joint one, I hope. Try some of this *capra*. It's rather good.'

I was feeling quite fearless. I can only put it down to my conquest of computers.

I said, 'I encountered the Francis Homer Gleesons again today.'

He said, 'Well, you get no sympathy from me. You should have taken my advice and remained in the cabin.'

I said, 'I won't be a prisoner, Bernard. I simply refuse. And as for taking your advice, I begin to question its worth. Your advice may be about to cause both of us embarrassment.'

He muted the television.

I said, 'Mr Gleeson turns out to have an enquiring mind. It flitters across vast areas and one of the subjects it alighted on today was titles of the British peerage.'

He put down his glass.

I said, 'He came dangerously close to asking me to explain my title. Fortunately we were interrupted.'

Bernard said, 'What nonsense! The man is clearly a half-wit. The intricacies of the peerage will be quite beyond him.'

I said, 'His team are currently in the lead in the Trivia Quiz.'

'Trivia Quiz!' he said. 'Trivia is right. And anyway, we're in the middle of the Aegean, may I remind you. What can he possibly discover? Do you imagine there's a copy of Debrett's in the ship's library? I can assure you there isn't. It's wall-to-wall Grisham. Just forget the subject ever came up.'

I said, 'To quote Mr Gleeson, he has a sister who watches nothing but period dramas and is sure to want to know every detail about the English lady he met. He may be a man of limited education but he likes facts. He collects them. And if he goes to a computer for information, which he may very well do, he's going to find things spelled out so clearly a child could follow them and it's going to be perfectly humiliating. Then what price following your advice?'

'Really, Enid!' he said. 'You must stop being so melodramatic.'

I said, 'And you must stop being so complacent. Have you never heard of the World Wide Web?'

He looked at me over his half-moon glasses.

He said, 'It sounds to me like you've been reading far too many bad novels.'

7

Santorini. We're at anchor in the waters of the caldera along with the *Carnival Excelsia*, the *Costa Fortuna* and the *Diamante Princess*, and according to Jesus, who went up on deck first thing in order to give us a weather report, the mists had dispersed and the sky was the colour of a Blue Lagoon cocktail.

I was still in bed, lingering over my second cup of tea.

Bernard said, 'You're very slow this morning. Do get a move on or there'll be a queue for the tenders.'

I said, 'I'm not coming. I've decided to stay on board today.'

He said, 'Are you sick?'

I said, 'I didn't sleep well.'

'But are you *sick*?' he said.

I said, 'No, but I will be if I have to take that bus ride up to Akrotiri.'

One hairpin bend after another. It's the most stomach-churning journey and when we get there I find I can't enjoy the Minoan frescoes because I'm so dreading the return trip.

He said, 'You've never complained before.'

I said, 'I also calculate that around nine thousand other passengers will be making landfall today and I have seen it all before.'

The cabin felt luxuriously spacious after he left. I showered and dressed and then took the lift up to C Deck for a cappuccino. Lori Snow, Destination Shopping Consultant, was in the Coffeeteria.

She said, 'I love your T-shirt. Where did you get it?'

As far as one could remember it was from the Salvation Army shop near Hanover Square.

She said, 'You mean like, a goodwill store? Wow! That is so ethical. That is so cool.'

Lori is from Phoenix, Arizona. This is her second season with Oyster Line and she loves her work.

I said, 'I'm afraid I'm playing truant today. I'm going to stay on board and indulge myself. I hear there's a hot stone massage that's rather wonderful. If it isn't horribly expensive.'

She said, 'Ask for Kim, tell her who you are and she'll probably give you a discount. You mind if I ask you something? What night cream do you use?'

Extraordinary. Americans will ask one anything.

I said, 'More often than not I use nothing. A small jar of Pond's cold cream lasts me for ever.'

'No!' she said. 'Because your skin is fabulous. I mean, I don't know how old you are but whatever it is you don't look it.'

I said, 'I'm fifty-five, Lori.'

'Wow!' she said. 'That is awesome.'

I made a list of all the people I wanted to look up on the World Wide Web: beastly Roger Joad and the Luxley-Greenwoods; my old beaux, Guy Lambton and Miles Brassey. And of course, Bernard. Because if someone like little me pops up several times, there must be pages and pages of mentions for more notable people.

The Spa and Fitness Centre is one deck down from Coffeeteria. The girl said a hot stone massage would cost forty pounds and she could give me an appointment for eleven o'clock. Or, she could offer me a special discount on the Head to Toes Pampering Package, inclusive of brow shape, French manicure and bikini wax. With a slight niggle of guilt about the extravagance I booked the massage and then went down to the Internet Point.

Brady said, 'Surfing already, Mrs Finch? I think you've caught the bug.'

When an email drops into the mailbox it makes a little plinking sound. It was a reply from Billa Thoresby! Brady heard the noise and gave me the thumbs-up sign.

Darling Eeny!!!!!

How hugely thrilling to hear from you! Are you still with the molto sterno Bernardo? I believe he rather disapproved of me. Rollo and I are divorced I expect you heard and he's been a total shit about money so I'm about to embark on marriage numero 3, don't laugh!!!! Laurence is French, has a respectable amount of lolly and a small chateau in the Touraine which I helped him decorate. We're going to hire it out as a wedding venue. They're quite the thing. Anyway I've simply HEAPS to tell you. Are you ever in town? I should so adore to see you.

Hugs. Billa

How time flies when one is surfing. I found the Luxley-Greenwoods immediately, in the *Daily Telegraph* obituaries. Colonel (retd) Roderick 'Tommy' Luxley-Greenwood, died 2 October 1998 in Rome. He served in the Desert Rats during the North African Campaign, the invasion of Sicily, and the battle for Caen in 1944. He was predeceased by his wife Joyce, née Trotter.

So they're both gone. I'm not sorry. I never liked them.

No success with Roger but I found a Rodger with a 'd' Joad who runs an *agriturismo* in Puglia. The beaches look divine and one sleeps in one's own private *trullo*. It's hard to imagine the Roger Joad I knew doing anything more energetic than reading a two-day-old *Times* but perhaps his circumstances have changed. Perhaps he too has had to roll up his sleeves, insert a 'd' and start a new life.

Guy Lambton I found very easily, complete with a photograph taken when he was joint master of the Tern and Weaver Foxhounds in the mid 1990s. My word, he'd piled on weight, and grown rather florid too. There was also a Davina Lambton, chair of Yeaton, Tern and Lullingfields Women's Institute. I'll bet that's the wife. And two junior Lambtons, Emma and Penelope, who seem to be on a winning streak at various Staffordshire gymkhanas.

Miles Brassey also had numerous mentions, mainly on boards of directors, but no picture. I should love to know what he looks like these days. He was losing his hair even in his thirties when I last saw him. He doesn't seem to play polo any more but I did find a Carmela Guzman Brassey photographed at a benefit for distressed ponies held in Gloucestershire. Very slender, very glam. Argentinian, one assumes.

The greatest surprise though was Bernard, who hardly appeared at all. He was named as guest lecturer on this and several other cruises, past and future, but otherwise nothing. Even I have more entries than he does. I'd rib him about that but as he doesn't believe in the existence of the Internet there doesn't seem any point.

Brady is right. I have caught the bug. I was just about to drag myself away when into my mailbox plinked a message from Araminta Fellowes.

Dear Enid,

Isn't this Friends thing marvellous? I've only been on the

Darnbrook list for a month or so and you're my first contact. Hope that isn't because people remember me as a rather strict Head of House! Well here I am, leading such a dull life while you're cruising the world. We've promised ourselves we'll travel when the boys are off our hands but we have a large dairy herd so it's jolly difficult to get away. I'm married to Charlie Percy-Quennell (he was at Eton with my brothers) and we have two boys. Tom-Tom has just left Dumbletons with an A level in Media Studies and hopes to go into films. John-John is in the Far East pursuing import-export opportunities. Are you in touch with Billa Thoresby at all? I saw her at Henley about five years ago and thought she looked awfully bloated. It could have been due to some kind of medication of course but one daren't ask. She was always so touchy about 'embonpoints'. From what I hear she still leads a hectic love life too. Where does she find the energy! But do let's meet up. Do you ever come to Rutland?

Best regards,

Minta.

Nothing from Flissie Philpott. Brady says I shouldn't read too much into that as some people don't check their mailbox every day but my guess is she's still in a sulk about the transistor radio. Heavens, I was only trying it out. It was a tinny little thing anyway. If it had been a halfway decent radio it would have survived such a brief submersion in water.

I must own I was a little nervous about the massage. For

79

two pins I'd have called the whole thing off but I gave myself a stern talking to and found that once one became accustomed to wearing nothing but a modesty cloth it was really very relaxing. I found my thoughts meandering along all kinds of pleasant pathways and even after I had dressed and gone to lunch I felt strangely mellow.

Which is the only explanation I can give for Don Harrington, Gentleman Host, approaching me as I was leaving the Sea Breezes Salad Bowl and complimenting me on my glowing complexion.

He said, 'You're looking very bonny today, if I may say so.'

Bonny! I don't believe anyone ever called me that before!

He said, 'I was thinking of going up to the Riva. Can I press you to an ice cream cone?'

It's his fifth time cruising this route so he too had decided to give Santorini a miss.

He said, 'All that steaming mule shit. A man can only take so much. What was your excuse?'

Don is from Leeds, twice divorced and has had a great number of jobs including, many years ago, modelling men's clothing for mail-order catalogues. He said, 'Littlewood's, 1963 to 1965. I was the guy in the Y-fronts, with a spanner in my hand and a faraway look in my eye.'

I suppose he does have the kind of clean-cut looks that one used to see in adverts.

His role on the *Golden Memories*, where there are many

more single women than there are men, is to redress the balance, to be available as a dance partner and so forth.

He said, 'Taxi-dancer and widow-walker on a floating hotel. The statistics are in my favour, you see. All those rich old boys dropping off the twig, leaving the ladies with more money than they can ever spend. It's a job with very good prospects, as long as I keep all my marbles. As long as I don't start dribbling.'

I said, 'But you must have to be pleasant to everyone. What if you don't like the women?'

He said, 'What's not to like?'

He usually works on the Caribbean cruises during the winter and stays at home for the summer so he can follow the cricket at Headingley, but this year he needs to buy a new car so he's working through the summer too.

He said, 'Every time I see you you're on your own. Doesn't Sir Bernard ever leave the cabin?'

I said, 'Of course he does. He lectures. He leads tours. He's leading one today, to Akrotiri. And it's Professor Finch, not Sir Bernard.'

'Is it?' he said. 'Oh well, pardon me. But he does look like a Sir Bernard, you must admit.'

It's true, he does.

He said, 'And that's a lot better than looking like a *Saint* Bernard.'

One can see how Don got the job. He chats away so easily and he's awfully good at asking questions. Where were my favourite places, what did I like to do in my free time? I suppose a stranger couldn't be expected to understand that I don't often get any free time. Bernard's work dictates where we go and when. There are two houses to run, as well as Bernard's diary to manage and vast numbers of his foreign friends who turn up and expect to be fed. I'm lucky if I can finish *The Times* crossword once a week.

He said, 'There must be something you like to do. Everybody has something. I'll give you an example. When I go to a cricket match, I keep a score book. Then, on winter evenings, I read it and relive it, stroke for stroke. I enjoy that nearly as much as watching the actual game. Which some people might find sad. But that's me. What about horses? You look the horsey type.'

I said, 'Well I used to ride, obviously. Everyone did.'

He said, 'But not any more, eh?'

He was leaning forward, resting his chin on the heel of his hand, studying me.

I said, 'No, not any more.'

He said, 'How long since you were in the saddle, Enid?'

It's been years. Not since St Gallen.

I said, 'I was never very good at it, you see. Strange, because I was practically born on horseback. Everyone expected me to be a natural, but I wasn't. Pathetic really.'

Mumsie was out with the Vale of Lune when her birth pangs began and absolutely refused to give in to them until the final fox had been flushed. Then she hacked home alone and according to Mrs Capstick's version of things there was a frightful row as to whether childbirth was likely to ruin Poppa's billiard table and Mumsie barely made it to the scullery, where I made my debut.

Don said, 'Not pathetic at all. You wouldn't get me on a horse. Too bloody skittish. One minute you're riding high, next thing you know you're in a plaster cast up to your neck. I'll tell you something really pathetic. I like untangling string.'

I said, 'Well, I save rubber bands.'

He said, 'And do you fashion them into balls?'

I do. They make very good balls.

He said, 'I can't sleep if I'm not sure I put the milk bottles out on the step. I have to get up and check.'

I said, 'We don't get a milk delivery any more. We buy our milk at the supermarket. Do you like popping the bubbles in bubble wrap?'

He said, 'I can take it or leave it. But I'm acquainted with a few bubble-poppers. There's no hope, you know? It's an incurable condition.'

His mobile telephone juddered across the table. He picked it up and squinted at the little screen.

I said, 'I expect you're familiar with email?'

'No,' he said, 'I never got around to that. It takes me all my time to read these text messages people send me.'

He fished out a pair of reading glasses.

I said, 'I think email and the World Wide Web have changed my life.'

'Is that so?' he said. 'Well, I'm glad something did.'

Whatever *that* meant. He got to his feet.

I said, 'Thank you for the ice cream.'

'It was nice chatting to you, Enid,' he said. 'You've got a lovely smile. You should let the world see it more often.'

8

Bernard returned from Santorini very hot and very cross, a mood that wasn't improved by having an audience of three for this evening's lecture. I'm sure it was no fault of Bernard's but Gavin Iles, the Cruise Director, has been hostile from Day One.

He said, 'You're not on one of those Smithsonian cruises now, Bernard. This is the *Golden Memories*. Sun, sea and all you can eat. Your average punter sees he's got the choice of going to a lecture on the *lares compitales* or a Treasure Hunt, first prize dinner for two at any *Golden Memories* eatery, you can't blame him for saying, "Fuck the *lares compitales*."'

Bernard said it was their loss.

But Iles said, 'It'll be your bloody loss if you don't pick up your act. You've got to make things sexier. Isn't Delos where they've got all those big carved stone dicks? That's the way to sell it. The Donkey Dicks of Delos. That'd get the ladies interested.'

Such a vulgar man. He fingers the edge of his nostril as he talks.

And tomorrow is Mykonos, never my favourite port of call. Bernard remembers it when it was nothing but sugar-cube houses and windmills and fishing nets but to me it means crowds, crowds and still worse crowds. And for Bernard's tour we'll have to take that sickening ride across to Delos by caique.

Iles left.

I said, 'You won't like my saying this …'

Bernard said, 'Then don't say it.'

I said, 'I must. Because I very much fear, if you don't make more of an effort to get along with the Gavin Ileses of the world, you'll never work for Oyster Line again.'

'What a loss that will be,' he said.

It will. It will be the loss of the necessary jingle to pay the road tax on my ancient Volkswagen and buy a new washing machine for Corte Tagiapiera.

I said, 'This is where the money is, Bernard. This is the future. I'm afraid the bijou niche you've been occupying has now shrunk to a narrow ledge.'

He sighed and said, 'The world is too much with us, Enid. You should have seen Fira today. It was an anthill. I found myself praying for another cataclysmic volcanic eruption. I felt no fear. It would have been worth losing my life to see all those baseball caps engulfed in lava. Mass tourism. It's like the Car of Juggernaut flattening everything in its path.

86

Just because people can afford to go to places doesn't mean they should be allowed to. It's quite unbearable.'

I said, 'Well until you invent a new career it's what you must do, so please try to be less grumpy about it. Think of it this way, you're educating people. I'm sure you make a difference to some people's lives. What was it that American gentleman called you? Remember? Last year, after your tour of Heraklion? An agent for change!'

Not amused.

'Agent for change!' he said. 'It made me sound like a bank clerk. You should have seen what I had to work with today. Base metal. Vacant faces. I talk about the Cyclopean fortifications of Akrotiri and all they care about is where they can get a cold Coca-Cola and whether the toilets are safe to use. And to make matters worse, you weren't there to deal with their more idiotic questions. I think you were very selfish to stay on board.'

So I was missed. Perhaps I should play truant more often.

I said, 'Yes, I was selfish, but I've had a lovely relaxing day and now you'll be the beneficiary of my good mood. And we're at the Captain's table tonight. You'll enjoy that.'

He took a long, long shower and emerged transformed. The sun has quite bleached his hair and his black linen suit set it off very flatteringly.

I said, 'Ready for drinkies?'

'Yes,' he said, 'I could use a stiff one. Buzz Jesus and tell him we need ice.'

I said, 'We're not drinking in the cabin, Bernard. There's a distinct odour of sweaty shoes in here. We're going to a bar, like everyone else. We're going to be seen. Do you realize people are talking about us? They wonder why they never see us together. They wonder why I'm so often alone.'

He said, 'Do they? And who are "they"?'

I said, 'Just people.'

'People?' he said. 'Have you been mixing?'

I said, 'I'm putting my foot down. Tomorrow we're going to do things rather differently. When you've finished your tour we'll have an early lunch, perhaps at the Pelican or the El Greco, and then come back to the ship and do things together.'

'Things?' he said. 'What things?'

I said, 'There are heaps of possibilities. I don't believe you've seen half of the features of this ship. There's an open-air cinema. There's an art gallery.'

He said, 'An art gallery? Do you mean one of those places where they auction worthless posters to rich fools?'

I said, 'There's also a very agreeable ice cream parlour. Their pistachio is excellent.'

'My word,' he said, 'you have been indulging yourself. Very well, very well. Tomorrow you can show me the *gelateria*. But no art, Enid. I absolutely refuse to be seen looking at fake Dalis.'

We had pink gins in the Trafalgar Bar before we went in to dinner.

I was seated between Captain Sylvester and a very shy Englishman called Green, or possibly Brown. Bernard was partnered by Myrtle from Surprise, Arizona, a matronly lady swathed in grey organza, and a Mrs Polder who picked at her food. Her face made me think of a mummified monkey. Mr Polder was a huge egg-shaped man who breathed very noisily as he ate. The Polders are from Fredericksburg, Texas.

Myrtle from Surprise said that as far as she was concerned this is the best cruise she's ever been on and the only thing the *Golden Memories* lacks is a dedicated sun deck and pool where those who wished to could take off *all* their clothes. And Captain Sylvester joked that she should suggest it to the cruise line but it would have to be placed out of sight of the bridge otherwise it might constitute a dangerous distraction.

Mr Polder said, 'On the subject of nudity, I have something I'd like to ask the Professor here.'

And Bernard looked up, expecting, I imagine, a question on Greek vases.

Mr Polder said, 'I read in the cruise brochure that you're a Cornell man, Professor, so you'll be able to straighten something out for me. Is it true at Cornell they make you take that swimming test in the altogether?'

I don't know when I've ever seen Bernard lost for words. Well, it was a bizarre question. There was a long silence while he chewed on a piece of rather stringy chicken, then he shot the briefest glance in my direction and said, 'No. It's not true.'

He turned away, practically presenting his back to Mr Polder, and began talking to Myrtle as though she were the most fascinating creature in the world.

But Myrtle was still interested in Mr Polder's question. She said, 'A swimming test? For a college?'

Mr Polder said, 'Oh yes. It's a well-known thing. Before you can graduate. And I heard the boys are expected to take it in the buff. But the Professor says not.'

She said, 'Well the Professor should know.'

'He should,' he said. 'And I'll take his word on it.'

But he said it as though he didn't really accept it at all. Mr Polder has very small red ears and was sweating profusely from the effort of eating not only his own serving of Chicken Marengo but also his wife's. I disliked him immensely.

I was about to say something but then Captain Sylvester asked me what gondola rides cost these days and then my thoughts on whether Venice is sinking, and the moment slipped away. But what I *could* have said was that the whole story about swimming tests must be a myth. It has to be because Bernard is sixty-five years old and he has still never learned to swim.

Usually, after dinner at the Captain's table, Bernard is euphoric. For the other guests it can be the highlight of their cruise. They're keyed up, like horses before the Off, and completely disposed to be charmed by everything. It's the kind of situation where Bernard does very well. Indeed sometimes he so bathes in the spotlight one comes away forgetting that it was actually the *Captain's* table and not Bernard's. But tonight was different. Tonight he was preoccupied. He wouldn't take a stroll under the stars, he didn't want to go for a nightcap or give me what I'm sure would have been his hilarious impersonations of our dinner companions. All he wanted to do was go directly to the cabin.

I said, 'A penny for them?'

'You'd be over-paying,' he said. 'I'm just not feeling quite the thing, that's all.'

I said, 'Probably the prawn cocktail.'

'You're right,' he said. 'The prawns. I think I'll make tracks. Get safely within range of a bathroom.'

I said, 'If you don't mind I'll stay out a little longer. It's a beautiful evening.'

'It is,' he said. 'Sorry, old thing. But you stay and enjoy yourself. I'm sure there's some conjuring show, some knobbly knees contest you'd enjoy.'

Even a bad prawn can't dampen Bernard's natural gift for sneering.

I went to the Internet Point. Plink! Another message from Billa.

E,

So you tracked down dear, dear Minta. Yes, I know she's married to Charlie Percy-Quennell, several times winner of my Prick of the Year Award. Rollo knew him from Lloyds. Then the father died, Charlie inherited and he now makes cheese in the East Midlands.

91

I've seen Minta a few times in various rain-sodden marquees, but she tends to look at me as though I'm a hand grenade minus its pin and give me a wide berth. I do know there are two boys, one of whom is out in Laos or somewhere on his nth gap year, presumably in retreat from Minta's relentless hovering. Darling E, I have a splendid plan. Let me know when the molto sterno Bernardo will be out of town and I'll come and visit. I haven't been to Venice in yonks.

Huggeroni, B

Bernard was still awake and reading the *Selected Poems of Yannis Ritsos*.

I said, 'Tum feeling any better?'

'Much,' he said. 'False alarm. Apologies to the prawn.'

We made spoons and chatted in the dark.

I said, 'Captain Sylvester is nice.'

'Acceptable,' he said. 'Lightweight, but acceptable.'

I said, 'Darling, he's the captain. He doesn't need to know about the Amphictyonic League of Delos. The main thing is that he knows how to drive the ship. The English couple seemed decent.'

'Did they?' he said. 'I don't believe I heard them speak. The woman I had on my left reminded me of a Zeppelin and the one on my right reminded me of an Amazonian shrunken head.'

I said, 'And what did you make of Mr Polder?'

'Polder?' he said. 'Which one was he?'

Oh, Bernard.

I said, 'He was Humpty Dumpty. The one who believed Cornell makes people take a swimming test.'

'Oh yes,' he said. 'The buffoon. What more can one say?'

I don't know, Bernard. I suppose one could say that Mr Polder let you off rather lightly.

He was drifting off to sleep.

I said, 'Bernard, do you think I have a lovely smile?'

'Never really thought about it,' he said.

Silence. For ten seconds, twenty seconds? How long does it take a man to formulate a sentence and pay his wife a compliment?

He said, 'But now I do think about it, allowing for the fact that you have a tendency to scowl and that you grew up in a country with no tradition of orthodontics, yes, you do. A very pleasant smile.'

9

Mykonos. Once again we came in behind three other cruise ships. An island that used never to see anything larger than a fishing smack now has to accommodate four or five sixteen-deckers a week. There was no space for us dockside so we're at anchorage and people taking Bernard's tour were asked to be aboard the first tender. Today is a long day. We don't sail again till midnight, to give people the opportunity to sample the nightlife on shore, but the earlier in the day one tours Delos the better.

After last evening's poorly attended lecture we found we had an amazing thirty-seven people signed up for the trip, which rather restored Bernard's spirits, even when he discovered that the number included the McCuddys. Gavin Iles appeared at the tender station just before we pushed off, rubbing his hands and shouting, 'See what I mean, Bernard? I told the girls on the Excursions Desk to push the carved dicks. Now we're cooking.'

My role on the tours is to bring up the rear: the stragglers and those who are too frail or too heavy to keep up with Bernard's brisk pace; the ones who linger too long taking photographs or wander off prematurely to the souvenir stands. One has constantly to do head-counts, particularly on an uninhabited island like Delos where one really can't afford to leave anyone behind. We always walk the Sacred Way first, to the Sanctuary of Apollo, then on to the Lion Terrace. That way, those who are flagging can potter around the museum or rest at the snack bar while the more energetic ones climb the steps to the summit of Mount Kinthos for the view across the water to Rhinia and Tinos.

Delos is such a desolate place. Nothing but lizards and rocks and a merciless north wind. Two of the stone lions that used to guard the Sacred Lake are in Venice now, guarding the Arsenale. Seeing their old companions always makes me feel homesick, but then, perhaps the ones in Venice are homesick for Delos.

I ordered cold drinks for those who'd decided against the climb, among them Chip McCuddy. Cricket was gamely following Bernard up the mountain.

Often, at this juncture, I find I'm being serenaded by the Bernard Finch Appreciation Society, but today everyone was very subdued. Perhaps it was the heat. And I certainly think Gavin Iles had oversold the stone phalluses.

One lady said, 'Not much fun for you, dear, is it? Seeing

the same old ruins time after time? You ever get to go anywhere livelier? You ever tried Acapulco?'

Chip McCuddy's head drooped onto his chest and his Coca-Cola grew warm.

The plan, once we'd landed back at the jetty and concluded the tour, had been to stroll down to the Alefkandhra for lunch, then take the tender back to the ship. Mykonos is the port of call where everyone runs like lemmings to the beaches and the ship is quite deserted till evening, so I had every hope of persuading Bernard to relax with me on one of the sun terraces instead of bolting straight for the cabin.

He said, 'You realize I'll be very annoyed if you drag me to some spot where those awful people are likely to gather. What was their name? Gimson? Gibson?'

'Gleeson,' I said. 'How unlike you to forget a name.'

He said, 'Unless it's a name that I can have no possible interest in remembering.'

I let it pass.

I said, 'I think I can promise you Mr Gleeson will be stretched out on a patch of sand somewhere and Mrs Gleeson will be basting him with Ambre Solaire every half hour.'

He laughed.

We were pushing our way slowly through the crowds when I heard someone call Bernard's name and my heart quite sank. I knew even before I turned around who it was. Stash Leontis, sitting outside Niko's, with a glass of ouzo and one of his vile little black cigarettes. Stash is one of

Bernard's myriad Greek friends but unlike Tsampi Karagiannis he doesn't own a beautiful shade-dappled terrace and he doesn't even pretend to welcome my company. He lives in Athens and it was the most rotten bad luck to run into him on Mykonos. I knew exactly what it meant. There would be drinks, then more drinks, and lunch would be delayed until well into the afternoon.

'Bernard!' he said. 'I just was thinking how long since I see you. Is too long time. And suddenly there you are. This is wonderful surprise. Where you are going? Sit! We get drink!'

I said, 'Actually, we were on our way to lunch.'

'Lunch!' he said. 'I just had shower. I just had coffee. You English! Always in big hurry.'

Bernard said, 'It is rather early for lunch, darling. Do sit down.'

I said, 'It may be early but it's what we agreed.'

He said, 'Don't make a fuss, old thing. It's not every day we bump into Stash.'

But I was quite determined. I'd tagged along all morning. I'd been pleasant and helpful to the people on Bernard's tour. I'd ordered their drinks, advised them on tipping, provided them with Kleenex, helped them with their small coins. I'd performed a hundred tiresome services and the afternoon was going to be mine.

I said, 'You stay if you absolutely must. I have no wish to spend the afternoon watching you drink. I have a good book to get back to.'

Bernard said, 'I'm afraid the wind on Delos makes Enid very disagreeable. It always brings on what I call one of her Meltémi Moods.'

Stash said, 'Ladies, eh? What can we do with them?'

Damned cheek. I should have said, 'Stash, I don't imagine *you* ever even *tried* to do anything with a lady.'

But I didn't think of it till much later.

Some cruise passengers never go ashore, no matter how famous the port or what the inducement. They worry about falling ill with food poisoning or getting robbed. But today the ship felt quite empty when I returned, even in the atrium where there are always people about, whatever the hour. As we have a late sail-away tonight some of the crew have been allowed ashore too. When I popped back to the cabin to pick up my thriller Jesus and his friends were just off on a four-hour break, all gaiety and laughter.

'Everything OK, Ladyship?' he called. 'Anything you need?'

Such a sweet boy. Nothing is too much trouble for him. Sometimes I think Bernard forgets we're not his only passengers. He has a whole corridor to look after.

I had the saltwater pool all to myself. I enjoyed the laziest of swims. Then I lay under a parasol and must have dozed off. I only woke because someone was flicking water onto me. Irene. She was in the pool riding, as a child might, on the shoulders of Don Harrington; I hadn't realized the duties of a Gentleman Host extended so far.

After a little horseplay they clambered out of the water and pulled up sun loungers beside me. Don H, eyes closed, stretched out in the sun. Irene determined to chat even though I'd picked up my book.

She said, 'Mom wasn't feeling well enough for sightseeing so I had to stay on board today. She can't be left.'

Virginia was apparently well enough to be left unattended while Irene frolicked in the pool. But of course one knows nothing of the particulars. An ageing parent, and no brothers or sisters. How does one cope? Mumsie is now eighty and in rude good health. Bobbie is slightly younger and prone to bad joints. Of course in her case one has no personal obligations, but if something were to crop up with Mumsie … She's absolutely vowed never to leave Lowhope except in a wooden box. Then, I have Bernard to consider. I couldn't simply dash off and leave him to fend for himself, but I very much fear that Bobbie would be awfully tight-fisted about paying for a nurse. One can only hope that Mumsie enjoys a sudden death, preferably predeceased by Bobbie.

Irene said, 'You and the Professor had any more trouble? You know?'

I said, 'None at all.'

She said, 'They could be waiting till you're off your guard. Lulling you into a false sense of security.'

I said, 'I don't think so. It was all just an innocent mistake. We all know what it's like to be convinced one has met a person before when in fact one absolutely has not.'

99

She said, 'Still, you want to be careful. People latch on to you and before you know it you've got a problem on your hands. I have some experience in these things. I took a cruise to Margarita Island, Venezuela in ninety-six, started palling along with a couple I met at a Getting-to-Know-You, very nice people, or so they seemed. Psychopaths, it turned out.'

Don Harrington sniggered.

She said, 'You can laugh, Don. I ended up fearing for my life. See, the husband started hitting on me, you know what I mean? Said his marriage was on the rocks, yadda yadda. Then the wife got jealous. I was getting phone calls in my stateroom, nobody there when I picked up. She'd see me in the dining room and give the throat-cut sign. And where can you go on a ship? I was like a fish in a barrel.'

It sounded horrendous. No hiding place.

She said, 'I was near to cracking up, I can tell you. Then the last night, I forced myself to go to the gala, and there they were on the dance floor, all lovey-dovey, whispering and looking my way and laughing. It was all a put-up job.'

I said, 'But why?'

She said, 'It's obvious. That's how they got their thrills. Tormenting people. Seeing if they could push me over the edge. It put me off cruising for a while, I can tell you. Now I always travel with Mom. People see you have a companion, specially one who walks with a cane, they're more respectful.'

An alarming story. If true.

She said, 'So all I'm saying is, you better be careful. The friendly types can be the worst.'

Don rolled onto his stomach.

He said, 'Who are you talking about?'

She said, 'The Gleesons. Formal Night? We'd finished dinner and you'd just come over to our table? The little guy with the bad wig and the loud wife? He said he was sure he knew the Professor from when they were kids, from some little town in New York state? He made a big thing about it. You remember.'

'No,' he said. 'Can't say I do. Which Professor?'

'Lady Enid's husband,' she said. 'Do keep up.'

He said, 'Bernard? But he's English.'

She said, 'No he's not. He just sounds English. He's been married to Lady Enid for so long I suppose he's picked up the lingo.'

Actually, it's nothing to do with his being married to me. Bernard already sounded like a true Englishman when I met him. I suppose he must have learned it from Clifford Dennis.

Don said, 'So then what happened?'

I said, 'Nothing happened.'

Irene said, 'You didn't see the look Gleeson gave his wife after you and the Professor had left the table. As if to say "he's not heard the last of this". And then *she* said, "There was no call for him to storm off like that, I don't care how important he thinks he is. Anybody'd think it was an insult to ask if he was from Painted Post." Then *he* said, "Willy always was a touchy beggar." And that's when I told them, lay off the Professor or you'll have me to reckon with.'

Don said, 'Hang on a minute. Who's Willy?'

'Willy,' she said, 'is the person Gleeson says the Professor used to be. But he isn't.'

Don said, 'Buggered if I can follow it. And where is our Professor today?'

I said, 'He bumped into an old friend. They're having lunch in town. Bernard likes to keep up his colloquial Greek.'

'Colloquial Greek, eh?' he said. 'That's a new one.'

Irene said, 'What's he a professor of exactly?'

The thing about Bernard's career is that it's been enormously varied.

I said, 'Basically, he's a classicist.'

Don said, 'Is he, by jingo! Try saying that ten times with a new set of dentures.'

Irene said, 'And I guess he's retired from some kind of college?'

Not retired in the sense of receiving a pension. If only. Obviously he had been associated with various seats of learning but by the time I met him his teaching days were already over. In Rome his energies were devoted entirely to assisting Clifford Dennis. To a certain extent one might say he sacrificed his academic career and little thanks he got for it in the end. As I recall, in those days he was known simply as Dr Bernard Finch. It was much later, after he began lecturing on cruise ships, that the 'professor' title somehow caught on. He has explained it to me many times but it's all so convoluted that one never feels much the wiser. But 'Professor' certainly suits him.

'Yes,' I said. 'Retired.' And I fixed my eyes firmly on the page I was trying to read.

An American voice came floating across the deck.

'Hi there, Don! Is that a flotation device down the front of your trunks or are you just pleased to see me?'

It was a woman, not in the first flush but clinging to the wreckage. She was wearing an animal-print bikini and a pair of mirrored sunglasses.

'Hello, Dorcas,' he said, rather wearily.

Irene sat bolt upright.

'Fuck off, witch tits,' she said. 'Don's spoken for.'

One sensed that some terrible cat fight might be about to break out and there one was, trying to read one's book and directly in the line of fire.

'Is that the time?' I said. 'I really must be making a move.'

10

I was still waiting for the lift when Don came hurrying along, tucking in his shirt.

'Going down?' he said.

Up, down, wherever. There's no peace to be had on this vast ship even on a day when everyone has supposedly gone ashore.

He said, 'Checking to see if the wanderer's returned?'

No, hellfire and damnation. In the remote eventuality that Bernard was sitting in the cabin wondering where I was, hard cheese for him. Not that it was any of Don Harrington's business.

I said, 'The lift seems very much in demand. You might find it quicker to walk.'

He looked at his watch. An expensive-looking piece for a man who wears British Home Stores' sandals.

'I've got time,' he said. 'It's only friends of Bill W.'

He said it as though it should mean something to me, but

I imagine there may be any number of Bill Ws on a ship the size of the *Golden Memories*.

'Of course, the walk would do me good,' he said. 'Trouble with these cruises. If you're not careful all you do is eat.'

But still he stood there.

I said, 'They say we may have thunderstorms tonight.'

'I hope so,' he said. 'Clear the air. Sorry about that little scene back there. Irene can be a bit …'

I suggested 'territorial' might be the word.

'Yes,' he said. 'That's it. Territorial. And she does enjoy a scrap. Start a fight in an empty room, could Irene. And the other one's not much better. Dorcas. She's supposed to be dancing with Ike Windhagen but she still seems to be playing the field. You wouldn't believe the trouble these dance contests cause.'

I said, 'It's a great compliment to you though. Two ladies fighting over you, at your age.'

He laughed and said, 'You're overlooking an important point.'

The lift doors opened.

I said, 'What's that?'

'They're nuts,' he said. 'Dorcas, Irene. Round the bend, the both of them.'

I stayed on past K Deck and went, swimmer still slightly damp beneath my towelling cover-up, directly to the library where a demonstration of paper crafts was about to begin. As Poppa always said, the best revenge is to enjoy life.

Someone sat behind me. Then I felt a tap on my shoulder. Cricket McCuddy.

'I make all my own cards,' she whispered. 'I'm always on the lookout for new ideas.'

An origami shamrock, a pop-up talking-mouth frog card, a Christmas angel made of quilled paper and a Hallowe'en skeleton, and those who'd like to try their hand can attend a workshop tomorrow afternoon. Perhaps I will. It's quite wonderful the skills one can acquire on a cruise ship. When Bernard lectured on the Gods and Gondolas Cruise last year I learned how to read a balance sheet. I've since forgotten but nevertheless I'm sure it's a jolly useful thing to have done.

Cricket claimed me the absolute instant the demonstration was over.

'We loved the tour this morning,' she said. 'That husband of yours is quite something. All those names and dates. How'd he ever remember them?'

Bernard remembers what interests him.

I said, 'It's a gift. Though strangely he can never remember the date of our wedding anniversary.'

'That's normal,' she said. 'What are you doing next? You got anything planned? I'll bet you don't. I'll bet that hubby of yours has his head stuck in some old encyclopaedia. Chip's napping. But I can't stay in bed when there's all these activities to enjoy. Let's you and me go do something.'

We looked at the schedule. Alec Fisher, the golf pro, was

running a swing clinic. Fr. Griffiths was offering an Interfaith Evensong in the Library. And there was a Music of the Seventies quiz in the Show Lounge.

'Here we are,' she said. 'The Martini Master Class.'

I hesitated. Fatal.

'Come on,' she said. 'It'll be fun. At the end they give you a real martini glass, to take away and keep.'

And so I allowed myself to be led to the Top Hat Bar. What did I learn?

1. One should never use the ice from the cocktail shaker but rather strain the martini from the shaker on to fresh ice cubes.
2. Citrus twists can be prepared in advance and kept in the refrigerator.
3. Barmen are now called baristas and one calls them anything else at one's peril.

We began with a classic 007 Vesper Martini. Gin and vodka, three to one, with a half measure of Lillet Blanc. I only took the tiniest sip. The Pepper and Salt Martini is made with vermouth and black peppercorn syrup and served in a salt-rimmed glass. A Stinkatini is garnished with a garlic-stuffed black olive. Both outstandingly good but as Cricket doesn't care for olives or for garlic I'm afraid I tasted rather more than I should have. She, on the other hand, adored the sweeter mixtures and knocked them back with reckless haste. A

Watermelon Martini, with a sprig of mint and a melon ball on a stick. A Banana Cream Pie Martini with a maraschino cherry and the glass rim dipped in cocoa powder. And a Cranberry Martini with a cinnamon stick, very cheery to look at and suitable, as the barista said, for the holiday season.

Cricket was terribly tipsy by the time we emerged and became quite emotional when I insisted she take my complimentary martini glass.

'You're so darling,' she said. 'I told Chip, the first night we had dinner. I said that is a darling girl.'

I said, 'I think a coffee might be in order.'

'Good idea,' she said. 'But first we better sit down a minute till the ship stops leaning.'

I steered her towards the Coffeeteria.

'This is my friend, Lady Enid,' she announced to the waitress. 'Us girls are looking for coffee.'

The waitress said, 'You came to the right place.'

Cricket said, 'Because the ship's rocking around. You feel that? Must be a storm blowing up. So me and Enid, we're gonna sit right here till it's safe to move. Bring us the best coffee you got. I'll take mine with extra cream. And marshmallows.'

The waitress said, 'Coming right up.'

And I believe I heard her say, 'One espresso, one Viennese with marshmallows, one sick bag to go.'

Cricket said, 'Enid. Glad I ran into you. It's nice to make a new friend, don't you think?'

She seemed to be waiting for an answer.

108

I said, 'Yes. Very pleasant.'

I had a vision of Christmas cards arriving, year after year without fail, and the day eventually dawning when one asks, 'Who on earth *were* the McCuddys?'

She said, 'What'll we do next?'

I said, 'I think I'll go back to my cabin and read.'

'Reading,' she said. 'I could never get into that. Is your hubby napping too?'

I said, 'No. He had an appointment in town.'

'See,' she said, 'that's what I mean. They have to go to business. They have to take a nap. It gets lonely for a girl.'

I said, 'But you have children. And grandchildren, I believe.'

'All married,' she said. 'All gone. I'm lucky if I see them once a week. Everybody's busy. We gave them our best years, didn't we? We didn't have time to make a friend. Now they say "Grandma, you should get a computer." They say, "Cricket, you should volunteer at the Veterans' Hospital." They say, "You're very fortunate. Your husband can afford to take you on cruises." They don't realize. Chip has to take a lot of naps. He says I wear him out. It's the age difference. Like you and your hubby. He's older than you, right?'

Ten years. They say the significance of the gap shrinks as one gets older and anyway, Bernard never seems to change.

She said, 'See, there's eighteen years between me and Chip. I guess I shouldn't complain. He's pretty good. We can't expect them to be studs, can we? Not at their age.'

We can't.

109

'Enid,' she said, 'you're an experienced woman. How often would you say is normal? Man and wife. At our time of life. You understand what I'm talking about?'

I was very much afraid I did, along with everyone else in the café. She had leaned in close to me but failed to lower her voice.

I said, 'Every case is different, one imagines. How is the cha-cha-cha coming along?'

'No,' she said, louder than ever. 'But. Just for argument's sake. We're talking about what, three, four, five times? We're just talking ballpark here. Just girl friends talking right? Gimme a number.'

Under the influence of alcohol one of her eyes has a tendency to wander.

I said, 'Well, if you insist. Shall we say four?'

As Bernard once coyly expressed it, 'paying one's quarterly dues'. He's actually rather shy in that department.

'Yeah,' she said. 'I reckon four is reasonable. Some weeks it might be more, some weeks it might be less.'

I said, 'I meant per annum.'

'Per annum!' she shrieked. 'I'm not talking about four times a year! I'm talking about four times a week!'

Two men seated at a nearby table roared with laughter.

'Shhhh,' she said to them. 'This is girl talk.'

I signalled for the bill.

She said, 'Are you serious? Four times a year? Did your hubby get that prostate procedure or something?'

It's not a thing one ever discussed. Bernard, being older and more experienced, has generally taken the lead in these matters and 'quarterly dues' is the habit we fell into. Of earlier liaisons in his life, I know nothing. Actually, I suspect he may have been too busy roaming the hills of Arcadia to have had any.

'Four times a year!' she kept saying. 'And he's a good-looking guy too. How'd you keep your hands off him? I guess you're not on hormones. See, I'm on hormones. Everybody should be on hormones. Me and Chip, we have separate rooms at home, because of his snoring. But we still get it together, you know? I just have to remind him to take his little blue pill.'

I said, 'The pill stops him snoring?'

'No,' she said. 'No, no, no. I'm talking about the pill that puts the lead back in the pencil.'

The waitress brought the chit.

Cricket said, 'I'll get that. I have money.'

I signed. It was only two coffees.

She said, 'I have bags and bags of money. My husband is a very wealthy man.'

The waitress said, 'Is that right?'

Cricket said, 'See my friend Enid? She only gets it four times a year. Makes you think. And you know something else? My husband, when he takes his little blue pill he's as good as new.'

The waitress said, 'All that and money too, eh? Some people have all the luck.'

I let Cricket off the lift at F deck and pointed her in the direction of her suite.

'Enid,' she said. 'My friend. Do you need money?'

I said, 'No, I don't need money.'

Not much.

She said, 'Because I can give you money.'

I said, 'Perhaps you should have a little rest before dinner.'

'Sure,' she said. 'Nighty-night. Give my regards to Willy.'

I said, 'Who's Willy?'

Arms flailing.

'Willy?' she said. 'You know? *Willy*. The Professor.'

I said, 'Why do you call him Willy?'

She leaned against the wall of the corridor.

I said, 'His name's Bernard.'

'Bernard,' she said. 'You're right. Frankie's the one calls him Willy. Silly. Mind how you go, Enid. Ship's still leaning.'

11

No emails. How flat one feels when one's mailbox is empty. I looked again at the Darnbrook page of Friends Reunited and sent messages to two girls who might conceivably remember me: Caro Griggs and Leonora Carisbroke-Cowles. They always went around together so one sort of has an image of them as one does of Tweedledum and Tweedledee, without being entirely clear which one was which. Still, worth a try.

Then I did something fearfully rash. I sent a message to Miles Brassey. Just a brief and breezy 'hello' but for lack of his personal address I followed Brady's suggestion and sent it to info@hoggmillerblandbrokerage.com. One prays one hasn't made a colossal fool of oneself.

People come and go all the time at the Internet Point but there's no chatting. Each person is intent upon his own computer screen and all one hears is the rattle of keyboard keys and the occasional sigh or stifled titter. It wasn't until

I got to my feet to leave that I realized Chip McCuddy was using the terminal back to back with mine.

I whispered to Brady, 'Mr McCuddy is very deep in concentration this evening.'

'Oh yes,' he said. 'A big card player, Mr Mac. He plays most days.'

Imagine! Playing poker without ever meeting the other players. Is there anything one can't do with a computer?

As the slight martini haze cleared I found I was ravenously hungry. I took a booth in the back corner of the Hash Sling, wolfed down corned beef with two fried eggs undetected by anyone eager to be my friend, and then walked it off going round and round the jogging track until the Chocoholic Buffet opened at nine thirty. They had one of those chocolate fountains on board the Aphrodite last year but Bernard rarely eats dessert and anyway he would rather go hungry than be recognized in the scrimmage of a buffet. One of the great advantages of having an unmemorable face is that one can return for second helpings of chocolate-dipped strawberries without anyone remarking.

Ten thirty and the cabin was still in darkness. It got to eleven and still Bernard hadn't returned.

Jesus said, 'Oh, Ladyship, what we gonna do with him? Last tender's leaving in ten minutes. If the Professor don't make it he'll have to swim.'

An option not open to Bernard.

I couldn't have been calmer. In fact I found I was very slightly hoping that he *would* get left behind. It would make an exciting end to the day and perhaps teach him a lesson. So when I heard him, bantering with the stewards in the corridor, I must confess I felt the teensiest bit disappointed. He appeared in the doorway looking very much the worse for wear.

As far as one could gather he and Stash had lunched far too well at the Yacht Club, then they'd fallen in with a crowd of Stash's friends and continued the party at a series of bars up by the windmills.

I said, 'Why must you always push things to the very limit?'

He said, 'Why must you always exaggerate?'

I said, 'What would you have done if you'd missed the last boat?'

'Oh for God's sake, Enid,' he said, 'I *didn't* miss the last boat. I never miss boats. I'm here, but you are so poisoning the pleasure of a wonderful day, I rather wish I weren't.'

We undressed in silence, with Bernard being very careful to avoid my eye or any other contact, which was no easy matter with so little room to move. I made a bid to thaw the chill.

I said, 'You look sunburned. Do you need calamine lotion?'
'No.'

I said, 'Are you hungry?'
'No.'

I said, 'Would you like first use of the bathroom?'

'I'm entirely indifferent.'

Then he lay on the bed, hiding behind Herodotus, though I'm sure he was far too squiffy to read.

I said, 'Yes, thank you, Bernard, I had a very enjoyable day in spite of being bumped by Stash Leontis. I swam, I relaxed in the sun and chatted to people, I had my body covered in oil and massaged by a seven-foot eunuch. I had three martinis, dinner with Omar Sharif, and an all-you-can-eat chocolate fountain dessert experience.'

He put down his book.

He said, 'Enid, are you going through the change of life?'

I said, 'What exactly do you mean?'

He said, 'I don't think there's any need to go into details. You are at that age.'

I said, 'I may be at *that age* but I feel perfectly well. Do you know, I was chatting today to a lady whose husband is considerably older than you and they still have sexual relations.'

He said, 'When we get home I think you should see a doctor.'

I said, 'I will not. I've never felt better.'

He said, 'Nevertheless, you're behaving in a very erratic manner. First you throw a tantrum because I elected to come over on the last boat, then you try to make amends by plying me with calamine lotion. And now it becomes clear that you've been roaming the ship, indulging in heaven knows what fantasies and talking to heaven knows whom about heaven knows what. You shouldn't even mingle with the passengers. I used to be able to trust you in these matters. You used to have an almost regal reserve.'

I said, 'How can I not mingle with the passengers? What else am I supposed to do if you take off with friends and leave me in the lurch?'

He said, 'You would have been perfectly welcome to stay and have lunch with Stash. You were the one who went off in a jealous huff. And now I think you're just being provocative. You never drink martinis and I don't believe for one moment that you discussed matters of such a personal nature with a total stranger.'

I said, 'Not a *total* stranger, at all. Mrs McCuddy. We went to a paper-crafts demonstration and then on to a martini tasting. I was quite glad of her company after you stood me up. But as I was saying, apparently Mr McCuddy had some waterworks problems a year or two ago but now he takes a little pill, to assist with the hydraulics, and Cricket says he's his old self. Better, in fact.'

'Cricket?' he yelled. 'Cricket? What kind of a name is that? Who *are* these people?'

I said, 'You have met them. Cricket and Chip McCuddy were at our table on Formal Night. They're from Delaware and they're friends of the Francis Homer Gleesons. Cricket sat between you and Officer Davenport with her ample cleavage on display, as I'm sure you perfectly well remember.'

He said, 'I remember no such thing. I remember nothing of Formal Night except that I was surrounded by mediocrity.'

I said, 'You're fibbing, Bernard. You have every reason to remember because that was the night you were cornered by Mr Gleeson and charged with being the identical twin of someone called Willy Fink.'

'Willy Fink!' he said. He brushed the name aside as though it were an annoying insect.

I said, 'And by the by, someone asked me something today and I couldn't for the life of me remember the answer. Where were you when you were made "professor"? Was it Pavia?'

He said, 'Someone asked you? Someone asked you that! Good grief, what is this, a budget cruise for the unlettered or a Papal Inquisition?'

I said, 'Neither. It's a simple question.'

'Ah yes,' he said. 'A simple question from a simpleton. This undoubtedly comes from the dogged Mr Gimson.'

I said, 'Gleeson, Bernard. Mr Gleeson.'

'I stand corrected,' he said. 'Well, what will he come up with next, I wonder? I suppose tomorrow he'll be querying my hat size.'

I said, 'I'm going to attribute your testiness to the amount of alcohol you've consumed. Perhaps in the morning, when you're sober, you'll give me a civil answer. As a matter of fact it wasn't Mr Gleeson who asked. And from everything I've seen he's a perfectly ordinary, decent sort of person.

Not Brains Trust material, perhaps, but not a complete ninny. He thought he knew you, he made a mistake and now he's quietly minding his own business and enjoying his cruise. I don't see any necessity for you to obsess about him.'

'Obsess?' he said. 'Is that really an intransitive verb?'

I said, 'Bernard, I'd like to turn off the light and go to sleep. As to Mr Gleeson, I think he's very unlikely to trouble you any further.'

And as the words left my lips there was the faintest noise from the corridor and a long, cream envelope slid under the cabin door.

Frankie and Nola Gleeson
invite you to cocktails,
Wednesday Nite, 6 til 8,
The Humidor Cigar Bar

Bernard dropped the invitation straight into the wastepaper bin but it was as though it lay between us all night.

12

I waited until we'd finished breakfast before broaching the subject.

I said, 'I should respond to the Gleesons.'

He said, 'There's no need. It's only a cocktail party.'

I said, 'It doesn't hurt to be courteous. Perhaps one of us could pretend to be unwell.'

He said, 'I don't need to pretend. I *am* unwell. I have a sore throat.'

I said, 'That's because you came home tight and snored all night.'

He said, 'I did not snore. As a matter of fact I hardly slept. I lay awake worrying about your erratic behaviour.'

I said, 'What do you mean?'

'Really, Enid,' he said. 'All this talk of Omar Sharif and banana martinis and omniscient computers. I very much fear you're going off the rails.'

I said, 'Omar Sharif was an ironic embellishment. And

actually, I think it would be easier to attend the Gleesons'
little party than to make excuses. I'll find you a throat
lozenge.'

He said, 'Please don't trouble. It's not *that* kind of sore
throat. I'm not going and that's all there is to it. I am on
this cruise to teach and to guide, not to adorn the cocktail
parties of strangers.'

I said, 'And what am I here for?'

He said, 'To be your husband's helpmeet and comfort,
not to cause him embarrassment and anxiety.'

I said, 'Well then, perhaps your helpmeet had better fly
the Finch flag and attend the party on your behalf.'

'No, Enid,' he said. 'I forbid it. We don't socialize. That's
our rule. You know that.'

I reminded him that on the Gems of Iberia cruise we not
only had cocktails with Lord and Lady Hallingby, we also
dined with them and then reciprocated with drinks and
nibbles in our stateroom, but he said that was an entirely
different case.

'A completely different case,' he said. 'The Hallingbys
were our kind of people. But these Gleesons, just because
they have money, do they think I'm on tap? Do they think
they can summon me, like a member of the crew? There are
certain lines one does not cross. I mean to say, look how
they've spelled "night" and "till".'

I said, 'At the very least I must send a note.'

He said, 'If you insist, but your politesse will be wasted

on them. Keep it short. Simply extinguish any possibility of our attending without going into explanations. Get one of the stewards to deliver it. And then you're to remain out of their sights today. Jesus will serve us lunch in here and we'll read our books.'

The very idea was unendurable. It was still early but the sky was already vibrating with heat.

I said, 'Bernard, I refuse to hide. The weather is perfect and we have a glorious day at sea. Now please stop being silly and come for a turn around the Sports' Deck.'

He said, 'There's nothing silly about a speaker being concerned for his voice. I'm lecturing on the History of the Olympiad at five o'clock and as I believe I already mentioned, I have a throat infection.'

I said, 'Then all the more reason why I shouldn't be cooped up with you. And if you really have a sore throat you should go to the infirmary.'

He said, 'What do you mean, "if I *really* have a sore throat"?'

I said, 'Your throat wasn't bothering you when you were gallivanting with your friends yesterday. You seemed to be in good enough voice last night, serenading Jesus with the Song of Seikelos. There seemed to be very little wrong with your voice when you were berating me. And I absolutely will not stay in here all day to humour you. All this nonsense about the Gleesons. To listen to you one would think they were savages, which they certainly are not. They may be unsophisticated and rather gaudy, but the mark of a true gentleman is that he can get along with anyone. Poppa used to say snobbery is the hallmark of an upstart and you, Bernard, are behaving like a snob.'

I didn't see it coming. The yogurt pot came spinning out of nowhere, and struck me on the cheekbone. One has read about domestic violence but never, ever dreamed that one would one day become a victim. I'm still trembling as I remember the shock of it.

He said, 'And you are behaving like an unruly child. You seem to have lost all sense of what is correct and appropriate. A loyal, solicitous wife would follow her husband's wishes without questioning them, but you seem determined to go your own self-indulgent way. You're a selfish bitch, Enid. A selfish, selfish bitch.'

This was deeply unfair. I respect Bernard's wishes almost all the time. I never cook devilled kidneys because he hates the smell. And the reason I haven't seen Billa Thoresby in so long a time is that Bernard found her to be irritating. Billa and I used to be such pals. And will be again.

Usually, after a tiff, he's quick to make amends. He hates to see one blub. But I could tell by the set of his jaw that he had no immediate intention of apologizing and, indeed, his last words to me as I left the cabin were, 'I advise you against running to any of your new-found friends with lurid tales. I advise you to remember whom you have to thank for your status on this cruise.'

Jesus was whistling his way along the corridor.

'Good morning!' he said. 'We got ourselves another beautiful day.'

One did one's best to manage a smile.

'Ladyship,' he called after me. And he pointed out that I had apricot yogurt splattered down the front of my blouse.

He said, 'Take it to the laundry for you?'

I said, 'No, I don't think I'll go back to change. Perhaps we can just dab it clean?'

We went to the steward's station and he gave me some water and a paper towel.

I said, 'Careless of me.'

'No worries,' he said. 'You go up in the sunshine, it'll be dry in no time.'

Jesus is always so open and friendly but his eyes never met mine this morning. He was embarrassed. Perhaps he'd overheard Bernard calling me a selfish bitch.

Mumsie and Poppa always behaved as though Olive and Mossop and Mrs Capstick were blind and deaf. It took me some years of not having a domestic staff for me to realize those people do have eyes and ears.

How lonely one can feel among four thousand people. All those couples strolling hand in hand along the decks, frolicking in the hot tubs, picking out jewellery in the shopping mall. I thought I'd mastered my tears until Lori Snow, Destination Shopping Consultant, greeted me so warmly.

'Hi, Enid,' she said. 'Wanna go get a coffee?'

And so it all came tumbling out.

*

124

I said, 'Bernard is under stress, of course.'

Self-inflicted, but still. He's such a perfectionist.

'Bullshit,' she said. 'He behaved like an asshole.'

Lori is thirty, maybe thirty-five. It's a different generation, a different attitude.

I said, 'I'll just stay out of his hair this morning. Allow things to cool down.'

She said, 'Stay clear of him all day, give him something to think about. You gotta draw the line, Enid. You know? Today it was a yogurt pot. Tomorrow it could be his fist. My cousin Sherrilynn, her boyfriend used to throw his dinner at the wall. Did it all the time. She even put up spongeable wallpaper. Then one day he threw the crockpot too, knocked her unconscious. She said she never saw it coming, but I did.'

I said, 'Then what happened?'

She said, 'The judge sent him to Anger Management.'

I said, 'And did it help?'

'No,' she said. 'He skipped too many classes.'

Lori is a sweet, friendly girl but one does have the impression that she and her cousin come from the type of background where that kind of behaviour isn't unusual. Bernard is an educated, cultured man. But the Gleeson episode has rather unstrung him, and then a day in the company of Stash Leontis won't have helped. A man who never married and who doesn't miss an opportunity to remind Bernard of various wild, bachelor jaunts they undertook together in the dim and distant past. All of this I can see might make a man feel a little out of sorts. Nevertheless I think Lori is right. A thrown yogurt pot should not be ignored.

I found a shady corner where I could sit and think. It was Virginia who interrupted my solitude.

She said, 'It's nice to see a familiar face. Ask me, this ship's too big. I like a cruise where you can get to know people.'

Irene was at Ballroom Boot Camp. Only four days till the big competition.

I said, 'They seem to take it very seriously.'

'Some of them do,' she said. 'Some of them would kill to win. Irene's only doing it for fun. She's more of a social dancer.'

I said, 'She seems to have hit it off with Don Harrington.'

'Yes,' she said. 'He's getting up in years, for Irene, but he seems nice. He has a very funny way of talking, though. I can't catch everything he says.'

I said, 'He's a Yorkshireman.'

'Is he?' she said. 'Well, he still has a good head of hair, I'll give him that. There was another woman had her eye on him. Dorcas. Mutton dressed up as lamb, if you ask me. Very pushy, very possessive. But she didn't reckon on Irene. Irene usually gets her man. She usually manages to have at least one little adventure per cruise.'

We found two seats outside the Verandah Lounge.

She said, 'I don't understand the appeal of it myself. You're just getting to know a person when it's time to say goodbye.

Because they never work out, you know, these vacation romances. They never amount to anything. How can they? You're living in Philly and he's living in Portland. But it doesn't bother Irene. She's not the type to settle down. I used to hope she would. I used to hope I'd get some grand-babies but I can't complain. We travel to all these wonderful places and she takes the best care of me. She's my only one, you see. Do you and the Professor have children?'

I suppose if children had come along we'd have managed, but they didn't and I've always felt it was for the best. Bernard was quite set in his ways by the time we met and babies would have been terribly disruptive. He isn't any old husband. He needs to be free to pursue his research interests. How could we have travelled if there were school fees to find and long summer hols to cater for? We couldn't have sent them to Lowhope. I always remember what Bobbie Snape said when Bernard and I announced our engagement.

She said, 'I hope you're not going to start podding out brats because we can't have them here. It wouldn't be fair on the dogs and Prim couldn't cope.'

'Prim' is what Bobbie calls Mumsie. It's short for Primrose. Funny, Poppa always called her 'Mumsie'.

Of course my being without issue means that when I go to my long home a whole branch of Mumsie's family will die out but she's never voiced any regrets about that. She's not a sentimental woman. But it could be the reason she's thrown herself so energetically into her dog breeding. A kind of sublimation. It may be the end of the line for Lunes at Lowhope Fell Hall but she'll long be remembered for her work with the Dandie Dinmont terrier.

'No,' I said. 'Sadly no children.'

'Taff!' she cried. And along came the Reverend Griffiths in a short-sleeved clergy shirt and a pair of cotton slacks.

'Virginia!' he said. 'Glad to find you. And Lady Enid too. Would you ladies care to join me in a Danish pastry?'

It seems that even an older person like Virginia can find herself a companion on a ship like the *Golden Memories*.

I said, 'I was sorry to miss your Songs of Praise last evening. I had a prior commitment.'

'Not to worry,' he said. 'I'm sure you were there in spirit and that's what counts. We had a pretty good turnout, considering we were up against the demon drink. They put us in the same slot as a Martini Master Class. Well you can't blame people. They come on holiday, they want a bit of fun. The flesh is weak.'

Virginia said, 'I hear you had another busy night.'

'I did,' he said. 'Who told you?'

Apparently Virginia looks in on the general information desk several times a day, for a chat. It whiles away an hour and she hears all the gossip.

She said, 'Night before last he had a stroke, didn't you, Taff?'

'Heart attack,' he said. 'He wasn't one of ours, as it turned out. He was a gentleman of the Hebrew persuasion. But a prayer never hurts.'

'And last night,' she said, 'they say there was a gun fight in the laundry.'

'It was knives, actually,' he said. 'Two Filipinos in the butchery department. They get over-excited and out come the blades. Plenty to be had down there, of course. Meat cleavers, boning knives. And then we had a croupier, very depressed. It's working below deck that does it. Some of them hardly see daylight. It affects the mind, you see. Ask any doctor. People spend too much time with nothing but a light bulb, it can make them very down in the dumps. Sometimes they threaten to jump. That's where I come in.'

He's never had an actual jumper. I think Virginia was rather disappointed.

'Well,' he said, 'Let me put it this way. I've been on two cruises where people have gone over the side but neither of them were jumpers. They were just silly buggers. One was a lad, had too many beers and did it for a dare. The other was a lady and I won't go into details. I'll spare your blushes. Suffice it to say that a stateroom balcony and a copy of the Kama Sutra were involved. How's the Professor, Lady Enid? I never see him out and about.'

I said, 'He's not so well this morning. His throat is troubling him.'

And his nerves. And his self-control.

He said, 'I'm sorry to hear it. Would he like a visit, do you think?'

Bernard loathes what he calls Liturgical Lukewarms.

129

Clifford Dennis was vertiginously High and one imagines may have flirted with Rome but Bernard has never actually signed up for anything. He just has strong opinions. On my side, the Lunes were recusant Catholics but Mumsie lapsed, the Oakhangers were firm believers in Sunday golf and I sort of fell between the cracks, so Bernard and I were married at Marylebone Register Office.

If he were to plump for a church I think it would be the Orthodox. He adores their prostrations and the incense and the stovepipe hats. Once a year he likes to retreat to Mount Athos, not that he's in the least holy or anything but they do have such marvellous antiquities there and of course he's so known and respected the monks allow him to handle everything. But as for Fr. Tudor 'Call me Taff' Griffiths, he's everything Bernard despises in a clergyman.

I said, 'That's awfully kind of you. I'm sure a visit would cheer him up enormously. We're in K19.'

13

I'd been thinking of attending a demonstration of ice sculpture but Virginia had a better idea.

She said, 'I'd love to go and watch the ballroom dancers practising. If I had you with me I bet they'd let me in.'

I said, 'Why would they not let you in?'

She said, 'Irene says only people taking part in the contest are allowed. Things are hotting up, you know. I guess they don't want distractions.'

Such nonsense.

I said, 'You're a paying passenger. You can go anywhere.'

'Except restricted areas,' Fr. Taff reminded me. 'Only people such as myself are permitted in restricted areas. Well, I tell you what, Virginia, why don't I come with you to see the dancing? They can hardly ban a man of the cloth. Matter of fact, I think I should go and give them a bit of a blessing.'

The three of us trooped down to the Show Lounge where all the tables had been stacked to one side and thirty or so couples were quickstepping to 'Blue Skies'. Irene and Don

Harrington, Dorcas of the famously pendulous bosoms, dancing with a Gentleman Host called Ike Windhagen, and the McCuddys. For so large a man Chip McCuddy is surprisingly light on his feet.

Geraldo said, 'Take five, everyone.'

Geraldo's the dance pro. I'd seen him around and from his name and his built-up shoes I'd rather assumed he was a Latino. Now I've heard him speak I think it would be sensible if he made up his mind whether to be Brazilian or French. Alternatively, he could just stick to his native Birmingham accent, which would probably be the easiest thing all round.

'Have a breather,' he said. 'Then we'll do a foxtrot and a Gentleman's Excuse Me waltz.'

Everyone groaned.

'They hate it when I make them change partners,' he said. 'But it's good for them. Keeps them on their toes. Nice to see you, padre. We don't get many visits from the vicar.'

Fr. Taff said, 'I like to do the rounds. From the bridge down to the bilge, I pride myself I cover my patch. A chaplain's job doesn't end when he hangs up his cassock, you know. And I think our Lord would approve. He was probably a bit of a dancer himself. They were great dancers, you know. The men of the Bible Lands. Marriage feast at Cana and all that. I'll bet they had a right old knees up.'

Geraldo said, 'Why don't you come and join in? I'm sure one of these lovely ladies would be happy to have you as a partner.'

Fr. Taff said, 'I'm very tempted, I must confess. I haven't danced a foxtrot in years. What do you say, Virginia?'

'Not me,' she said. She held up her cane. 'My dancing days are done. But what about Lady Enid?'

'Well,' he said, 'I don't know. Lady Enid's husband might have something to say about that.'

Ah yes. The thought of me in the arms of a pocket-sized pastor would drive him wild with jealousy.

I said, 'I think we can risk a couple of dances without causing a scandal.'

'Right you are then,' he said. 'You're on. You're familiar with the basics?'

More than familiar. One had them drubbed in during one's final year at Darnbrook and again at St Gallen even though by then the Bee Gees had come along and all that was required at dances was to jiggle on the spot, with or without a partner.

I realize we cut a rather comical figure, Fr. Taff no more than five feet two to my five feet ten. I had an irresistible tendency to look down at his scalp through his Brylcreemed comb-over. If nothing else, it distracted me from the smirking I knew must be going on. He danced well though. Very firm and decisive.

'Funny how it comes back to you,' he said to my chest. 'Like riding a bike.'

The waltz was a slow arrangement of 'Fascination'. Chip McCuddy cut in almost immediately and we left Fr. Taff to

133

find himself another partner. Chip has a different style. He leads with his belly, taking very long, comfortable strides, but then he sprung a whisk turn on me and I got into a terrible tangle, witnessed by Irene who happened to be dancing by with Geraldo.

'See?' she called. 'You can't expect to turn up halfway through the week and dance to our standard.'

And to my great delight Geraldo let go of her, tapped Chip on the shoulder and spun me away to the middle of the dance floor.

'A word of advice,' he whispered. 'Keep your head and your buzzies up. It'll help you keep your balance. You'd make a nice dancer if you didn't slump.'

I said, 'Are you from Rio?'

He said, 'I've been there. Carnival. What a town. Like four Saturday nights in a row.'

I said, 'But you're not *from* there?'

He said, 'You're a naughty one, you are. No, I'm from Wolverhampton actually, but don't you go saying anything. The ladies like me being South American, especially the Japanese ones. It's only a bit of window dressing. Harmless.'

I said, 'I completely understand. Your secret is safe with me.'

The dance was almost over when Don Harrington claimed me.

'Fancy seeing you here,' he said. 'Are you and the Reverend going in for the contest?'

Don wears a rather pleasant cologne but he pushes one around the dance floor like a lawn mower. Irene is welcome to him.

I said, 'Good Gordon Highlanders, no. We only popped in to have a look. Irene's mother wanted to see how things were going. And then Taff got the itch to dance.'

'Good for Taff,' he said. 'If you got an itch, scratch it, that's what I always say. And where's our famous Professor this morning?'

I said, 'He has a sore throat.'

'Oh dear,' he said. 'I suppose that's the drawback with his line of business. All that talking. I never see him around. I never see him socializing.'

I said, 'My husband doesn't see himself as being here to socialize. He's here to provide cultural enrichment.'

'No, ducks,' he said. 'He's here to keep the punters happy, same as I am.'

The last bar of music had barely died away when Irene reclaimed her trophy. She slipped her arm through Don's.

I said, 'That was fun.'

She said, 'It was a waste of our valuable time. We don't want to have to dance with beginners. We've got a competition coming up. And why did you have to bring Mom with you? I hate her watching. She jinxes me.'

I could see Fr. Taff approaching, with Virginia on his arm.

I said, 'I think she finds the days a little lonely, while you're so busy dancing.'

'Beautiful,' Virginia said. 'It was beautiful to watch. And Lady Enid too. You looked like a different girl when you took to the dance floor.'

Irene said, 'What are we doing tonight, Don?'

He said, 'I'll let you know. There's this cocktail party for starters. I shall have to go to that.'

'What party?' she said. 'Why aren't you taking me?'

'Come if you want to,' he said. 'I don't suppose they'll mind. It's some people called Gleeson.'

She liberated her arm.

She said, 'Not Frankie and Nola Gleeson?'

'Yes,' he said. 'I think so. Why, who are they?'

She said, 'You know, the *Gleesons*. I told you about them enough times. They're those awful people that attacked the Professor on Formal Night.'

I said, 'Hardly *attacked*.'

She said, 'The Professor thought so. He couldn't get away from them fast enough. But excuse me, it's none of my affair. I'm only the friend who stood up for you. I'm only the friend who warned them to lay off.'

Don said, 'Keep your knickers on, Irene. No need to get narky. It's only a little party.'

She said, 'Then don't go. Why are you going?'

He said, 'Because they asked me, and being nice to passengers is what I'm paid to do.'

She said, 'What about being nice to me?'

He touched her hand.

'Come on,' he said, 'don't act mardy. I'll see you later.'

He left.

She called after him.

She said, 'Maybe you won't see me later. It'll be a pathetic party anyhow. I bet no one'll show up.'

She was studying me.

I said, 'I will, for one.'

She said, 'You. Are. Kidding.'

That's how she said it, with the most withering of looks.

I said, 'Bernard and I are in rather the same position as Mr Harrington. We're here to oblige, and as my husband is unwell, tonight it will fall to me.'

'Mom,' she said, 'it's time for your lunch.'

And she hurried Virginia out of the Show Room. Well jolly bad luck to her.

Fr. Taff said, 'Lady Enid, I wonder if I might have a word?'

He was pink-cheeked from the Gentleman's Excuse Me.

He said, 'This contest? It's probably a silly idea, but would you be interested at all, in taking part? Not for the prize, mind. I've got cruises booked right through to New Year's and I daresay you have too. But for the participation. Stop me if I'm out of order, but I think we could give some of these couples a run for their money.'

I said, 'I think it's too late.'

'No,' he said, 'it isn't. I asked Geraldo. He said it's never too late.'

I said, 'I don't have a gown.'

He said, 'But I'm sure you have something suitable. I know what you ladies are like. You always pack too many frocks.'

I said, 'But we'd need to practise. Can you spare the time?'

Contestants have to select two ballroom dances and one Latin American. There was no argument about the samba and we agreed that the quickstep would be a better option than the waltz. It suits Taff's staccato style. The problem was the second ballroom choice.

He said, 'I'll be candid with you, Enid. If it was up to me I'd go with the tango. You know what they used to call me at the Patti Pavilion in Swansea? Tango Taff. They used to say I danced like a tightly coiled spring. Like a crouched jaguar.'

I insisted on the foxtrot.

'Very well,' he said. 'Lady's privilege. And your husband? Will you mention it to him or will I?'

I said, 'If you're going to visit him this afternoon, you'll see him before I do.'

'Leave it to me,' he said. 'Only we don't want any misunderstandings, do we? We don't want people thinking there's any hanky panky going on.'

I found I was trembling in the lift. Partly it was a flashback of this morning's yogurt pot incident, partly it was a different, excited kind of trembling. There was so much to think about. A new dress. A shampoo and set. My natural sense of rhythm, remarked upon by Geraldo. And my dance partner. A crouched jaguar in white socks and open-toe sandals. Bernard, one could imagine, was going to be beside himself.

14

Another message from Minta.

Dear Enid,

You mentioned you have a place in Venice. Our son Tom-Tom is
planning to Inter-Rail this summer and hopes to time things so he
catches the Venice Film Festival. It would be such a weight off my
mind if you could put him up. One hears the most alarming things.
My niece Lucy slept on the pavement outside the Gare du Nord
last summer and came home with a rat bite.

A couch would be absolutely fine and his two friends would be
perfectly okay with sleeping bags on your floor. I won't offend by
offering to pay but needless to say there's a bed for you and your
husband at Barleythorpe Grange if you should ever find yourselves
in the vicinity.

M.

Lord! What has one started! And nothing from info@. I
mean, all Miles need do is say 'how nice'. It's not as though

there's bad blood between us. I went off to Florence in search of culture and he continued trawling through the debutante pond. And it's not as though one were trying to reignite anything. I'm sure I made that crystal clear.

The earliest a stylist was available to do my hair was three o'clock but I was determined not to return to the cabin. It can take hours for Bernard to realize he's been sent to Coventry. Besides which, I didn't want to interrupt Fr. Taff's pastoral visit.

I felt so restless. No longer trembling, but simply unable to sit still and concentrate on Inspector Montalbano. I climbed up to B Deck to explore new territory. At the bow end there's an open-air cinema and a games arcade and a bar called the O-zone where they have discotheque dancing late at night. Aft, there's a children's playground and a shallow pool, practically deserted, where one can bring floating toys, and best of all, the entrance to the Big Tube water slide. It runs, glass-sided at first and at a slight incline so that one has the sensation of speeding along high above the sea then, suddenly, one is plunged into a dark blue gloom as the tube corkscrews down and deposits one, rather thrillingly, in the splash pool two decks below.

As I clambered out, dripping, a lifeguard rushed over.

He said, 'Hey! You! Out!'

I said, 'I am out.'

He said, 'One. You're not correctly attired. Two. You didn't shower before entering.'

I said, 'How do you know I didn't shower?'

He said, 'Don't get smart with me. Three. Shoes are not permitted.'

Which I thought was rather nit-picking of him because I wasn't *wearing* shoes, I was carrying them, but anyway his reprimand was quite eclipsed by the round of applause I received from a party emerging from the wedding chapel. A couple called Sol and Zibby Straub, married for fifty years, had just renewed their vows, witnessed by their daughters and their sons-in-law, and asked me to be in their souvenir photograph, dripping clothes and all. Then I sat outside Knickerbocker Soda Fountain and had a hot-fudge sundae while my clothes dried. All traces of apricot yogurt had been washed away.

At home Graziella always drenches my hair in Amami lotion and puts it in rollers. Then I sit under a dryer hood and read ancient magazines until it's baked. Graziella has done me for years and charges a fraction of what one would have to pay in London. But the girl in the Waves Salon said no one styles hair that way any more. She said my hair has natural body which needed a good wet cut followed by a scrunch-dry with an anti-frizz volumizing product. I do hope Graziella won't be offended when she sees what I've had done. It makes me look quite different. I walked right by Gavin Iles on my way to the shopping atrium and he didn't even recognize me. And Lori Snow gave me her seal of approval.

'Wow,' she said. 'Look at you.'

I said, 'It's a choppy tousled bob.'

She said, 'It sure is. You look great.'

I said, 'It's not too young?'

'Get outta here,' she said. 'You must be about the same age as my mom and she's got a pink streak.'

I said, 'And now I need something to wear. But I can't afford very much.'

'I'll find you something,' she said. 'It's what I do.'

I thought black would be the best plan. A simple little cocktail dress that one could wear again and again, but they have very little black on the *Golden Memories*, and not much beige either. They have things mainly from the Nola Gleeson palette.

Lori said, 'OK, now are we talking leisure wear or formal wear?'

I said, 'I need something for Gala Night. Reverend Griffiths and I have decided to have a go at the dance competition. And it has to be suitable for a cocktail party too.'

She said, 'You going to Frankie and Nola's party tonight? Me too!'

I said, 'We hardly know them.'

She said, 'I do. I know them from previous cruises. They are the sweetest people.'

She was rattling through the racks of evening wear.

She said, 'My advice to you. In a word. Separates.'

The fabric is crushed silk, full of tiny creases and in a gorgeous lapis lazuli shade of blue.

'Sapphire,' she said. 'If you ask me, this has your name on it. It brings out the colour of your eyes. Easy care, too. Cold wash in soap flakes, cold rinse, then you twist it into a rope, get hubby to hold on to the other end. The tighter you twist, the better. Then you put a rubber band round each end, let it twist back on itself and leave it to dry. Couldn't be simpler. You can roll it up in your luggage, no need for an iron, and you've got the skirt, put it with a nice little top for a cocktail party, you can ring the changes and wear this top with a different skirt, or you can put them together and *voilà*, it looks like a dress. All you need is a little shawl for the cooler evenings. You have a pashmina? I'll throw one in, slightly imperfect.'

The amber tear-drop earrings were her suggestion too. They pinch a little but I believe I can endure the pain for an hour or two.

She said, 'You should always wear earrings. They draw the eye up, see? They finish an outfit.'

I do have earrings at home somewhere. A pair of rather grubby diamond clips that I inherited from Grandma Oakhanger. The family jewels. Cousin Tig got the tiara which she must have little occasion to wear in Torremolinos. One assumes she's sold it by now to bolster her sangria fund. As for the Lune inheritance, all one managed to rescue was a strand of pearls and a very ugly cameo brooch. By the time one arrived for Granny Lune's funeral Mumsie had already sent the emeralds to Phillips to be auctioned. I believe Bobbie Snape brought undue influence to bear there, having set her heart on a new, all-mod-cons whelping wing with infra-red heating for her Dandie pups.

Jesus waved to me from the door of the steward's station.

'Ladyship!' he said. 'You got new hair. Very nice. I like.'

He was looking me in the eye again, this morning's little incident forgotten.

I said, 'Has my husband gone up to give his lecture?'

I was hoping to have the cabin to myself, to try on my new togs.

'No,' he said. 'Talk's been cancelled. Professor's not moved all day. He had company, though. Fr. Taff sat with him a spell. We love Fr. Taff. Then the big boss come. Mr Iles. Then nurse came, gave him something for his throat. Don't you worry. He ain't been lonely.'

Bernard was in his pyjamas and dressing gown, sipping a glass of lemon cordial. I had decided to be bright and cheerful, but firm.

I said, 'Did you absolutely have to cancel your lecture? We shall never hear the end of this from Gavin Iles.'

'My lecture,' he whispered, 'is the least of it. Where the hell have you been all day? And why did you give that insane Welshman our cabin number?'

I said, 'He visited then?'

'Visited!' he said. 'He practically moved in. I thought he'd never leave.'

I said, 'Well he is the chaplain. Visiting the sick is one of the things he does. Did he pray with you?'

145

'He did not,' he said. 'He gave me the overly detailed story of his life and asked permission to dance with you in some kind of competition.'

I said, 'And you gave him your blessing?'

'I told him to help himself,' he said. 'Anything to get rid of the man. Is he some kind of fantasist?'

Only in comparing himself to a crouched jaguar.

I said, 'He's completely harmless.'

He said, 'But what was he talking about? Dancing? You don't dance.'

I said, 'No, *you* don't dance. It's for Gala Night. The Ballroom Blitz. We're going to dance a waltz, a foxtrot and a samba. Such a lark. Don't worry, we won't win. Although Geraldo did say I have great natural ability as a dancer, and Geraldo should know. He's the pro.'

He stared at me.

'Why, Enid?' he said. 'Why are you doing this to me?'

I said, 'Oddly enough Bernard, you started the ball rolling. You were in a perfectly foul temper this morning and as it seemed politic to stay out of your way I've spent the day entertaining myself. Yet again. "Where's the Professor?" they ask. "We never see the Professor." It's hardly surprising if men have begun buying me Danish pastries and asking me to dance. I gather the nurse visited. What did she advise?'

'He,' he said. 'Aspirin. Hot lemon. Rest.'

I said, 'Then you won't be well enough to come to dinner. I'll tell them to give someone else your place.'

'No,' he croaked. 'I'll try to rally for dinner.'

I said, 'If you're not well enough to lecture you're not well enough to be seen in the dining room. What if you have something catching?'

I stripped off my clothes, still chlorine-scented from my trip down the water slide.

I said, 'You'd be far better off ordering some ice cream from room service and getting an early night.'

I dressed in the bathroom. My gorgeous new top with a pair of ancient but perfectly serviceable black trousers and a slightly imperfect shawl. Bernard looked at his watch when he saw me ready to leave.

I said, 'I'm going to pop in to the Gleesons' party before dinner.'

He was stunned.

I said, 'Well why not? It's easier than making excuses. And it would be nice to have some company for a change.'

'Company?' he said. 'Ah yes. The company of a demented Welsh gnome in a dog collar, no doubt.'

I said, 'Jealous, Bernard? Surely not. Who could possibly be interested in me?'

He hunched down behind *The History of the Peloponnesian War*. No mention of my new top or my new earrings. No mention of my choppy tousled bob. And no apology for the yogurt pot.

15

Four messages in my inbox!

From Leonora Carisbroke-Cowles:

Dear Enid, I think I remember you. Were you the one who had a
front tooth knocked out by a lacrosse stick?

No, I was not. That was Araminta Fellowes.

From Billa:

Eeny,
That is so typical of Minta. You don't hear from her in years and
then she immediately wants a favour. Anyway I imagine her
precious boy child would prefer to stay in a hostel with all the
other spotty youths. I must say though, kids are so lucky now with
all this Inter Rail stuff. When you consider we were hardly let off
the leash until after St Gallen and even then one was never

allowed to slum. Have checked on flights. Is Ryanair too grim? Is Treviso horribly far from you? Do you have a driver who could pick me up?

Kisses, Billa

From Miles Brassey:

Enid, How very modern of you! So glad to learn that you're thriving. I heard you'd married one of our brainy American cousins and were travelling the world, feted everywhere you go. Carmela and I divide our time between Buenos Aires and the Great Wen. Still having to work for a crust but one hopes to wind down ere long and do nothing more than play the occasional geriatric chukka. Best regards to you and your lucky man. Any Nobel prizes in the offing? Miles

And from the desk of Dr Ibrahim Ekowolo, Union Bank of Lagos:

Dear Sir,

I sincerely write to seek your co-operation to carry out urgent and confidential business opportunity. I am Senior Management of Foreign Remittance Department. Some years in past client Mr. Tunde Agbaje have deposited in Two Year Saving Plan sum of 51 million United States Dollar. Upon maturity of Plan it is come to my notice that Mr. Tunde Agbaje is dead in year 2000 in automobile accident without next of kins or Will and Testament. In accordance of Nigerian banking law if this monies is not claimed (51 million

149

United States Dollar, with interest) it will revert to ownership of Nigerian government. My proposal is to find foreign person of good standing to claim the monies as next of kins. All you must do is send me details of your banking account and I will arrange transfer of funds of which you will retain 30 percent, no question asked. This transaction is guaranteed no risk. Kindly reply, dear Sir, to my private email, dribekow79@yahoo.com. Do not reply directly to Union Bank of Lagos as this transaction will be organized strictly by my own self.

Trusting in a mutual benefit of our business relationship.

Yours most sincerely

Dr. Ibrahim Ekowolo

I said to Brady, 'I have no idea who this person is.'

He looked over my shoulder.

'Oh congratulations,' he said. 'The scammers have found you. That didn't take long.'

Apparently once one has an email address one is prey to all kinds of tricksters. They get their hands on one's bank particulars and make off with one's money. Brady said I can expect to receive many more similar messages. I begin to see that embracing the communications revolution isn't without its downside. Presumptuous requests from Minta. Bland notes from former lovers. Letters from Nigerian thieves. On the other hand, Brady warned me I may also receive offers of cut-price Viagra, Chip McCuddy's little blue pill.

It was time to make my entrance at the Gleesons' party.

The Humidor Cigar Bar is on N Deck, next door to the casino. It has a smell of stale carpet and a feeling of perpetual night.

I felt terribly nervous. I don't remember the last time I attended a party without Bernard. He cuts such a figure and more often than not he's the star of the evening. One can simply slipstream behind him and not worry about what to say.

During my last term at Darnbrook we had Wednesday afternoon socials when boys from Upwell would come over for tea and buns and conversation, and of course at St Gallen one learned how to address absolutely everyone, from God down, but chit-chat still doesn't come naturally to me. We have no tradition of it in the family. Poppa and Grandpoppa belonged to White's and the Turf Club which catered to any conversational needs they had. But Mumsie is impatient of all company except that of Bobbie Snape. Like several Lunes before her, she's quite liable to fire her air rifle at any car that passes the Gate House uninvited.

My nerves weren't helped by my new togs. In front of the bathroom mirror I'd liked what I saw. In fact I'd even wished I had a dab of lipstick to apply. But when it came to it, when I stood on the threshold of the room and heard the hum of conversation, I suddenly felt ludicrously over-dressed. If it weren't for having to face Bernard I'd have gone back to the cabin and changed into some old favourite, or even skipped the party altogether, but then other guests came upon me from behind and swept me before them into the bar.

Nola Gleeson was all in coral: a chiffon trouser suit with floating sleeves, satin high-heeled shoes, and a silk cabbage rose with beaded net leaves perched on the side of her tower of hair. I was not over-dressed.

'Lady Enid,' she said, 'it's darling of you to come. We heard the Professor's not so well. We heard he had to cancel his little talk.'

There were several familiar faces: the McCuddys, of course; two couples from Chicago who had taken Bernard's tour of Izmir and very much enjoyed it; and Mr Polder, Bernard's egg-shaped interrogator on the subject of Cornell, with his monkey-faced wife. Also Don Harrington *sans* Irene, Second Officer Scott Davenport, and Lori Snow, who whispered, 'Was I right about those earrings or what?'

There was much talk of cruises already taken and cruises planned. Antarctica seems to be the destination of choice for next year. Heaps of opportunities for lecturers, one imagines; all those long days without shopping opportunities. Perhaps Bernard needs to become an expert on penguins.

The drinks were delicious. Apricot juice and a shot of grenadine cut with a light, sparkling wine.

Cricket said, 'The barman designed it specially. It's called A Nola.'

I said, 'And the barman is called a "barista", remember? Our Martini Masterclass?'

'Oh my Lord,' she said. 'Was that last night? Was that you?'

Chip McCuddy said, 'Frankie! You and Nola thought about Antarctica?' and there was Frankie Gleeson, minus his toupee, bearing down upon me in a remarkable dinner jacket. Not quite coral, but certainly close to pumpkin.

'Enid,' he said. 'Have a beetroot kettle chip. They're our newest flavour.'

The Gleesons apparently made their money in crisps and never travel without a box of samples.

He said, 'Root vegetables. There's a lot of excitement about them this year.'

I said, 'I had no idea.'

'People don't,' he said. 'They sit in a bar or on a plane, they consume a snack without giving it a second thought. Now myself, I gained an early appreciation of the potential in snack foods. I used to sell pretzels at Pioneers' games at Dunn Field. Pretzels and Crackerjack. Then I married my late first wife, Phyllis, which opened up the world of pork rinds. Phyllis's folks had a pig farm out near Batavia.'

Batavia is on the New York State Thru-Way between Buffalo and Rochester.

Frankie Gleeson omits no detail.

'First year,' he said, 'we tried our hand at cracklings and we couldn't bag 'em up fast enough. Later on we branched out into corn chips and then much later along came your extruded snacks, cheese puffs, prawn crackers and the like, but cracklings is where we started. The market's changed a lot, of course. Potato chips still lead the field but nowadays folks are looking for the low-fat, low-sodium options. I'm semi-retired now. Sold the business in 2000 because that's what I promised Nola I'd do. So now I get more time for fishing and Nola likes us to take these cruises. I still keep in touch with the business, though. I like to stay current. Compressed snacks in pellet form, that's the future.'

Fascinating.

I said, 'I mustn't monopolize you, but I did just want to ask you something. About your old school friend? They say each of us has a double somewhere in the world, don't they? It's so fascinating to think we may know the name of Bernard's. I even took a tip from you and searched for him on the World Wide Web.'

'Me too,' he said. 'You won't find him. Well, you'll find a few Willy Finks, same as you'll find any number of Frankie Gleesons, but you won't find Willy. He's disappeared.'

The last time Frankie Gleeson saw him was in 1958. A lifetime ago. Pre-Bobbie Snape. I was eight years old, Poppa still lived at Lowhope and all was well with the world.

He said, 'I can picture him now, with his big old leather valise, going off to college, off to catch the Greyhound to Albany. He was quite the scholar, Willy. Couldn't hit a ball to save his life but anything out of a book, he was your man.'

I said, 'And you lived on the same street?'

'Right next door,' he said.

I said, 'And his people never mentioned what became of him?'

'No,' he said. 'But you have to understand, the Finks weren't the kind of folk you jawed with over the fence. They were a bit out of the ordinary, if you know what I mean? I guess that's why Mom took pity on Willy. Mothered him a bit. We were a houseful so what was one more? There was times he sat at our table more than he sat at his own. Mrs Fink wasn't much of a homemaker. Those days, the ladies didn't go out to a job of work. But she did. When you're a kid you don't realize things but now, when I look back … I mean, in those days, nobody on Brewster Street wore lipstick. I'm trying to remember her name. It was something unusual. I'll think of it in a minute.'

Poor Willy Fink. As a girl with all too many memories of finding a cold, deserted kitchen when one hoped supper might be ready, one can empathize. The food at Darnbrook was vile but it at least appeared at regular times.

I said, 'I do hope you find him. Wherever he is in the world, I'm sure he'd be thrilled to see you again.'

'Serafina,' he said. 'That was it. Serafina Fink. She must have been quite a handful.'

Nola interrupted him.

'Frankie,' she said. 'Snacks. Circulate.'

I moved off, planning to say a few words to Second Officer

Davenport and then leave, duty done, but I was intercepted by Mr Polder.

'Point of information,' he wheezed. 'I find Professor Finch isn't the only Cornellian on board. Tell him there's a Mr Erikson, from the Class of Fifty-five. He's usually to be found in the Card Room between four and five.'

Bernard will be thrilled.

He said, 'On a further point of information, Mr Erikson provided me with a detailed answer to my question about the swimming test. Anyone who graduated before 1970 would certainly have taken the test naked. Not the ladies, of course. But in the gymnasium and the pool the men followed the fashion of Ancient Greece. I'm surprised Professor Finch didn't remember that, being a Classics man.'

I said, 'I'm afraid my husband is incurably vague about things that don't interest him.'

Mrs Polder stood holding one of Frankie Gleeson's beetroot crisps as though it were a used Kleenex.

Polder said, 'But he'll be interested to hear of my findings. Grateful, even. It is his alma mater, after all.'

I was desperately trying to catch the eye of Lori Snow or Don Harrington. Anything to escape from the direction Mr Polder seemed to be drifting, but Lori was deep into snack foods with Frankie Gleeson and Don Harrington failed to notice me. In fact I believe he may have turned his back on me deliberately. I do hope Irene hasn't begun another of her campaigns.

Polder said, 'An inaccurate answer about such a signal

feature, it could give a puzzling impression. Don't you think, Lady Enid?'

I said, 'I suppose it would. I'll mention it to him.'

My plan was to slip away, with no more than a wave of thanks, but it wasn't to be.

Nola and Cricket headed me off with a pincer movement.

Nola said, 'You're anxious to get back to the Professor. Of course you are. I know what these guys are like when they get a sniffle. You'd think they were dying.'

We laughed.

Cricket said, 'Ask her then, Nola.'

Nola said, 'Well, we were wondering. As soon as ever the Professor's feeling better we'd like to take you guys to dinner, me and Frankie, and Chip and Cricket. To the Burlington. Did you try it yet?'

The Burlington Grill, Oyster Line's attempt at *fin-de-siècle* luxury. We haven't eaten there. It's rather beyond our purse. And anyway, thanks to a casual remark from *your* husband, Nola, *my* husband has been taking all his meals on a tray.

'You'll love it,' she said. 'Leather chairs, electric candles, beautiful crystal stemware. The real thing.'

I said, 'Thank you. We'll look forward to it.'

The fact that Bernard would rather have a red-hot poker shoved up his bottom than have dinner with you is neither here nor there. I'll certainly mention your kind invitation.

'Great,' she said. 'You just let us know. The minute the Professor's back on his feet we'll make a reservation.'

157

Cricket said, 'They make this great cocktail. A blackberry bourbon cobbler. And wait till you see the size of the steaks.'

Nola drifted off to greet two new arrivals.

Cricket squeezed my arm.

She said, 'You're looking wonderful tonight. I guess that's what having an admirer does for a girl.'

I said, 'An admirer?'

'The Reverend Father,' she said. 'I saw the way he was looking at you in the ballroom this morning.'

I said, 'We're only dancing together. There's absolutely nothing more to it than that.'

'If you say so, dear,' she said. 'Still, a little flirtation wouldn't hurt, would it? Anything to keep hubby on his toes, hunh?'

Lord! I do hope this isn't going to become complicated.

Bernard was already seated when I got to the dining room. He had his rainbow cashmere scarf wound loosely around his throat and a lilac-rinsed American lady hanging on his every word. He didn't rise.

I said, 'No need to get up. I see you've made a dramatic recovery.'

He said, 'One must do one's best. I shall eat nothing but the soup.'

There was an empty seat beside a gaunt, jaundiced-looking American. He was something to do with the Federal Reserve but seemed not to want to talk, which suited me very well.

I'd had my quota of small talk for one evening and I was very much distracted by the sight of Bernard, who was toying with a bread roll and drinking heavily.

One minute he'd be whispering hoarsely, then he'd warm to his theme, forget himself and speak in his usual, well-projected voice. Twice I suggested he might benefit from an early night, twice he pretended not to hear me. He sat and sat and drank and drank.

'What *is* the urgency, Enid?' he said, when I got to my feet in exasperation.

I said, 'We have a very busy day tomorrow. Olympia, darling? Remember?'

'Olympia!' he said. 'I can do Olympia tied hand and foot. Oh, but you have dance practice. Of course! My wife, ladies and gentlemen, who is a scion of the noble houses of Lune and Oakhanger, has elected to take part in some uncouth ballroom battle.'

The other guests were all studying their empty glasses.

He said, 'And her partner in this vulgar display will be none other than our shipboard sky pilot, the Reverend Taff Griffiths. My wife will be dancing with the Welsh runt.'

I said goodnight and walked away. I didn't look back but I could tell he was finally leaving the table.

'Lady Enid Finch,' he said, 'otherwise known as Dances with Parsons.'

He laughed. No one else did.

I said, 'That was fairly embarrassing.'

He said, 'It's no more than you deserve. You're the one leading the field in embarrassing behaviour.'

We walked back to the cabin in silence. A sheet of paper had been pushed under the door. He groaned.

'Not another bloody invitation,' he said. 'Why can't people leave me in peace?'

He scanned it, balled it up and tossed it into the bin.

'Nothing of interest?' I said.

'Nothing of interest,' he said, 'unless you needed a reminder that we have only till tomorrow morning to apply to take part in an entertainment called Name That Tune.'

I hung up my beautiful new top. I'd found, as the evening passed, that I grew more and more accustomed to looking glamorous. By the time dinner was over I wasn't even conscious of it any more.

'Well,' he said, 'I suppose one must ask. How were the gruesome Gleesons?'

I said, 'They were charming.'

'My word!' he said. 'What an easy conquest you are. I gather then they've lost interest in the provenance of your title.'

I said, 'It didn't come up.'

He said, 'I find myself wondering what one would talk about with such people. Baseball teams, perhaps? Or the convoluted rules of ice hockey.'

He had a moment of difficulty with the word 'convoluted'. When Bernard is very drunk his face seems to slip out of focus.

I said, 'We found plenty to talk about. The shopping possibilities on an Antarctic cruise. Fishing. Sore throat remedies. The pleasures of small-town life.'

'Ah yes,' he said. 'Ice Cream Socials? Pageants? Foliage Festivals?'

I said, 'All of that. But mainly we talked about snacks. Frankie Gleeson has built an empire on bacon rinds and potatoes.'

'Snacks!' he said. 'The very word makes one shudder! A snack millionaire. One couldn't invent these people.'

He was starting to enjoy himself.

I said, 'By the way, Mr Polder was at the Gleesons' party.'

'Polder? he said. 'Polder?'

I said, 'Large waistline. Small red ears. Cornell. Swimming Test.'

A creditable attempt at looking vaguely bored.

'Really?' he said.

I said, 'Yes, he rushed to tell me he'd met another passenger who was at Cornell and so has been able to clear up the whole swimming-test question to his satisfaction. He asked me most particularly to tell you they *do* still have the test but no one has taken it in the nude in more than thirty years. So there it is. I've delivered the message. Mr Polder seems more than a little obsessed with the subject, I must say. He's a strange man. And his wife never speaks.'

Bernard shook his head.

'Swimming test!' he said. 'What an idiot.'

I said, 'But anyway, mainly I chatted with Frankie Gleeson who is really very pleasant and so terribly enthusiastic about his chosen path in life. He explained to me how those little cheesy, puffy, snacky things are made. You know, the kind Mumsie serves as an hors d'oeuvre?'

A faint smile. Relief, one imagines, at leaving behind the treacherous waters of Cornell and reaching the shallows of Cheese Puffs.

'Why do you do it, Enid?' he said. 'What masochistic streak persuades you to listen to these freakish people? Cheesy, puffy, snacky things?'

I said, 'But it's interesting, Bernard. One can always learn something. What they do is, they take cornmeal, add a little water and cook it under pressure till it forms a kind of glop. Then they force it through an extruding machine, rather like a cake-icing nozzle one imagines, and out the other end oozes the little shape. Which they then dry, spray with oil and coat with a cheese-flavoured powder. Isn't that fascinating?'

'Astonishing,' he said.

I said, 'But the other amazing thing that emerged this evening was that Willy Fink, Frankie's long-lost school pal whom you so strongly resemble, and whose middle name is Bernard, and with whom you share a birthday, has something else in common with you.'

He unscrewed the top of the whisky bottle.

I said, 'More drink?'

162

He said, 'A: I need an anaesthetic for my throat and B: if I'm to be forced to listen to a reprise of Mr Gleeson's *doppelganger* fantasies I need an anaesthetic for my brain.'

He poured himself a very generous measure and gargled with the first mouthful.

I said, 'Not a reprise. Just a rather charming coincidence.'

He said, 'I'm turning in. If I don't get some rest I'll be in no condition to tour Olympia tomorrow.'

I said, 'You're right. It's late. But while you're getting ready for bed do tell me what you think of the extraordinary fact that you and the ghostly Willy Fink both had a mother named Serafina.'

There was a brief silence.

'Really, Enid!' he said eventually, shirt over his head. 'This is so tiresome. I'm sixty-five years old. My mother, had she lived, would now be ninety. Serafina wasn't at all an unusual name a hundred years ago.'

He went into the bathroom and brushed his teeth much more thoroughly than usual. By the time he reappeared I was in bed with Inspector Montalbano. Bernard slipped between the sheets, turned his back to me and clicked off his reading light. Did he really think the subject was closed?

I said, 'Such a pretty name. If we'd ever had a daughter I suppose that's what we might have named her. Serafina Finch.'

I heard him sigh.

I said, 'I imagine it comes from the same root as seraphim. Cherubim and seraphim continually do cry, et cetera.'

'Yes, Enid,' he said. 'From the Hebrew, *seraf,* a fiery serpent.'

I said, 'Was your mama a fiery serpent, Bernard? You've never told me about her.'

He said, 'There's nothing to tell.'

I said, 'But there's something to tell about *everyone*. Who were her people?'

'Her people?' he growled. 'You should hear yourself! Who were her people! I'm afraid we can't all have marquesses and viscounts in the attic. Most of us have families too boring or too dead to be worth a mention.'

I'm sure I always showed an interest in Bernard's family. It was simply that he preferred not to talk about it and one sensed a tragedy in the background, something perhaps best left undisturbed.

I said, 'Well from what Frankie Gleeson said that wouldn't apply to Willy Fink's family. He hinted that there was some kind of *scandale*. I shall ask him about it when we have dinner.'

'What?' he said.

I said, 'We're invited by the Gleesons. To the Burlington Grill. It's fearfully expensive and the steaks are apparently the size of a dustbin lid.'

'Over my dead body,' he said. 'And over yours too. I know you too well, Enid. I don't believe for one minute you've agreed to such a thing.'

I said, 'Just tell me one tiny thing. Did your mama wear lipstick?'

He fumbled for the whisky glass on his night table.

I said, 'Don't you think you've had enough?'

He said, 'I have acute laryngitis. And since I'm to be deprived of sleep and plagued with ridiculous questions, I think I'm at least allowed to choose my own poison.'

I said, 'But did she? Wear lipstick? Frankie Gleeson was saying that in a town like Painted Post, where he grew up, the wearing of lipstick was hugely significant. It was practically like hanging a red lantern outside one's door. Whereas in my family it was rather a matter of taste. The Lune women didn't, but the Oakhangers did. Very much so. Grandma Oakhanger applied it so generously it always used to end up on the table napkins and on her teeth. And Cousin Tig likewise, perhaps because she has a similar overbite. But what about your mother, Bernard? Was she lippy or no lippy?'

'I neither remember nor care,' he said. 'I have more important things on my mind, such as your rapid descent into feeble-mindedness. Dancing with a clerical troglodyte. Discussing cosmetic aids with a cheese-puff manufacturer. You're losing your grip, Enid. And it won't have been helped by the kind of company you've been keeping. I should never have allowed you to go to that bloody party.'

I said, 'Allowed? You should be grateful I flew the flag while you skulked in here in your pyjamas.'

'I have never skulked in my life,' he yelled.

I said, 'You have a lot to be thankful for, Bernard. Your laryngitis has cleared up, as if by magic. And you're blessed with a wife who does her duty *and* entertains herself. So in future, please don't throw away notices that may be of interest to me. In between trudging the ruins of Olympia and dancing with the Welsh troglodyte I might just like to take part in Name That Tune. Did that ever occur to you?'

I jumped out of bed, rescued the screwed-up paper from the waste basket and smoothed it out.

BERNARD FINCH OF WORLD REPUTE
STRIKES A POSE IN HIS LINEN SUIT.
I SAY IT'S ALL BALONEY.
I SAY THE MAN'S A PHONEY.

I said, 'Darling! This isn't about a quiz show, at all. What were you thinking?'

He said, 'Perhaps I wanted to shield you from a sick joke thought up by an idiot prankster. Did that ever occur to *you*?'

I said, 'Who do you imagine sent it?'

He said, 'I'd have thought that was blindingly obvious. The Bacon Rind King.'

I said, 'But Bernard, this is a limerick! Surely a man as limited as Frankie Gleeson wouldn't be capable of composing a limerick.'

A heavy sigh.

'A clerihew, Enid,' he said. 'It's a clerihew.'

I put out my light.

I said, 'Goodnight.'

No reply.

I said, 'Still, one has to wonder, who could have written it? And why? There's Gleeson, with his Willy Fink obsession. Or could it be Mr Polder? He was hinting rather darkly about your time at Cornell.'

Silence.

I said, 'It's all too silly for words. I mean, what would it matter if you did grow up in Painted Post and changed your name and omitted to go home for funerals? One might have one's reasons. No family is perfect, after all. Poppa's Great-Uncle Ootie lost a whole tea plantation in a game of cards and there have been legions of Lunes who've suffered from mental wanderings. What would it matter if a person's mother did wear lipstick? Jolly good luck to her, I say. And who could give a fig which university a person attended? To have attended one at all seems to me a great achievement. I can't think of a single Oakhanger or Lune who did as much.'

He said, 'Are you going to keep up this drivel all night?'

I said, 'It's just that it's all such a puzzle to me and you know how I love a puzzle. I find myself wondering what the chances are that two people born in New York state on January the twelfth 1940, one named Wislaw Bernard Fink, the other named Bernard Finch, should not only greatly resemble one another but both have mothers called Serafina too. Darling, you know about probability theory. What do you say?'

Silence again.

I said, 'Also, I do find it remarkable that there are so few references to you on the World Wide Web. Gracious, even Bobbie Snape's brother has more mentions than you do and apart from having bred a rather successful three-day eventer his main claim to fame is that he lives on bought pies and never throws away a foil pie dish. He has rooms full of them. But anyway, all I wanted to say was that if there were something in your past that you haven't shared with me, perhaps now is the time. Because I do feel that our little encounters with Polder and Gleeson should alert us to the information revolution. "An explosion of information" is how Brady described it. He's the computer boy. He runs the Internet Point downstairs. We're entering an era where one can discover anything about anyone at the click of a mouse. And as I do sometimes find myself in the position of answering questions about you, I'd simply like to know if there's anything you're not telling me.'

He sat up in the dark. I couldn't see him but I could tell something was about to happen. The air was so electric I was braced for a blow. When a man is the worse for drink who's to say that the morning's yogurt pot won't be followed by a heavy-bottomed tumbler? But it didn't come. He just spoke, and his voice vibrated with anger.

'Foil pie dishes?' he said. 'Mice that click? Your insanity

is further advanced than I'd feared. But very well, Enid, since I'm to be kept from my sleep and pushed beyond endurance. Yes, yes, yes. There *is* something I haven't told you. But I'm going to tell you now. Frankie Gleeson is a pathological liar. And always was.'

16

The nurse's name is Quincy. He's from Toronto and he wears a white tunic that buttons along the shoulder.

He said, 'Well, his throat looks OK but his temperature's slightly raised and he says he's got a dull, throbbing headache.'

I said, 'So he's not well enough to work?'

He said, 'Shall we call it a 24-hour viral infection?'

I had to tell the Excursions Desk something, and quickly. Of all the items on the Cultural Enrichment programme the excursion to Olympia is always the most popular and there's often fierce competition to be in Bernard's group rather than tag along with one of the local guides.

Gavin Iles was in his little office, flossing his teeth.

He said, 'Lectures cancelled, tours cancelled. And I hear he was three sheets to the wind in the dining room last night. It's not good. Not exactly covering ourselves with glory, are we, Lady E? I was promised Bernard Finch would be a big draw. I was told it'd be like getting Nick Nolte and Master fucking Mind for the price of one stateroom.'

One inside stateroom. Next to the funnel uptake shaft.

I said, 'I imagine Bernard isn't the first guest lecturer to be indisposed, particularly when you house people in such poorly ventilated accommodation. But there's no need to cancel today's tour. I'll lead it myself.'

He said, 'You? You're not serious?'

It seemed to me to be the perfect solution. To get me out of that horrid sickroom for the day and to do something that might salvage Bernard's dwindling prospects with Oyster Line. He has no pension and until such time as he actually commits to paper the many books he plans to write it's essential that he works.

I said, 'I'm absolutely serious. Why not?'

He said, 'But can you do it? Do you know any dates and stuff like that?'

The Sacred Truce, 776 BC. The Temple of Hera, 650 BC. The Statue of Zeus, 430 BC. The sacking of the Altis, 85 BC. The Pax Romana, 31 BC. That deflated the little popinjay.

'OK, OK,' he said. 'No need to go over the top. You need just enough to give the punters the impression you know what you're talking about.'

I said, 'So I'll do it?'

'Yes,' he said. 'Off you go. The tour guide will be Finch, E instead of Finch, B.'

They were already warping us in to the pier at Katakolon. I ran back to the cabin to get my sun hat and Bernard's paperback edition of Pausanias. He raised himself on his elbows, hot-looking and rumpled, and croaked, 'Where are you going?'

I said, 'To Olympia. I'm standing in for you.'

He threw himself back onto the pillow, hands raised to the gods.

He said, 'No, no, no! You cannot. The very idea is ludicrous.'

I said, 'Bernard, I realize some of the ladies will be disappointed not to be led by you but better that than getting any deeper into Gavin Iles's bad books. I expect he'll pay you a visit later. He was quite concerned about you. And if the Reverend Griffiths looks in, remind him we have foxtrot practice at five o'clock.'

I received a very warm welcome from my tour group. They made sympathetic noises when I announced that Bernard was ill and then gave me a little round of applause when I said I'd do my best to make sure they didn't miss anything.

One lady said, 'You must have heard it so many times, I'll bet you know it by heart.'

And a gentleman at the back of the bus called out, 'And you're nicer to look at too.'

Bernard's method at Olympia is to plunge straight in to the site: the Prytaneion, where the athletes used to stay in five-star splendour; the Gymnasium and the Palestra, where they trained; Pheidias's studio, where they went to get their statues carved, rather as one might now go to one of those machines for a passport photograph. But I decided on a different approach. I took them to the terrace by the Treasuries first, on the lower slopes of the hill where the women and slaves used to stand. From there one can look down on the ruins of the Stadium and try to imagine the colour of the spectacle and the roar of the crowd.

I remembered most of Bernard's anecdotes. Where he'd raise a laugh telling how Nero invented new competitions and then had the rules bent so he could win them. Where he'd pause for dramatic effect outside the ceremonial gate, with an imaginary victor's palm in his hand. Of course I wasn't able to read to them from Pindar, for which I apologized, but they seemed not to mind.

One lady, dressed rather appropriately in a tracksuit, said, 'Don't give it another thought, honey. We're ready for the gift shop and a cold beer.'

I can't say that I entirely overcame my nerves but after I'd finished and we were driving up through the trees to have lunch at a taverna I felt exhilarated. Now I understand why Bernard is often in a good humour after a tour, even one that he judges to have been beneath his expertise. The delivery saps enormous amounts of energy but one is left feeling one has done something worthwhile. One feels one has made a difference, however small, to people's view of the world.

By the time we reached our lunch stop the terrace was packed with early arrivals and waiters were running back and forth with enormous platters of grilled meat. I had no choice but to perch next to Mrs Polder.

'Lady Enid,' she said. She handed me a sachet of antiseptic wipes.

'For your cutlery,' she whispered. 'If you're going to risk the food.'

Polder leaned across her.

'The Professor still out of sorts?' he said.

I said, 'He has laryngitis.'

He said, 'Throats. You can't be too careful. But I guess he's being well looked after. I'm sure they'll do everything they can. An important figure like Bernard Finch. They were damned lucky to get him.'

Mrs Polder was pecking at a piece of pitta bread.

She said, 'What are they giving him? For his throat?'

Aspirin. Glucose drinks. The benefit of the doubt.

Polder said, 'He won't have been well enough to seek out the other Cornell gentleman yet. Mr Erikson.'

I said, 'No. Not well enough to do anything really.'

'Pity,' he said. 'But there's still time. They'll find a lot to jaw about, I'm sure.'

Mrs Polder said, 'I could let you have a little Cefadroxil for him.'

I said, 'Thank you, I'll bear it in mind. But I have a feeling he'll be over the worst by this evening.'

Then the bouzouki band started up. Mrs P put her bony hand on mine.

'Don't touch the salad,' she shouted. 'I learned that lesson the hard way the year we went to Cozumel.'

It was late afternoon when the bus dropped us back at Katakolon and I was awarded my second round of applause of the day. Entertaining, informative and very considerate of those with mobility issues, that was what my report card said.

I wandered slowly towards the pier. I was in no great hurry to find out what awaited me in the cabin. And there, sitting on a bollard by the souvenir shops, gazing out to sea and quite lost in thought, was Frankie Gleeson.

I said, 'Has Nola abandoned you?'

'She's in one of these joints,' he said. 'Buying more necklaces. I'll never know why. She's only got one neck.'

I said, 'Thank you for the party last night.'

He said, 'It's a thing we always do. Nola likes to bring a personal touch to these cruises. And how's the Professor today?'

I said, 'He's still in bed. Doctor's orders.'

'Dear, oh dear,' he said. 'That's bad luck.'

I said, 'I'm glad I bumped into you. Last evening, when you were telling me about your old school friend, you mentioned his mother's name. It was something quite unusual. Remind me, what was it?'

'Serafina,' he said. 'You're right, it is unusual. I don't believe I ever met another one. They were Poles, of course, the

Finks. Old man Fink called himself Charlie. I don't know if that was his real name. I don't know if they have "Charlie" in Poland. And Willy's real name was Wislaw. Still, at least they gave him Bernard for a middle name. Everybody knows how to say Bernard.'

Which brought our conversation to a natural break. I could easily have said goodbye and continued on my way towards the ship. But that moment passed.

I said, 'There's something I feel I must say. You're going to think this very odd.'

He looked at me.

I said, 'It's just that I have the strangest feeling my husband *is* your old friend, Willy Fink.'

He took off his baseball cap and studied the words ELMIRA PIONEERS.

'Oh yes,' he said. 'I know he is.'

17

There were very few people about. Just two Greek boys playing pinball at the open-air bar. Four o'clock on a summer's afternoon, it's still the dead hour in Katakolon. Frankie Gleeson and I stood in silence for a while, as though we were paying our respects at the laying to rest of Professor Bernard Finch of Newburgh, New York.

I said, 'I'd like you to tell me some more about Bernard. About Willy.'

He said, 'What kind of thing?'

I said, 'Anything you can think of.'

'We lived next door,' he said. 'We'd lark around some-times.'

I said, 'I know nothing about his childhood.'

'Well,' he said, 'I guess we felt sorry for him. See, he was all on his own, no brothers, no sisters and we had Gleesons hanging from the rafters. I had four brothers older and Junie who's a year younger than me.'

I said, 'You included him in your games. That's nice.'

At Lowhope one was left to entertain oneself. On the one occasion Cousin Andrew was brought over to visit I remember throwing a tremendous tantrum because he wanted to play Snakes and Ladders and I had no idea that it was a game intended for more than one player.

Frankie said, 'Willy was an indoors kind of kid. He spent a lot of time at the lending library. Hanging out with us must have made a change of scene for him. Like, we might make a camp in the back yard, a piece of tarp and a cap gun and maybe a water canteen, and we'd play at Ambush the Japs. It was always the Japs, or the Germans. We didn't think about all this Outer Space stuff they have these days. And we'd make Junie fetch us Dixie cups of Kool Aid because she was the girl. Wouldn't get away with that today, would we? He'd come fishing sometimes, too. Or he'd go out with me and Dad, hunting for squirrel. Happy days. We had a big Airedale terrier called Booger. He was a wonderful hunting dog. He'd go through water and take a rat. Willy loved that dog. He was always trying to lure him round to his place but Booger knew what side his bread was buttered.'

It's true, Bernard does like dogs. He even likes the Jack Russell Bobbie Snape keeps as a house dog and he's a hateful little snapper.

I said, 'It sounds like such a happy time. How strange that he's erased all this from his life.'

He said, 'Darned if I can explain it. I mean, there's nothing

178

wrong with going away, getting yourself an education. Good luck to them with the brains to do it. But why wouldn't you want to come back once in a while? Why wouldn't you want to be where everybody knows your name?'

I said, 'Something must have happened. Was there a girl, for instance?'

'A girl?' he said. 'Well my sister Junie was sweet on him but he wasn't interested. No. I don't ever recall him having a sweetheart.'

He paused.

'Tell you the truth,' he said, 'I was kinda surprised to find out he was married.'

I said, 'You didn't think he was the marrying kind?'

Several of Bernard's friends said the same thing. Some of them were quite resentful. That's why we chose to have a very quiet wedding.

'You're right,' he said. 'As a matter of fact, there were some in Painted Post who thought Willy was a bit light on his toes, if you know what I mean?'

I believe I understood the drift of it.

He said, 'What I say is, it don't matter to me. People are as God made them. Just so long as they don't shove it down my throat. Anyhow, turns out they were wrong because here he is, married to your lovely self. He was just a late developer, that's all. He was a real Dapper Dan, though. Oh my! His pants were always pressed and he must have done it himself because his mom wouldn't have. I'll wager the only thing Mrs Fink ever did with a smoothing iron was throw it at poor old Charlie.'

Bernard pressing his own trousers! There's a skill he let slide after we were married.

He said, 'And I'll tell you another thing about Willy. He always favoured a bow tie. He started that when he was about fourteen, fifteen. Nobody on Brewster Street ever did that. Well, maybe for a prom, but not for day wear. That must have took some guts. Funny, he's done so well for himself. You'd think he'd enjoy meeting somebody who knew him from way back. You'd think he'd enjoy blowing his trumpet.'

You would. But since Francis Homer Gleeson stepped out of the mists of his past, Bernard's trumpet has been strangely muted.

I said, 'There's a very private side to Bernard and much as I think it would do him good to talk over old times, I know he absolutely won't. I'm terribly sorry.'

'Nothing to be done about it,' he said. 'A guy says he doesn't know me, I can't insist, can I? It'd have been nice to yarn about things, but there it is. He doesn't want to know me, and that's that.'

I said, 'I'm sure it's nothing personal.'

He laughed.

He said, 'Now if he was one of my old girlfriends I'd understand it. Some of them saw me coming, they'd probably jump ship.'

*

Jesus saw me getting out of the lift.

He said, 'Professor'll be glad to see you back. He's been buzzing that buzzer every five minutes. You wait while you see what he's got in there.'

I couldn't fully open the cabin door. It was blocked by an enormous arrangement of chincherinchees, gladiolus, and a bird of paradise, covered with cellophane and garnished with a gigantic bow made of shiny paper ribbon. A selection of things Bernard loathes assembled into a floral monstrosity.

There was a note attached: *TO THE 'PROFESSOR' FROM 'A FRIEND'*.

He looked terrible. His pyjamas were so creased and he hadn't shaved. The moment he saw me he began yelling.

'Get rid of it! Get it out of here! It's hideous! Why are you never here when I need you?'

I said, 'If you find them so objectionable why didn't you put them outside the door yourself?'

He said, 'Because I'm too ill to get out of bed and too weak to lift the damned thing, but I suppose that detail has slipped your mind.'

I said, 'Then why didn't you get Jesus to do it?'

'Because,' he said, 'Jesus has apparently decided not to respond to the ringing of my bell. Well he can say goodbye to his gratuity.'

Actually, we never leave gratuities. Bernard always says these people earn very good money and have practically no living expenses. He says they stash it away and then send it home to Mother.

I said, 'Jesus does have other passengers to look after.'

I hauled the damned thing into the corridor. Raoul, the junior steward was just passing.

I said, 'Could you possibly? We can't have flowers in our cabin. Such a shame but Professor Finch has an allergy.'

Raoul said he'd take them down to the cold store directly. One imagines the florist will be able to recycle them.

Bernard lay back against his pillows.

I said, 'That was a jolly lavish bouquet. You must have quite an admirer. Who do you think it is?'

He said, 'It wasn't a bouquet. It was an abomination, sent by people who have no sense of beauty. A bird of paradise! That says everything about the Gleesons. I expect they put paper parasols in their drinks too. Did they? You'd know. You went to their shindig. You're their big catch.'

I said, 'Why do you assume it was sent by the Gleesons?'

He said, 'It's obvious. You saw that sly use of the inverted comma. "Professor". That's Gleeson all over. The insidious hint that there's something provisional about my title, that I'm merely a "professor". Don't you understand what this means?'

I said, 'Yes, Bernard, I do. It means that in spite of your protests and your lolling in bed all day, you were actually well enough to get up and read the note attached to those flowers.'

Before he could say anything Nurse Quincy arrived. He took Bernard's temperature and checked his blood pressure.

I said, 'What's the verdict?'

'Alive, if not kicking,' he said. 'Blood pressure's fine, temperature's normal, coat's glossy, nose is cold, pyjamas could do with being changed.'

I said, 'Should he have antibiotics?'

'I don't think so,' he said. 'The chances are it's viral.'

Bernard said, 'I feel like death.'

Quincy said, 'Well, these viruses can be tricky things. Keep up the fluids and I'll look in on you again before Lights Out. Would you like something to help you sleep?'

Bernard said, 'I'd like something to put me out of my misery.'

'Oh dear,' Quincy said. 'Well, if Lady Enid would like to pop along with me to the Medical Centre, I'll give her one of our kits. Which would you prefer, cyanide or rope?'

The infirmary is below, on P Deck. We walked towards the lift.

Quincy said, 'Lady Enid, am I missing something here? Is there some reason the Professor doesn't want to get out of bed?'

I said, 'You think he's malingering.'

'Now, now,' he said. 'We don't use words like that aboard the *Golden Memories*. This is a happy ship. We're all here to enjoy ourselves. As a matter of fact, most of our clients end up in the Medical Centre because they've been enjoying

183

themselves too much. But for a healthy man the Professor does seem very determined to have something wrong with him.'

I said, 'He's been very tense, almost from the start of the cruise. He has this idea that someone's stalking him. It has been known to happen. Bernard's very charismatic, after all, and it's very hard to avoid people even on a ship as big as this.'

'Yes,' he said, 'I know it can happen. We sometimes get ladies turning up to see the ship's doctor twice a day. But the Professor? *Is* somebody stalking him?'

I said, 'No. But I think someone may be having a bit of fun with him. Like today, a bouquet was delivered.'

'Yes,' he said. 'It arrived just as I was leaving him this morning. A nice gesture. He didn't seem very pleased about it though. I notice he's had it taken away.'

I said, 'He hated it. Bernard has a very finely tuned sense of aesthetics. Ugly things can actually make him feel ill.'

'Oh dear,' he said. 'Life must be a minefield.'

I said, 'Tell me, Quincy. Is it possible my husband is having some kind of breakdown?'

'Oh, Lady Enid,' he said, 'let's not go there. Anyway, a diagnosis like that is way above my pay-grade. Do you want the doctor to see him?'

I said, 'I'd hate to bother the doctor unnecessarily.'

He said, 'And this isn't a very good time of day, doctor-wise.'

I said, 'Do you have a lot of people sick?'

184

'No,' he said. 'But the sun's over the yard arm.'

I said, 'I should tell you, it's the Cruise Director I'm concerned about. He was terribly cross about Bernard not working today. If he cries off again tomorrow I imagine Mr Iles will be well and truly on the warpath. He'll be asking questions and one would rather like to be ready with some convincing answers.'

Quincy said, 'I understand. Then you definitely don't want to involve the doctor. It kind of ups the ante, if you see what I mean. And there's a risk. If they hit it off, fine. They can agree to call it a viral infection and the Cruise Director'll just have to lump it. But the Professor can be quite sharp and between you and me, the doctor's pretty highly strung himself. He's Serbian. If they got off on the wrong foot …'

I said, 'Then let's wait and see how Bernard is by tomorrow morning. He may be so fed up, looking at the same Canaletto hour after hour, he'll decide he's well enough to get up and go to work.'

'My thinking exactly,' he said. 'The boredom cure.'

Bernard lay flat on his back, staring at the ceiling.

'Ah,' he said, 'the whisperer returns.'

I said, 'What can you mean?'

He said, 'I may be feverish but I haven't lost the use of my brain. It was all too clear you went outside with that boy so you could talk about me.'

I put the sleeping pill on the night stand.

I said, '*That* was the reason I went with him. Sleep is a great healer.'

He said, 'But what did he say? I know he said something.'

I said, 'That you're baffling medical science but he has every hope you'll have recovered by tomorrow.'

'I very much doubt it,' he croaked. 'I don't have the greatest confidence in that nurse. Heaven knows where they recruit these people. From the bottom of the swamp, you can be sure. When we get to Corfu I'm inclined to call Pippo Vlachos. He'll know someone at that private clinic.'

I said, 'In any event, don't worry. Everyone was very pleased with my tour of Olympia today, so if you are still unwell in the morning I'll feel perfectly confident about standing in for you again.'

'Will you indeed?' he said. 'Don't overreach yourself, Enid.'

I said, 'I'm only trying to help. Since your *raison d'être* aboard this ship is to provide a service and since ill health prevents you from doing so, it seems only sensible that I do what I can to compensate.'

Because it isn't so very hard, Bernard, as I discovered today. The facts and figures, your little anecdotes and asides, they were all there at my fingertips, absorbed over the years of being your devoted disciple.

His eyes were closed. He was weighing up which would be the lesser evil: to get out of bed and face his public or to hand over his work to me, a woman who has a Grade C in O Level Needlework.

186

I said, 'About those flowers. Should I make enquiries? I'm sure I could find out who sent them.'

'Absolutely not,' he said. 'I know who sent them and I will not rise to his bait.'

I said, 'Yes, probably the best plan. When I spoke to Frankie Gleeson earlier he seemed to have accepted that you have nothing to say to him but it could just be a ploy to make you lower your guard, to lure you out into the open.'

He said, 'Damn it, Enid, you've been talking to him again!'

I said, 'I could hardly avoid him. As you well know, on these cruise ships, no matter how large, one sees the same faces again and again. Indeed the less one wishes to see them the more frequently they pop up. Gleeson was down on the pier just now, waiting for his wife. I couldn't walk by him without speaking. It would have been too rude. Oh, but listen. I also talked to Mr Polder. He's awfully keen for you to meet Mr Erikson, Cornell, Class of Fifty-five. I think he sees himself orchestrating a meeting of great Cornellian minds. I find the man rather repulsive myself but you'll be pleased to hear I was all charm. Given the generally low intellectual level on board I imagine you'd enjoy meeting someone with whom you have something in common.'

He said, 'Why were you talking to Polder?'

I said, 'I sat with them at lunch. Up at the Pyrgos taverna. It was a frightful crush. They'd taken far too many coach parties. So I ended up squeezed in next to Mrs Polder. Well, one had to eat.'

He said, 'Why on earth didn't you walk down to the Kladhios? If you'd mentioned my name Dimitri would have rustled up something for you. There was certainly no need for you to sit with the rabble.'

I said, 'I'd hardly call the Polders "rabble". Anyway, you must bear in mind today I wasn't merely Enid Finch. Today I was Enid Finch, Assistant Guest Lecturer. One is here to keep the punters happy, after all.'

'Punters?' he said. 'Punters! What kind of a word is that?'

I said, 'With regard to the Gleesons, I've decided my best strategy is to get along with them. They've been perfectly charming to me, in their nouveau riche way, and after all, I have no personal reason for avoiding them. Think of me as your lightning rod, Bernard. And now we've established that I'm quite capable of standing in for you, you can relax and concentrate on getting back to good health. This virus has given you the perfect escape hatch from "the rabble" as you call them. I daresay Nurse Quincy might even be persuaded to quarantine you. As to Mr Polder, I'll keep him at bay until you're feeling stronger. I'm sure school reunions can be the most terrific fun but not when one is under the weather.'

He said, 'You're taking rather a lot upon yourself all of a sudden.'

How very much easier it is to deal with one's husband when he's lying in bed with a two-day beard.

I said, 'Am I? I'm sorry. Would you like Polder to bring

Mr Erikson to visit you in here? I'm sure he'd be willing. We have whisky, we have gin. I can get extra tooth mugs from Jesus and I'm sure the Gleesons would let me have some of those cheesy, snacky things.'

'Don't you dare,' he snapped. 'You've done quite enough harm, meddling, encouraging these people. Just stop interfering.'

I said, 'You might be a little more gracious. It's not as though I'm enjoying this. Frankie Gleeson is simply a childhood friend who was rather thrilled to rediscover you and life would have been a good deal easier if you'd simply grinned and borne it without all this fuss. It is only a ten-day cruise. Properly handled you might never have been troubled by more than a brief reacquaintance and then an annual round-robin letter. But no, you had to throw up that silly smoke screen. And you were less than truthful with me, insisting that you knew nothing of Willy Fink or Painted Post. Actually, Bernard, you made me look a perfect fool.'

He said, 'You are a fool, Enid, if you believe Gleeson would be satisfied with a drink and a Christmas card. An utter, utter fool.'

I snatched up my cardigan. He reached out to grab me but I was too quick for him.

He said, 'I'm sorry, I'm sorry. I didn't mean it quite the way it sounded. It's this fever. I'm not myself.'

No. Who are you, Bernard?

I said, 'I'm going up on deck.'

Away from the smell of your unwashed hair.

'Don't leave me,' he said.

I said, 'I have an appointment. With the Welsh troglodyte.'

'Of course,' he said. 'The dancing. You need your fun. I quite see that. Of course you must go. Just tell me I'm forgiven.'

I said, 'Try to sleep. Why not try the pill?'

He said, 'But am I forgiven?'

I said, 'Forgiven for what? For telling silly fibs? Or for calling me an utter, utter fool?'

He said, 'I've been alone all day.'

I said, 'Hardly. You've had Jesus at your beck and call and you've had at least two visits from Nurse Quincy.'

He said, 'But no one can fill the place of one's wife.'

Ah. The soft soap.

He said, 'And when one has a fever things can seem quite nightmarish, quite out of proportion.'

The soft soap followed by the mitigating circumstances.

I said, 'You could always get dressed and come with me. I think you're well enough to manage that. Do you realize Katakolon is our fifth port of call and so far you haven't joined me at the rail for a single sail-away?'

'*Mea maxima culpa,*' he said.

But stubbornness got the better part of remorse and he remained in bed.

'Enid,' was all he could say, as I closed the door behind me. 'Oh Enid!'

18

Taff Griffiths was waiting for me outside the ballroom. He was still in his white socks and sandals.

I said, 'No dance shoes?'

He said, 'I'm very sorry about this but I'm going to have to disappoint you. I'm needed below deck. There's a bit of a flap on.'

I said, 'Heavens, do tell.'

He said, 'I shouldn't really talk about it.'

I said, 'Don't tell me I have to apply to Virginia. She hangs around the Information Desk and finds out everything.'

'Well,' he said, 'as it's you. I know it'll go no further. Demonic possession. One of the laundry hands. And that's as much as I can say.'

I said, 'Gosh! So far from land and no one to assist you.'

There's an on-board rabbi but I'm not sure they do that kind of thing.

I said, 'Will you use the chaplet of St Michael?'

'Possibly,' he said. 'But sometimes a cup of tea and a chat works just as well.'

I doubt the Pope would agree.

I said, 'I suppose we could practise later?'

'I suppose we could,' he said. 'But the thing is, I wonder if we should? You know what I'm getting at? On further consideration?'

I said, 'You mean not dance at all? You mean pull out of the competition?'

'Upon sober reflection,' he said, 'yes.'

I said, 'Are you worried your bishop wouldn't approve?'

'No, no,' he said, 'bugger the bishop. To be honest, Enid, it's your husband. He didn't seem happy about the arrangement. Not happy at all.'

I said, 'Bernard doesn't mind.'

He said, 'That's not the impression I got. Quite abrupt, he was.'

I said, 'I think you caught him at a very bad moment yesterday. But almost the last thing he said to me as I came out just now was "Enid, you need your fun." So you see?'

'Well,' he said. 'Perhaps it's not the dancing. Perhaps it's me he objects to. He's a romantic. It could be he detected the chemistry between us.'

He was sweating.

I said, 'Chemistry?'

'Now, Enid,' he said, 'we're both adults. We both have appetites. We both know where the samba might lead.'

I said, 'But I bought an outfit. Blue crushed silk.'

He said, 'I dare say they'll give a refund.'

I said, 'This is so silly. It's just a dance. And Bernard is so uninterested he won't even know whether or not we dance.'

He said, '*I'd* know. And I'd never forgive myself. Those whom God has joined together. I'm sorry, Enid. I blame myself entirely. I got carried away.'

And off he scuttled, leaving one totally in the lurch at the very moment Irene and Don Harrington walked by.

Don said, 'Where's Taff running off to?'

I said, 'Duty calls. He's too busy to practise.'

Irene said, 'Oh dear. And you'll never get another partner now. It's far too late.'

Don said, 'What about the Professor? He wouldn't want to see you disappointed.'

I said, 'No, dancing isn't his thing. And anyway, he's unwell.'

Irene said, 'Yeah, I know. I heard Gavin Iles cussing about him.'

As soon as one sits in front of a computer one thinks of something one would like to look up. The only reference I could find to the Reverend Tudor Griffiths was a photograph taken aboard the *Pacific Princess* in 2002 on the occasion of a Renewal of Commitment ceremony between Nathan Roach and Sylvia Whittle. He seems not to have had a parish, at least not in recent years.

Just one email. From the pestilential Minta.

Enid,

I fear you may not have received my last message. Where on earth (or perhaps off earth!) do these emails go before they land on our computer screens? It's all quite beyond me. Anyway, re Tom-Tom, I'd be most enormously grateful if you could put him up in La Serenissima. If it's a question of money I imagine there are ways of getting the necessary to you, bureau de change or such like, though perhaps horribly complicated. Perhaps I could send you one of our farmhouse cheeses in lieu? Our Skeffington Blue Wedge won a bronze at the All England last year.

Fondly.

M

Skeffington Blue Wedge is a medium-soft, lightly-veined cheese with a strong blue bite. It is made from the milk of Jersey cows and fashioned into one-kilogram rounds with a natural mould-ripened rind.

I was about to leave the Internet Point and find myself a secluded spot for yet another solitary dinner when the McCuddys arrived.

'Hi honey,' she said. 'Don't tell me you caught this computer bug too. We missed you on the dance floor. We expected to see you and the Reverend practising. Only three nights to go!'

The slightest whiff of drink on her breath.

I said, 'I'm afraid my dancing is no sooner begun than it's ended. Fr. Griffiths is too busy.'

She said, 'But you mustn't give up. We'll find you a new partner. Chip, who can we get for her?'

But Chip wasn't listening. He was clicking through a long list of emails.

Cricket said, 'He's checking to see how Kayla's doing.'

The grandchild, with the chicken pox.

She said, 'How's your hubby?'

I said, 'Feverish. Confined to bed.'

'I swear,' she said, 'you are getting all the bad luck this trip. Well, you know what we're gonna do? We're gonna take you to dinner and while we eat we're gonna put our thinking hats on. We're gonna find you a new dance partner.'

I said, 'No. Really. I should get back to Bernard. I can grab a sandwich.'

'No way,' she said. 'If he's not well, he needs to sleep. And nobody eats alone when we're in town, isn't that right, Chip?'

'Nobody,' he agreed. 'Not when the McCuddys are around.'

'Tell you what,' she said. 'Why don't you and me head across to Sam's Bar while Chip looks at the stock prices? He takes for ever. We'll get a little drink and I'll tell you what Geraldo said about you.'

I said, 'Geraldo? About me?'

'Oh yes,' she said. 'You have been talked about.'

I said, 'Well, one drink.'

'Good,' she said. 'Chip, tell Kayla Grandma says don't scratch the spots. And tell the boys I got them all sweatshirts from the actual, original Olympics.'

Geraldo has apparently mentioned my dancing skills on no fewer than three occasions.

Cricket said, 'And it didn't go down too well with certain people I could mention. With a certain man-eater whose name begins with I. She was just plain jealous.'

Cricket had downed two Manhattans by the time Chip joined us.

'Dow dropped four hundred yesterday,' he said. 'And Tyler got his finger caught in Biff's car door.'

Another grandchild.

'Well why wasn't Biff watching him?' she said. 'See what happens when I'm not there?'

Chip said, 'Hospital says it's not broke though.'

Cricket's mobile telephone rang. It plays 'Yankee Doodle'.

'In Sam's Bar,' she said. 'Where are y'all?'

'Great,' she said. 'Yeah. We'll see you there. And you'll never guess what. The Reverend pulled out of the contest. He's too busy. Loada hooey if y'ask me. I'm not kidding. You can ask her yourself because we're bringing her to dinner. The Professor's still sick *and* she lost her dance partner. She's having one very bad day.'

'That was Nola,' she said.

*

There were six of us to dinner at The Old Sea Dog's Burger Bar: me, the Gleesons, the McCuddys and the elephant at the table. The Gleesons strike me as the kind of couple who tell each other everything, so anything Frankie knows about Bernard, Nola also knows. But what about the McCuddys? Are they in on this? I think not. Cricket was drinking steadily. If the Willy Fink Question has been discussed between them it would have been remarkable if she'd managed to stay off the subject as the Manhattans loosened her tongue.

Everyone else was drinking Coca-Cola with lots of ice.

Frankie said, 'But you must have whatever you'd like, Enid. Wine. I know that's what you folks drink over here. You'll have to order it yourself though. Me and Nola never got the hang of wine. Funny really, because they make it just up the road from us, all around the Finger Lakes. Cayuga, Seneca. They make white wine and red wine and all sorts. And my sister Junie and her husband, they make apple cider, which is a very healthful beverage. We drink that sometimes.'

Nola said, 'And champagne, Frankie. We always have champagne on our anniversary.'

'We do,' he said. 'Even though it gives me gas pains, pardon my French.'

I ordered a glass of the house red.

Frankie said, 'You sure that's OK? Don't stint yourself, now. Get yourself something good. Doesn't matter what it costs. You know a good one when you see one.'

The Gleesons have a very free and easy attitude to money. I mean, Bernard adores a good bottle but he'd never dream of buying one. When we're in Venice I'm afraid I take an empty carboy along to the loose wine shop and have it filled with *il cheapo sfuso,* and in London if we have guests I decant Bulgarian Country Wine into oft-recycled French bottles. No one seems to notice.

We exchanged histories. Chip and Cricket are from Georgetown, Delaware, home of the Perdue chicken. They grew up in the same street. In fact Chip remembers the day Cricket was born, there being almost eighteen years between them.

Cricket said, 'He saw me in my bassinet and decided he'd wait for me.'

Which Chip confirmed.

She said, 'And while he was waiting he upped and founded McCuddy Home Security. Started as a locksmith and never looked back.'

They have three sons and though they changed houses as their family grew they haven't moved more than two miles from where they started and neither have their children.

Cricket said, 'And the other remarkable thing is, while Chip was waiting for me to graduate high school, my sister Muffy married one of his brothers. Isn't that neat?'

They have more than thirty people to seat at Thanksgiving. How jolly it all sounds.

The Gleesons live in a house built by Frankie and his first

wife. It's in a town called Horseheads, only ten miles or so from Painted Post where he grew up. Such colourful names. Horseheads. Painted Post. Horseheads was apparently the burial ground of hundreds of army pack horses used in General Sullivan's campaign against the Iroquois during the Revolution. They were so broken down by months of trekking that Sullivan ordered them to be shot. Then the Iroquois dug up the skulls and put them on display, as if to say 'look what'll happen to you if you try to settle on our land'.

Frankie said, 'Didn't stop us though. We've got twenty thousand people in Horseheads now and none of them's Iroquois that I know of.'

Nola is from Watertown, New York, about thirty miles from the Canadian border.

She said, 'Know where I met Frankie? You'll never believe this. In the bleachers at Dunn Field, Elmira. The Pioneers were playing the Yonkers Hoot Owls. My kid sister was working in Elmira and I was visiting with her. I'm no great baseball fan but she was keen on one of the umpires, so she dragged me along to the game.'

Chip said, 'You sit in the bleachers, Frankie? I'd have thought you'd have your own box.'

'No,' he said. 'I did try one, years back, but I didn't care for it.'

Nola said, 'So I'm sitting there with my sister Connie and I hear this voice saying "Hey, beautiful, I got a bag of pork

199

rinds here has your name on it." And that was Frankie. Things didn't work out for Connie and her umpire but they turned out good for me.'

Frankie said, 'The two smartest things I ever did. Inventing Gleeson's Pork Rinds and offering Nola a free sample at the game that day. I'd been on my own five years by then and that's too long for a man.'

Nola was a widow when they met.

'I'd done a lot of living,' she said. 'Married at seventeen. He was a soldier boy from Fort Drum. Divorced at nineteen. Remarried at twenty-two and widowed at forty. Heart attack. He'd waxed both cars, which he always did on a Sunday afternoon, and he said he wasn't feeling so good so he was going upstairs for a nap. Never woke up. It was a terrible shock. I mean, I was OK for money. I had my own chain of nailtiques by then. But it takes a long time to get over something like that. I wasn't looking for anybody when Frankie came along. It couldn't have been further from my mind. Still, he did come along, and he's a treasure. He's a keeper. Now, how'd you and the Professor come to meet?'

They thought our story very sweet.

'Rome!' Nola said. 'That is so romantic. I've been in Rome, New York but I didn't make it to the real one yet. We have to go there, Frankie. Next year.'

'Yeah,' said Cricket. 'Us too. And Sorrento. And Capree. I want to see that Blue Grotto.'

Frankie said, 'Will you listen to these girls? We haven't

200

even finished this trip and they're planning another one. See Rome and die, they say. And I probably will. You'd think a guy'd be allowed to stay home in the twilight of his years.'

Chip said, 'You'd think so, Frankie.'

Cricket said, 'But you're not in the twilight years, Chip. You're in your prime.'

When she drinks a Manhattan she saves the maraschino cherry till last and savours it in a rather repellent, porcine way.

'Least you are,' she said, smacking her lips, 'when you remember to take your pill.'

There was an awkward silence and in careless haste I rushed to fill it.

I said, 'I'm afraid you'll find Capri very crowded. Every bit as bad as Santorini. My grandpapa used to adore it there but that was in the days when it was a kind of retreat.'

'Cah-pri,' Nola said. 'Don't you just love the way she says that? Cah-pri. And "grandpapa". I love it.'

Frankie said, 'And he'd have been a lord, right? Your grandpop? Or a baron? And that's how you come to be Lady Enid. I think I see how it works.'

19

It was so damned stupid of me, mentioning Grandpapa. Of all the subjects one might have brought up. Why does one always feel a compulsion to rescue others from their drunken gaffes?

I said, 'My grandpapa was a marquess.'

'Wow!' he said. 'You hear that, Nola? A marquess! And what about your other grandpop? He a marquess too?'

I said, 'He was an earl.'

'My, oh my,' he said. 'Give me a pen, Nola. You got a notepad in your bag? I gotta write this down. A marquess and an earl. Ain't that something!'

Chip raised a finger.

'The Marquess of Queensberry,' he said. 'Invented the rules of boxing.'

'That's right, Chip,' Frankie said. 'No hitting a man when he's down.'

'And the wife of a marquess,' said Cricket, with a triumphant wave of her empty glass, 'is a marcasite!'

Frankie Gleeson was sitting with his biro poised.

I said, 'My mother is the daughter of a marquess and my father was the son of an earl. And a marquess's wife is actually called a marchioness. And that's really all there is to tell.'

Frankie said, 'But I'll trouble you for their names. Because my sister Junie's gonna love this. She'll really go into it, you know?'

Nola was playing with her bangles, watching me. My cheeks were burning.

She said, 'Frankie, why don't you get the check? I could do with a breath of air and I think Cricket could too.'

They insisted I was their guest, for which I was grateful. Thirty euros seemed awfully expensive for a hamburger in a bun. People imagine that because one's family is titled one must be rolling in wealth when in fact one is effectively on one's uppers. Mumsie and Bobbie make a little with the caravan park but that's seasonal and they don't even advertise. It's probably barely enough to keep them in gin. There certainly doesn't seem to be anything to spare for repairs to Lowhope which, like all the other Lune properties is in an advanced state of decay.

Cousin Andrew was living at Lune Grange but it became so mildewed he had to move into the dower house and even there he's had to patch the roof over the kitchen and scullery with corrugated metal. And Oakhanger House is no more. It was sold to some kind of Eastern cult in order to pay the death duties and Cousin Tig now ekes out her funds in an apartment on the Costa del Sol. And of course Bernard contributes very little to the pot. He writes the occasional article, for which he's paid a pittance or, more likely, with two free copies of some obscure magazine. He has no family money and one begins to understand why. Serafina Fink squandered it on lipstick! So here we are, scraping by every month, while people like the Gleesons and the McCuddys have millions.

Their intention was to go down to the Top Hat Bar to see the floor show. Mine was to make my escape as quickly as possible. To find a chair in the remotest corner of the library and read until such time as Bernard would be soundly asleep. And all might have gone according to plan had the lifts not been so busy and had Nola not been so anxious about securing a floor-side table for the cabaret.

I said, 'We could always walk.'

They looked at one another.

I said, 'It's only six levels. And it is down.'

Nola said, 'Enid's right. We can do it.'

One would have thought I'd suggested trekking across the Kalahari.

Chip said, 'Take my arm now, sweetheart.'

But Cricket was full of the kind of bravado generated by five Manhattans.

'I don't need no arm,' she said, taking the steps at speed. 'I'm the youngster around here. You take care of Enid. She's six months older than me.'

Nola and I were hurrying after Cricket, calling to her to

wait for us, while Chip and Frankie huffed and puffed far behind. They didn't witness her defiant jump three steps from the bottom of a flight or the way one of her shoe heels caught in the metal carpet trim and she clawed for the rail, missed it and sagged to the ground, like a punctured hot air balloon. By the time they reached us on the mezzanine landing her knee had already started to swell.

Nola hailed one of the J Deck stewards who called the Medical Centre and a small crowd of passengers gathered to examine the carpet trim and give their opinion on the likely success of a lawsuit. Then Dr Lupin couldn't be located so conjecture turned to the subject of medical negligence. Cricket was meanwhile very gung-ho to try walking.

'All I need is a hand to get me up,' she kept saying. 'Nola, Frankie, go ahead and get us a good table.'

Nola said, 'I'm going nowhere. I'm staying here, make sure they look after you right.'

The knee grew larger. After the longest time Nurse Quincy appeared.

'Sorry about the delay,' he said. 'Busy night.'

He looked at Cricket's knee. Just a sprain, he said. But a bad one.

Frankie said, 'You qualified for this work? Because Mr McCuddy here'd as soon wait for the doctor to be available. He'd as soon wait on a proper medical opinion, wouldn't you, Chip? No offence, son, but we don't want any slip-ups, do we? You can't mess around with knees.'

Quincy was very good-humoured.

He said, 'I'm a qualified nurse, sir, New Brunswick registered, but if you'd rather wait for the doctor to take a look I quite understand. I just can't say how long you'll have to wait.'

Cricket whispered, 'Is he attending the exorcism?'

Quincy's eyebrow twitched.

'No,' he said, 'No. He's … dealing with a drink-related incident.'

I said, 'Could we at least move Mrs McCuddy to somewhere more comfortable?'

A steward brought ice cubes wrapped in a towel, Quincy telephoned for a wheelchair and Chip hummed tunelessly, bo-bo-bo-bommmmm, bo-bo-bo-bommmmmm, until Cricket burst into tears. The Manhattans had turned on her.

'My knee,' she sobbed. 'It hurts. And what about the dance contest? Chip, what are we gonna do?'

Chip seemed quite at a loss. Frankie feared she might need surgery, Nola glared at him and said the swelling would probably go down as fast as it came up, and Quincy said not to get her hopes too high. They lifted Cricket into the chair and wheeled her, still sobbing, along to the service lift.

I said, 'I'll leave you here. Too many cooks, et cetera.'

Nola said, 'No, Enid. I'll need you to help me get her to bed. Guys are no use at a time like this.'

The McCuddys, like the Gleesons, have a king suite, with two enormous beds, a large sofa, a balcony, complete with cane furniture, and a bathroom with a proper bath tub. Very luxurious. But their counterpanes are exactly the same unpleasant shade of mustard as ours and they have the same cheaply framed Canaletto, so money doesn't buy one everything.

Quincy said, 'So what did we decide about the doctor?'

Frankie said, 'We want him.'

Quincy said, 'I'll ask him to come as soon as ever he's free.'

He left.

Cricket said, 'I need the potty.'

Nola said, 'Frankie, wait outside.'

Chip sat on the other bed with his head in his hands.

'Oh dear, oh dear,' he kept saying. 'Oh dear, oh dear, oh dear.'

Nola said, 'Chip, wait outside with Frankie. Second thoughts, Frankie, take Chip down to the Hash Sling and get him a strong, sweet tea. He's in shock.'

Nola said I had to help her take Cricket to the bathroom though Cricket was hopping so determinedly I felt *de trop*, to say the least. I tried to avert my eyes from the marshmallow thighs bulging over her stocking tops.

We got her back onto the bed. Her knee had grown to the size of a honeydew melon.

She said, 'We're gonna miss the Dance-Off and Chip'll never forgive me.'

Nola said, 'Now, honey, Chip don't care about some little

dance contest. He just wants you to take care of that knee. Anyhow, you could be A1 again by Gala Night.'

Cricket said, 'I won't be. Look at it. Everything's ruined. And Chip's gonna be mad because we put a triple chassé in our quickstep and he's worked so hard to get it right.'

Her eyes were glistening with tears.

Nola said, 'I know! Enid doesn't have a partner either. Chip can dance with Enid. Only thing is, you'd have to work out what to do about the prize, if they win. I guess you could toss for it.'

The suggestion didn't go down well. Not with me, not with Cricket. She howled.

'Noooo,' she sobbed. 'Noooooo.'

I said, 'Please, Cricket, don't upset yourself. It was just a silly suggestion. Nola didn't mean it.'

Nola said, 'Yes I did. Land sakes, if Chip's gonna be disappointed about his triple chassé, why not? It's only a dance. Enid'll give him back at the end of the contest.'

Cricket was hiccuping through her tears.

She said, 'I oughta be brave, didn't I? I just don't know if I could bear it. To see him in the arms of another woman.'

Nola said, 'We're not talking about Sharon Stone, honey. We're talking about Enid.'

Good old Enid, with whom any husband is as safe as the Bank of England.

I said, 'But anyway, as a matter of fact I wouldn't do it.'

Cricket turned her pink, swollen eyes on me.

She said, 'You won't dance with my Chip?'

I said, 'No.'

'Why?' she said. 'My husband not good enough for you, hunh? *Lady* Enid.'

Oh, the switchback moods of a five-Manhattan drunk: the over-hasty intimacy, the bravura, and then the snotty, sniffing, maudlin melancholy that turns on a sixpence into belligerence. I dropped by the Excursions Desk before I went back to the cabin. Cricket McCuddy had just given me another reason for making myself scarce tomorrow.

The James Bond Experience and Corfu Crafts Village Tour were fully booked but the girl said there were still spaces on Bernard's tour of Corfu Town. I was gratified to see that both the Polders and the Gleesons had signed up for it, optimistic of his recovery. It will do him good. Sometimes one must face one's demons.

I reserved one of the two remaining seats for the Paradise Beach Excursion.

Bernard was not only awake when I returned to the cabin but out of bed and with his hair combed.

He said, 'I believe I feel a little better.'

I said, 'I do hope so because frankly I don't feel equal to standing in for you again tomorrow. Olympia is one thing, Corfu quite another. My iconography is pretty shaky.'

Worryingly shaky, he agreed.

I said, 'And I'm not at all sure I can be trusted to recount the miracles of St Spiridon, which would be a disservice to the tour group as well as to the great saint himself.'

He said, 'You're right, it would be unforgivable. I must force myself. I've decided, no matter how ghastly I feel tomorrow morning I shall put my best foot forward and give them their money's worth. You were gone a very long time. I suppose you've eaten?'

I said, 'Yes, I did.'

In the Old Sea Dog's Burger Bar, dear, with your arch-nemesis and his friends.

He said, 'Then I hope you went Dutch. Taffy Twinkle-Toes struck me as the type to play the poor church mouse. I know what you're like, Enid. You'd be too bloody polite to make a parson pay his way.'

I said, 'I didn't eat with Fr. Griffiths. He was called away. Someone down in the bilge had gone loopy.'

He said, 'You ate alone again. I'm sorry.'

To tell all or to glide over the events of the evening and allow the moment to pass? Well, when a person is recovering from a viral infection and still in a debilitated condition, mightn't it be rather cruel to burden them with unnecessary and possibly distressing details?

I said, 'Eating alone doesn't bother me. One gets accustomed to it.'

He smiled.

He said, 'That's my girl! Nothing daunted. You know, I

210

believe you were dining alone the first time I ever saw you. It must have been at dei Monti.'

I said, 'It was Da Felice, actually.'

'You're right,' he said. 'Da Felice! And Clifford said, "Look at that dear creature sitting alone. Do let's invite her to join us." Which I did and you brought your plate of *bucatini amatriciana* over to our table and you had sauce on your chin.'

It wasn't the first time you saw me, Bernard. It was the first time you *noticed* me.

'Da Felice,' he said. 'The superb saltimbocca, remember? With buttered spinach.'

I said, 'Bernard, were you and Clifford lovers?'

He looked at me over the top of the Room Service menu.

'Rule Number One, Enid,' he said. 'Rule Number One.'

Rule Number One is that we don't talk about Clifford because Bernard was so terribly hurt when Clifford's family bundled him out of the house immediately after the funeral, and also by the way old friendships faded away. It was rather cruel that all those people who had seemed to admire Bernard so much turned out not to admire him at all once Clifford was gone.

Nurse Quincy tapped on the door.

'Sorry I'm late!' he said. 'It's been one of those days. We've had earache, mosquito bites, sunstroke, voices in the head, a Fanta ring-pull stuck on a toe, explain *that* one if you can, and then the sprained knee.'

211

I caught his eye and he understood immediately. I wasn't there. I know nothing of the McCuddys and their friends, or of Cricket's little accident.

He was delighted to find Bernard not only out of bed but also ordering a Club Sandwich and a bottle of Merlot.

'Excellent!' he said. 'That's what I call a full recovery.'

Bernard said, 'I'd hardly call it "full", but I believe I am feeling a little stronger.'

Quincy said, 'Was it my nursing skills or Mother Nature's?'

Bernard said, 'It was mind over matter. Sometimes one has to ask that bit extra of oneself.'

Quincy said, 'That's the spirit. As long as you take things steady for the next day or two.'

Bernard said, 'I will, as far as my responsibilities allow.'

Quincy said, 'Just remember to drink plenty of water and don't push yourself unnecessarily. If you start to wilt, Lady Enid can always take over. She was a big hit this morning, apparently. Everyone's talking about her.'

Bernard said, 'I'm sure my wife very stoutly did her best at Olympia but she cannot possibly lead people around Corfu. She knows far too little about the Paleopolis mosaics or the Damaskinos icons. And can she give them Homer? Of course not.'

And he got to his feet and began to recite.

'When earth-encircling Neptune heard,
He went to Schiera where the Phaeacians dwell

*And there he stayed until the ship, making its rapid way, got
    close in.
Then he went up and turned it into stone
And drove it down, to root it in the ground.
And then he went his way.'*

'Well then,' Quincy said. 'I can't top that, so I'll wish you
good night.'

20

Having drunk deeply of the Merlot Bernard is asleep. I am not. But one simply daren't switch on the bedside light so one is reduced to sitting on the throne in the Littlest Room, trying to jot things down and clear one's head. The fact is, Frankie Gleeson, in all innocence, has touched upon something rather delicate. My title. And, being the kind of man he is, he keeps returning to it, as one's tongue returns to a troublesome tooth or one's fingers play with a loose thread. One always feared this moment would come.

I was the Hon. Enid Nellish. When I married I became the Hon. Mrs Finch. But Bernard, perhaps because he's from the colonies and lacks certain instincts, felt I'd been very poorly served by the rules of the peerage. And I very feebly allowed myself to be persuaded to do something about it. Something rather shameful.

Grandpoppa Oakhanger was the 5th Earl and Poppa, who was the only son, had the title Viscount Moyle. Quite soon after his divorce from Mumsie, Poppa remarried. His new wife was an American person called Paige, a dancer recently retired from the Tiller Troupe. She became the new Viscountess Moyle and a year after their marriage they had a baby boy, Ripley, of whom one never speaks in front of Mumsie. She felt that Poppa's sexual incontinence had led him into a sentimental error and that as a consequence he'd ruined the Oakhanger blood line. Not that it was really any concern of hers. Grandpoppa Oakhanger certainly didn't seem worried about it. I once heard him describe Paige as a nicely paced filly with no apparent vices, so one got the impression he liked her.

So Ripley, of Ripley's Pre-Owned Autos, is my half-brother, though we met only once. Poppa and Paige lived in town until 1975, when Poppa's gout drove them to the warmer climes of Florida. He always said I should visit, but one felt so awkward. It was too far to go for a short visit but three days is the absolute limit either for being a house guest or having a house guest thrust upon one. Also, Poppa was very much changed. He'd become almost, one hates to say it, not *our* kind of people. Under the influence of Paige he began wearing synthetic trousers and referring to the drawing room as 'the lounge'.

The last time I saw Poppa was in 1977. He came back to England for Great-Uncle Ootie's memorial service and took me to lunch at Fortnum's. I had no idea he'd been unwell so it was a great shock to see how gaunt he'd become and it was made no easier by his insistence on joking about it.

'Your old Poppa's ready for the knackers,' he said. 'Next stop, the glue factory. They say it's due to the cigs but I don't subscribe to that myself. I've always smoked top quality and never more than two packs a day. I've always been a Dunhill man. Not like those filthy hand-rolled things your mother smokes.'

Whether it was a question of the quality or the quantity of the cigarettes, it made no difference. Poppa had lung cancer and within little more than a year he was dead. And then, because Grandpoppa outlived him by several years, it was Ripley who eventually succeeded to the title and became the 6th Earl Oakhanger. The fact that he had a title really couldn't have mattered to me less. If one has grown up an 'Hon.' one doesn't mope around wishing for something different. But Bernard greatly resented Ripley's title, and after we heard that Ripley had married and would no doubt soon father an heir, he allowed his mind to dwell on the subject far too much.

He used to say, 'Enid, it's iniquitous that you, the offspring of two noble English houses should be a mere "Hon." while the wife of a car salesman is swanning around calling herself "Lady Shelly-Mae".' Though actually we never verified that Ripley's wife uses her title. One imagines that in Gainesville it might be regarded as a joke.

But Bernard insisted on my consulting Mr Lineham at Snagge, Lineham and Pink, which put us to enormous and unnecessary expense, and when Mr Lineham delivered his opinion, which was that nothing could be changed, Bernard still wouldn't let the matter rest.

He said, 'As far as I'm concerned you're a Lady and from now on I shall refer to you as such.'

Which he promptly did. I felt rather uneasy about it at first but our circumstances made the change fairly easy. We lived for much of the year in Italy where they're quite promiscuous about titles, and we never saw people from my old circle so there were no tricky moments. The only thing I had to insist upon was that the matter be concealed from Mumsie. She absorbed the peerage rules with her nursery rusks and has nothing but the utmost scorn for those who slip up, let alone those who quite deliberately transgress.

There it might have rested until the day we were flying out of Gatwick airport and I, having foolishly left behind my passport at the check-in desk, was paged as Mrs Finch and asked to go back and collect it. It couldn't have mattered less. No one else in the airport knew or cared what I was called but Bernard was livid.

He said, 'How can you smile so gaily, Enid? It's insufferable. There's only one thing for it. You must change your name so there can be no further argument about it. You must take Lady as a new first name. Then everything will be completely legal and puffed-up little airline clerks won't be in a position to humiliate you.'

Of course, I hadn't felt humiliated. I was very happy to be The Hon. Mrs Finch. But Bernard wouldn't let go of the idea and the real humiliation came when I followed his wishes and made my application for change of name by deed poll. It was refused, on the grounds that the insertion of the name 'Lady' was liable to mislead, whether in a calculated manner or not. They said they might approve 'Lady' as a middle name if I cared to reapply but I was so sick of the whole affair by then I simply dropped it. Bernard wasn't very pleased but he realized it would be counterproductive to make a fuss, so he just continued calling me 'Lady Enid' as before.

He does it with the best of intentions and I've grown accustomed to it, but it was inevitable the day would come when questions might be asked. I suppose I rather imagined it would be someone from my past, someone like Billa Thoresby, or a distant Lune cousin pitching up on a package tour to Venice. I certainly hadn't expected the threat to come from an American in white plimsolls. And I do feel a little threatened by Mr Gleeson. He's awfully friendly, in that American way, but he's not the fool Bernard makes him out to be and one senses there's something jolly determined about him. This evening his questions made me feel like a small, woodland creature who's just seen a terrier's snout poking into the mouth of its burrow.

Bernard was up, showered and shaved by seven, singing the Toreador song as he selected a shirt and bow tie. The telephone rang. Gavin Iles.

Bernard said, 'Flying in the face of medical advice, yes. The tour goes ahead. There'll be no need for a stand-in. The maestro is back.'

I said, 'It's wonderful to see you back on your feet. And Mr Iles must be very happy.'

'Iles!' he said. 'The man hasn't a clue. The fact that he sent you to Olympia in my stead speaks volumes. He has no concept of the years and years of study and experience that give me my stature. No offence, Enid, but honestly!'

I gave him my well-practised Good Sport smile.

I said, 'None taken. You're the one the public want, Bernard. As you rightly pointed out last evening, I can't give them Homer.'

'No,' he said, 'but you do have your role, Enid, and I don't underestimate it. You chivvy the stragglers. You help the nitwits understand their euro coins. A tour without your assistance would be such a trial.'

I said, 'But not impossible, as today will prove. I'm going to Paradise Beach in a glass-bottomed boat.'

He stood, in his socks and his boxer shorts, quite lost for words.

I said, 'Think of it as our new regime. We've been so quarrelsome this week. Perhaps we're too much in each other's company. And of course, since my success standing in for you at Olympia, our working relationship can never be quite the same again. So today you can go your way and I'll go mine. To Paradise Beach.'

'Why, Enid?' was all he could say. 'Why?'

I said, 'Because one will be able to swim off the boat. And then there's going to be a barbecue on the beach and it all sounds like the most wonderful fun. I think I'm entitled to a little pleasure, Bernard. You had your nine-hour lunch with Stash Leontis, after all.'

'Ha!' he said. 'So you're still simmering about Stash! You can be so childish. Well, enjoy yourself with the lowbrows. A barbecue! How very suburban.'

He hogged the looking glass for simply ages, trying on all his ties until he settled on the mauve spot.

He said, 'Needless to say you'll be among your new-hatch'd friends on this jaunt. Tiny Taff. The Pork Rind Gang.'

I said, 'No. I'm going alone.'

He said, 'Don't split hairs, Enid. You may be *going* alone but I'll wager you'll find some familiar faces when you climb aboard. A glass-bottomed boat sounds right up Gleeson's *strada*.'

I said, 'No. I seem to remember the Gleesons have their names down for your tour. And the Polders. The core members of the Bernard Finch Fan Club. You could be in for a very interesting day.'

I thought he carried it off rather well. His face showed nothing. Only someone who knows Bernard as intimately as I do would read anything into the way he fiddled with the pocket flaps of his jacket.

He said, 'I hope you won't have cause to regret abandoning your post today. Just remember what happens to people who lie down with dogs. And I very much hope you'll find time amidst all this selfish junketing to go to HellaSpar and stock up on my kumquat marmalade.'

21

Bernard's group had already moved off, Frankie and Nola clearly visible in canary shades of leisurewear. They were heading up the hill to their first stop; the church of St Spiridon.

'Spiridon, the Cypriot shepherd who became a bishop and in death, a worker of miracles. His incorrupt body lies in this silver casket but four times a year he is paraded, in his shroud, around the city and once a year he's given a new pair of slippers. Why? Because he's still busy, running around performing miracles and wearing out his shoes.'

Pause for laughter.

'And what were his miracles? Principally he saved Corfu from plague, from famine, and from something Corfiots would regard as worse than both put together: the Turks.'

Boom-boom.

There were coaches waiting for us on the pier. It was a mainly younger group, with only a couple of faces I recognized.

Dorcas in a batik sarong, Don Harrington. I sat with four very merry secretaries from Kansas: a Lindy, an Avril and two Sallies. It was bliss to be anonymous.

We drove along the coast road to Barbati where there was a flotilla of caiques to take us on, further north, twelve to a boat. We sailed towards Nissaki past white cliffs, pitted with caves and running sheer down into the clearest sapphire water. Two of the cavern entrances were big enough for us to sail right in. To explore the smaller ones, one just dived off the side of the boat and swam inside. Some were filled with a greenish light, some with blue, and one with the most heavenly rosy pink. We stopped for lunch at a tiny cove, inaccessible except by boat and quite deserted except for the eighty or so in our party. Sardines grilled over brushwood, Greek salad and cold beer. I sat with the Kansas secretaries while we ate.

Two of them are married, two are divorced although seeing people, and they take a cruise together every year, ladies only, and seem to have the most enormous fun. I suppose this is an advantage of having a job of work, especially in a large company. One would get to know a lot of people and could strike up friendships. When I did my stint at the gallery all those years ago there was no fellowship because one manned the desk alone. It wasn't a terribly busy gallery either. Sometimes a whole day could pass without any clients ringing the bell.

I think perhaps I should have enjoyed being a secretary

and going on excursions with chums, if only I'd thought of it at the time. Mumsie wouldn't have raised any objections. She always encouraged me to go away from Lowhope and keep busy with projects. But one simply didn't know any secretaries. One didn't think of such things. In our circles one went off to St Gallen or wherever and then it was assumed one would marry soon after. Which one did, eventually. Billa has been rather more enterprising than I have, starting up her little curtain and cushion business, but purely out of necessity, one imagines, after Husband No. 2 invested so recklessly and then absconded with a Lithuanian fashion model. I'm sure there was no previous history of Thoresbys working for a living. Perhaps I could still do something. If Minta Fellowes can sell cheese, going into business can't be so terribly difficult.

After lunch everyone relaxed, except for a few energetic types who played volleyball. I grabbed one of the few patches of shade, stretched out on my towel, closed my eyes and drifted off to sleep. But I was jolted out of my snooze by the thud of Don Harrington, Gentleman Host, throwing himself down beside me on the sand.

'Afternoon, Enid,' he said. 'And how are you today?'

I said, 'I'm well, thank you.'

He said, 'And what about dear Bernard?'

I said, 'He's well too.'

He said, 'Really? The word on the lower decks is that he's cracking up.'

223

I'd have expected a little more discretion from Quincy.

I said, 'Not at all. He had a touch of laryngitis but now he's very much recovered. This morning he conducted his tour as scheduled.'

He said, 'Would that be the Corfu: Homer to Holocaust Tour? That sounds like a barrel of fun.'

I said, '*De gustibus non disputandum est*.'

'If you say so, ducks,' he said. 'If you say so.'

He offered to rub sun cream onto my back. I declined.

He said, 'Have you found a new dance partner?'

I said, 'I'm not looking for one. It's far too late. Things didn't work out and that's that.'

He lit a cigarette.

'Pity,' he said. 'You're a nice dancer. I reckon you and Taff'd have been in with a chance.'

I said, 'Then you should be glad we dropped out. It improves your chances.'

'Me?' he said. 'I couldn't give a tinker's.'

I said, 'Well Irene certainly could. She was furious about us competing. I wouldn't have put it past her to trip us up.'

He laughed.

He said, 'No. Her bark's worse than her bite. I'll tell you Irene's problem. I think she had her sights set on you as a new friend, you know? The *Lady* Enid thing? It would have been a bit of a feather in her cap.'

Hellfire and damnation, why do people attach so much

importance to that? Bernard included. In that respect he's really no better than many of the people he despises.

I said, 'That's so tiresome.'

'I'm sure it is,' he said, 'but you know how it is? Some people love all that stuff.'

Dorcas called to him to go and join the ball game. He ignored her.

He said, 'Why don't you just drop the "Lady"? Who's to stop you?'

I said, 'I'd love to, but Oyster Line rather latched onto it. They seemed to think it would add to Bernard's appeal.'

'Load of bullshit,' he said.

Dorcas called to him again.

I said, 'Don't let me detain you.'

'You're not,' he said. 'Last thing I need, leaping around after a bellyful of sardines.'

I said, 'You seem to be a big hit with the ladies.'

He said, 'I tell you, this is some cruise. I've never met so many nymphomaniacs. It must be something in the drinking water. I like your swimsuit, by the way. I like the little skirt. Very retro. Anyway, I'm glad to hear Bernard's all right because nobody likes to see a colleague in difficulties. *Esprit de corps* and all that. A happy, healthy ship, that's what we all want. And believe me, if I hear any more gossip I'll squash it, flat.'

I said, 'Good.'

He said, 'Obviously I don't really know Bernard myself.

I haven't had the opportunity, what with him thinking he's too bloody grand to mix, and then with him being ill. But his reputation goes before him, of course.'

He fell silent for a while, smoking his cigarette.

Then he said, 'This story that's going around, about him thinking people were watching him, and about Gavin Iles calling him a malingering cock-sucker, you've got to wonder how they ever get started, don't you? I mean. Professor Bernard Finch! And Gav Iles is such a nice, easy-going guy.'

Even when I closed my eyes he refused to take the hint. He rolled onto his stomach and leaned on his elbows.

'Let's see,' he said. 'Malingering. Well we can cross that off the list. He had laryngitis, as can happen to anyone and now he's OK. Antibiotics, eh? Where would we be without them? Hundred years ago, a bad throat and you could be a goner. Then there was "cock-sucking"? Now where can that have come from? That's not a thing you say lightly. Is it?'

A tiny, remote beach. Behind me, steep cliffs, in front of me, the sea. There was nowhere to escape.

He said, 'When I hear something like that I don't rush to judgement. I examine the evidence. As my old dad used to say, if it looks like shit and it smells like shit, it's likely not chocolate. And I have to say, when a man's more interested in the busboy's arse than he is in any of the fair sex lovelies at his dinner table, it rings a little bell with me. I think to myself, hello-oh. What do you say, Enid? Is your husband a cock-sucker? Because a wife would know.'

226

He stubbed out his cigarette. He was looking at me very intently.

He said, 'I watched you dive off the boat this morning. The nicest bum I've seen in a long while.'

I said, 'Please go away.'

'I'm going,' he said.

But he leaned over and tucked a strand of hair behind my ear. Miles Brassey used to do that. Extraordinary that such a silly little thing can make one tingle.

'Tell me, Enid,' he whispered, 'when was the last time you had a really good fuck?'

At which moment, thank heavens, our driver told us it was time to use the porta-potty and board the boats.

One of the Kansas Sallies said, 'You OK? You look real hot and bothered.'

The sail back to Barbati still seemed endless. I had a fearful headache from the sun and I had Don Harrington's insinuations going round and round in my mind. Have people been talking? Did someone see Bernard lunching with Stash Leontis and leap to a silly conclusion, or has he really slipped back into the tendencies of yesteryear? He may have been guilty of the occasional muddle in the past, but isn't every man? Oakhanger boys always went to Marlborough and the Lunes to Ampleforth and one has the impression it used to be quite the norm to hug one's chums and show one's affection by sharing the contents of one's tuck-box. Nowadays both schools admit girls so I suppose that side of things will rather have changed.

As we boarded the coaches Dorcas began shouting, 'They pay you to join in and look after the singles, not loaf around talking to married women. Ask me, you're past it.'

It was only when I heard Don Harrington answer her that I realized he was standing right behind me.

'You're right,' he said. 'I'm just a poor old geezer. I needed a day off.'

Dorcas made a very rude gesture and boarded the other coach.

I felt Don's hand touch the small of my back. The same inexplicable tingle.

'Get a seat at the rear,' he whispered. 'Away from the silly-billies.'

And I'm ashamed to say I did. The beer must have been stronger than I realized.

The coach was far from full. There was absolutely no necessity for him to share my seat.

I said, 'You needn't think I'm going to talk to you.'

He said, 'And I'm not going to talk to you. How about I slip my hand inside your blouse while we take a nice little afternoon snooze?'

The physical side of things has never been important with Bernard. It's not what makes our marriage tick. He's very attractive, of course. Tall, commanding, patrician, even. And he dresses very well. I'm always proud to be seen with him.

But first and foremost he's an intellectual. When he gets his head in a book he doesn't feel the heat or the cold, or hunger or thirst or any other of those fleshly appetites. I've often joked that I could serve him lunch stark naked and he wouldn't notice.

I have no illusions. I know I'm no beauty. I have the long Oakhanger nose added to the Lune tendency to heaviness in the hocks, but growing up one was discouraged from attaching any importance to appearances. Mumsie certainly never did. She was against pandering to the tastes of men long before the feminists thought of it and at Lowhope the only looking glass was in Poppa's dressing room. She and Poppa met at a shooting party in Hampshire and married quite soon after at, I think, Grandma Oakhanger's suggestion. It wasn't a hugely successful marriage but neither was it totally wretched. They were generally civil to one another. Apart from a brief tussle over custody of the bound copies of *Horse and Hound* I never heard any unkind words between them and I honestly think if Bobbie Snape hadn't manoeuvred herself into Mumsie's affections with tickets to the Horse of the Year Show, Poppa might have been persuaded to return.

When I reached the age of self-consciousness Mumsie's advice was that if I truly wished to marry I should simply station myself in the drawing room of any of my Oakhanger aunts for the duration of the Season and someone was sure to come along and make me an offer, someone who saw no necessity to study the mantelpiece whilst poking the fire. In fact my Season was a nightmare of teas and balls in borrowed frocks and quite barren of marriage offers. But in the long run she proved right. I made no running for Bernard. He simply came to me, in his hour of need, and he's never raised any objection to the length of my nose or the conformation of my hocks.

Neither was I wholly inexperienced before Bernard. Guy Lambton was awfully keen on me at one time, as was Miles Brassey. One would go to parties in town and sometimes there would be warm moments in the back of taxis. But Bernard was my first real lover; always considerate and not at all as demanding as friends had warned me a new husband could be. Heavens, when Billa married husband Numero 1, a terribly good-looking but entirely gormless waiter she met whilst holidaying in Cyprus, he hardly allowed her out of the bedroom for the first few months.

But the most ardent of suitors cool with the passing of time. And then the years take their toll. The old bod is neither as energetic nor as attractive as before and one's expectations diminish. So how do I begin to account for my behaviour this afternoon? I drank just one glass of beer with my lunch. And I had every reason to despise Don Harrington after his scurrilous hints about Bernard. But I did sit with him at the rear of the coach and I did allow him to unhook my brassiere as we bumped and swerved down through Dhassia and Kontokali, and with the Kansas secretaries sitting only a few rows away too.

230

At first one felt it would be embarrassing to object. One hates to make a fuss. And then somehow one found it all too agreeable and got swept along. I returned to the ship, as though in a feverish dream, and sleepwalked to Don's cabin.

He has a lot of white hair on his chest. He has a bottle of Milk of Magnesia on his night stand and a Tom Clancy novel. He has kind eyes.

I remember saying, 'I don't do this kind of thing.'

And I remember him saying, 'I only stop when a lady asks me to.'

His accommodation is a single, so even more confined than ours. I washed and tidied myself up as best I could but I couldn't bear to look at myself in the mirror. He lay on the bed wearing only a sheet.

He said, 'Don't fuss. You look wonderful.'

I said, 'I don't want to look wonderful. If I look wonderful my husband may ask questions and I'm hopeless at telling untruths.'

'What, dear Bernard?' he said. 'He won't notice. I'll bet he never looks at you.'

I said, 'Why do you dislike him so much?'

He said, 'He is quite dislikeable.'

He is.

He said, 'It's his airs and graces. I don't care about the bullshitting. As a matter of fact I'm a bit of a bullshitter myself. But he thinks he's too good for this cruise. It's written all over him. What is he, fucking American royalty?'

No. He's just Willy Fink from Brewster Street, Painted Post.

He said, 'But the thing is, Enid, I don't like to see a lady being neglected. When I see a lady who needs something, I respond. If she needs somebody to light her fire, even if all she needs is someone to light her cigarette, I'm there. That's me. It's what I do.'

Don Harrington, twice-divorced.

I said, 'But not well enough to keep a wife, apparently.'

'Touché,' he said. 'Let me put it this way. I'm not cut out for marathons. I'm better suited to the hundred-yard dash.'

I said, 'And obviously very experienced.'

He said, 'Look, I'm retired, I'm single, I've got a full head of hair and a machine-washable dinner jacket. Oyster Line needs men like me. They pay me to dance with the single ladies and squire them at the roulette tables. Now it can happen, at the end of the evening, that a lady asks to go *à la carte,* in which case I do my best to oblige. Some of them come back for seconds. Some of them like to express their gratitude, usually with a little something from the Gentleman Jim outlet, which I return unused as soon as is decent and get a cash refund. But in case you're wondering, this one was on the house. The pleasure was mine, but I hope it was yours too.'

I wasn't sure how one concludes these things. A hand-shake seemed too formal, but a kiss too intimate, in spite of what had gone before. It was five o'clock. Bernard was lecturing on Dubrovnik: Pearl of the Adriatic at five thirty.

232

I said, 'I have to go.'

'Me too,' he said. 'Friends of Bill W.'

I said, 'Who is this Bill W people talk about? He seems to have a great many friends.'

He laughed.

He said, 'I don't know where in the world you've been all your life, Enid, but don't ever change. It's nice to meet someone who doesn't know all the bloody answers. It's Bill Wilson, pet. William Griffith Wilson. The chap who started Alcoholics Anonymous. Friends of Bill. That's what we call ourselves.'

I said, 'You don't seem like an alcoholic. My Cousin Tig hides bottles down the side of her couch.'

'Oh yes,' he said. 'We've all done that. Down the arm of the chair, back of the wardrobe, in the sock drawer. Now here's what we're going to do. I'll leave first. Give it five minutes, open the door a crack, make sure the coast's clear and walk smartly down the corridor. And if anybody says anything, you were never here.'

Which made me feel even more like a floozie.

I was lucky. It was the time of day when people are going back to their staterooms to change for the evening, but I managed to get clear of Don's corridor without seeing anyone and went directly down to the Internet Point. Chiefly I didn't want to see Bernard just yet. I wanted time to compose myself.

Two emails.

From Minta:

Enid,

We Darnbrook girls always had it dinned into us to answer our correspondence with dispatch so can only suppose you're sailing through some kind of black hole at present. Look forward to hearing from you soonest.

M

From Leonora Carisbroke-Cowles:

Enid Nellish! Now I know who you are! Having put on my thinking cap and consulted sister Harry (one year younger and in Bronte House) I realize I'd confused you with Minta Fellowes. So sorry!!!!! You were the dark horse who did madcap things like flying Big Bertha's bloomers from the flagpole on Founders' Day, and no one ever suspected you because you looked so terribly pi. Gosh, how long ago it all seems. My three girls all went to Darnbrook and I can tell you they got up to much worse things, sicking up their food, smoking weed, charging horrendous amounts to their credit cards. We were angels in comparison.

Anyway I imagine you're now something fearfully respectable like a Justice of the Peace. You'll remember Caro Griggs who actually was an angel, always sucking up to oldsters and getting full marks? In prison, my dear. Bumped off her husband with anti-freeze! Must fly. So nice chatting. Lenny C-C

234

I should so have loved to spill the beans about my afternoon and was about to send an email to Billa when the awful thought occurred to me that when one clicks on SEND one has no idea how the message reaches its destination. It may be out there somewhere, where anyone can come along and read it, like a letter left unsealed on a desk. Brady said it *is* feasible for such a thing to happen but not very likely. So difficult. But I was just longing to tell someone so I sent a slightly coded message.

> Billa, Had a surprising little lower-class adventure between lunch and dinner. Quel surprise! Eeny

Jesus said, 'Professor's gone up already, Ladyship. He's giving his talk.'

I said, 'He's quite well then?'

'Oh yes,' he said. 'Nurse Quincy come down about four o'clock to check him over. He says Professor's got a touch of reflux euphoria but don't seem anything wrong with him to me. He was smiling and whistling. I'd say he's fit as a flea.'

I took a very hot, very soapy shower and walked in to the library just in time to hear Bernard's opening line.

'"If you want to see heaven on earth, come to Dubrovnik." So wrote George Bernard Shaw. Though one might ask what a repackaged atheist would know about heaven.'

Pause. Smile archly.

22

I sat at the back. There was the usual good turnout for Dubrovnik including, I noticed, Mr and Mrs Polder, who were seated on the front row. The Byzantine years, the Venetian years, the Habsburg years. Bernard tripped gaily through the lecture I've heard him give so often, pacing back and forth, here a witty aside, there a theatrical fermata, finishing in relaxed, conversational style, perched on the edge of the table, arms crossed, fielding questions about the best place to buy embroidered tablecloths and with such good humour. He'd changed out of this morning's seersucker and was wearing his café-au-lait linen and a green silk ascot.

One of the dangers of Bernard's self-absorption is that he doesn't remember faces. I now see that it must take an enormous effort to maintain the towering creation that is Bernard Finch. I suppose there's little left over for paying close attention to others. Which is why he failed to notice Mr Polder or to pick up that the dry old stick of a man being propelled towards him by Polder's big, fleshy hand must be Mr Erikson, of the Class of '55.

'Professor Finch,' I heard Polder say. 'This is Gunn Erikson, another Old Cornellian. He's been most eager to meet you.'

I hurried to Bernard's side. I was, at one and the same time, soothing my guilty conscience by playing the protective wife, and ghoulishly anticipating the fate of a bug caught in a spider's web.

Polder said, 'Gunn here was in the department of electrical engineering.'

A chilly smile from Bernard. He offered Erikson his hand.

Mr Erikson said, 'And you? Classics, I'm guessing.'

Bernard cleared his throat. Erikson was peering up at him through thick spectacles.

'Glad to meet you,' he said. 'Theta Xi.'

One of those American college fraternities. Bernard paused. Not knowing the etiquette of these situations one wondered whether Erikson hadn't committed some terrible gaffe, declaring himself so openly. Like announcing that one banks in Switzerland.

But Bernard recovered.

'Alpha Epsilon Pi,' he murmured. Then he picked up his papers and pushed against me, trying to move away.

Erikson said, 'A E Pi? Really?'

Some little thing passed between him and Polder. Bernard noticed it too. I don't ever remember seeing him blush before.

He was very quick though. He only had a few seconds to decide whether to fold or raise. He raised.

'No,' he said, 'not A E Pi. A E *Phi*.'

Erikson tugged on his earlobe.

'Deaf as a haddock,' he said. 'Gets me into no end of trouble. A E Phi. Well, well. Now let me see, Classics, fifty-eight, would that have been in Harry Caplan's time or had Kirkwood taken over by then?'

Bernard said the only thing he could.

'I knew them both. And now if you'll excuse me, gentlemen, Lady Enid and I are late for another engagement.'

Polder called, 'What a pity, sir. We were hoping you'd have time for a drink. I'm sure you have a lot to talk about.'

But Bernard kept on walking.

Erikson said, 'Some other time then.'

Bernard said, 'Indeed. Some other time.'

And he positively hustled me out of the library.

I said, 'And where are we going so urgently?'

He said, 'Don't be a dimwit, Enid. We're going to our room, safe from the reach of Mr Erikson and his Pandarus. Allow that type to start reminiscing you'll be there all night. Do you really want to spend your evening listening to the droning of an electrical engineer?'

I said, 'No, I don't. But I'm sure that wasn't what he intended. Gracious, the man only wanted to exchange a few pleasantries.'

He said, 'Please don't interfere in what you don't

understand. Different years, different faculties. I have absolutely nothing to say to the man.'

I said, 'Nevertheless, no need to have been so abrupt. And you'd better not be planning on going into hiding again. I'm not dining in the cabin, Bernard. I refuse. We're going to go to a restaurant like normal people and you'll just have to take your chance. From what I hear Mr Erikson spends much of his time in the Card Room and if you take me anywhere half decent for dinner you'll avoid Polder because his wife doesn't eat. We'll go to da Beppe.'

He said, 'You're very mettlesome this evening. You have quite a glint in your eye.'

He was still pushing all the lift buttons with great impatience.

He said, 'Yes, very well, we will go to da Beppe. But we'll have drinks in the cabin first. I'll get Jesus to bring us a couple of large gin and tonics. You'll want to change for dinner.'

I said, 'I've already changed.'

I was wearing my lovely new sapphire-blue skirt, and my slightly imperfect rust-red shawl.

I said, 'I don't want a gin and tonic. You go to the cabin if you must. I'm going to check my emails on the computer. I'll meet you in the Sorrento Bar at seven thirty.'

'Emails!' he said. 'Computers! What will you get up to next? I do hope you're not going to become addicted, like all those blank-eyed teenagers.'

I already am addicted, Bernard. I love the way I can look up anything that takes my fancy. Even the names of fraternities hosted by Cornell University. I love the way I can be sitting on a ship in the Straits of Kerkira, tap out a message to Billa Thoresby in South Ken and receive a reply within the hour.

Eeny!

Do you mean what I think you mean? Is it one of those hunky poolside lifeguards? Lucky old you. It's grey and cold and piddling rain here and there you are loafing off some sun-baked Greek island and getting extra-mural jiggy. It's too unfair. Not that I have any complaints about Laurence. He's perfectly adequate in the bonkeroo department and, more importantly, he does own un petit chateau. But tell me more you wretched girl. Name? Nationality? Size of meat ration? And how on earth are you managing to keep things secret on board ship? Or is your intention to be discovered in flagrante and rouse Bernardo to jealous passion? You know, the old 'buttered bun' phenomenon? Well anyway, enjoy! And though one hates to sound like one's mother, be careful too. The trouble with a young stud is one can never be sure where he's been dipping his pen. Green with envy. Billa

Chip McCuddy arrived. He said Cricket's knee is still swollen in spite of having rested all day. One felt one should offer to visit but feared the offer might be accepted.

I said, 'Can I send her some magazines?'

'No need,' he said. 'Don't you worry about Cricket. She's got her handicrafts. Matter of fact she's just now making a card for our young granddaughter, Kayla. You open it up and inside it's like a frog. Very clever with her hands, my wife. Very gifted.'

He sat down at the computer terminal back to back with mine. Then his head popped up.

He said, 'She's awful cut up about missing the dancing. She said I should maybe look for another partner, but I reckon she was just putting a brave face on it. I couldn't do that to her.'

I said, 'No. Of course not.'

He said, 'Unless it was somebody, you know, somebody she didn't have to worry about?'

I delved busily in my handbag.

He said, 'Somebody such as yourself.'

I said, 'I don't think that would be a good idea, Chip. Whatever Cricket may say, I'm sure she'd be terribly upset if you were to dance with anyone else.'

Particularly after a couple of Manhattans have gone down the hatch and stoked the fires of jealousy.

'Yes,' he said. 'I guess so.'

I closed my mailbox. It's called 'logging off'. One is enjoying all these new words.

Chip said, 'I hope you didn't think I meant you're not an attractive lady. I only meant Cricket wouldn't mind because she *knows* you. She knows you're not like *that*.'

I said, 'But better all round if we just sit on the sidelines and watch, don't you think? Have a lovely evening.'

241

'Well,' he said, as I was leaving, 'so long as I've not offended you. Because you're a very attractive woman, Enid. And I'm not too old to appreciate it.'

All the other computer users remained hunched over their keyboards, listening to every word. Lord! Billa's right. The buttered bun phenomenon.

23

It isn't at all difficult to avoid searching questions from Bernard about one's day. He's always happiest when talking about himself.

I said, 'I gather today went well? You seemed to be in good voice for your lecture.'

'Still slightly sore,' he said, 'but I struggled through.'

I said, 'And no awkward encounters? No Willy Fink moments with Frankie Gleeson?'

He said, 'Gleeson had a tendency to stand right at the front of the group and beam at me in buffoon-like fashion but I simply ignored him and he gave me no trouble. The wife was wearing an enormous yellow sun visor. She put me in mind of Daffy Duck.'

I said, 'And you wisely decided against mentioning the flowers?'

'Flowers?' he said.

I said, 'The floral extravaganza delivered to your bedside.

I believe I heard you threaten to tell Mrs Gleeson where to stick her bird of paradise.'

'Good grief,' he said. 'The flowers. I'd completely forgotten.'

Those inverted commas around the word 'Professor' still trouble him, I can tell.

He said, 'As far as I'm concerned the fewer words that pass between us and the Gleesons the better. Indeed it was probably just as well you weren't there today, the way you've been fraternizing on this voyage you've left us very exposed.'

I said, 'Fraternizing! You make it sound like high treason.'

He said, 'Yes, fraternizing. You've been quite promiscuous with your hobnobbing. Then people use your over-friendliness to gain my ear. But today I made it clear from the start I was there to educate, not to socialize, and it all went off very well.'

I said, 'Perhaps there's a lesson in this? Perhaps I've become more of a liability than an asset. I can easily stop accompanying you on your tours, you know.'

'Darling,' he said, 'what nonsense. Of course you're an asset.'

An opinion you'll no doubt revise when you discover I forgot to buy your kumquat marmalade.

He said, 'Anyway, as soon as we'd finished I deposited them all on the Liston, pointed them in the direction of coffee and baklava and shot off to see Pippo. He took me

244

to lunch at the Orestes which was quite superb. He insisted on paying but of course he gets a huge discount.'

Pippo Vlachos is another old friend of Bernard's from the Clifford Dennis years, still very good-looking, black-cherry eyes and silver temples, and always very sweet to me. He had something of a career in films, almost always wearing bathing trunks, and was quite a heart-throb in the early sixties, but it fizzled out as fashions changed and he went back to Corfu to rescue homeless cats. He never married. I'd have regretted missing lunch with him if I hadn't had such an exceptional day myself. Deep-water swimming. Fresh sardines. Sexual intercourse.

He said, 'As a matter of fact I discussed the Gleeson farago with Pippo and he agrees with me. The best thing is to deprive it of all oxygen.'

I said, 'I feel sorry for Frankie Gleeson. We don't know that he sent the flowers. We don't know that he sent that poem. And it seems all he's been guilty of today is smiling at you. Poor little man.'

Hand raised, palm open, all differing opinions stopped in their tracks.

'Enid,' he said, 'when will you ever learn? In the modern world the wrong kind of people have money. Here we have a man who barely graduated high school and now has too much money and too much time on his hands. It's also a well-established fact that on cruises people get up to all kinds of things they might think twice about on dry land.'

I blushed to the roots of my hair.

I said, 'How was Pippo?'

'On top form,' he said. 'Carrying more weight than the last time I saw him. He's involved with a new boy, rather sulky-looking I thought. They may be in Venice for the Film Festival. I said we'll do dinner. Enid, you're looking extremely pink this evening. What *have* you been doing? Spending too much time in the sun by the look of you.'

But without waiting for a reply he began drawing me a sketch of the goat tower Pippo is building in his garden and so the stickiest moment passed.

He said, 'In spite of my magnificent lunch, I must say I'm ravenous.'

We ordered linguine primavera, veal cutlets and a delicious, peppery Chianti.

I said, 'Do you realize this is the first time we've eaten *à deux* during this cruise? I began to think you'd never leave the cabin.'

He said, 'Don't remind me. It's been quite hellish. You can count yourself lucky you didn't catch it. But then, you never succumb, do you? Strong as an ox. It must be all those Cumbrian winters you endured.'

The fact is there was little inducement to be ill either at Lowhope or at school. One's sleeping quarters weren't heated in either place and the only remedies Mumsie believed in were brisk walks and a vile drink made from raw eggs and sherry which she invented for ailing Dandies. In childhood the habits of a lifetime are formed. Now one simply never thinks of becoming ill.

I said, 'Well you're back from the jaws of death and that's all that matters. So let's make the most of it. Let's make a kind of fresh start. A renaissance!'

If you're capable, Bernard. Are you, I wonder?

He said, 'What kind of fresh start?'

I said, 'No more silly secrets. For instance, I'd love to hear about your life in Painted Post.'

He sipped at his wine, gazing over my shoulder, deciding which way to play it. To dig in deeper or to fly the white flag.

Eventually he said, 'There's really nothing to tell. I remember nothing about the place, because it was completely unmemorable.'

A tentative surrender.

I said, 'Bernard, you have the finest mind I know. You have perfect recall of every ruin you ever visited and yet you can't remember your childhood home? What nonsense.'

He was saved by the arrival of the Reverend Taff Griffiths, with Virginia on his arm.

'Professor Finch!' he said. 'You've recovered, I see. Well that is good news. I'm sorry not to have made another house call but between you and me I've been run off my feet. Quarrels and depressions and spiritual crises. I've never known a cruise like it.'

He was speaking to Bernard but his eyes kept flicking to me.

Virginia said, 'But things are quiet tonight, knock on wood, so we're getting dinner.'

Griffiths said, 'Anything in particular you'd recommend? I'm rather fond of spaghetti Bolognese myself.'

Bernard said, 'Then you probably needn't venture into any deeper culinary waters.'

A sneer that failed to hit its target. The Reverend Taff has a non-stick surface.

Virginia said, 'Irene's got a date. I told her not to worry about me. She needs to relax. She's very tense about the dancing tomorrow night.'

Taff said, 'Yes, the dancing. Sorry that didn't work out, Enid. No hard feelings I hope?'

I said, 'Absolutely none.'

'Probably for the best, eh?' he said.

I said, 'Yes. I'm sure you're right.'

He said, 'But I expect we'll see you there, you and the Professor? Ringside seats, I expect. It promises to be a very entertaining evening.'

Bernard said, '*Lady* Enid and I have other plans.' And he turned away, looking for our waiter, on the spurious grounds that his salad lacked balsamic vinegar.

'Oily little Celt,' he said, almost before they were out of earshot.

I said, 'I think it's rather sweet of him to look after Virginia. Her daughter leaves her on her own far too much.'

He said, 'Looks after himself, more like. I know his type.

Goes into a revolving door behind you and comes out ahead of you. You can be sure the old lady will be paying for dinner.'

I said, 'Darling, don't be such a curmudgeon. His only offence was to ask me to dance and you soon scared him off.'

He said, 'Yes, I did. And it annoys me enormously when people take advantage of your good nature and start calling you "Enid" when they've known you for barely five minutes.'

And it annoys me enormously when you make such a fuss about a made-up title.

How glad I shall be to start afresh with a clean slate. On our next cruise I shall be known as The Hon. Mrs Finch. Perhaps not even that. It sounds so stuffy. I may style myself simply as Enid Finch. But tonight wasn't the time to go into that. It wouldn't be right to pull all those rotten teeth in one session.

I said, 'Now, where were we? Yes. Painted Post. You remember nothing but you must concentrate and see what you come up with. Otherwise I shall have to apply to Mr Gleeson for further particulars.'

He smiled but he wasn't amused.

I said, 'I'll get you started. Painted Post is in the Finger Lakes area of Western New York, just a few miles north of the Pennsylvania state line. Continue.'

He said, 'You're in a very kittenish mood this evening, Enid. And looking damned comely too. Perhaps you should go to barbecues more often.'

He ordered limoncello.

24

Painted Post is a tiny town – we'd call it a village in England – at the confluence of the Tioga River and the Conhocton, or the Cohocton as it's often written. It gets its name from an actual painted post, long disappeared, that was believed to mark the burial place of a Seneca Indian chief and when Bernard was last there, in 1958, there was a replica post and a bronze statue of an Indian warrior in the main square.

I said, 'Next time we're in America we must go there. I should so love to see where you grew up.'

'No you wouldn't,' he said. 'What do you imagine you'd do when you got there? A little turkey hunting? A little canoeing? You could take in the whole town in fifteen minutes.'

I said, 'I'd still like to see it. You're familiar with Lowhope, after all. Gracious, you can even name the people in most of the portraits.'

He said, 'I think you'll allow that there's a world of difference between the country seat of a noble English family and a pile of rotting clapboard in western New York. Anyway, I doubt it's still standing. Anyone with any sense will have knocked it down.'

Frankie Gleeson would know if that's the case.

I said, 'I think seeing where you grew up would help me understand you better. You always say I have Lowhope stamped all the way through me, like a stick of Brighton rock.'

He said, 'You do. Nobility, lightly worn. Scorn for the fripperies of life. And, dare one say it, a tendency to gloominess. But Painted Post would tell you nothing about me. Italy, Greece, Istanbul, those are the places that shaped me. The only thing Painted Post did for me was prompt me to pack a bag and leave. Anyway, what is this awful fashion for *understanding* people? I've never had any desire to be understood. You've done something different with your hair.'

I said, 'Actually, I've been wearing it like this since Mykonos.'

'Have you?' he said. 'Well I approve.'

He ordered more limoncello. Then, little by little, he unburdened himself.

Yes, he grew up on Brewster Street, Painted Post, New York and he left as soon as he was able because the place stifled him. Yes, his birth name was Wislaw Bernard Fink, but he changed it to something more universally pronounceable and he did it so long ago he doesn't think of the person called Willy Fink as being remotely connected to him. And no, he didn't go home for his mother's funeral because he was exploring the rock-carved monasteries of Cappadocia and didn't even hear of her death until several weeks after the obsequies.

I said, 'There! Telling me wasn't so terribly hard, was it?'

He said, 'It's not a question of being hard. It's a question of being pressured into reopening closed books for absolutely no good reason.'

I said, 'Doesn't allowing your wife to know you better constitute a good reason?'

But he doesn't think I've learned anything of significance. His argument is that by the time we met, the boy called Willy Fink no longer existed. That the man I married was Bernard Finch, cultured, scholarly and European.

He said, 'The clock can't be turned back, Enid. I left Painted Post in 1958. I've never returned and God willing I never will.'

I said, 'But of course in Frankie Gleeson's mind Willy Fink still exists. He can't be blamed for that.'

'Frankie Gleeson's mind!' he said. 'There's a contradiction in terms. The man is mindless.'

I said, 'He's made an awful lot of money.'

He said, 'He's sixty-five and he's still only ten miles from where he started. Well, he was never going anywhere. I couldn't stay around people like that. Why do you think I moved to the other side of the world? I had to be with *my* kind of people.'

252

I said, 'And you did it, with enormous success. You went from little Painted Post to some of the greatest universities in the world. You should take some pleasure in meeting someone from your past. He's certainly thrilled to have rediscovered you. And when he gets home he'll spread the word. I expect he'll contact your alumnus association.'

He said, 'My point exactly. He'll be on the telephone to all the other deadheads who never left town. Then you'll change your tune. We'll be plagued. People will hear I have a place in Venice and come crawling out of the woodwork, presuming on some vague, long-dead acquaintance to get themselves a free bed.'

It amuses me the way Bernard always says *he* has a place in Venice.

The fact is it was bequeathed to *me* by Grandpa Lune and the timing couldn't have been more providential. After years of judgements and appeals and counter-appeals Bernard had just lost his claim even to a tiny share in Villa Peruzzi. As our lawyer said, it was a cruel miscarriage of justice and Clifford Dennis must have been spinning in his grave, but the net of it was that we were left considerably out of pocket and still without a place to call our own. There was also the awkwardness of sides having been taken. Bernard's Italian friends were entirely supportive but people like the Luxley-Greenwoods and Roger Joad had orchestrated such a spiteful campaign against him one really didn't feel one could stay on in Rome. It was the end of an era.

Then, just when we were thinking we'd have to decamp to Eaton Mews, Grandpa Lune passed away and left me his little house in Corte Tagiapiera. That he even owned a place in Venice came as a colossal surprise to Granny Lune and Mumsie, who had never paid very great attention to his foreign meanderings. They accepted that the Cumbrian winters brought on his annual attack of the glooms, but they were baffled by the cheerful way he accepted his doctor's prescription for sunshine *ad libitum* and regarded it as little short of tragedy that he was forced to winter in Italy and miss the best of the hunting season.

When Bernard and I went to Venice to inspect my inheritance we discovered that Grandpa was most fondly remembered there, by boatmen and porters and, well, by just ordinary young men. He had been a nice English gentleman, they said, *molto simpatico*, who always had a pleasant word for them. However, the house was in a shockingly bad condition and sparsely furnished. It was a bachelor retreat without a single comfortable armchair. According to the neighbours Grandpa spent very little time inside. He preferred to be out and about, rowing his *pupparin* across the lagoon or simply sitting in the sun with a glass of wine.

Bobbie Snape who, I may say, has never travelled further than the Crufts Dog Show, advised us to sell and invest in somewhere sensible, like Southport or Lytham St Anne's, but that would never have suited Bernard. It was as though the house in Corte Tagiapiera had been waiting for him. He walked in to what had been Grandpa's dressing room, with its window overlooking the canal, and claimed it for his study.

I said, 'Don't worry about people proposing themselves as house guests. They'll receive our standard reply. A: we have no guest room, and B: we know the names of several jolly reasonable locandas. Or one can simply not respond, which is what I'm doing with Minta Fellowes because she won't be deterred by the lack of a bed. It's for her son and she insists a floor would do.'

'Who?' he said. 'Minta who?'

I said, 'Araminta Fellowes, although actually she's now Percy-Quennell. We were at Darnbrook together. We're only just back in touch but she's already trying to trade a Venetian holiday for some of her stinky cheese.'

He looked perplexed.

'Cheese?' he said. 'Darnbrook?'

I said, 'An old school chum. She makes cheese. And she's hoping we'll accept a wodge of it in payment for putting up her son and his friends. They're about to embark on a Grand Tour, twenty-first-century-style, and as Billa remarked, she has some sauce.'

'Billa?' he said. 'Do you mean the Thoresby woman? But how have these people barged back into your life?'

I said, 'They haven't. I opened the batting. Email, darling. It's the easiest thing in the world. I'm eenymeeny@smallworld.com.'

He said, 'Too damned easy by the sound of it. I do wish you'd be more careful.'

I said, 'And I wish you'd be more adventurous. Surely it would be so much easier if you'd just humour Frankie Gleeson? Only one more day left. And he certainly won't be looking for a free bed. They've booked the Palladio suite at the Cipriani.'

Eye-wateringly expensive.

'Typical,' he said. 'For how long?'

Bernard adores the Cipriani buffet. He likes to sit beside the pool, but always suitably attired for possible lunch invitations, and although he reads he keeps his radar switched on. In the course of a summer morning any number of influential and hospitable people are likely to happen along.

I said, 'Several days, I imagine. And I'm sure he'd love nothing better than to treat you to luncheon.'

He looked very grave.

'Enid,' he said, 'you're such a pure soul. You never think ill of anyone. Gleeson pretends to be my friend but I can tell you, there were times when he made my life hell.'

I said, 'Truly? But he told me you used to go fishing together.'

'Very, very occasionally,' he said. 'Sometimes you have to parley with the enemy and fishing can be a pleasant pastime. Even a poet can enjoy fishing.'

'And hunting, too,' I said. 'With a dog called Booger.'

'An Airedale,' he said, quick as a flash. I believe I saw a little sadness in his eyes.

'Yes,' I said, 'and you hunted for squirrel.'

'It was Gleeson Senior who did most of the shooting,' he said. 'Then the mother would cook them. That's the kind of family the Gleesons were, Enid. Squirrel-eaters.'

I see no shame in that. I may well have eaten squirrel myself. When Mrs Capstick ran the kitchen at Lowhope she had a rather chewy pie crust into which she threw anything Poppa bagged. Definitely rooks. Almost certainly starlings. And I've often wondered about a miniature dachshund of Mumsie's which sank its teeth into Poppa's ankle one Sunday morning and then unaccountably disappeared. Poppa said he'd yelled at it and it had run away in a neurotic funk typical of its breed, but I do remember that Mumsie left her helping of pie uneaten the next evening and she and Poppa were on Non Speaks for ages.

I said, 'More, please! If not about you then about the squirrel-eaters.'

He thought for a moment, then smiled.

He said, 'One of Gleeson's crackpot ideas was to sell squirrel tails to the fishing-tackle store. He predicted vast earnings and went around promising to treat all the girls to vanilla phosphates. He was always dreaming up commercial schemes. Then he discovered that the tackle store didn't deal in hard currency. They'd only pay for tails with merchandise. So he was left with the choice of accepting fishing lures as payment or disposing of bags full of malodorous squirrel tails. Such an idiot.'

Though the cost of a new roof wouldn't trouble him, which I suppose must be a source of some comfort.

I said, 'Not such an idiot. He can now afford the Palladio Suite.'

'He's welcome to it,' he said. 'Let him wallow in its luxury and may he come no nearer to my city than the view from his panoramic windows.'

Bernard is very proprietorial about Venice. He hates to see the Box Tickers, as he calls them, trudging through our narrow streets in beach attire. Rialto, tick! San Marco, tick! Glass pendant made in China, tick!

He said, 'He no doubt thinks Bellini is a name invented by a barkeep. Frankie Gleeson was and is a jock, Enid, and a jock regards anyone who reads or paints or listens to classical music as a candidate for mockery. They go around with other jocks in brainless, guffawing mobs and pick on anything they don't understand. Believe me, as someone who played piccolo in the school band, I know what I'm talking about.'

The piccolo! Yet another facet of Bernard I never knew about.

We moved outside the restaurant and sat in deckchairs. He seemed to find it easier, talking in the dark. That his father had been an official at the Town Hall, I already knew, but it was in Elmira, New York and not in Newburgh.

I said, 'Don't tell me he was the mayor!'

He was some kind of general administrator.

I said, 'And your mama?'

He shrugged.

'She was just one's mother,' he said. 'There's really little more to say.'

Her maiden name was Smolak and his Smolak grand-parents lived in Nanticoke, Pennsylvania and spoke only Polish. His Fink grandparents lived just a few miles from Painted Post in Beaver Dams and as far as he knows they spoke English but they disliked travel so he never saw them. He had no brothers or sisters, and in a small town like Painted Post there were no kindred spirits for a twelve-year-old boy who saw a photograph of Michelangelo's David in a library book and knew from that moment what he wanted to do with his life. Bernard's childhood was possibly even lonelier than mine. At least I had Olive to talk to, and Mossop. At least I had Mercury. The Finches, or more accurately, the Finks, had absolutely no staff. They didn't even own a horse.

I took his hand in mine.

I said, 'How sad that your parents both died so young. Do you miss them?'

'Obviously not,' he said. And he fell silent.

We went up to the Observation Deck before turning in. It was a starry night, with just a fingernail of moon and the occasional light twinkling from the Albanian shore.

Bernard said, 'We should take a break after this. Go up to Asolo for a week or two, or Trento. Recharge the batteries.'

He was standing very close, his arm around my shoulders. I wondered if he might smell Don Harrington's cologne on me in spite of my having showered so thoroughly, but he said nothing.

We took the express lift, first stop the atrium on L Deck, a place where one is bound to encounter people and sure enough, as we crossed the Piazza, who should be coming towards us but the Gleesons, dressed in matching terry bathrobes.

Bernard groaned, very quietly.

'Just nod and keep walking, Enid,' he whispered. 'Do not linger.'

But it would have been too rude. I grabbed his arm and forced him to stop.

Nola said, 'Well there you are! And don't you make a handsome couple. Did you guys get a romantic dinner at long last?'

I said, 'We went to da Beppe.'

'Good for you,' she said. 'A plate of spaghetti can be fun. You don't want to be eating fancy every night. By the way, very nice tour today, Professor. We thoroughly enjoyed it, didn't we, Frankie? And I hear *you* had a fun day, honey.'

My first sickening thought was that someone had noticed Don Harrington's attentions to me on the motor coach or seen me leaving his cabin.

But she said, 'We were just in the hot tub talking with four sweet girls from Kansas. They said you were swimming like a fish today, diving off the boat like a real water-baby.'

I said, 'Yes, it was the only way to get in to some of the caves. It was quite beautiful.'

'I'll take your word for it,' she said. 'You wouldn't catch me swimming into any caves. And I hope you rinsed well afterwards. Salt and sun and all, they're ruination to the hair. Do you have a conditioner? You just let me know if you need anything.'

Frankie Gleeson was studying his towelling slippers. He seemed almost shy in Bernard's presence.

Nola said, 'Here we are, only one day left and we still didn't get to take you to dinner. And tomorrow night's Gala Night so that's no good. But don't worry, we haven't forgotten. We'll do it when we get to Venice. There's a place called Sips.'

Cips.

I said, 'It's pronounced "Chips".'

'Is it?' she said. 'Chips? That's cute! Sounds like just the place for us, eh, Frankie? Chips! They say it's the best. They say George Clooney eats there and it's real hard to get a table, but Frankie belongs to Platinum International Dining so we won't have any problem.'

Bernard said, 'They say no one goes there any more. It's too crowded.'

Nola shrieked with laughter.

261

She said, 'You got a droll sense of humour, Professor. I love it. *Monty Python*.'

Frankie said, 'Bernard, a little test of your memory. I wonder how many names you can recall from Brewster Street. I'll start you off. Corner lot, the Ketchums. They were a big family. Worse than us Gleesons. They musta slept in shifts. Next door, the Vanderhoffs. Remember Verna? A real blonde? Her hair was nearly white. She married a boy from Dansville, did chassis repairs. I'll think of his name. Your turn. Next to the Vanderhoffs?'

Bernard said, 'Go away, Gleeson. Just bugger off.'

Frankie laughed.

He said, 'Now I've rattled him because he can't remember. Next to the Vanderhoffs was the Millers. I can tell you exactly where Harold is these days. Victory Village. He's got one of those park homes and he does paintings. Bowls of fruit, vases of flowers, that type of thing. He only does them on cardboard but people buy them. Let's try you on the other side of the street. Across from the Ketchums? The Donahues. Remember Marcella? Had a gap between her front teeth? She had that fixed. I used to see her sometimes in Izard's department store, in Elmira. She worked in Men's Apparel. I don't know where she is now. Next to the Donahues? You're not doing very well, Bernard. Next to the Donahues was the Arnotts and next to them was the Mantles. Mr Mantle drove an old Plymouth. We were across the street from the Donahues, then you, and next door to you, the Whipps. He worked at Bement's Dairy and they had a houseful of cats.'

Bernard said, 'Excuse me. Goodnight.'

Frankie winked at me.

'Goodnight,' he said. 'Enid, Bernard. Sleep well.'

I said, 'There! That wasn't so bad, was it? A breakthrough actually. He called you "Bernard".'

'Sips!' he said. 'Did you hear that? Sips!'

I said, 'Now, now, don't be cruel! We can't all be linguists.'

He said, 'Nor can we all be the toast of the cruise. The understudy goes on and her tour of Olympia is the talk of the town. Pursued by ballroom boyos, hairdressers and wealthy snack merchants, she dives off a boat with the greatest of ease. Upon my word, Enid, what else have you been getting up to?'

A useful side effect of after-dinner drinks is that they deaden all pangs of guilt.

I said, 'You might be a little more gracious. I took over your tour to help you. You should be glad people are praising it.'

'Praising it!' he said. 'You surely know that understudies always get thunderous applause. As do dogs for walking on their hind legs.'

Dear Bernard, why must you be so mean-spirited?

He said, 'Needless to say, we will not accept any dinner invitations from the Gleesons, no matter how desirable the venue.'

Not even to Cips, Bernard? Gosh. Frankie Gleeson really does have you on the back foot.

An envelope had been pushed under the door to our stateroom. It was addressed to Bernard. He scooped it up and went directly into the bathroom and when he came out it was stuffed into his inside pocket.

I said, 'A fan letter?'

'No,' he said. 'Just tomorrow's schedule.'

I said, 'How odd. The activity schedules are always delivered in the afternoon, on a sheet of foolscap. Is there something special going on tomorrow?'

'Oh for heaven's sake, Enid,' he yelled. 'Who are you? Miss bloody Marple?'

And he threw his jacket on the bed.

It was a kind of greetings card, hand-made; a simple drawing, gaily coloured and crowded with dozens of tiny human figures. The sort of thing one might send to a child.

On the front was written WHERE'S WILLY? and inside it said NOT AT CORNELL, AND NEVER WAS.

I said, 'Darling, there's only one place for something like this.'

I threw it in the bin.

He said, 'Which is where I was about to put it when you interfered. I tried to spare you, Enid. I try to bear these things alone.'

I said, 'You don't need to spare me. I'm your wife.'

He clasped me rather woodenly to his chest. Not at all

264

like Don Harrington who lowered one onto the bed in a frenzy of hot fumbling and unzipping. But one mustn't think about that. It never happened.

We chatted in the dark.

I said, 'I'm so glad we've talked. I can't tell you how exciting it is to find out new things about you. Polish grandparents, hunting for squirrel, playing the piccolo. It's like discovering a hidden room in one's house. And I expect there will be much, much more. Perhaps an entire wing!'

He said, 'There will not be more. I've said all I ever intend to say. The subject is now closed.'

One can throw a lifebelt to a man who's out of his depth but if he's convinced he can walk on water one can't force him to reach out and grasp it.

I said, 'But to have risen from such inauspicious circumstances to the great heights you've achieved. I'm awfully impressed. To have gone from a little dot on the map like Painted Post, to have attended a prestigious university like Cornell and even belonged to one of those Greek fraternity thingies. You know, I had a feeling about Mr Polder from the very first moment we met. The way he questioned you about the swimming test, and then the way he insisted on your meeting the desiccated Mr Erikson. I'd say he's one of those envious people who failed to obtain a degree himself and now enjoys trying to undermine the achievements of others. It would explain the horrid, juvenile card.'

He said, 'I don't agree. As far as I'm concerned the finger of suspicion still points towards Gleeson.'

I said, 'But think how Polder and Erikson practically mobbed you after your lecture this evening. I expect Polder planned it that way, to throw you off balance. He was hoping you'd make some kind of silly mistake he could then seize upon. Which of course you did.'

He was silent for a while, calculating.

He said, 'What do you mean?'

I said, 'Well, you know, the way you got into a jumble about Alpha Epsilon thingummy? I mean, it must be so easily done. There you were, at the end of a long, hard day, your mind still on the Maritime Republic of Ragusa, when they ambushed you and began firing heaven knows what arcane questions at you. If you ask me it was the most rotten luck that you slipped up and gave the name of a Jewish sorority when you obviously had the correct name right on the tip of your tongue. It was your fraternity, after all.'

The skill of using torture lies in knowing when to end the session.

25

We're at anchorage off the Old Harbour. I went up on deck just before seven to watch the approach to Dubrovnik and there was a misty rain falling, predicted to continue all day. There are also two other cruise ships in town and Bernard is not in a good mood.

'I can hear it now,' he said. 'The thunder of obese gawkers in ridiculous sports' shoes. The clack and whirr of their cameras. Their loud inanities echoing off those ancient limestone walls.'

No mention of last night.

He said, 'I hope you're not abandoning me again today, Enid. I see there's a safari through the Dalmatian bush on all-terrain vehicles. I pray you haven't signed up for that.'

Jesus was whistling his way along the corridor.

'All ready for Gala Night, Professor?' he called. 'You got anything needs pressing?'

Bernard said, 'The only thing I need for Gala Night is my earplugs and a sleeping pill.'

Jesus laughed.

He said, 'I know you kidding me, Professor. Ain't nobody gonna sleep tonight. You gonna be dressing up in your best threads, taking Lady Enid to the dancing.'

I said, 'Yes, do let's. Just to watch. It'll be such fun. There are two Japanese ladies who dance together and take it terribly seriously. And Don Harrington's dancing with that fright named Irene.'

'Don who?' he said.

My lover, Bernard. The man who did to me something you've never done. He kissed me on the end of my long Oakhanger nose.

I said, 'Harrington. Gentleman Host.'

'Well, well,' he said. 'Yet another character from your wide acquaintance. Don Harrington, Mr Rent-a-Date. How you do get around! But I think I'll pass. After a morning spoon-feeding the dunderheads on gobbets of history I shall be fit for nothing but a rest and a quiet little dinner in the cabin.'

Jesus heard him.

He said, 'No Room Service tonight, Professor. They got the Gala Dinner to serve then it's clean-up night in the galleys. Turnaround Day tomorrow.'

I said, 'So, Bernard, you'll jolly well have to come to the Dining Room and join in the fun.'

'I will not,' he said. 'We'll eat a decent lunch in town and then you can catch a bus to Lapad. You can go to that mini market, buy a bottle of wine and something to nibble on this evening.'

I said, 'Perhaps Frankie Gleeson would let us have a selection of his snacks.'

He said, 'I must warn you, Enid. I'm in no mood for your attempts at humour.'

The rain was coming down steadily. We entered the city through the Ploce Gate with only thirty or so passengers in tow. Quite a number of people have elected to stay on board today, given the bad weather. Apparently there's also fierce competition for hair and nail appointments.

Bernard has his preferred route around Dubrovnik as he does for every other city where he guides; first the Lazareti, then the synagogue on Zudoska Street, then the Sponza Palace. There's something about rain that makes tour groups difficult. They go into huddles with their umbrellas and will chat while Bernard is speaking, something he finds intolerable. But as I've often reminded him, these are paying customers not students who can be dealt sarcasm and withering looks.

He wasn't at all himself, seemingly quite distracted. So much so that when it came to the Latin sign over the Sponza arch he completely lost his thread and I had to help him out. *FALLERE NOSTRA VETANT*. Basically, 'we don't tolerate cheats'.

'Thank you,' he said, through gritted teeth, and we moved on swiftly to the church of St Blaise. The rain had stopped.

Bernard's greatest strengths in Dubrovnik are its city walls and its fortifications. As he likes to pun, the forts are his *forte*. But some people were anxious about walking on stones made greasy by the rain.

I said, 'I think you're going to have a few refusers.'

He said, 'I couldn't care less. It's their loss entirely.'

I said, 'Actually, I think I'm going to be one of the refusers. It's not as though I can be useful.'

Though I've heard it all countless times I still get in a fearful muddle about bastions and casemates and scarp walls.

'As you wish,' he said, *so* testily. 'Hurrying back to the ship, are we? What is it this time? An exhibition of paint drying? A seminar on bead-threading?'

I said, 'No. I'm meeting my lover.'

He conceded a weak smile.

I said, 'Bernard, do buck up. It's almost over. We'll be home tomorrow.'

He said, 'You mean it's almost over till the next time. I'm tired of lecturing to *dummkopfs*, Enid. Did you hear what that woman just asked?'

I did. She wondered which country she was in. Well, a cruise can be confusing. One goes to sleep in one place and wakes in another.

He said, 'But even though my coat is drenched, my throat is giving out and my wife is buggering off to our warm little cabin, I shall do what I'm obliged to do.'

Recently Bernard has grown somewhat resentful about our financial situation though one has really done the best one can. I got a very decent price for three Dutch oils left me by Grandpoppa Oakhanger. And I've found tenants for both houses for the months we'll be away on the Voyager Line world cruise. I do think I pull my weight. And I can hardly be held responsible for certain paths Bernard chose even before I knew him.

Ideally he should be in a cloistered, university environment, but somehow it never happened. After Cornell, or wherever it was he truly studied, he seems to have been constantly on the move. Montpellier, Ferrara, Pavia, Thessaloniki. How he ever found the time to complete his doctorate I can't think, though of course he does have an extremely fast and brilliant mind. I used to imagine we'd end up in a rackety old house in Oxford or Cambridge, with his students dropping in for cups of tea and lots of lovely college feasts to go to. But it wasn't to be. He said he needed intellectual freedom, that he couldn't bear to be tied to one place or to someone else's timetable. Guiding educated, well-connected people suited him very well.

They used to say he opened their eyes to history in a way no one else had ever done. And he was more than happy to have lunch with them, or dinner. They were his kind of tourist, 'real travellers' as he preferred to call them. But clients of that kind don't come along every day and as one's investments languished and property repairs devoured more and more of one's income it became vital to bring in more jingle. So when Oyster Line offered him a little work it was a godsend. It's difficult for him, I know, tailoring his presentations to the mass market, but I really see no alternative.

I whispered, 'They're not *dummkopfs*, dearest. They're the valued clients who are helping to pay for a new roof. And if it's any consolation I'm not going back to the ship. I'm going to stroll along the Stradun and sit in a café with my crossword puzzle. You can look out for me when you come down off the ramparts. I believe I heard you promise me a decent lunch.'

'Did I?' he said. 'Are you sure? Why don't you get something on the ship? Don't wait for me. All I shall be fit for is a whisky and hot water.'

He set off, the brim of his Borsalino still dripping. There were ten stalwarts determined to walk the walls with him, anticlockwise past the Revelin Fortress and the Minceta Tower, round by Fort Bokar and completing the circle at St John's. A good two hours.

26

I wiped off a seat and sat outside the Café Sesame. A few of Bernard's refusers followed me. It often happens. When people go ashore from the haven of a cruise ship they can be stricken by terrible anxieties. Principally, that the ship will leave without them. The sight of a familiar face comforts them. Well, they think, *she's* still here and *she* knows what she's doing so we must be all right. Little do they realize that one of these days I intend to get left behind, just to see how it feels.

I hadn't been there long, sipping a hot chocolate, when I saw a rather glum-faced Frankie Gleeson heading my way in radioactively white gym shoes and a transparent mackintosh worn over his shorts. I waved and his face lit up when he saw me.

I said, 'Come and join me.'

No Nola. She'd taken a taxi to the Excelsior hotel for a day of beautification and Frankie had been to the Sveti Ivan tower where there's a small aquarium. He'd found it disappointing.

'Just a few eels and stingrays,' he said. 'You'd think they'd make something of it. Fish of the Adriatic. They could do. You look around this place, there's a bunch of old buildings you can look at but there's nothing else much to do. People bring kiddies here on vacation, a good aquarium could be a big attraction.'

I said, 'But you see Dubrovnik doesn't need any big attractions. It's a tiny, fragile treasure. One has to be very careful.'

'Is that right?' he said. 'Well, they oughta make up their minds. All these big ships putting in, you've got to have something to offer. People are on vacation, they expect to find something to do. Now could you get that boy to bring me a soda? I can't understand a damned word they say.'

I ordered a Coca-Cola for him.

'Thank you,' he said. 'What the heck country is this anyhow? Nola couldn't remember.'

Croatia. The Republic of. Formerly part of Yugoslavia.

'That's it,' he said. 'Croatia. One of those new countries. Willy off guiding, is he? Bernard, I mean. I keep forgetting he's Bernard now. I suppose he'll always be Willy to me.'

His drink arrived with a tiny bowl of peanuts.

'Stale,' he said. 'I haven't been impressed with the standard of bar snacks in this part of the world.'

I said, 'I made something of a breakthrough the other evening, over dinner. Bernard actually talked a little about Painted Post and his childhood.'

'Good,' he said. 'I'm glad to hear it. A man shouldn't run away from his roots.'

I said, 'He even remembered your Airedale dog.'

'Couldn't but help it,' he said. 'Booger was some dog.'

I said, 'And tell me about when you used to go fishing. What did you catch?'

'Oh well now,' he said, and he settled back in his chair. 'Started off, we'd go down to the creek and fish for crappies. Early morning or just before it gets dark, that's the best time. Course, when you're a kid that makes it more of an adventure. You can catch trout in the Conhocton, if you know where to look, and pike and bass, but when we were kids it was panfish we were after. Blue gill, bullheads, yellow perch. Yellow perch make the best eating. If we went home to Mom with a few yellow perch in the pail we knew we could get away with murder for a few days. Worst thing were the brook suckers. You'd need to be hungry to eat one of them. If I caught a brook sucker I'd throw him right back. Good times, though. We were lucky growing up where a boy could be outdoors, entertaining himself. Kids today, they hardly stir off the couch. We were blessed, no two ways. And I'm still fishing. I've got the Catherine Creek in my back yard, Seneca Lake just up the road. No, I couldn't live any place where I didn't have good fishing.'

The rain started up again. I suggested we move inside. He hesitated.

I said, 'You have to go?'

'No,' he said. 'I got time. It's just I get the feeling Willy don't appreciate you talking with me. Bernard, I mean to say. I wouldn't want to be the cause of any bad feeling.'

I said, 'Not at all. It was obviously very hard for him, opening long-closed doors, but now he's begun he'll find it easier. Which is why I thought it would be very helpful for me to learn as much as I can about those lost years. I'm sure you can tell me all kinds of things.'

'Well,' he said, 'if that's what you'd like. If that's what you think'd help. I wouldn't care to interfere, you know? Strikes me he's of quite a nervous disposition, Willy? Bernard.'

Oh he is, Frankie. He's a veritable hothouse bloom.

I said, 'Yes, his nerves are delicate but there's also something very determined about him. When he decides to do something, as he's now decided to face the bogeymen of his past, he'll grasp every means and every opportunity. I think you'll find that away from the confines of the ship and the pressures of work he'll welcome the chance to spend time with you.'

He said, 'You think so?'

I said, 'I do. Perhaps while you're in Venice you and Nola will come to tea?'

'We will,' he said. 'Tea with an English lady and a chance to yarn about old times with Willy Fink. I wouldn't miss that for the world.'

Me too.

I said, 'Now tell me everything you remember. Tell me about his father. Was he tall and handsome, like Bernard?'

He chuckled.

'Charlie Fink?' he said. 'No, he was a ratty-looking little guy. He had those type of eyes, you know, when one of them's looking at you the other one's looking at the floor? No, there's nothing of his old man about Willy. Unless, of course … Well no, I shouldn't say it.'

Serafina had a certain reputation.

He said, 'See, Mrs Fink, she'd been in the theatre. She'd been a dancer. Buffalo or somewhere. You got to keep in mind this was back in the fifties. People on Brewster Street, you know, they were a bit wary of theatrical types. Particularly the ladies. Any mention of chorus lines, any mention of the Shea Theatre, they'd start locking up their husbands. And then with Willy not having any look of Charlie Fink about him, not an eyelash, well I guess folk talked. But they're all dead and gone so I don't suppose we'll ever know. Anyhow, it didn't seem to bother Charlie. He raised Willy as his own, if you can call it "raising". It wasn't like now, all the fuss they make. We were dragged up in those days.'

I said, 'Bernard has never spoken of his father. Was it a troubled relationship, would you say?'

'Troubled?' he said. 'I don't know about that. I guess his old man used to take his belt to him once in a while. Not that Willy was a kid who got into trouble. Matter of fact, in school he was a bit of an apple-shiner. But we all used to

277

get whacked in those days. Our Dad used to give us the strap sometimes when we hadn't done anything. He'd say it was on account, payment in advance for the next time we stepped out of line. You couldn't do it now, of course. Nowadays a kid'd whack you right back. But no, I don't think there was any trouble between them. Maybe it didn't occur to old Charlie that he mighta had a cuckoo in the nest. He wasn't the sharpest tool on the workbench.'

The Sesame was getting quite crowded. The windows were steaming up.

I said, 'I think Bernard said his father worked in local government.'

'Did he?' he said. 'My recollection is he didn't do anything much, and those days there was plenty of work for anybody who wanted it. We had the glass factories in Corning and Elmira. That's where my dad worked. But now you mention it, now I'm thinking, Charlie mighta done a stint at the Town Hall, as a janitor. Couldn't have lasted long though. All those years, there wasn't many days when you didn't see Charlie sitting on the porch.'

Well, janitors are jolly essential people and probably quite interesting when one gets to know them. Still, one couldn't help but feel the briefest twinge of sympathy for Bernard. But Serafina had a theatrical background, which is far more interesting.

I said, 'And what about Bernard's mother? Was she beautiful?'

278

He dropped his gaze for the first time. He actually looked bashful.

'Well,' he said, 'I don't know about that. I was only a kid, of course. But she wasn't like any of the other moms, that's for sure. She was a one-off!'

One can empathize with that. Mumsie is perhaps a little out of the ordinary. Certainly not one of those fragrant, pearl-wearing mothers who'd drive up to Darnbrook in shining cars and take their daughters to tea in Lancaster. And one did once find a little anonymous note in one's locker. It said, *Your mother is a lezzie.*

I said, 'And was her theatrical past Painted Post's only objection to Mrs Fink, or did she do something scandalous?'

There was an awkward silence. He was jingling the ice in his glass.

He said, 'Nola seen me with this she'd kill me. They tell you not to get ice in foreign places on account of bacteria.'

I said, 'You needn't worry about spilling the beans. In my family we have every kind of aberration and Bernard knows about every last one of them.'

He's often joked that I'm the first Oakhanger-Lune in centuries who isn't either mad, bad or both.

Frankie said, 'I'll put it this way, Mrs Fink enjoyed life.'

I said, 'Was it drink? Was it men?'

He said, 'I think she was game for anything going. But what it was, she was known around the young guys. You understand what I mean? Young guys wanting to lose their cherry? She'd kinda get them started. Show them the way.'

I said, 'You mean she was a prostitute?'

'No, no, no,' he said. 'I'm not saying that. I don't think she ever took money. It was more like a service she offered. There was probably somebody like Mrs Fink in most towns.'

Not in Carnforth, I'm sure. Though one does remember a General Girl we had before Olive. Edith. She wasn't with us long. She left after it was brought to Mumsie's notice that she was better known as Edie the Witherslack Bike.

I said, 'But where did she do it? Not in her home?'

'Back of cars,' he said.

It was almost noon. I ordered a glass of wine for myself and a small beer for Frankie.

I said, 'Perhaps it was just gossip.'

'Yes,' he said. 'Cudda been. Although my brother Jimmy reckoned she took care of him and he wasn't given to untruths.'

He looked at my crossword puzzle for a while. Then he said, 'I've shocked you.'

Perhaps a little. But what an interesting bond between Bernard and the Gleeson family.

I said, 'And where is Jimmy now?'

'Chapel Knoll Cemetery,' he said. 'He was killed in Korea, Battle of Heartbreak Ridge, but they sent his body home eventually. Twenty-one years old. So it's no bad thing Mrs Fink saw him OK before he shipped out. As things went, she gave him a nice send-off.'

I suppose one could think of it as a kind of war effort.

I said, 'And what became of Mr and Mrs Fink? They are both dead?'

'Oh yes,' he said. 'Long since. Well what happened was, Mrs F got herself a paying job, in Elmira. It was a good while after Willy went away, 1965 maybe, or '66. I know me and Phyllis were married. Phyllis was my first wife, may she rest in peace. So Mrs Fink would have been getting older. I guess the demand fell off for, you know, the other thing. She was too restless to stay a home-maker, that's for sure. And then one thing led to another.'

I said again, 'Was it drink?'

'Yes,' he said, 'in a way it was. She was working in a liquor store.'

It seems Serafina met a man at a dance at the Mark Twain hotel in Elmira and decided to run away with him. She emptied the till at the liquor store and, under the influence of alcohol and wearing no panties, drove her car into the Conhocton River, drowning herself and her paramour.

I said, 'It must have been a great scandal in a small town like Painted Post.'

'Not only in Painted Post,' he said. 'She'd enjoyed a wide acquaintance. After the accident everybody and his Uncle Louie had a story about Mrs F.'

There was some suspicion of the car brakes having been tampered with and Mr Fink was questioned, as were several other local figures who might have harboured fears of blackmail. The blame was finally pinned on poor car maintenance and Swiss Colony sherry, but the repercussions were felt for many years.

Frankie said, 'You know, people usen't to like Charlie Fink but after the car incident everybody felt sorry for him. And he really went down, after that. He'd just sit in the house, wouldn't shave. Mom'd take him a casserole but he wouldn't touch it. He was just eating out of cans and drinking rotgut.'

Poor Charlie Fink. Bernard never visited him.

I said, 'And then he died?'

'Yes,' he said. 'He sat out on the porch in the snow one winter's night, fell asleep and never woke up. Nice way to go, so they say.'

I said, 'And then what happened?'

'Nothing much,' he said. 'They made enquiries, tried to get in touch with Willy but he'd vanished. Charlie was in a drawer at the morgue for quite some time waiting for somebody to pay for the burying.'

I said, 'Who did pay?'

He shrugged.

'The parish, I guess. I don't know where he ended up. Maybe he's in Chapel Knoll too. My sister Junie might know.'

I said, 'Bernard was probably travelling. There were many years when he didn't have a fixed base. He would have been fearfully difficult to contact.'

'Yes,' he said. 'That'll be it.'

282

But you were just being polite, Frankie. What you're really thinking is what kind of a man doesn't bother to bury his father?

I said, 'And the house?'

He said, 'The house was a rental. My, oh my, that was some task, clearing it out. There was so much stuff in there. I don't know that it was ever lived in again. It was in bad shape. Then somebody bought the lot and tore it down. There's a house stands there now but it's not the one the Finks lived in.'

I said, 'And Bernard never came back.'

'Not that I heard,' he said. 'And I think I woulda heard. There's plenty of folk in Painted Post'd still remember him.'

I said, 'I think he felt stifled in Painted Post.'

'Stifled?' he said. 'I don't see why. You couldn't ask for a nicer place. Hard-working, neighbourly people. Fresh air. Good fishing. People choose to leave, so be it, but I won't have Painted Post blamed. I won't hear a word said against it.'

He was quite sharp.

I said, 'But I imagine life wasn't easy for him there, what with his mother, and his own style. You said yourself he was always rather *different.*'

He said, 'He wasn't the only one. One of the Ketchum girls had a hare lip, made her talk funny. And there was Harold Miller. He was a few pickles short of the full barrel. I guess we used to have a bit of fun with him too. And nobody forced Willy to wear that bow tie. Anyhow, we're talking about fifty years ago. Seems to me he oughta be over it by now.'

The door opened and Don Harrington backed in, shaking out his umbrella.

'Ah,' he said. 'Friendly faces! Mind if I sit with you for five minutes? Only I've got a lady in pursuit. I thought I'd duck in here, let her cool off a bit.'

Frankie said, 'Pull up a chair.'

I said, 'I thought Irene had established sovereignty. Don't tell me they're still fighting over you.'

I found I couldn't look him in the eye. If the rain hadn't been lashing against the window I'd have put on my coat and left immediately.

He said, 'It's because there's not enough of us to go round. They need to up the numbers. Six Gentlemen Hosts on a ship this size, it's madness, particularly with this dance competition. Ray Middleton's just about out on his feet. Course, he's coming up for seventy.'

Frankie said, 'I wouldn't have your job. I hope they give you danger money.'

Don said, 'They should, but they don't. They give us a bit of walking-around money and that's all. Well, you get your accommodation and your keep, and while you're working you can let your own place, get a bit of an income from it. That's what I do.'

Frankie said, 'And you'll be dancing tonight, I guess?'

'Oh yes,' he said. 'There's no rest for the wicked. Enid, I think you're wanted.'

He gestured towards the window where Bernard, hat dripping, jaw set grimly, was peering in. He saw me at the same moment I saw him. I hurried to the door but by the time I reached it he'd already begun to walk away.

I called, 'Darling, why don't you come in and dry off? Have a coffee.'

He turned.

'Judas,' he hissed. And he strode off, head and shoulders above the throng.

Frankie was preparing to leave.

'Got to get to the Excelsior Hotel,' he said. 'My beautified wife'll be waiting for me to buy her a bar snack.'

Don said, 'The Professor not in the mood to join us?'

I said, 'He was in a hurry to get back to the ship. He's not feeling well.'

'Oh dear,' he said. 'And what's wrong with him this time?'

I said, 'It's his throat again. I must say I don't think the air is terribly healthy in those inside staterooms.'

Frankie said, 'They put you in an inside cabin? A Professor and a Ladyship? That's not right. I wish I'd known. I cudda got you moved. The money I spend with these people, I cudda had a word to Hospitality.'

How Bernard would have loved that. Moved to the suite he has so desired, but at the behest of Frankie Gleeson.

I said, 'Well, no matter. We've survived, and now we only have one more night.'

He insisted on paying for everything, even Don's pot of tea.

'Don,' he said, 'perhaps you'd share your umbrella with Lady Enid, if you're heading back to the ship?'

Don said, 'It'd be my pleasure.'

Frankie pumped his hand. He said, 'It might help keep some of the other ladies at bay, eh?'

He left. Such a comical little figure in his foldaway raincoat, like a rainbow squash ball in a bubble-pack.

Don said, 'Nice chap.'

I said, 'I should go too.'

He said, 'Or we could wait a while, see if the rain stops?'

It seemed like a reasonable idea.

He said, 'We don't want to go bowling down the street and rear-end dear Bernard, do we now?'

He put the emphasis on the second syllable of 'Bernard'. I've noticed people do that when they want to demonstrate their dislike of him.

The café door opened again. Frankie Gleeson had returned, slightly breathless.

'Twenty-two Across,' he said. 'Something fishy about this alloy of gold and iron. Orfe. *Or* stands for gold, *Fe* stands for iron.'

Of course. I thanked him.

He said, 'A nothing fish, the orfe. A garden-pond fish. It

came to me as I was walking along. See you tonight! Best bib and tucker. I expect we'll see everybody tonight.'

And he was gone again.

The rain showed no sign of easing. Don finished his tea and we gathered up our belongings.

I said, 'You'd better turn up your collar and put on your sunglasses. Who's chasing you this time?'

'Dorcas,' he said. 'She never gives up. Walk closer to me. You're getting dripped on.'

I said, 'I'm absolutely fine.'

'Are you, Enid?' he said, and he brushed against my bosom as he slipped his arm through mine. 'Are you sure?'

The tenders were in great demand. The rain was driving everyone back to the ship.

Don said, 'So, what do you have planned for the rest of the day? Another sandwich on a tray in the black hole of Calcutta? Another afternoon doing your crossword puzzle while Bernard gargles with TCP? Or would you like to come and play in my house? I have 7UP. I have peanuts.'

27

There were a hundred enjoyable ways I might have passed the afternoon. They were showing a film called *The Pirates of the Caribbean* at the cinema. The final of Name That Tune was taking place in Sam's Bar. And there are often people looking for a fourth for bridge. Or I could simply have returned to our quarters and chatted to Bernard about his father's career as a janitor. That would have been fun.

I know a kind of madness can overtake people on a cruise. I've seen it so often. They drink too much and make exhibitions of themselves, like those idiots on the Gems of Iberia cruise who lunched too well, missed sailing time in Cadiz and hired a motorboat to chase after the ship, all to no avail. I've shuddered at the folly of such people. Now I'm one of them. I have stepped out onto a parapet and jolly thrilling it is, too.

Don and I had very energetic sex, then both fell asleep afterwards. I only woke because he sprang up in bed and said 'Shit! Irene! I'm late.'

I found the best thing was to remain beneath the covers with one's eyes closed while he dressed. It obviated the need for small talk. I heard the buzz of his electric razor. I heard him zipping up his trousers.

He said, 'You'll close the door behind you when you leave?'

I uncovered my head.

He said, 'And you'll be gone by the time I get back. You're not going to doze off again?'

I said, 'Why? Do you have someone else booked in?'

Which I suppose made one sound rather possessive, though nothing could be further from the case. The last thing I wanted was to linger in his fetid little room. Nevertheless, Don misinterpreted my words.

'Now then, Enid,' he said. 'We're both grown-ups.'

He ruffled my hair.

'Cheer up,' he said. 'Worse things happen at sea.'

And he left.

Even his bathroom made one feel tawdry. The bottle of fake tan, the corn plasters, the sad little stub of supermarket deodorant. Worst of all, the bristles in the sink. Bernard wet shaves. He uses a good badger-hair brush from Trumpers, like Poppa used to do, and Oxford Blue shaving soap. Poppa used to wear West Indian Extract of Limes which I can never smell without feeling sad, but Bernard prefers Eau de Portugal. And he would never, ever leave bristles in the sink.

I was dressing when she tapped on the door.

'Don?' she called. 'You in there? We're meant to be practising.'

It was Irene.

I went back into the bathroom and stayed very still. My heart was hammering.

She knocked and called a second time, then she slipped a note under the door, a page torn raggedly from a diary.

WAITING IN BALLROOM YOU BASTARD. IRENE

I sat on the bed in my raincoat and headscarf and waited for ten minutes to pass. I heard a few voices in the corridor, passengers returning to their rooms, but mainly it was quiet out there. Five o'clock. People were resting, painting their nails, getting ready for Gala night. I looked through the spy hole. No one in sight.

I opened the door just enough to peep out. That was when she flew at me with incredible speed.

'Where is he?' she yelled. 'Where is the fucking fucker?'

She pushed me back inside the cabin, kicked the door shut and pinned me against the wall, breathing heavily. She was so close one could notice the pores on the side of her nose. It was Dorcas. She had her hands at my throat. And then she stopped in her tracks.

'You?' she said. 'He's humping you?'

I said nothing.

She said, 'Where is he?'

One's mouth was so dry it was difficult to speak.

I said, 'He had an appointment.'

290

'Oh yeah?' she said. 'Don's appointments. What is it? Friends of fucking Bill W?'

I said, 'He's not here.'

She said, 'I can see he's not here.'

She looked at the rumpled bed. She laughed but her eyes were still blazing.

She said, 'Still warm, is it?'

The room smelled of old shoes. And something else.

She said, 'I know who you are. You're somebody.'

She was still between me and the door.

She said, 'What's your name?'

I just wanted to be out of that beastly room.

I said, 'Finch.'

'Weird name,' she said. 'You're some kind of duchess.'

I said, 'No.'

'Yes you are,' she said. 'Don't fuck with me. What are you?'

I said, 'Not a duchess.'

She said, 'What then?'

It was too ridiculous, being obliged to explain one's lineage to that miserable creature, but there was something awfully edgy about her. One had the strongest feeling that at any moment she might pick up a coat hanger or some other innocent-looking object and attack. That one would be found murdered in an inexplicable location, as happened to Second Cousin Cosmo during one of his frequent trips to Thailand.

I said, 'My grandfather was a marquess.'

'My grandfather was a marquess,' she said, trying rather ineffectively to mimic my way of speaking.

'Same thing,' she said. 'I've heard them talking about you. You're the one married to the faggoty guy who gives the talks. Don take pity on you, did he? Well, Finch, you're out of bounds, same as that other cow. I mean, I don't care about him dancing with her. Matter of fact, she did me a favour because he's not all that, not on the dance floor. But in here …'

She looked at the bed again.

She said, 'In here he's got a reserved sticker on. You understand how this works? Two Ralph Lauren shirts and a pair of mother-of-pearl cufflinks, that's what I paid. And I got in first, see? I don't care how much you spent, I got in first.'

At which point I felt the situation tilt gently my way.

I said, 'I didn't spend anything. I don't pay for men.'

I was taller than her by several inches.

She said, 'What was this then, a charity performance?'

I said, 'You're in my way.'

She said, 'What'd you do, beg him for it? You must have done. Know what you remind me of? You look like one of those fucking llamas. All ass and teeth. I could feel sorry for you only you've been helping yourself to what's mine and that's not nice. There's gonna be a payback for this, Duchess.'

Her neck was a web of little creases, just like my lovely lapis lazuli crushed silk.

She said, 'Wait till this gets around. Don Harrington gave the poor old duchess a freebie. That'll raise a laugh. I think I'll take a picture. It'll make a nice little souvenir to show everybody.'

She took out her mobile telephone and tried to push me towards the bed. I stood my ground.

I said, 'I really recommend that you don't do that.'

She mimicked me again.

'You'd really recommend, would you?' she said.

All she had to do was put away her telephone. If she chose to obstruct me, if she chose to mock my accent and derogate my looks, one can hardly be blamed for losing one's temper. 'Good old Enid,' they all think. 'Laugh at her, take advantage of her, treat her as though she's a total nincompoop. Good Old Enid won't mind.'

Well, I'm afraid Good Old Enid does mind. I'm afraid Good Old Enid snapped. A person can only take so much. If she had simply stepped aside and allowed me to leave one wouldn't have been provoked into pushing her out of the way and setting in motion her fall against the edge of the bathroom door. It was simply a chain of events. It was one of those silly accidents that can happen to anyone.

I went first to the Coffeeteria. The girl behind the bar didn't understand what I meant by a *caffè corretto*.

I said, 'Then just give me a double espresso and that bottle of Fundador.'

She rolled her eyes. And I'd no sooner poured a slosh of

brandy into my cup than I felt someone slither onto the stool beside me. Alec Fisher, golf pro.

He said, 'I hate Gala Night.'

I said, 'Push off, Alec. I want to be alone.'

'I know the feeling,' he said.

But he didn't budge until he'd slurped down a cappuccino, infuriatingly slowly, and then scraped up every last fleck of *schiuma* from the cup. The girl charged me for four shots though I'm sure I hadn't had anything like that much. I felt very clear-headed.

I saw Lori Snow as I walked through the Piazza. She was chatting to the sales girl in the Murano Glass outlet and waved at me to go over.

She said, 'All set for the big night?'

For a moment I couldn't think what she meant.

'The Dance-Off?' she said.

I said, 'I'm not dancing. The Reverend Griffiths got cold feet.'

'No!' she said. 'Oh that is such a tragedy. But I hope you're still going to wear your crushed silk. An outfit like that, you can wear it anywhere. Are you OK?'

I said, 'Do I look not OK?'

'A bit,' she said. 'Last-day doldrums, eh? Back to earth with a bump.'

Or crack! Against the bathroom door.

I said, 'Yes. Cooking, laundry, paying the bills.'

No more afternoon sex.

'Not for me, though,' she said. 'I'm on board till October, then I've got a month off before we start the Caribbean season.'

That's Lori's life. We dock in Venice tomorrow morning and by Wednesday evening they'll be on their way again. Bari, Catania, Civitavecchia, Livorno, Monte Carlo and Barcelona. Some of the passengers will be staying on too, doing two cruises, back to back.

I said, 'Do you happen to know if Bill W's friends are meeting today?'

She said, 'Far as I know they meet every day. You'll find them in the library.'

She was gazing at me with a rather annoying expression of sympathy, as though one had just announced a death in the family.

She said, 'Good luck.'

I said, 'It's not for me. Somebody asked me about it and I didn't know what to tell them.'

'Yeah,' she said, 'I guess we all know *someone* who has a problem.'

One felt as though the entire population was on the move, even behind closed stateroom doors; packing bags, dressing, limbering up for a great transhumance to the final session at the feeding trough. Gala Night Dinner. The Internet Point was deserted.

Brady said, 'Come for one last surf, Lady E?'

I said, 'I shall miss it.'

He said, 'No need to miss it. Get yourself a laptop.'

It's a kind of slimline computer one can carry around in an attaché case and no doubt horrendously expensive.

I said, 'A pipe dream, I'm afraid. New roof to pay for.'

He said, 'Get away! You can afford it! Treat yourself. You can't stop now.'

Lord, how people do assume one is rolling in lolly. I hope he wasn't expecting a gratuity.

From Billa:

Eeny, awaiting news from the boudoir with great impatience. Expect you're having a divinely fabbo time and so too busy (or exhausted!!!!) to write. Does Bernardo suspect? Word of advice. Say goodbye before the gangplank. These things never transplant to Life on Earth. Xx B

From Minta:

Enid,

Your replies still not getting through. Tom-Tom arrives Venice some time between July 28th and August 15th. Should he call you from the station? If so, send number. Or are you sufficiently well known for him to jump into a taxi and ask for the Finch palazzo? On his arrival please have him call home. I shall be out of my mind with worry till I know he's in safe hands. He'll have his asthma puffer with him plus a spare but as long as he doesn't eat shellfish, eggs or cow's milk he should be fine. Can one obtain soy milk in Italy, I wonder? If not he should be all right with goat's milk. Also please ensure he baths every day, tepid water with a tablespoon of the Dead Sea Salts you'll find in his toilet bag. If he forgets, his eczema tends to worsen, but you know what teenagers are like. But perhaps you don't. You must insist he doesn't lounge around all day playing with his electronic game. This is a quite wonderful opportunity for him to immerse himself in art and so forth so you must be ruthless with him and drag him around the important galleries, etc. no matter how much he squeals. The Accademia, obviously and the Guggenheim, and the Uffizi. Or is that Florence? Fondest love,

Minta

PS: hope you don't have any long-haired cats!

Enid to Minta:

Three elderly Persians who are shedding horribly.

I could see the door of the library from where I was sitting.

A woman in Nevada claims to have seen the face of the Virgin Mary on a pepperoni pizza. A Siberian tiger has given birth to twins. Tomorrow's weather forecast for Venice, temperature rising to 23 degrees, thundery showers towards evening. After a blow to the head a medical check-up is recommended even if the loss of consciousness is very brief.

The library doors opened and people began to emerge. Don was almost the last to leave and jolly cross he looked too when he saw me waiting for him. As though one were the pestering type. As though one *wanted* to be lurking in the shadows.

I said, 'You had visitors, after you left. Irene knocked, pushed a note under the door and went away. Then Dorcas.'

He sighed.

He said, 'Didn't I tell you to get dressed and get the hell out of there?'

I said, 'She ambushed me. She waited for me to open the door then she overwhelmed me.'

'Great,' he said.

He started to walk away.

I said, 'I haven't finished.'

More sighs.

He said, 'Well we can't stand here. Stand here, we might as well get it put out on the *Ten O'Clock News*.'

He pulled me into the Cigar Bar. It was quite empty.

I said, 'I'll have a whisky, with water.'

He said, 'This isn't a party. You were saying?'

I said, 'Dorcas threatened me.'

'She's all talk,' he said. 'What do you mean? Threatened what?'

I said, 'She tried to take a photograph of me. With your bed in the background.'

He said, 'Well that won't be worth a light. Haven't you noticed? Every bed's the same, every room's the same.'

I said, 'I stopped her taking it.'

298

'Good,' he said. 'So there's nothing to worry about. Subject closed. We can all go home.'

He started to get up.

I said, 'Not quite. There may still be repercussions.'

'What?' he said. 'You worried she's going to tell your old man? Forget it. Who'd believe her? Lady Enid getting laid? Lady Enid, who's never seen without her Marks and Sparks cardie? I think even Bernard'd recognize a fruitcake when he sees one. And say he doesn't, what's he going to do? Challenge me to a duel? Pocket silks at dawn?'

As a matter of fact, with all that Polish ancestry I think Bernard would rather suit a duel.

He softened for a moment.

He said, 'Listen, ducks, generally I make it a rule not to go with married ladies. I don't need to. A cruise like this, I get as much action as I can handle without stooping to that. The trouble is, some of these girls have very high expectations. Cruises have that effect. Everything for the asking at the push of a bell. Non-stop entertainment, non-stop grub. It means you can't serve the same old meat and potatoes every time you take a lady to bed. You understand what I'm saying? You have to keep changing the menu. It can get very wearing. I'm not a young guy any more. Now *you* were a different case. I didn't really count you as married because well, how can I put it, Bernard doesn't strike me as the jealous type. I'm sensitive to these things. Soon as I saw you I knew you'd be grateful for meat and potatoes. And I was right. Wasn't I right?'

I said, 'I wish I'd never met you.'

He said, 'You didn't. I don't even remember your name. Lady who? Nothing happened. Dorcas is nuts. End of story. Enjoy Gala Night.'

He stood up.

I said, 'She may still be in your cabin.'

He said, 'You left her in there?'

I said, 'I didn't have much choice.'

'Jesus Christ!' he said. 'She better not have done any damage.'

I said, 'I don't think she will have done. I expect she'll have left, as soon as she felt well enough.'

Then I had his attention.

I said, 'She fell. She banged her head. But she'll be all right.'

He said, 'What did you do to her, Enid? What have you done?'

I said, 'She had no business crowding me like that. She had no business threatening me and mocking me.'

He said, 'She banged her head? I don't want to hear this. You attacked her, and then you left her in my cabin? Fucking Nora!'

I said, 'I was only defending myself.'

He seemed not to know whether to sit down or walk away. His shoe heels are worn right down.

He said, 'Was she conscious?'

I said, 'She lost her balance. I'm sure she'd been drinking.'

He said, 'But was she conscious? When you left her?'

I said, 'Not exactly. It was only the door frame. She fell awkwardly, that's all.'

His face looked rather saggy all of a sudden. I think he flogs himself too hard.

He said, 'Christ Almighty, Enid. You haven't killed her?'

She was definitely breathing when I left her. The only thing very slightly bothering me is that according to head-injury.com people can collapse some time after a blow to the head. But I saw no reason to alarm Don Harrington with that.

28

Jesus called to me as I came along the corridor.

'Oh Ladyship,' he said, 'there you are. Good thing you come back. We were just going to put a call out for you. Professor's took a bad turn. Nurse is in with him now.'

Bernard was in the armchair with a blood-pressure cuff around his arm.

He looked at me with such loathing.

'Get out!' he yelled. 'Get out you treacherous bitch.'

Quincy said, 'I tell you what, why don't I come back later?'

I followed him out of the stateroom and Bernard called after me, 'Yes, go on. Go and find a little corner where you can whisper about me.'

We walked towards the steward's station.

Quincy said, 'It's none of my business. I don't want to intrude. But health-wise we seem to be back to square one.'

I said, 'Throat?'

He said, 'Razor blades in his throat, blinding headache, and a global conspiracy to destroy him. The trouble is I can't see anything wrong with him. He definitely doesn't have a fever.'

I said, 'He's just cross because I've been out all afternoon. And he got wet touring this morning. Rain always puts him in a vile mood. He'll get over it.'

Quincy said, 'Well, if you say so. But you should have heard him before you came back. He was raving. Names of people who've got it in for him. Some guy called Boulder?'

I said, 'Polder. Poor Mr Polder. He tried to introduce Bernard to another passenger he thought he'd be interested to meet. That's his only crime. But Bernard can be such a grouch.'

Quincy said, 'And he gets like this often?'

I said, 'No, it's taken an amazing confluence of events and circumstances to bring him to this desperate pitch today. You know, my husband attracts a lot of attention on these cruises, not all of it welcome. People sometimes try to get too close to him, which can be stressful in itself. He always keeps his distance. Bernard is very firm about boundaries. But some people get upset when they're rebuffed. They can make nuisances of themselves in other ways.'

He said, 'So something did happen. Did he report it?'

Hardly. That would have made him look even more of a precious chump.

I said, 'Nothing happened. All I'm saying is, a man in Bernard's position, a man of his sensibilities, can easily feel hounded.'

Quincy said, 'I see. I think. What about drugs? Could he have taken something, to help him relax? Something to take the edge off a bad day?'

On that point too, I was able to assure him. Neither Bernard nor I ever dabble in mind-altering substances. As a matter of fact, no one has ever offered me any.

Quincy said, 'Lady Enid, I should probably call the doctor. But I don't want to.'

I said, 'Then don't. We'll be in Venice by tomorrow morning. As soon as we're home I'll get our doctor to give him a thorough check-up. He probably just needs a rest.'

A rest from what? Being Professor Bernard Finch?

Quincy still hesitated.

He said, 'You don't think he might, you know, get violent?'

He might, I suppose. The flung yogurt pot of yesterday may become the hurled ashtray of tomorrow.

I said, 'I really don't think so. Bernard's strongest weapon is his tongue.'

He said, 'Because if you needed a doctor later on you might have a bit of a wait.'

I said, 'Are lots of passengers ill?'

Any cases of post-concussion collapse?

'No,' he said. 'But tonight being the last night, we'll be running a kind of reduced service, if you know what I mean. I can let you have a Valium.'

When I returned to the stateroom Bernard hadn't moved. He just sat, gripping the arms of the chair. He glared at me.

I said, 'Before you start, kindly don't call me any more horrid names, particularly in front of the staff.'

He said, 'I speak as I find. I saw you with him, hugger-mugger.'

I said, 'Hugger-mugger? What can you mean?'

'Oh yes,' he said. 'Smiles. Animated conversation, albeit with that idiot Gleeson. Yes, I think any reasonable person would describe that as "hugger-mugger".'

I said, 'Oh, I see! Now I understand. I sit for an hour in the Café Sesame, sheltering from the rain. I chat to various *Golden Memories* passengers and because one of them just happens to be Mr Gleeson I'm now accused of some kind of clandestine meeting. A secret meeting on the main street of Dubrovnik in the middle of the tourist season? Really, Bernard!'

'Just *happened*?' he said. 'Out of three thousand passengers you just *happened* to be chatting to that jumped-up little Crackerjack vendor. And no prizes for guessing what, or rather whom you were discussing.'

Ah yes. Professor Bernard Finch, the centre of the solar system.

I said, 'Frankie Gleeson and I discussed a great many things. Tourism opportunities in Croatia, the shelf-life of peanuts, the best way to cook yellow perch. But yes, we did touch on a few things that relate to you, such as your mother's colourful career and your father's lonely end.'

He remained stony-faced but his foot twitched.

He said, 'How easily duped you are, accepting Gleeson's word on anything.'

305

I said, 'Why would Frankie Gleeson make up stories about your family, Bernard? Why would anyone? It's not as though you're anyone of interest or importance.'

Silence.

I said, 'And I may be easily duped. No one better to vouch for that than you. But at least I didn't leave my father to be buried out of the public purse.'

Dearest Poppa. He died in Fort Lauderdale and he'd no sooner passed away than he was cremated, with great American speed and efficiency, before one had the chance to book an aeroplane ticket. Paige promised to send a portion of his ashes for scattering at some significant English location but we then discovered that FedEx had a prohibition against transporting human remains so my portion of Poppa had to wait on Cousin Tig taking a holiday in Florida and bringing him home in her laundry bag. Then there was the whole question of where Poppa would have liked to be scattered. Certainly not at Lowhope where there was the risk of his being trampled beneath Bobbie Snape's size 9s, and not at Oakhanger because his favourite hack across to Froxfield now lies beneath an executive housing estate. I eventually drove him to Newmarket Heath early one summer morning and peppered him onto the Gallops. He would have liked the idea of proximity to some future Guineas winner.

I said, 'Aren't you ashamed that you allowed someone else to bury your father?'

'No,' he said, 'I am not. I knew nothing of it until

306

long after it was done. What was I supposed to do? Have him disinterred and reburied to make some kind of filial gesture?'

I said, 'You knew your mother was dead. You knew he was alone. Why didn't you visit him?'

He said, 'Because I didn't like him.'

As though that has anything to do with anything. I don't like Mumsie but I wouldn't dream of not visiting her.

He said, 'And you conducted this wide-ranging discussion over refreshments too. Cups and glasses on the table. At Gleeson's expense, I hope.'

I said, 'Yes, he paid. He's nothing if not generous. He paid for Don Harrington too. You'll have noticed him sitting with us.'

'Ah, yes,' he said, 'Harrington. The superannuated gigolo. The man in the chain-store blazer. Where did he fit into this high-powered colloquium?'

I said, 'He didn't. He was simply admiring my thighs.'

He almost laughed. But then he remembered he was supposed to be sick.

I said, 'I welcomed their company, Bernard. I've done rather too much sitting alone on this trip. A person can tire of it.'

'Only a person with an unfurnished mind,' he said. 'Personally I never tire of solitude. Gleeson was minus his floozie, I noticed. Where was she? Buying another trowel for her rouge?'

I said, 'Beneath that rouge Nola Gleeson is a very well-meaning person. And as for Frankie Gleeson, I find him refreshing. He's so artless.'

'Witless would be more like it,' he said. 'Well, Enid, congratulations. You seem to have found your level. And after this meeting of great minds was adjourned, then what? A tiddlywinks tournament? Another dip into the buffet-lunch nosebag? You've been missing for hours and you knew I was feeling below par. You knew I needed you.'

I felt perfectly composed. All the impressions that flickered through my mind, the smell of Don's cologne and the faint squeak of the bed frame, the warmth of his skin and the terrifyingly delicious way one melted inside, like a jelly left in the sun, everything is safely filed away, to be savoured at leisure. If only one didn't keep getting interrupted by flashes of the thud Dorcas's skull made against the door frame. But there's really nothing to worry about. Everyone cracks their head once in a while.

I said, 'Needed me? You, who never tires of solitude? You rather gave me the impression that I was the last person you needed. Dash it, Bernard, you were the one who walked off in a huff. And don't think it wasn't noticed by others. It wouldn't have hurt you to step inside the café and say good day to Frankie and Don instead of stomping off like a petulant child. One really grows tired of making excuses for you.'

He said, 'I did not stomp. And you still haven't explained your long absence.'

I said, 'My time is my own. But if you're suddenly so interested in my life, I was here and there. There's so much to see and do on a ship this size. I was in the Coffeeteria listening to the woes of the golf pro, I was at the Internet Point answering emails, I was in the Murano Glass shop chatting with Lori Snow.'

A sarcastic shaking of the head. Not the Murano Glass shop!

I said, 'Oh yes, and I also fitted in an hour of wild sex with my lover. So all in all, quite a hectic afternoon. Then I came back to the cabin to be met by a very unpleasant welcome.'

He said, '*You* had an unpleasant welcome!'

He pulled a piece of paper from between the pages of his *Stones of Venice* and skimmed it onto the bed.

He said, 'How about *that* for a welcome?'

> *There was an old faker named Fink*
> *Whose tastes were decidedly pink.*
> *He made a good match*
> *But in spite of his catch*
> *His credentials undoubtedly stink.*

I said, 'This is what has upset you?'

'Can't you see?' he said. 'They're out to destroy me.'

I said, 'Darling, don't you think you're being a little melodramatic? It's only a silly old limerick. It *is* a limerick, isn't it? Or am I wrong again?'

No reply.

I said, 'Too clever for Frankie Gleeson, in any event. Far too clever to have been written by a man whose head is full of rocks.'

'Indeed,' he said. 'But now I know there's more than one of them in on it. I have the evidence.'

When dealing with the insane it can be useful to accept, temporarily, their view of the world.

I said, 'Evidence? Well good gracious, tell me about it.'

He said, 'Let us leave aside for a moment the home-made cartoon. The clerihew, you'll recall, was written with a cheap ballpoint pen, and in capital letters. A sure sign of a limited education. This, on the other hand, is typed, albeit on poor-quality paper. Here we are, Enid, on board ship, off the Croatian coast. Hardly a situation where many people can have a secretary type a limerick. I imagine even you can see the trail leads to the office of Gavin Iles. *Quod erat demonstrandum.*'

Dear Bernard. In his universe, correspondence must either be written with a Waterman fountain pen or typed by a secretary.

I said, 'You mean Gavin Iles is in cahoots with Frankie Gleeson? But why?'

'Because,' he said, 'he's in Gleeson's well-lined pocket and because he's another envious, anti-intellectual oaf. But it doesn't end there.'

I said, 'You mean there are others involved?'

'Oh yes,' he said. 'Polder, Erikson, they're all in on it.'

I said, 'What about Jesus?'

'Don't be ridiculous, Enid,' he said. 'Let us stay within the realms of reality here. But that nurse, so-called, he's a different proposition.'

I said, 'Nurse Quincy?'

'Nurse Quincy!' he laughed. 'You don't imagine he's a real nurse, do you? I'm fairly sure he's spying on me.'

I said, 'Gosh. That was a stroke of luck for Gleeson, that you developed laryngitis and needed a nurse.'

'Not *luck*, Enid,' he said. 'They obviously put some kind of toxin in my food. Room service, remember? Step one, they make it impossible for me to dine in peace in a public place. Step two, they contaminate my food.'

I said, 'Quincy certainly had me fooled. He's awfully convincing. He inspires confidence. But then I suppose fakes often do.'

A light, glancing blow, but I believe it didn't pass unnoticed.

I said, 'But why would anyone go to all this trouble? Can you please explain it to me because I'm afraid I'm being rather thick, as per.'

Since I married Bernard I've become painfully aware of the deficiencies of my intellect and my education. At Darnbrook one was channelled towards the lighter-weight subjects: drama, fabric crafts, tennis. I have conversational French and Italian. I can drive a car, which is more than

Bernard has ever learned to do and I'm rather a dab hand at hanging wallpaper. But I do lack his training in logic, grammar and rhetoric.

He said, 'Gleeson is a man obsessed. For almost fifty years he's nursed his resentment of me. He may have made a fortune but money can't buy you brains. He's searched the world for me, determined to pull me down.'

I said, 'You mean he actually came looking for you?'

'Of course,' he said. 'Why else do you think he takes so many cruises?'

I said, 'I thought it was because his wife enjoys spending his money.'

He said, 'Not at all. He targeted me. He identified me from my photograph in the Oyster brochure and then with lavish inducements he recruited Iles.'

I said, 'And where does Mr Polder come in?'

'Masons,' he said. 'They're all goddam'd Freemasons.'

I excused myself to the sanctuary of the Littlest Room and took a shower. When I emerged Bernard still hadn't moved. His lips were moving, his fingers were moving, as he quietly enumerated the strands of his theory.

I began dressing.

He said, 'You're not off out again?'

I said, 'Of course I am. It is Gala Night.'

He said, 'But I'm not well.'

I said, 'Then you must sleep.'

'How can I,' he said, 'with all this crowding in upon me?

312

There have been telephone calls as well. I didn't mention those. I didn't want to alarm you. The telephone rings and there's no one there. It happened twice this afternoon.'

I said, 'Did you report it?'

'What's the point?' he said. 'They're all in on it.'

I said, 'Perhaps going up to Asolo would be a good idea. A change of scene might help.'

'Yes,' he said. 'Let's go where the world recedes.'

I said, 'But for this evening I think you should change your strategy. I think you should come out and face your enemies like a man. Since they've succeeded in unmasking you why allow them the pleasure of torturing you any further? Admit your fabrications and laugh off their campaign against you.'

'Fabrications?' he said.

All sickness and vulnerability forgotten for a moment. There was a challenging tilt to his chin, an excited glitter in his eyes.

I said, 'Well, there is now no dispute that you began life as Willy Fink. But as you yourself said, thousands of people change their name and Bernard Finch does have a much better ring to it. I don't know that I'd have liked to be Mrs Fink. We've also established that your father was unemployed for most of his life, but then so were all male Lunes and Oakhangers, with the exception of Grandpoppa who went occasionally to the House of Lords. And if your mother dipped her fingers in the till I'm sure it was because she was rather desperate. Stuck in a miserable little clapboard hovel, surrounded by unsympathetic neighbours. The men finding her so alluring and the hausfraus hating her.

'Life must have been hell. I'll bet she encouraged you to go away. Being a theatrical type she would have completely understood the attraction of reinventing yourself. It's no more than any young man might do, trying to make his way in the world. At least one had a rationale. Unlike Cousin Andrew who used to go around claiming close acquaintance with Jeremy Irons for no reason any of us could discern.'

Silence.

I said, 'And as for the Cornell business, honestly, who cares? Why not come clean and put this silliness behind you? You could have studied through a correspondence course for all it matters now.'

That found its mark.

I said, 'You know, Bernard, I've come to the conclusion that on a cruise ship people's qualifications aren't terribly significant. I mean, obviously, one wants someone on the bridge who knows how to steer and so forth, but apart from that surely the main thing is that the passengers are happy? If the dancers weren't quite good enough for Broadway, if the Gentleman Host used to sell vacuum cleaners or the Guest Lecturer never actually completed his doctorate, does anyone care? I don't think so.'

He said, 'You've thrown your lot in with them too. I

314

knew it! And now you expect me to surrender to Gleeson, to go like a lamb to the slaughter? Never!'

I said, 'Then I can't help you. You'll just have to skulk in here and wait for the next silent phone call. I'm certainly not spending the evening in here, cooped up in this airless room with your so-called throat infection.'

'So-called?' he yelled. 'So-called!'

He was furious.

I said, 'I'm getting dressed.'

He said, 'I have influenza.'

I said, 'I don't think so. I think your influenza is about as genuine as anything else about you, Professor Finch.'

He lunged towards me and tried to grab me by my bathrobe but I was too quick for him.

He said, 'What about your own little secret, *Lady* Enid? Wait till your new friends find out about that.'

I said, 'It's over, Bernard. I've resolved to end that silly piece of make-believe. I was minded to do it anyway and now Billa Thoresby is coming to visit it's become essential. If Billa ever found out she'd have a field day.'

'Billa Thoresby,' he said. 'You invited Billa Thoresby? But we decided to stop seeing her.'

I said, 'No, *you* decided. I've rather missed her. But you don't have to endure her company. You can go off on one of your scholarly wanders. Go to Pavia and renew your library ticket. Go up to Asolo and start that damned book you're always threatening to write.'

He began to unbutton his shirt.

He said, 'I have nothing more to say to you. I'm going to bed.'

I said, 'And I'm going to the Gala Dinner.'

'Off you trot then,' he said. 'Go and enjoy whatever hideous entertainments they have in store for you. Dancing waiters, no doubt, and the lights extinguished while dessert is carried in bedecked with sparklers. My word, Enid, what uncouth tastes you turn out to have.'

I laughed. It was just too much to see him putting on his pyjamas at six thirty in the afternoon.

I said, 'You're right. All those years you thought you knew me, I was concealing the awful truth from you. I like eating banana splits, I like dancing the hokey-cokey and I've never read Proust.'

And neither have you, Bernard, at least not the copies on our bookshelf. All those uncut pages.

I said, 'And I'll tell you something else. I hate films by Einstein.'

'Eisenstein,' he murmured, and he slid between the sheets.

29

I threw a suitcase on the bed.

He said, 'Kindly turn off the light.'

I said, 'Out of the question, I'm afraid. I have to pack.'

'No you don't,' he said. 'It's only a five-minute job and we don't dock till eight tomorrow morning.'

I said, '*My* packing may be the work of five minutes but yours takes far longer as you would know if you had ever done it. *Your* suits have to be layered with tissue paper. *Your* ties have to be carefully rolled.'

Hand raised. Silence in the ranks! Don't plague me with your tiresome housekeeping details. I will not allow your petty facts to disturb my personal convictions.

I said, 'And I'm not leaving the job till tomorrow morning because I'll be tired. Tonight could be a very long night. Cocktails, and dinner and then the Ballroom Blitz Dance-Off. I expect it'll be well past midnight before I get to bed. So you're going to have to endure the light for a little longer. That is the drawback with these tiny cabins. It's a pity I didn't get to know Frankie Gleeson earlier in the voyage. He said he could quite certainly have had us moved to a superior suite.'

He pulled the sheets over his head and didn't stir even when Quincy came to the door with a pill.

He whispered, 'How is he?'

I said, 'Sleeping.'

I spoke up, to make sure Bernard heard me.

Quincy said, 'Probably the best thing.'

I said, 'It is. If he were well enough to take part in the evening's festivities who can say what indignities he might suffer? He might win a tombola prize. Or be expected to wear a paper crown. So better all round if he just stays in this bloody cabin and sweats it out of his system. Whatever it is. And if his condition should deteriorate, he can always press his buzzer.'

Quincy said, 'He can. But I must warn you, buzzers won't be answered very promptly tonight. Once the stewards start hitting the Gatorade it'll be like Sodom and Gomorrah.'

I was ready just before seven. My hair revived by hanging my head down and spritzing it with water, just as the stylist showed me, and my new skirt and top worn together for the first time. I liked what I saw in the mirror. I just wished I'd splashed out on new pumps too. My black courts weren't quite the right look.

I said, 'Are you awake?'

He pulled the sheet off his head.

He said, 'Of course I'm awake. How could anyone hope to sleep when their legs are being crushed by suitcases and they have klieg lights shining into their eyes.'

I said, 'I'm going down to have a drink before dinner. Can I get you anything before I leave?'

A shot of castor oil in your gin, dear? A sprinkle of senna powder in your cocoa?

He said, 'A little tender, loving care would be nice.'

Ah. A change of tack. Beneath that sheet some thinking had been going on.

I perched on the bed.

I said, 'Bernard, do buck up. This is too boring.'

He said, 'It's all such a mess.'

I sensed he might be about to deliver a long confession, full of tedious explanations and self-absorbed silences. But it was far too late in the day for that.

He said, 'We have to talk.'

I said, 'Very well. But not now.'

'Yes,' he said. 'Now.'

He took my hand.

He said, 'I am entitled to call myself "Professor", Enid. It's not a question of passing an examination. It's a distinction accorded by one's peers, in recognition of one's contribution to the advancement of a field of research.'

I said, 'And yours is a very large field. Byzantine iconography, mercantile Venice, the Delphic Oracle, the Crimean War, the Caliphate of Cordoba.'

319

A weak smile. A deprecatory brush of the hand, as though to say, 'Don't over-egg the pudding, dearest.'

He said, 'Well, I wouldn't describe myself as professorial in *all* those subjects. But I flatter myself I'm a retentive student and I certainly have a firmer grasp of my subjects than is required by the passengers on an Oyster Line cruise.'

I said, 'Of course you do. And so if for reasons beyond your control you weren't able to complete your studies, who can gainsay that given the chance you would have been awarded the highest marks. Degrees! They're only pieces of paper, when all's said and done.'

A non-committal grunt. A man without a degree who can't quite bring himself to commit the heresy of saying it doesn't matter.

I said, 'And how could you be expected to publish when Clifford Dennis monopolized your every waking moment? All that travel. Heavens, you were never anywhere long enough to unpack your pencil sharpener, let alone concentrate on writing a monograph.'

His jaw was less clenched. A little colour was creeping back into the cheeks.

'True,' he said. 'Clifford did rather consume my best years. Though of course it's not strictly true to say I didn't publish.'

Yes. There was the pamphlet on the mediaeval roots of Calabrian Greek. Not widely read, admittedly, but it was greatly welcomed by the appreciative few and its sequel, on the Albanian dialect of inland Attica, has been far too long

320

in coming. Mumsie enjoyed a similar moment in the spotlight with her Roneo'd information sheet on the history of the Dandie Dinmont as an otter hound in the Cheviot Hills. Mass appeal isn't everything.

I said, 'And you do *look* like a professor. So I would say, even if Gleeson and his conspirators go to the press with this, nobody will take them seriously.'

'The press?' he said.

I said, 'It's not as though it would make a huge splash. It's the kind of non-story one might read about in August, when there's nothing happening in the world. And anyway that may not be their intention. My guess is they've had their bit of fun and now they'll let the matter drop. But you know Frankie Gleeson better than I do. How do you think he'll play it?'

He looked quite ghastly. Like a winged bird. A golden eagle brought down by a lie.

I said, 'The danger, if you're right about there being several parties involved, is that one of them will go off and do something independently. A whisper in someone's ear. Best to be prepared, I suppose. You have nothing to lose by preparing a statement. Just in case.'

He said, 'A statement?'

I said, 'You know, the kind of thing MPs put out when they get caught fiddling their expenses. A small misunderstanding that led to an error of judgement. No intent to mislead or to profit by it in any way. With the benefit of hindsight, one should have sought an opportunity. No one harmed except yourself. A deep sense of shame one must live with for the rest of one's life, et cetera, et cetera.'

'No,' he whispered. 'A victory for Gleeson? I'd rather die.'

I stood up.

He said, 'Don't go, Enid. Stay with me. We don't like these last night parties. All that vulgar bonhomie.'

I said, 'No, Bernard, *you* don't like them.'

He said, 'You're wearing earrings.'

I said, 'They're amber. They bring out the colour of my eyes. Do you like them?'

He said, 'You're meeting someone.'

I said, 'Possibly. Though not by arrangement.'

He said, 'What does that mean?'

I said, 'This is the *Golden Memories* cruise ship. With three thousand passengers milling around it would be extremely hard not to meet people. One would have to hide in the darkest depths of the bilge.'

He was slumped against his pillows with the kind of imploring look dogs have when they know one intends leaving the house without them.

He said, 'Do you really mean to leave me alone?'

I said, 'Yes, I do. If I don't put in an appearance tonight of all nights there certainly will be talk. I'm going to go out there and fly the flag. No one will ever know from looking at me that there's a crisis going on inside this room. It's going to be business as usual, Bernard. And you can savour a little more of that solitude you so enjoy. It will give you time to reflect.'

'How changed you are, Enid,' he said. 'I feel I hardly recognize you.'

I said, 'One must do what one must do. One must rise from the smouldering ashes.'

He said, 'But you seem so hard and so distant. Whatever happened to the sweet English girl I sailed with out of Istanbul?'

I said, 'She discovered she was married to someone called Willy Fink.'

I slipped my wrap around my shoulders.

'Yes,' he said, 'of course you must go. You can't be expected to sit here all evening. You have your own life to live. A younger wife, seduced by merry-makers. I suppose one knew this time might come. And if it had to happen, now is a fitting moment. When my life is over anyway.'

The party atmosphere was palpable the moment one stepped outside. Women in party dresses, their men coaxed out of shorts and into full-length trousers, a pianist playing show tunes in the atrium, and the unmistakable throb of humanity surging towards the bars where complimentary glasses of Asti Spumante were being served.

The Reverend Taff Griffiths was the first to claim me. He was coming out of the convenience store with a mentholated nasal spray.

'It's this air-conditioning,' he said. 'It gets me every time.

And may I say how lovely you're looking this evening. A man could have regrets.'

The buttered bun again.

I said, 'Regrets are silly. One must live with one's choices.'

'You're right, Lady Enid,' he said. 'You're so right.'

I said, 'And please don't call me "Lady Enid". I've decided to be plain "Enid" from now on.'

'Fair enough,' he said. 'Very egalitarian. "Enid" it shall be. But not "plain", mind. Far from it. Ravishing, I'd say. The Professor still middling, is he?'

'Just resting,' I said.

Just living with his choices.

'That's the ticket,' he said. 'Rest is a great healer.'

The Gleesons passed by and indicated that I would find them in the Top Hat Bar.

'Well then,' said the Reverend Taff, 'I must let you go. I see your friends are expecting you. But perhaps later on you'll allow me to take you for a twirl? When they open up the floor for the social dancing?'

I said, 'Perhaps.'

As long as you don't get any silly ideas, Taff Griffiths. As long as you understand you'll merely be my vehicle to the dance floor.

'Lady E,' said a voice behind me. 'The very person I was hoping to run into.'

Gavin Iles.

He said, 'I wonder, could I trouble you for a minute of your time? Perhaps we could go to my office?'

30

On land one can imagine Gavin Iles as the manager of a small supermarket but on board the *Golden Memories* he's the great panjandrum. Cruise Director. He's in his early forties, has hairy knuckles and always the hint of a barrow-boy smirk on his face.

'Got a bit of a mystery here,' he began. He had a sheet of paper in front of him on his desk. 'A bit of a strange one, you might say. I didn't know quite what to make of it, but then I thought, "Ask Lady Enid. She's fond of a puzzle."'

I said, 'I do wish you wouldn't call me that. Call me Mrs Finch. Call me Enid.'

'As you please,' he said. 'Enid. I've received a very strange communication.'

He pushed the paper across the desk to me.

fINc*H* iS A faKe
*F*RoM a wELL-WiS*h*Er

With the letters painstakingly cut out from a newspaper and glued to the page, just as blackmailers do in murder mysteries.

'Any thoughts?' he said.

I said, 'Only that unsigned letters should always be consigned to the wastepaper basket.'

'Oh, I agree,' he said. 'Interesting though, isn't it? That somebody's gone to all that trouble?'

I said, 'It never ceases to amaze me what people get up to on cruises.'

'I know what you mean,' he said. 'I could write a book. But this. Scissors, glue. Who'd bother? And why?'

I said, 'You're showing this to me because of the name "Finch". You think it refers to me, or to my husband?'

He said, 'Not your good self, no, no, no. A Lady's a Lady and who's going to argue with that? But Bernard, well, he is the only other Finch we have on board. And he's, how shall we say, not the most popular member of the line-up? He doesn't mix. He's not friendly with the paying customers. Not to put too fine a point upon it, there are a lot of people who think he's a toffee-nosed git.'

He tapped his Oyster Line biro against his teeth.

'And this word "fake",' he said. 'Where's that come from? What can they be getting at? Are Bernard's credentials in less than perfect order? Has somebody been snooping? Do we have a bogus professor on board? Do we care? I ask you, Enid, would any of these happy campers know a Greek ruin from a hole in the ground? Still, they wouldn't like it at head

326

office. It wouldn't look good, would it, if one of their Guest Lecturers turned out to be a dud? Particularly Professor Finch. "The star in our crown", that's what they told me about Bernard. "You're very lucky to get him", that's what they said.'

I said, 'Surely if you think this refers to Bernard he's the one you should be talking to?'

He sat back, pretending to think. Every gesture is done for effect.

'You're right,' he said. 'Where will I find him?'

I said, 'In our cabin. Why don't you pop along and show him this? He'll enjoy the joke. You'll find him there all evening.'

'What!' he said. 'Not coming to Gala Night? Missing all the fun of the fair? Don't tell me he's sick again.'

I said, 'I'm afraid so.'

'Dear oh dearie me,' he said. 'What are we going to do with him?'

The Gleesons and the McCuddys were halfway down a bottle of Louis Roederer rosé champagne. There was an empty glass waiting for me.

Nola whispered, 'It's a bit sour to my taste, but that bubbly they're giving away tonight, Cricket knocks it back way too fast.'

Cricket said, 'Enid, you come sit by me. Poor Enid's on her own again. She can't dance because she don't have a man and I can't dance because I've got a busted knee but we'll be OK. We'll be good pals.'

She appeared to have started the evening ahead of everyone else.

Nola said, 'No hubby again?'

I said, 'He had a setback.'

'What a disappointment,' she said. 'And just when he seemed like he was on the mend.'

Frankie said, 'I reckon there's something about this ship don't agree with him.'

Chip put it down to the recycled air. Nola blamed vibration from the engines. Cricket thought it was in the stars.

'Look at me,' she said. 'My horoscope said I was in for a week of ups and downs and it was right. I fell down and had to sit with this knee raised up. What sign's the Professor?'

'Capricorn,' Frankie said, quick as a flash.

Cricket said, 'How the heck did you know that, Frankie?'

'Just guessed,' he said.

Nola's gown was blood-red satin decorated with sparkles around the neckline and hem. Frankie was wearing his bird's nest toupee and a maroon dinner jacket. Chip was in ivory and Cricket was in gold taffeta with an elastic bandage around her knee.

I said, 'You all look very glamorous. I feel rather under-dressed.'

Nola said, 'Not a bit. You look swell, honey. I think this cruise has done you good. You're glowing.'

Cricket leaned in.

'Must be because she's getting plenty,' she said, in the loudest of whispers.

Nola patted her hand.

'Steady, Cricket,' she said. 'Hey, know what I got today? A frangipani scalp rub. Heaven. You ever get the chance, try it.'

I said, 'What a pity you saw so little of Dubrovnik.'

She said, 'I've seen postcards. I get the general idea. But dragging around in the rain, looking at old archways? No thank you! That's not my idea of a vacation. And you know, there was nothing in the shops worth buying. You'd think they'd smarten up their act, all these cruise ships coming in. They could put a glass roof over part of that main drag, get some label stores and some clerks who speak English. They'd make a lot of money. Now Venice, *that's* going to be something else.'

Cricket said, 'Yes! Pocketbooks. That's what's top of my list. And scarves. I'm getting scarves for the girls.'

She has three daughters-in-law.

The Gleesons will have five days in town but the McCuddys are staying at the Gritti Palace for just one night. They fly home on Wednesday.

I said, 'You'll see so little of Venice in one day.'

'It'll be enough for us,' she said. 'We're experienced travellers. We don't make the mistake of trying to see everything. Just tell me the best place to buy real Italian purses. And how we get to Harry's Bar.'

I said, 'Harry's is easy. From the Gritti you can walk there in two minutes.'

'Not with this damned knee, I won't,' she said. 'We'll get a limo service.'

Nola said, 'Cricket, didn't you ever see *Everyone Says I Love You*? Julia Roberts? You can't get a limo service in Venice. It's all canals.'

Cricket looked very cross. Her lipstick had seeped into the creases along her top lip.

She said, 'Well I know that. I'm not stupid. But they gotta have *some* place for the cars. How else are they gonna deliver stuff?'

Some things are just too improbable to try and explain. Sometimes it's better to allow people to discover things for themselves. As to the best place to buy handbags, I had no idea. It must be ten years at least since I bought one and I'm almost certain it came from Marks and Spencer.

I said, 'At the very least you must see the Basilica of San Marco, inside and out.'

She said, 'If you say so. But if you ask me, when you've seen one church, you've seen them all.'

'Tell you what,' Frankie said, 'gets to this stage of a vacation, all I can think about is that long trip home.'

'Me too,' Chip said. 'If I had my way we'd stick to cruises out of Miami or Tampa. You're home a lot faster.'

Cricket said, 'Chip gets Restless Leg Syndrome. Me, I'm OK. You get a reclining seat, and there's a full bar service.

330

Or you can take a pill and you're there before you know it. Know what I did on the way over? Christmas shopping. Ordered everything from SkyMall. The boys, the wives, the grandbabies. By the time we changed planes at Frankfurt I was all done.'

Chip said, 'We land at Philly middle of the afternoon but we still have a ways to go to Georgetown.'

Frankie said, 'Then you got to get behind the wheel.'

Chip said, 'One of our boys meets us, but it's still a drive. Then there's the time difference.'

Frankie said, 'By the time you get home you've been up eighteen, twenty hours. You don't hardly know what day it is.'

Nola said, 'Will you listen to yourselves! All the interesting places we've seen, all that neat stuff we bought. Ask me, it's been well worth the effort. How about you, Enid? You have far to go to get to your place?'

Hardly any distance at all. Retrieving one's luggage and getting on a shuttle bus are what take the time. But once we get to Piazzale Roma we can walk and be home in no time. I can even pick up bread and milk as I cross Campo Santa Margherita. Bernard refuses to queue in shops so he goes ahead of me. I usually arrive to find him sitting in the gloom, hat and coat still on, sifting through the mountains of mail for anything that catches his eye. I don't mind. Actually I prefer to throw open the shutters myself and say hello to my geraniums.

I said, 'On foot we can be home in ten minutes.'

Cricket said, 'On foot? What's with all this walking? You some kind of outdoors person?'

I said, 'In Venice it's often the quickest way. If we waited for a water bus it could easily take half an hour.'

Nola said, 'But we can drop you, can't we, Frankie? We gotta boat meeting us, because the place we're staying is an actual, actual island. We'll get the guy to swing by your place. You gotta dock?'

In fact there is a spot where a boat could deposit us. A greasy little step beneath the *sottoportego,* where one might step very gingerly ashore, hauling one's bags through the green slime. How Bernard would enjoy that, especially if he had Frankie Gleeson to thank for the favour.

I said, 'Thank you. If you're sure you don't mind going a little out of your way.'

'Sure we're sure,' she said. 'It'll be fun to see where you guys live.'

Cricket said, 'Sounds weird to me. How come you ended up in a place like that anyhow?'

I said, 'My grandpa left me a little house there.'

She said, 'Couldn't you sell it, get something more convenient?'

Unthinkable. It doesn't matter how the walls crumble or the floors sag, as far as Bernard is concerned it's *his* little piece of Venetian heaven. He feels it was preordained. As though Grandpa Lune would have been at a loss how to dispose of the property if I hadn't had the foresight to marry a man of Bernard's sensibilities. Of course, he'd love to afford something more substantial, perhaps a second *piano nobile* or at least something with an *enfilade* and an important door or two, and were it not for the fact that it would mean sacrificing Eaton Mews he might have pressed very hard for us to trade up, but Bernard does enjoy having a decent London address too. And so we perch in our little backwater.

It's terribly amusing that Bernard, apparently the son of a Polish janitor and a chorus girl, has managed to raise our social standing in Venice so far above that of Grandpa who, by all accounts, never attended parties and was only interested in messing about in boats. But as soon as we took possession of Tagiapiera Bernard made a great study of the Libro d'Oro families and cultivated friendships with practically all of them. Indeed one rather dotty old Contessa, having heard vaguely about Grandpa and then having met Bernard, got in a fearful muddle and still insists on addressing him as 'Marchese', an error Bernard has been in no great hurry to correct.

I said, 'I don't think we'll ever sell. Most of the time the honour of living there outweighs the inconvenience.'

Cricket said, 'Honour? With no place to park your station wagon?'

31

On Gala Night photographers stand outside each dining room snapping people in all their finery. Cricket insisted we all be photographed together, Gleesons on one side of me, McCuddys on the other. You can buy prints as souvenirs. What fun it will be to have a memento of such an eventful cruise and of Bernard's long-lost school friend too.

We went our separate ways for dinner, the Gleesons and the McCuddys to the Staff Captain's table and I to Radio Officer Casey's table where I found three Australians, brother, sister and elderly mother, the dreaded Polders and an empty seat where Bernard should have been. Officer Casey made rather more of a fuss about filling Bernard's vacant seat than one would have wished and I very much feared Don might be conjured up as a suitable replacement. Fortunately another of the Gentleman Hosts, Wilbur Lom, was prevailed upon. Wilbur doesn't usually take a seat at dinner. He avoids rich, heavy meals because of a peptic ulcer but he's always willing to make up the numbers at a table and sip a glass of milk.

Disorders of the digestive system being very much Mrs Polder's field, she totally monopolized him, leaving me with the pineapple farmer from northern Queensland. He sells machine-harvested fruits for the juice and canning markets and his greatest problem in life is a disease called Mealy Bug Wilt. All this I learned whilst avoiding eye contact with Mr Polder. He was pretending to discuss golf courses with Officer Casey but I suspected he was only waiting for an opportunity to delve deeper into Bernard's academic records.

A most festive dinner: shrimp cocktail, a choice of filet mignon or grilled swordfish, followed by jubilee cherries flambée. The waiters were all decked out in gay bow ties and before dessert was served they went from table to table picking out guests, some willing, some not so willing, to make up a conga line and dance around the room. Wilbur Lom was on his feet in an instant and so was I. By the time we returned to the table the talk had turned to the subject of crime. What if, the pineapple farmer's sister wished to know, a murder was committed on board ship? Who would investigate it? Who would have the authority to make an arrest?

Officer Casey said, 'Heck, I know there's a lot of tension over this dance contest tonight but I hope it doesn't come to murder.'

Gentle laughter. And then the snuffling, wheezing sound of Mr Polder building up a head of steam and preparing to hold forth.

'I think you'll find,' he said, 'that the flag under which the vessel in question sails is relevant to the case.'

Officer Casey said he thought the *Golden Memories* was registered in Liberia.

'Furthermore,' puffed Polder, 'it would depend on the exact location of the ship when the crime is committed. It might be within the territorial waters of a country or it might be on the high seas, if indeed the location could be pinpointed. By the time a crime is discovered the vessel could have moved many miles. The *locus delicti* might never be known.'

Officer Casey said, 'I guess you must be a lawyer.'

'No,' Polder said. 'But as a frequent traveller on cruise ships I make it my business to know these things.'

Tables were emptying as people went off to the evening's entertainments and waiters were busily setting for second service. Nola called to me as they passed.

'Got to get to the ballroom,' she said, 'before all the good seats are taken.'

I stood up to leave.

Polder said, 'I'm sorry not to have seen the Professor this evening. Damned pity, we never did find time to talk. There were a number of things I'd have liked to discuss.'

I'll bet.

I said, 'I'll tell him you asked after him.'

'Do,' he said. 'Tell him I'm sure our paths will cross again.'

The ship was starting to pitch a little. Officer Casey had

said we might expect the odd storm before morning. Several times on the way back to the cabin I had to steady myself against a door post. I opened the door a crack. The overhead light, the bathroom light, the bedside lights were all burning. The bed was empty.

Dressing gown thrown on the chair, pyjamas dropped on the floor and tomorrow's clean shirt, gone. Bernard had risen.

Jesus said, 'Yeah, I seen him. He buzzed for a bottle of water around eight. I told him, he didn't have no business lying in bed on Gala Night. I told him he oughta put his pants on and go to the party. I bet he's walking about looking for you.'

Just what one didn't want. Bernard grouching around like a death's head, intent on ruining one's evening. He used to do that when one had friends to supper. The last time I ever invited Billa to Eaton Mews he went to bed immediately after dessert and then appeared later, wearing his dressing gown, wanting to know if we intended depriving the whole street of sleep with our shrieks of laughter. And it was only eleven fifteen. A less self-assured person than Billa would have left her nightcap undrunk and hurried apologetically away. Well, I was absolutely determined he wasn't going to drag me away from the Ballroom Blitz.

I scribbled a note to let him know I was with the Gleesons.

There were fourteen couples competing, of whom I recognized three: Don Harrington and Irene, the two middle-aged Japanese ladies who always dance together, and Ike

Windhagen and Dorcas, mercifully none the worse for her little accident. I could relax and enjoy the contest, relieved of all worries.

The foxtrot was over by the time I found Nola's table. The Gleesons were rooting for Couple No. 8, Camille and Jack Appleyard, because they were from Buffalo, New York. Cricket sniffed.

She said, 'I'm not rooting for them. They had no spring in their chassé. I'm not rooting for anybody. I can't believe me and Chip aren't out there dancing.'

She ordered another Manhattan.

She said, 'Don't look at me like that, Nola. It's for the pain. Nobody knows what I'm going through.'

It was during the quickstep that the ship began to roll again. The music was Benny Goodman's 'Sing, Sing, Sing'. We were in darkness but the dance floor was lit by shifting coloured lights reflected off a mirrored ball. The Appleyards seemed to have quite a following but Ike Windhagen and Dorcas were better dancers by far. She was wearing a sea-green gown and a fixed smile. Irene was in pink with a very short, bouncy skirt and was doing a great deal of winking every time she and Don passed the judges' table. But Don was dancing like a man with things on his mind, which is probably why he staggered slightly as the floor tilted and caused him to commit a foul against Couple No. 5. Apologies were made and accepted but one sensed that from that moment, no matter how well Don and Irene danced, their chance of winning was gone.

There was a break after the quickstep, to allow time for those who wished to change their outfits for the Latin American Medley. Geraldo, the Dance Pro, danced a showcase paso doble with a cabaret dancer called Mallori. Nola crossed the room to congratulate the Appleyards on their performance and returned with inside information.

'Those Japs,' she said, 'are professionals, so they're not in the running. They're sisters and they've got a dance studio in Tokyo but they can't win because that wouldn't be fair. The woman in green is called Dorcas, she's from Trenton, New Jersey, and she nearly didn't go on tonight because she's not feeling well. And Don Harrington's partner's over there giving him the rough side of her tongue because they got penalty points for obstructing another couple. Remember her, Frankie? She's the one tried to pick a fight with me? Anyhow, the couple they interfered with, they're honeymooners from South Dakota, second marriage for both of them, and he had a hip replacement six months ago.'

Frankie said, 'Any time you want to know a person's life story, hire Nola.'

The rumba is certainly not Don's dance, still less the samba. He lacks the necessary looseness around the hips. Actually, he looked quite exhausted 'South of the Border (Down Mexico Way)'. The lighting changed to orange and blue, criss-crossing beams that gyrated to the beat and made nauseating patterns on the floor. The Japanese sisters danced

339

perfectly but like robots, Irene and Dorcas waggled their bottoms at each other like duelling baboons and Frankie Gleeson played a football game on his mobile telephone.

There seemed to be growing support for Couple No. 5, though Cricket wasn't impressed by their jitterbug.

She said, 'I don't care if he does have a titanium hip. They're all flash and no technique.'

Then the floor was thrown open for a social waltz while the judges conferred.

Chip cleared his throat.

He said, 'Enid? I wonder, would you care to?'

Cricket said, 'No, Chip. She wouldn't care to. Enid needs to go check on her hubby. He's sick, remember?'

He subsided into his seat.

Cricket said, 'I'm not being funny or anything, but let her find her own dance partner.'

And right on cue the Reverend Griffiths stepped forward.

'Here I am,' he said. 'As threatened. Taff Griffiths reporting for dance duty. If you're not already spoken for.'

I know Don was watching me and I suspect Dorcas was too, though I could never catch her doing it. I also had the faint hope that Bernard might be out there in the dark, hanging around at the back of the crowd, witnessing my triumph. If Taff and I had practised all week we couldn't have danced better.

'Superb,' he murmured. 'Poetry in motion. A different time, a different place, the Celtic beast in me might have gained the upper hand. But don't worry, Enid. I've got a firm grip of myself.'

I didn't respond.

He said, 'I don't think you appreciate the effect you have. It's that elegant English reserve. It gets me all fired up.'

I said, 'Just as well then that we didn't compete. I should have hated to be the cause of a man's self-immolation.'

He pulled me tightly into a final whisk turn and one felt an alarming surge of heat below the waist: a farewell nudge and wink from the Celtic beast.

The big moment had arrived. The 'top of the night' as they style it. It had been, Geraldo said, a very tough decision, the judges had been very impressed by the standard of dancing and it saddened him that he could only give away one cruise voucher. Cricket whimpered.

Nola whispered, 'I'll bet it's only good for three months. I'll bet it's for one of those little cabins without a window and then they whack you for an upgrade.'

The runners-up and recipients of a fifty-dollar gift certificate redeemable at any branch of CocoLoco Dance Wear were, Couple No. 5, Bette and Sidney Jansen from Pierre, South Dakota. The winners, for their thrilling combination of footwork, body flight, personality and creative choreography were Couple No. 3, Dorcas Siegal of Trenton, New Jersey and Ike Windhagen. And Ike, being an employee of Oyster Line and living up to his title of 'Gentleman Host' will of course be surrendering his portion of the prize to his lovely partner.

Dorcas screamed and punched the air, the Jansens kissed everyone in sight and I saw Irene's tail feathers as she stormed off the dance floor and pushed through the tables towards the exit. Don didn't follow her.

Frankie said, 'All done? Can we go now? How about we get the tab and go up on deck? I think Cricket could use some fresh air.'

She said, 'Excuse me! Cricket could not. Cricket could use another drink.'

The band began to play 'Que sera, sera' and Dorcas and Ike took to the spotlight for their victory waltz. One circuit then the Jansens joined in, another circuit and other couples flooded onto the floor.

I'd have loved one last dance, but the Celtic beast was nowhere to be seen. I was just one solitary female among many, without an offer even from a Gentleman Host. One felt terribly flat.

Then, suddenly, as the waltz segued into a gentle cha-cha-cha, there was a strange, soft ripple of sound, the dancing stuttered to a halt and a space cleared to reveal a heap of pickled skin and spangled satin crumpled in the middle of the floor. Dorcas had collapsed.

32

Opinions on the reason for Dorcas's collapse were being voiced practically before she hit the floor. The stress of the contest. Dehydration. A skipped dinner. Nola thought drugs were involved.

She said, 'You must have noticed the way she was smiling all the time. Completely unnatural.'

I noticed Don Harrington slipping out of the room, loosening his tie and Ike Windhagen could be heard saying, 'We were just dancing away, happy as you like, and then down she went, whump. I figured she musta mislocated her knee but no, she was stone cold out.'

Over and over he said the same thing.

I put on my wrap.

Nola said, 'You're not leaving?'

I said, 'I should check on Bernard.'

She said, 'You can't go now. Don't you want to find out if she's dead?'

Cricket said, 'She won't be, Nola. That type never are. You go, Enid.'

On the dance floor there was a big discussion as to whether Dorcas should be moved. Those who felt she should at least be straightened out a little and made more comfortable were overruled by Geraldo who has a certificate in CPR as well as a shiny gold boiler suit.

'She's breathing,' he said. 'That's all that matters. Now leave her as she is till the doctor's seen her.'

As the word went round that she was breathing one sensed a certain amount of disappointment, perhaps because Dorcas wasn't the most popular of winners, perhaps because a death on the dance floor would have made such a thrilling end to the cruise. People drifted away but outside the ballroom the story was spreading like fire in brushwood. It was the heat, it was the lights, it was a jab from a poison-loaded safety pin. She was tall, short, dark, blonde, she was a party girl, she was a saint, she was a hag from hell with switchblades fitted to her ankle-straps.

I went up to B Deck. In the O-zone they had declared the outside dance floor off-limits because of worsening weather. A man was using the karaoke machine, singing '(Is This the Way to) Amarillo', to an emptying room. People were leaving, making their way to lower decks and midships where they might be less affected by the pitching and rolling. I ordered a sambuca.

The barman said, 'You'll have to drink it fast. I'm closing.'

I said, 'In that case, give me two.'

I felt a damp paw on my arm. Alec Fisher.

'Hell, isn't it?' he said. 'Why do we do it?'

He was at the lugubrious stage of drunk, but talkative. Even when the barman slammed down the grille he didn't pause. Lived most of his life in New Hampshire. A PGA pro who never quite made it, three times divorced with various children he rarely sees and every ex-wife a she-devil. He's caddied for big names, enjoyed a five-minute career as a commentator on a golf channel, opened and soon after closed a golfing accessories shop, and where has it all got him? Drinking alone on a cruise-ship bar stool.

I said, 'As cruise-ship jobs go I'd have thought you had one of the best. Out in the fresh air, taking passengers to local golf courses, playing on a simulator when business is slow.'

'It's not as easy as it sounds. You're up against all the other stuff people can do. Quiz shows. Excursions. People like your old man. Everybody's heard about the *Professor*. But me, I'm on commission. I have to sell myself. On a bad day I might only get a couple of takers for my swing clinic. Then there's the ones who keep coming back. No-hopers who're never going to improve. Where's the job satisfaction in that?'

Another embittered man, face to face with disappointment, and oozing self-pity.

I said, 'A woman collapsed in the ballroom tonight. She'd just won the dance contest and suddenly she was on the floor, unconscious.'

345

He said, 'Then people think if you work on a cruise ship you've got sex on tap. They think you've got women throwing themselves at you. Ha! Most of them are dogs.'

I said, 'Perhaps she's diabetic and forgot to take her medication. In the excitement of the evening.'

He said, 'When I was on the circuit, I had some issues, required medication. Then they said I failed to provide a urine specimen. It was an oversight, you know? You've got some bitch wife after you for child support, you've got lower back pain, you can easily forget to provide a specimen. Next thing you know your career's lying at the bottom of a water hazard.'

I said, 'I wonder what happens on a ship like this if someone were to become seriously ill. Perhaps they put in to the nearest port.'

'Chopper,' he said. 'They radio for a chopper.'

I said, 'But where could it land? Would there be room on the golf links?'

'No way,' he said. 'Can't be done. They'd have to winch 'em up.'

I said, 'But in the dark? And it's windy tonight.'

He said, 'You know your trouble? You worry too much about other people. This woman? She probably took a little something to get in the party mood, know what I'm saying? They're all doing it. Stupid cow's got nobody to blame but herself. Let's get another drink.'

I said, 'No, not for me. Really.'

'Yes, yes,' he said. 'Another drink. For two fucking refugees from fucking Gala Night. Now where's the fucking barman?'

He rattled the grille then set off around the deserted bar in hopeless search of someone to serve him. His gait was strange, as though he were climbing a steep hill. It was only when a large potted palm slid clear across the floor and knocked him into a tub chair that I realized it was the ship that was leaning, not him.

'I'm OK,' I heard him say. 'No damage done. Close one, though.'

But I was already skittering for the door, before the ship tilted back and sent any of the furniture crashing my way.

'Goodnight, Alec,' I said. 'Time to go below.'

Virginia hailed me from across the atrium, waving her walking stick. She was sitting alone.

'Lady Enid!' she said. 'Isn't this exciting! Do you think we're going to sink?'

I said, 'Most unlikely. These little storms happen in the Adriatic at this time of year. It's nothing to worry about.'

'Oh well then,' she said, 'I guess my time hasn't come. But you know I've always hoped to come to a sticky end on one of our vacations. A shipwreck or a volcano or something. Even if it's just a little bite from a poisonous spider. I'd sooner that than turn into a vegetable and be a burden to Irene.'

I said, 'Have you seen her? I imagine she's upset she didn't win tonight.'

347

She said, 'She's heartbroken. And it was all his fault, you know? Don Harrington? He wasn't concentrating, and then he caused them to interfere with those people who were runners-up. But I always say it's the taking part that counts. And then, look what happened to the one who did win. They say she might have had a bump on the head.'

I said, 'You mean when she fell?'

'No,' she said. 'Prior. They say she might have delayed concussion.'

I said, 'Who told you that?'

'Nobody in particular,' she said. 'I heard people talking. Sit here long enough you get to hear everything.'

The ship pitched again.

I said, 'I should go. Can I walk you to your cabin? You should take someone's arm with the ship rolling so much.'

She said, 'Oh I'm not going to bed, dear. I always stay up on the last night. I always leave Irene the cabin to herself on the last night, in case she finds herself a beau. Besides, I want to be awake when we sail into Venice. They say it's a sight worth getting up for.'

It is. In fog, in rain, in sun, a floating miracle. The pilot comes aboard just off Malamocco, then we turn through the Lido channel and after the green, leafy islands of Vignole and Certosa we begin the slow swing around Sant'Elena and into Venice. I know every bell tower.

'My best regards to the Professor,' she said. 'Tell him we'll be sure to look out for his name on future cruises.'

33

Eleven o'clock and Bernard still wasn't in the cabin. I couldn't imagine where he would have gone, on Gala Night of all nights. The library was in darkness. The upper, less frequented decks were closed because of the weather. It crossed my mind that he might have gone in search of Doctor Lupin in a final bid for sympathy, but P Deck is off-limits to passengers after the Medical Centre closes in the evening. One needs a special code to open the doors. And anyway, in all likelihood Dorcas was down there. What if one happened upon her, restored to consciousness, and she pointed an accusing finger?

I returned to the cabin and tried to read but even Inspector Montalbano couldn't hold my attention. I found I was checking my watch every ten minutes, then every five minutes and, as midnight passed, then twelve thirty, the faint, fluttery feeling I'd been trying to ignore flared up into the full-blown certainty that Bernard had gone missing.

The steward's station was deserted. What to do? Prepare

for bed and keep the vigil a little longer? *Lady Enid, when did you first suspect something might be amiss?* One o'clock seemed about right. Just on the off-chance that he'd been caught up in the climax of Last Night silliness, or drunk too much and fallen asleep in a chair.

It was 12.55 when I went up to the atrium. The four secretaries from Kansas staggered by wearing paper hats. One of the Sallies remembered me.

'Enid!' she called, 'Come and have a drink!'

They stopped.

She said, 'Hey, you OK?'

I said, 'I was hoping the Information Desk might still be open. I really need to speak to someone.'

She said, 'Are you kidding? On party night? What's the problem?'

I said, 'It's my husband. It's probably nothing. I'm probably being silly. But he seems to have disappeared.'

She said, 'But he'll just be enjoying himself somewhere. He'll be sitting in one of the bars shooting the breeze. He'll have forgotten the time. That's men for you. You come with us. We're going to the Top Hat. Maybe we'll find him in there.'

I said, 'My husband doesn't like sitting in bars.'

Least of all on the night when the Fun Enforcers are determined to make everyone join in the Chicken Dance.

'Don't worry,' she said. 'He'll turn up. Then you can come and have a farewell drink with us.'

350

There were now two Enids: the one who knew in her bones that Bernard wouldn't come striding across the atrium and the one who sat and waited anyway. One felt rather conspicuous, sitting alone in an evening gown and a cardigan while the rest of the world partied. I wished I'd thought to bring my book with me. Then, at one thirty, just as I'd decided I should check Bernard hadn't returned to the cabin and fallen asleep, the door to Gavin Iles's office opened and Lori Snow emerged followed by Iles himself, adjusting his dress.

'Hello, hello,' he said, one arm in the sleeve of his jacket. 'If it isn't Lady E.'

I said, 'You're working late. I'd given up hope of finding anyone.'

'Yes,' he said. 'Just catching up on a bit of paperwork, weren't we, Lori?'

She laughed.

He said, 'So? How can we help?'

I said, 'I just wondered, what would be the procedure on a ship like this when a person hasn't been seen for several hours?'

'Generally,' he said, 'nothing. They always turn up. We had three people missing last night. They have a few drinks, they forget the time. One girl heard them paging her and didn't even bother to pick up a phone. She'd had a row with her boyfriend and decided she'd give him something to think about.'

351

I said, 'But presumably there is a point at which one would raise the alarm?'

He said, 'Is this dear Bernard we're talking about? Don't tell me he's finally got out of bed.'

Lori said, 'Gav, be serious. You can see Enid's worried.'

She sat beside me while I recited the evening's sightings. In bed at seven, claiming to be at death's door, buzzing for bottled water at eight, then up, dressed and gone by nine. Not seen since.

I said, 'And I'm certain he won't be in any of the public rooms. Bernard hates Gala Night.'

'Naturally,' Iles said, under his breath.

Lori said, 'I'll page him.'

She was missing an earring.

All over the ship Lori Snow's voice asked Professor Bernard Finch to please pick up any courtesy telephone and contact the Information Desk. We waited ten minutes, then she repeated the message.

Iles said, 'One more time.'

He had begun nibbling the skin around his fingernails.

'Lady E,' he said. 'That little business we talked about earlier? You don't think there's any connection? Stuff on his mind? Know what I mean? Maybe he's gone on a bender?'

I said, 'That's hardly Bernard's style. And anyway, he prefers to drink in the cabin.'

Lori said, 'Shall I call Security?'

'Not yet,' he said. 'Before we start running around let's

352

be sure we're not missing something obvious. Lady E, Enid, when you do these cruises, does Bernard ever, how shall I put it, indulge in a bit of slumming? Does he make any little night-time trips down to the bilge? Getting to know the crew? Know what I mean?'

I said, 'Yes, I know what you mean and no he doesn't.'

Lori said, 'Gav! This is the Professor we're talking about.'

He said, 'You'd be surprised. We've got a bloke does the Creative Writing talks during the winter season. He likes a bit of rough. Men in singlets. Sweat and cigarettes and machine oil. You wouldn't think it, to look at him. He's quite a smart gent, but there it is. And of course it's not encouraged. Actually, it's against the rules. They're down there, we're up here and never the twain. But. It does happen.'

I said, 'Not Bernard. He only likes beautiful things.'

A little twitch of a sneer.

'Fair enough,' he said. 'I had to ask.'

He leaned forward with his elbows on his thighs, gazing at the floor.

'Bernard, Bernard, Bernard,' he said, eventually. 'Why are you doing this to me? It's been one fucking thing after another, ever since we left Istanbul.'

'There she is!' I heard Nola say, and she came tip-tapping across the atrium in her backless mules, with Frankie behind her, trying to keep up.

She said, 'We heard the message go out and I said to

Frankie, "That's weird, because he's in bed sick. Enid told me so." You lost him?'

I said, 'It's so silly. He's probably somewhere terribly obvious. One hates to make a fuss.'

She said, 'But what are they doing about it?'

I said, 'I'm not sure what the next step is.'

Lori said, 'Gav?'

Iles said, 'Next thing is, you go with Lady E and check the cabin one last time. If he's not turned up there, give me a bell. I'll have to alert Fazakerly. Two fucking a.m. He's going to be thrilled.'

Brian Fazakerly is the Chief Security Officer.

Frankie said, 'I'd be glad to go with Lady Enid. Leave you free to set the wheels in motion for a thorough search. How do you go about it? Top down or bottom up?'

Iles said, 'And you are?'

'Gleeson,' he said. 'Frankie Gleeson, old friend of the family.'

Iles said, 'Well, Mr Gleeson, we have our way of going about things and our way is for a member of the crew to make another check of the missing person's quarters. And that'll be Lori here.'

Nola said, 'And I'll go with them. You stay here, Frankie. Make sure they get things moving. They oughta be calling the Captain right now. They oughta be telling him to stop the ship.'

Iles said, 'We don't stop the ship, madam, until we're sure

the missing passenger isn't sitting in a bar. Or asleep in somebody else's cabin.'

Our stateroom was still empty.

Nola suggested I stay down there, away from the public gaze until Bernard was found but Lori said that wouldn't be possible.

Nola said, 'I don't see why not.'

But I did. When a person goes missing the last place they were seen is of interest to those conducting the investigations.

Enid Finch, where were you on the evening of June the twenty-second?

Lori said, 'You all right, Enid?'

I was.

Nola said, 'Of course she's not all right. Her husband's missing and you people didn't even start looking for him yet.'

Lori said, 'We do have to follow procedures, madam.'

There's an amazing kind of telegraph on a cruise ship. The word passes around that they're going to be serving lobster at the midnight buffet or that a fight has broken out and a crowd soon gathers. By the time we got back to the Information Desk there were already a few people hanging around, sensing that something of interest might be happening.

Brian Fazakerly is a big, comfortable man, formerly of the West Mercia Constabulary.

'Nosy bloody parkers,' he said. 'On your way please, ladies and gentlemen. No congregating. There's nothing going on here.'

He took me into Gavin Iles's office. Nola wanted to come with me but he insisted that she remain outside.

'Don't worry, madam,' he said. 'I'm only going to get a bit of information. I'm not going to eat her.'

He adjusted the height of Gavin Iles's chair and picked up an earring from the rug.

'Now,' he said, 'from the beginning.'

Did I have any reason to be concerned about Bernard? Anything odd about his behaviour? Had he said anything to cause me concern? Had he been drinking?

Sometimes, as much as one knows that questions will be asked, one doesn't decide until the very last second whether to tell the full truth or selected details.

I said, 'He's been rather stressed. It's all too silly but Bernard isn't strong in that way.'

Security Officer Fazakerly has that unnerving ability to listen and say absolutely nothing. Not even 'Mm'. Then, to fill the vacuum left by his silence, one continues to talk.

I said, 'Mr Gleeson, the gentleman outside with his wife, knew my husband many years ago and when he recognized him on the first day of the cruise he tried to revive the friendship. Bernard refused. It was a rather tricky situation for a while, though all resolved quite amicably now. But there were other people trying to get close to him, asking lots of personal questions. It happens, you know? It's not the first time Bernard has attracted unwelcome attention on a cruise, but this time he found it very distressing. My husband's a terribly private person. He conceived the idea that people were talking about him, that there was even a plot to destroy him. Too ridiculous, of course, but Bernard isn't a strong person. He has a brilliant mind and he's awfully creative, but psychologically he's rather delicate.'

He said, 'But you hadn't quarrelled? Nothing untoward?'

How difficult it is to paint a true picture of a marriage in just a few words. Every couple quarrels, after all. When I was very little Mumsie and Poppa occasionally threw riding boots. In later years they just left each other notes.

Gavin Iles put his head round the door.

'I've got the Padre out here,' he said. 'Taff Griffiths? He wonders if Lady Enid would like some moral support?'

Brian Fazakerly said, 'You want the Reverend to sit in?'

I said, 'No, I don't think I do.'

'Quite right,' he said. 'He's another nosy little bugger. Now, where were we? You left your husband in the cabin in bed around seven?'

I said, 'Yes.'

He said, 'And he didn't, for instance, ask you not to go? He didn't say anything that made you wonder if he should be left on his own?'

I said, 'I felt sleep was what he needed. When a person

is saying irrational things one can't argue with them. It's a waste of time.'

He said, 'I don't disagree. I'd probably have done the same thing myself.'

The Deck Officer arrived.

'Brian,' he said. 'How's it going? Who are we looking for?'

Brian Fazakerly said, 'Professor Bernard Finch, age sixty-five, hair dark blond, eyes blue, height 6 feet 4, weight 13 stone, probably wearing white linen slacks and a lilac Nehru shirt. That means it doesn't have a collar. Shouldn't be hard to spot, should he? And this is his wife. Lady Enid.'

The DO nodded.

He said, 'Last seen?'

Fazakerly said, 'A bit hazy. Their regular steward definitely saw him around eight. The Professor's been in bed with the flu and the steward took him a bottle of water. We've got another steward thinks he might have seen him on the corridor later on, but frankly, he's had a couple of bevvies so I don't think we can rely on that.'

'Cabin searched?'

'I've got two men on it now. It's an inside stateroom, so it won't take long.'

The DO said, 'What about the Crew's Bar?'

Fazakerly said, 'Not his style.'

The DO said, 'Could he be in a card game somewhere?'

I said, 'My husband doesn't play cards.'

The DO said, 'Anything else? Any history?'

Fazakerly said, 'Not really. It's his first time with Oyster. He's the chap who does Classical Greece. No major health problems but he's not been quite his usual self this past week, is that right, Lady Enid?'

Arrogant, imperious, unkind, infantile, slippery. No, Bernard has been completely his usual self.

I said, 'Just a little tense.'

The DO said, 'He ever gone missing before?'

Never. On the day he was evicted from Villa Peruzzi he went for a long, solitary walk in the rain before he finally resolved to ring my doorbell. I remember him labouring up my narrow stairs at Panfilo Castaldi in that marvellous Australian stockman's raincoat he used to wear and throwing his hat at my feet.

Gavin Iles appeared in the doorway again and this time forgot to leave after he'd delivered the message that our cabin had been searched and nothing had been found. No note, no signs of a struggle or injury. Just Bernard's pyjamas thrown on the floor, as normal.

In the eventuality of being questioned about a missing husband, what is the recommended comportment? Should one pace the floor and demand action? Or should one abdicate, leave the experts to swing into action and sit politely wringing one's hanky? I found I didn't quite know where or how to look. There was a long silence broken only by the sound of Gavin Iles scratching his armpit.

Then the DO said, 'So. Headcount?'

Brian Fazakerly cracked his knuckles. He gazed at the inevitable Canaletto as though it might contain the answer.

'Yes,' he said, eventually, easing himself out of the chair, 'headcount.'

A call was made to the bridge, to the Officer of the Watch. The ship was to be stopped until Bernard was found. Or not found.

Iles opened the door.

'Lori,' he said, 'can we get a little something for Enid? Cup of tea?'

I said, 'I'd prefer a black coffee. With brandy.'

That seemed to strike the right degree of desperation.

Lori said, 'The Reverend Griffiths is still outside. And Mr and Mrs Gleeson. Would you like them to come in and keep you company?'

I said, 'I think I'll come out to them. I find the air rather stale in here.'

The excitement had quite taken my legs from me. I genuinely staggered a little as I stood up and Gavin Iles caught my arm.

I said, 'It must be the smell of late-night paperwork.'

34

Here is what they say.

This is an important security announcement. Passengers are asked to leave all public areas and go immediately to their accommodation while a search of the ship is conducted and all passengers are accounted for. Passengers are asked to remain in their cabins and listen for further announcements. Thank you for your cooperation.

But people weren't cooperating. In fact some of them were jolly annoyed about the bars being closed. They said it was Gala Night and they were entitled to carry on drinking. Some of them were excited because word was spreading that there might be, almost certainly was, a man overboard. One couple tried to get into the express lift to the Observation Deck and when the security guard stopped them an argument broke out.

The guard said, 'Didn't you hear the announcement? Everybody's to go to their cabins till they've been counted.'

The man said, 'Yes. And now you've counted me, so get out of my way, pal. I'm going up where I can get a good view.'

His wife was trying to calm him.

But he said, 'Fuck it, Tina, whose side are you on? If there's a body in the water we want to get a good picture, right? It'll be worth something.'

The guard said, 'There isn't a body in the water. Now are you going to do like I asked you nicely or do I have to throw you in the brig?'

The wife said, 'Leave it, Steve. It's not worth it.'

'Bunch of fucking Nazis,' he shouted. 'You haven't heard the last of this.'

Frankie introduced himself to Officer Fazakerly.

'Gleeson,' he said. 'Friend of the Professor. I'd like to offer my services, for the search.'

Officer Fazakerly said, 'Sorry, sir. I've got my own men. We have our procedures, you understand? We can't allow any freelancing.'

Frankie said, 'I can follow orders. I did a spell in the Coast Guard years ago.'

The DO said, 'Our goal is to complete the headcount, locate the missing passenger and get under way again as quickly as possible. We've got worsening weather conditions. The outside decks are closed to all but essential personnel, sir. We don't want a mystery turning into a needless tragedy do we now?'

He said there were thundery squalls coming in from the west and the waves were swelling to six feet.

I said, 'What if you don't find him? What happens then?'

Taff Griffiths said, 'Don't say it, Enid. Have faith.'

He used the occasion to knead my elbow. Officer Fazakerly said that with the water temperature at around twenty degrees a person could survive for several hours, particularly if he knew how to assume an energy-conserving flotation position.

I said, 'My husband can't swim.'

And Iles said, 'Energy conservation! Our Bernard's a dab hand at that. He's spent more time in bed this trip than he has out of it.'

Frankie said, 'One thing I can tell you. Willy's not a jumper.'

'Willy?' the DO said. 'I thought we were looking for a Bernard?'

He said it was quite rare for passengers to jump. He said the way many people end up overboard is they have too much to drink, then they climb on to the guard rail, perhaps for a dare, and then just miss their footing.

Frankie said, 'Well that's not Willy. Bernard. He wouldn't do anything so dumb. No, he's still on board somewhere, you can bet your last dime. He's hiding some place. See, you have to understand who you're dealing with. You have to know how his mind works. If you're going after a large-mouth bass you won't get far treating him like a smallmouth. See what I'm saying? And if you ask me, Bernard's a large-mouth.'

363

Smallmouths swim in schools, apparently. They like deep water and cool currents, and if you catch them they'll put up a big fight.

He said, 'I've seen smallmouth jump clear out of the water, trying to throw the hook. That's not Bernard. Ask Lady Enid. He'd run to ground instead. He'd go some place quiet and work out his next move.'

Nola said I shouldn't be drinking alcohol.

I said, 'I'm fine, truly.'

'No,' she said. 'You think you're fine but you're in shock. They should let you go lie down.'

I wasn't allowed back to our cabin. It was sealed until Bernard had been found.

Routine procedure, they said.

Gradually the place emptied. All music was turned off, all the shops were shuttered and the atrium fell silent. The engines had stopped. The *Golden Memories* had become a ghost ship.

Frankie was still applying fish psychology.

He said, 'I feel so damned useless. I wish they'd let me help. There's nobody understands the largemouth bass better than I do. He's a loner, see? Then, he don't exert himself much. He don't need to because he's king of the hill. Nobody eats him. He'll dive, but not like a smallie. More likely he'll just hang in slack water, lie there, wait for something useful to happen along.'

Deck by deck the reports came in.

A Deck, a couple behaving erratically on the golf links, suspected of using a controlled substance.

B Deck, male passenger, intoxicated, asleep in the open-air cinema, wanted to know if he'd missed dinner. Not Bernard.

C Deck, clear. D Deck, clear. E Deck, clear.

N Deck, female passenger found trapped in one of the casino toilets. A carpenter was on his way to force the lock.

Taff Griffiths said he'd been chaplain on a cruise from Hawaii to Honolulu in 2001 and a passenger disappeared and as far as he knows she never was found.

'Disappeared into thin air,' he said. 'No note. No sign of violence. It was a complete mystery.'

And Nola said, 'We don't wanna hear stories like that. A guy in your line, you oughta have more sense.'

But I didn't mind. I was experiencing a delicious thrum of excitement.

G Deck, three passengers and two crew members found naked in a mini-suite, unaware of the search operation.

L Deck, clear. M Deck, clear.

The odds were lengthening. All that remained was to identify several confused passengers, discovered in cabins other than their own, and to search the spaces of the bilge decks: the engine rooms, the steering gear, the thrusters, bow and stern, the electrics' station, the sewage tanks, the crew's quarters and the stores.

My mind began to turn to practicalities. If Bernard was

lost at sea his body might not be recovered. What does one do in such circumstances? A memorial service, I suppose. Tsampi Karagiannis, Stash Leontis, they'd all contribute. Or perhaps a pilgrimage, on the first anniversary, to throw a wreath onto the waters, somewhere off Croatia. But are there complications when a person is lost at sea? Does one have to wait years for the case to be closed? Not that Bernard actually owns anything, no houses to be sold, no heirs to be seen right, but one would like to be free to move on. It occurred to me that I might sell Eaton Mews. It has really become nothing more than a chilly repository for Bernard's overspill library. And if my rediscovered Darnbrook friends are going to invite themselves to Venice so freely, I'll surely never want for a bed in London.

I wondered how Mumsie would take my widowing. In principle she disapproves of all husbands but Bernard could be very flirtatious. He always insisted we take a lavish gift when we visit Lowhope. A side of smoked salmon or a bottle of Bombay Sapphire. And he'd express a totally fake interest in gossip from the world of the Dandie Dinmont terrier. He was very clever at keeping relations cordial, but it's no secret that Mumsie feels I could have married more judiciously.

On several occasions she's said, 'Your father may have come to a regrettable end but I'm glad to say he didn't cost me a penny.'

And once she said, 'I really don't see the necessity for you to travel so much. There's a farm cottage at Lune Grange I'm sure Andrew would let you have. Then Bernard can go off without you. Probably be glad to. What do you find to talk about all the time? All that foreign muck you're obliged to eat, and all those strange, foreign types he associates with.'

Which I thought was pretty rich considering some of Bobbie Snape's idiosyncrasies. I mean to say, there's nothing wrong with a short hairstyle *per se* but she could as well go to any ladies' salon to get a trim instead of sitting so obviously in the barber's shop, in full view of the street. And she had absolutely no right to appropriate Poppa's Harris tweed suit practically minutes after he left. It was a very good three-piece from Henry Poole which Poppa certainly intended to have sent on.

I suppose I always expected to be a widow some day. Bernard is ten years older than me, after all, and from a family not noted for its longevity. I wouldn't remarry. I now know that the companionship I longed for back in Panfilo Castaldi can easily be found without hobbling oneself to a husband. One can go on cruises.

The walkie-talkie crackled.

Gavin Iles said, 'What was that?'

Officer Fazakerly said, 'Unexplained rise in temperature in the 3D store. They're checking the sensors.'

Nola said, 'Where's the 3D store?'

'Q Deck,' he said.

Iles said, 'Remind me, we got anybody in there?'

Fazakerly said, 'Just the one. Heart attack between Santorini and Mykonos.'

'That's right,' Iles said. 'The old guy. Well, that's all we fucking need. A missing passenger *and* a resurrection.'

I said, 'What's in the 3D store?'

Brian Fazakerly said, 'It's the cool room used by the flower shop.'

Iles said, 'It's the cool room used for bodies. Deceased passengers.'

I said, 'Why is it called 3D?'

Taff Griffiths said, 'Just one of those bits of shipboard jargon.'

'3D,' Iles said, 'stands for Definitely Done Dancing.'

Officer Fazakerly said, 'Steady on, Gav.'

And Nola said, 'Disgusting. You should show more respect.'

I said, 'So someone did die, during the cruise?'

'Yes,' he said. 'Sadly. An elderly gentleman. I'm afraid it does happen. All in a day's work for us.'

I said, 'I'm glad the rumours weren't true then, about the lady who won the dance competition. Some people were saying she'd actually passed away.'

'No, no,' he said. 'Just a bump on the bonce. As far as I know she's in the clear.'

The walkie-talkie coughed again. Nothing found in the 3D store. Q Deck searched and clear.

'Damned sensors,' Fazakerly said. 'They need replacing but you can talk till you're blue in the face.'

35

A call was made to the bridge. All decks had been searched and Professor Finch was still not accounted for. Nola took my hand, which was rather a mistake because having taken a person's hand one then has to decide the right moment to release it. Not during the delivery of bad news, certainly. And probably not immediately afterwards. One could be hanging on for hours.

I said, 'What happens next?'

Brian Fazakerly said, 'I'm afraid this is where we hand over to the air-sea search guys. Nothing more we can do.'

An announcement was made that the headcount had been concluded, that the ship would soon be under way and the estimated time of docking in Venice was now ten a.m.

Taff Griffiths said, 'Perhaps a prayer would be in order?'

Gavin Iles said, 'Say one for the Purser while you're on your knees, Taff. Now the fun begins. Extra breakfasts. Three hours late getting in for the turnaround. Passengers missing their flights. Oh boy.'

Nola said, 'What about poor Enid? She needs to lie down. She needs a doctor.'

I truly didn't. I felt a little frightened for Bernard. I hoped he hadn't suffered. But I felt perfectly calm. Our bags were packed. All I had to do was change into my day clothes.

Brian Fazakerly said, 'When we dock, you can either be first off or last. Personally I'd recommend waiting. It's very hard to give you any privacy the other way.'

I said, 'I'll take your advice.'

He said, 'The police might want a word, or they might come and see you later, seeing as you'll be at home. And then there's the press. The word soon gets out. A water taxi might be your best plan.'

Nola said, 'Don't you worry about her. She's riding with us. We'll take her home.'

Frankie had been silent since the engines had started up. He shook his head.

'Can't believe it,' he said. 'Willy wasn't a jumper. No way. It had to have been a rogue wave.'

Jesus asked to see me. He was crying.

'Ladyship,' he said, 'I feel so bad.'

I said, 'But you mustn't. You've been a very good cabin steward. My husband thought very highly of you.'

Which made him cry all the more.

Then Nurse Quincy came, pale and anxious.

I said, 'Don't say it. Don't even think it.'

He said, 'I can't help it. I know what I know.'

I said, 'And I can tell you, my husband didn't jump. He must have gone on deck against all advice and been swept away.'

He said, 'We don't usually lose patients in this job. Well, heart attacks. But you'd lose them wherever you were.'

I said, 'The lady who collapsed tonight? Dorcas, is that her name? Is she all right?'

'Yes,' he said. 'She can't remember what happened but she seems OK. She's going to the hospital when we get to Venice, just to be on the safe side. And she's very happy about winning. She's been going around kissing everyone.'

My tears came from nowhere. One was relieved, obviously. Frightful though Dorcas is, one wouldn't have wished her any harm. But she hardly merited tears.

Quincy said it was the shock. He said it makes people do weird things.

He said, 'You sure you don't want a pill? It might be a good idea to try and get some sleep till we dock.'

But I didn't want to sleep. Actually, I was roaringly hungry and could have demolished a plate of bacon and eggs though it didn't seem at all fitting to ask for it. Besides, on Arrival Day there's never much breakfast to be had.

I said, 'The storm seems to have passed. Perhaps I'll go up on deck.'

He looked at me.

I said, 'It's all right. I'm not going to throw myself into the water like a Hindu widow.'

371

'No,' he said. 'But you should still have somebody go with you. One of your friends? You've got a whole bunch of people waiting outside.'

I said, 'The Gleesons. Yes, I know. And the chaplain.'

'More than that,' he said. 'Loads of people.'

Chip and Cricket were there, and the four Kansas secretaries. Irene and Virginia, Mr and Mrs Polder, and even Myrtle from Surprise, Arizona, whom one had only ever spoken to once. There was one face I was strangely warmed to see. Don Harrington. Cricket started blubbing the instant she saw me.

Polder said, 'I do hope …'

And Virginia made a silent gesture of sympathy.

Nola said, 'You come with me, honey. Frankie's fixed it so we can stay in our suite till everybody's disembarked. You can be nice and private.'

I said, 'What I'd really like is a cup of coffee and a walk on deck. With a Gentleman Host.'

Don offered me his arm and we took the lift. They were serving cappuccino in paper cups at stations on all the outside decks. We stood and looked at the sea.

I said, 'Dorcas is all right. The nurse told me.'

He said. 'So I heard. I was on pins there for a bit.'

I said, 'You weren't the one who pushed her.'

'Maybe so,' he said, 'but it happened in my crib. She was waiting for me, you know? When I got back she was sitting on the bed. Only thing was, she couldn't remember how she got there.'

I said, 'I hope she doesn't suddenly remember.'

He said, 'I'm not going to lose sleep over that. And I'm sorry I was narky before. I know it wasn't your fault. Bloody Dorcas. She'd try the patience of a saint, that one.'

I said, 'She told me I look like a llama.'

He laughed.

He said, 'And you didn't whack her? You should have done.'

It's not what we do in our family. Poppa was the most patient person in the world. When he left Lowhope for the last time he didn't even slam the door. And once, when he and I had luncheon in town and I was lamenting the creeping influence of Bobbie Snape, he said, 'Eeny, don't be bitter. I'm glad Mumsie found happiness. It would have been too awful if she'd been left alone in that rotting heap while I'm enjoying daily golf in Palm Beach.'

I said, 'They think Bernard was washed overboard during the storm.'

'Yeah,' he said. 'I'm sorry.'

He stood behind me and wrapped his arms around me.

I said, 'He had things on his mind, you see. And I wanted to see the dancing, so I left him to it. I suppose he went up on deck to think, to get away from the noise of the parties.'

'Must have gone up before they closed the decks,' he said. 'I've done it myself. I love watching a big sea. It's one of those daft things you do.'

Not Bernard. How distracted must he have been to go out there in the wind and the rain, and without even his waterproof?

I said, 'Imagine being in the water and seeing your ship disappearing into the dark. All the lights blazing, music playing and you're all alone. Nobody can hear your cries for help.'

'Don't,' he said. 'Don't.'

The morning sea was like glass. A Turkish ferry passed us, going south.

I said, 'Do they usually find the bodies? When people are lost overboard?'

'Don't know, pet,' he said. 'Did the Purser get in touch with your family? So there'll be somebody to meet you? So you won't be on your own?'

I said, 'There isn't anyone really. A few cousins, but one never sees them. They'd think it very odd to be sent for. I'll be fine. The Gleesons have a water taxi organized so they're going to take me home in grand style. Funny. Bernard always longed for us to afford water taxis.'

Don said, 'I never did get to talk to him. He was always either striding along with his nose in the air or hiding in your cabin.'

I said, 'He wasn't a bad husband.'

'No,' he said. 'Course not.'

I said, 'He was very cultured and dashing and handsome.'

'Yes,' Don said. 'He was.'

374

Unfortunately it was all veneer. And once veneer starts to peel off it can look terribly sad and shabby.

He said, 'What do you think you'll do?'

Repent, that's what you'd better do first, Enid Nellish. Repent of taunting your husband with mysterious bouquets and anonymous notes. Repent of driving the silly man out onto a storm-swept ship's deck.

I said, 'Just go home, I suppose. Wait to see if they find Bernard's body. There are always things to do when one's been away. I'll keep busy.'

And at the earliest decent opportunity I'm going to catch the free bus to the Panorama shopping centre and buy myself a little computer. But that's not the kind of information a newly widowed woman shares.

I told Don the names of the bell towers as we slipped into Venice. San Pietro in Castello, gleaming white, San Francesco della Vigna with its towering spire, and tiny Sant'Isepo. San Antonin with its pretty bulb dome, San Giorgio dei Greci, which every year seems closer to falling into the canal. Canzian, Salvador, Apostoli, even Madonna dell'Orto, across on the northern edge of the city, with St Christopher standing on top, though he's too far away to make out. As we made the tight turn into the Giudecca Canal we dashed to the port side. San Giorgio Maggiore with an angel on his weather-vane, then clumsy, plain-Jane Zitelle, followed by triumphant Redentore with its twin minarets, and last of all the stocky little turret of Santa Eufemia, before we turned into the maritime station and dock. Home.

Then the stampede for disembarkation began. As we swung into our berth the Sanitrans boat sent for Dorcas nosed onto the dockside and Frankie and Nola's water taxi fussed around our stern like an excited dog.

I said, 'You'd better go. They've asked me to stay on board till everyone else has gone. Lest I prove to be such an object of macabre interest that I cause a traffic jam.'

'Oh yes,' he said. 'The rubbernecks'll be out in force. Poor old Bernard'll be something to tell the folks about when they get home.'

He gave me a hug.

'Take care then, Enid,' he said. 'You going to be all right up here on your own? Shall I tell your Gleeson pals where to find you?'

I said, 'No need. Nola and Frankie always know where to find people.'

He lingered a little, as though he shouldn't really leave me, as though I was just being fearfully brave.

I said, 'Go. Truly. I'm fine.'

He walked away, backwards.

I said, 'And thank you for the meat and potatoes.'

'My pleasure,' he shouted. 'And by the way, I like llamas.'

36

Nola's face was a picture when she saw our house in Corte Tagiapiera. *My* house. The outer door that sticks, the boot-hole full of rubber wellies, and then the steep narrow stairs. People assume one has Tiepolo frescoes everywhere and are rather astonished to see mildewed plaster and cracked ceilings. My neighbour, Mirella, had heard the American voices and was waiting at her kitchen window when I threw open the shutters. We *tutto-bene*'d each other.

Nola said, 'Aren't you going to tell her?'

I said, 'It didn't seem quite the moment.'

What does one say? My husband is lost at sea and now you must excuse me because I want to go to the Internet Point in the Crosera and send an email to my friend Billa.

Frankie said, 'The boat guy? Does he have the meter ticking?'

I said, 'This is Venice. There is no meter. He'll think of a figure and double it. You really should go. Please.'

Nola said, 'What, and leave you all alone?'

I said, 'I have so much to do I won't notice I'm all alone. Provisions to buy, calls to make, post to open.'

Including what looks like a cruise contract from Ocean Blue addressed to Professor *Sir* Bernard Finch. Four words and every one of them fake.

Nola said, 'I don't know. I don't think you should stay here tonight. Come with us to the hotel. Frankie'll get you a room.'

A room at the Cipriani, on Frankie Gleeson's account! I felt Bernard toss in his watery grave.

I said, 'Absolutely not. We'll have dinner one night. I'd like that. But being here on my own doesn't bother me.'

In a sense, Nola, I've been alone more often than not, even when Bernard was sitting across from me in that chair.

I did cry a little after they left. Less than twenty-four hours without Bernard and already the sting from his snapping and snarling had begun to fade. I found myself remembering moments of tenderness instead. The time we were caught in a snowstorm in Castel del Monte and he shared his loden green cloak with me. The time I had my wisdom teeth extracted and he went all the way to Canareggio to find me oil of cloves. One of the first things I unpacked was the meerschaum letter opener I'd bought for him in Istanbul. I'd picked it out so carefully and then I hadn't even given it to him.

I began to sort the laundry, opened Bernard's suitcase and closed it again immediately. The dead don't need clean shirts. I gave the geraniums a good, long drink, and watched a pair of lizards climbing the wall above Mirella's kitchen window. Then I telephoned Lowhope.

Bobbie answered. She always does. If it's a caravan-park enquiry and Mumsie were to answer there's every likelihood she'd frighten people off. Eventually I heard Mumsie shuffling to the phone in her sheepskin bootees.

I said, 'I wanted to speak to you before you read about Bernard in the papers.'

'Stopped getting them,' she said. 'They're full of rubbish and such a price. Why, what's he been up to?'

I said, 'He's missing. We were on a cruise ship. He was lecturing. And he went missing on the last night. He's lost at sea.'

Mumsie began relaying the news to Bobbie sentence by sentence.

I said, 'There was a storm and they think he must have been washed overboard. They're searching along the coast of Croatia but the chances are very slim. We have no idea what time it happened so the area he might be in is vast.'

'Sounds pretty hopeless,' she said. 'Will they send you a bill for the search?'

I said, 'I don't know. I didn't ask.'

She said, 'Well you should. You don't want them going around in pointless circles for days on end and landing you with an enormous bill.'

I said, 'Anyway we docked this morning. And now I'm back home, in Venice. Without Bernard.'

Silence.

I said, 'And that's it, really.'

She said, 'Dear me, Enid, this is going to cost you a pretty penny. Getting him declared dead. It can take years.'

I said, 'So I believe, but it doesn't matter. There's no hurry.'

'No,' she said, 'I suppose not. It's not as though he had any money.'

I said, 'How are you?'

'A1,' she said. 'Serenade Molly Malone won Best Terrier Bitch at Manchester.'

Another silence.

I said, 'Well, I just wanted to put you in the picture.'

She said, 'I imagine this is a horrendously costly phone call.'

One of the house dogs was barking.

She said, 'What will you do?'

I said, 'Nothing. I don't know. Billa Thoresby is flying out in a day or two anyway. She was coming for a holiday and I see no reason for her to cancel.'

'Good,' she said. 'Quite right. Billa Thoresby. You'll be glad to have someone cheerful around. I'd offer to come myself but it's such a difficult time. Serenade Lady Blaney is about to whelp and we're waiting for a new septic tank. We've had seepage.'

I said, 'And anyway, you'd need a passport.'

'Oh Lord,' she said, 'so I would. And that can take years.'

I said, 'And it's not as though there's anything to organize. One can't have a funeral because there's no body.'

She said, 'Well that will be a saving. I gather one doesn't see much change out of a thousand pounds these days.'

I said, 'Goodbye, Mumsie.'

'Goodbye dear,' she said. 'I'm very sorry for your troubles but chin up. Life goes on, et cetera. We Lunes are made of stern stuff. And perhaps you'll pop up to Lowhope now your time is your own.'

I heard Bobbie's voice, muffled.

Mumsie said, 'Although as Bobbie points out you may wish to wait until they've finished excavating for this damned tank. We're in quite a pickle.'

Nola called me practically every hour through the afternoon.

She said, 'I've been through it. I remember what it's like. When my Mitch had his heart attack I couldn't stay in the house. I went to my sister's place. It took me months to get over the shock.'

I said, 'I'd be glad to see you tomorrow, but tonight I really want to be alone.'

'OK, honey,' she said. 'Alone with your memories. I understand.'

I heard the *Golden Memories* sound its departure horn at six. If I'd chosen to I could have clambered up to our rickety *altana* and watched her smoke stack pass but I popped the cork on a bottle of prosecco instead, sat in Grandpa Lune's saggy old armchair and fell asleep. I dreamed I was guiding an enormous crowd of tourists among the ruins of Olympia and everyone was wearing a lifebelt. Then the scene changed to Lowhope and Bernard was there, being pushed in some sort of antique invalid carriage by Gavin Iles, and Bobbie Snape was breeding llamas.

I woke just before midnight with a crick in my neck. The prosecco had gone flat and I'd had nothing to eat all day. I caught Pizza-al-Volo just before they closed.

Billa came in on an extremely late flight to Treviso on Thursday. Piazzale Roma was quite deserted by the time her bus pulled in and she climbed out squealing, 'Quel adventure, Eeny! Do you know, one had to pay for one's luggage *and* pay for one's booze! I quite expected one would be asked to take a turn at pedalling or flapping the wings or however it is they keep the thing in the air.'

We didn't go to bed. There was so much to talk about.

'Well?' she said. 'Did he jump or was he pushed?'

I said, 'Actually, I think it was an accident. But in a sense he was pushed. I was quite hateful to him those last few days.'

'Such tosh,' she said. 'He'd been an idiot and a bounder. You're better off without him.'

That's what people will say now, among themselves if not to my face. I know they're right. It's just that his presence was so enormous I feel I have to learn everything anew. Like

382

learning to walk again after losing a leg. There were things I always left him to do, like circulating at parties. And there were all those things I felt obliged to do for him: lunch on the table at one thirty sharp; driving him to Heathrow so he could fly off on his various academic jollies; settling his account at Hatchard's, no questions asked.

Billa is making me sort out his personal effects. She says it's like ripping off an Elastoplast, best done quickly and by someone else. Such beautiful things though. Italian suits, silk bow ties, good English shoes. She sent me out for cigarettes and fresh supplies of Bardolino and by the time I returned everything was in black plastic sacks, ready to go to the charity bins.

She said, 'Onward and upward, Eeny. This room is wasted as a study. It would make an excellent bedroom for a paying guest. Think of it, darling. Lots of lovely lolly coming in without your having to vacate the premises and lock away the silver spoons. Better still, you could make this *your* room and let the double. Assuming you're not going to rush into another liaison and honestly, if I were you I wouldn't.'

Things with Laurence aren't panning out very satisfactorily. Since Billa completed her work on his chateau his interest in her appears to have cooled and all talk of weddings has ceased. His mother seems to be a significant factor.

Billa said, 'Take my advice. Confine yourself to cruise-ship flingettes.'

I begin to regret telling her about Don Harrington. She's

built up an image of him as a bronzed Lothario and keeps asking for further details, but there are none she would understand. And allowing her to meet Frankie and Nola Gleeson was such a mistake. It was their last day in Venice and they had really seen nothing of the city, devoting their time to me and running up heaven knows what expenses for water taxis. They had been so kind. But Billa thought them a pair of frights.

She said, 'You're their tame English aristo, darling, like an exhibit in a zoo. They'll be over every year, mark my words. She'll be poking those ring-laden fingers through the bars of your little Venetian cage.'

I think Billa is somewhat shocked by the modest size of my house.

She said, 'You'll never be rid of them. And they'll send all their friends and relations too.'

But I don't want to be rid of them. They're such comfortable, generous people. I may even visit them in Horseheads. Frankie can give me a guided tour of Painted Post and I'll take some flowers to poor old Charlie Fink's grave. It's not as though I can take any for Bernard.

I've been glad of Billa, though, in spite of the way she tends to thunder through one's life like the Royal Horse Artillery. She whistles and sings and is perfectly happy to live on red wine and slices of Sachertorte from Tonolo. She also initiated me into the art of sending messages from my lovely new mobile telephone, though I waited until she was tucked up for the night before I sent the message I'd been longing to send.

Thnk u 4 meat & pots. Llama.

A reply came buzzing through in no time at all.

Seconds? Xx Gent. Host.

37

The memorial service for Bernard was held at St Peter's, Eaton Square. Cousin Andrew drove the Lune contingent there and back in a day. It's very difficult to get people in to feed the dogs. Mumsie brought a splash of colour to the proceedings in a scarlet windcheater, five pounds from Age Concern in Carnforth.

Bobbie Snape was arrayed in Poppa's old Henry Poole Harris tweed which, I may say, is wearing extremely well.

There was a splendid turnout, particularly from overseas. Bog Stevovic, Pippo Vlachos, Gaetano Borin, Tsampi Karagiannis. Mumsie was very taken with Tsampi and issued an open invitation for him to visit Lowhope at the earliest opportunity.

I said, 'You're highly favoured. The rest of the world has been told to stay away pending a new septic tank. But anyway, don't think of accepting. The beds are damp and they live on canned soup.'

'Dear Enid,' he said. 'I can't believe this sad, sad day. Let me give you hug. I'm surprised Leontis didn't come. He was such big friend of our Bernard.'

Stash Leontis has been silent though I'm quite sure he got my note. I sent it to both his addresses.

I said, 'Well, people are busy. It really doesn't matter.'

'People *are* busy,' he said, 'but not Leontis. He never does a damn thing, only sits puffing little black cigarettes telling everybody else what they must do.'

I said, 'He hates me. I expect that's why he didn't come. He always felt I'd dragged Bernard away from the life he should have been living.'

'Nonsense,' he said. 'You were best thing for Bernard. When he was in Rome, eh, with Clifford Dennis, he was like little puppy dog. Run here, go there, yes, Clifford, no, Clifford. You make man of him. You take care now. You come visit us at Villa Petaloudi, eh? Any time.'

As she was leaving Mumsie said, 'It was a very pleasant service. Very appropriate. Well, best foot forward, dear. My advice is not to sit around moping. Get involved in something. You know, if you weren't always gallivanting you could get yourself a little dog.'

I caught an early flight back to Venice. It was a perfect, crisp blue sky day, more like October than November. The telephone was ringing as I came through the door.

'Enid?'

I knew the voice. Stash Leontis.

I said, 'You missed Bernard's memorial service. It was yesterday.'

'Yes,' he said, 'I know. I couldn't come. You alone?'

I said, 'Yes.'

'Good,' he said. 'Because now we must talk. Now is time to do something, to send money. I give you address.'

I said, 'What are you talking about?'

'Bernard,' he said. 'Fucking Bernard. I had him four months. Is enough. Now you must send money, so he can get little place. Not Rome, somebody will recognize him. Maybe Naples. Maybe Athens.'

I said, 'Stash, Bernard is dead.'

'Sure,' he said. 'OK. He's dead. You tell him.'

My legs had turned to water. I had to steady myself against the sink. Mirella was pulling in her string bag of mozzarella from the hook outside her kitchen window, starting to make lunch. We waved. Then I heard his breathing.

'Enid,' he said. Resigned. 'I fear I owe you an explanation.'

I said, 'I don't think the dead owe anyone anything.'

He said, 'Look. I realize it was an impetuous thing to do but at the time it seemed to make sense. There was that whole Cornell mix-up.'

I said, 'It wasn't a mix-up. It was a lie.'

He said, 'I concede I may have acted rather rashly but as a matter of fact I'm pretty certain I'd had an adverse reaction to whatever medication it was that so-called nurse gave me. I don't think I can be held entirely responsible for my actions. And the last thing I wanted was all this fuss.'

The last thing you wanted and the last thing you get.

I didn't answer.

He said, 'You're shocked, naturally. But please remember what I was going through, Enid. I had that bastard Gleeson hounding me, sending flowers, pushing notes under the cabin door.'

I said, 'Actually, that was me. I made up the limerick, and the clerihew. I was trying to dig you out of a hole. I was pushing you to confess all and make a clean breast of it, but you damned well wouldn't. You just piled lies on top of lies. And now it turns out even your death was a lie.'

It was his turn to be silent.

I said, 'The hideous flowers were from me too. I sent them out of sheer mischief. You were horrid to me on that cruise, Bernard. You were perfectly beastly.'

He said, 'I'm sorry. That's all I can say. And I'm determined to make amends. We can start anew. Buy a little place where no one knows us. Slovenia is very lovely. But in the meanwhile I need to lie low. And I am in rather urgent need of funds.'

I said, 'Don't talk to me about Slovenia. Where the hell were you?'

'In the bilge,' he said, 'moving from place to place to avoid detection. One of the boys down there helped me out.

One of the oilers. Well, I paid him a little something, obviously.'

He had stayed aboard the *Golden Memories* until she sailed again. Shaved his head, allowed his beard to grow and walked ashore wearing an Oyster Line T-shirt and a nautical cap when they docked at Civitavecchia.

'Thence by train to Bari,' he said. 'A ferry to Igoumenitsa and a bus to Athens. I've been staying with Stash but now the hue and cry has died down I think it would be a good plan to move on. Obviously one will have to rethink the future. Take a new identity.'

I said, 'Try Wislaw Fink.'

A mirthless laugh.

He said, 'You can pack up my things, as though intending to dispose of them, and then ship them to me as soon as I have an address.'

I said, 'I anticipated you. I packed up your clothes weeks ago.'

'Good girl,' he said.

I said, 'Yes. They're now being worn by various grateful Moldovan guest-workers. A happy thought.'

He said, 'You gave away my clothes?'

I said, 'You drowned, Bernard. In high seas off the coast of Croatia, after a week of increasingly bizarre behaviour. The ship was stopped and searched. You weren't found. You're dead. And Gaetano Borin gave the eulogy at your memorial service yesterday.'

'Well then, my books?' he said.

'Donated to the university.'

'Not my books!' he cried. 'Why were you so hasty? No. I'm sorry. I have no right. You're in shock. Of course you are. It never occurred to you. You're too innocent to have imagined such a thing. But don't worry. You can simply tell Ca Foscari you've changed your mind about the books. Say they're of sentimental value and you disposed of them with undue haste. They'll understand. And the clothes hardly matter. If you could send me a few thousand, care of Stash, I'll start afresh.'

I said, 'Yes, a very good idea. Start afresh. A new name, new shirts. Stash can take up a collection from some of those wealthy boys he drinks with on Mykonos. But I'm afraid I have nothing to spare. We widows have to watch our pennies.'

A change of tone. An edge.

'But Enid,' he said, 'now we *both* know you're not a widow after all.'

I said, 'You're right. It's called complicity. And as you know, I'm a law-abiding sort. I could never live with that. I'm going away. I'm leaving on a trip next week and I'll be gone until January. That gives you time to go to the police and declare yourself. Otherwise I shall simply have to do it myself when I get back. But much better if it comes from you. People have more sympathy for a person who summons the courage to own up than they do for someone who stays down his rat hole and hopes to get away with it, don't you agree?'

'A trip?' he said. 'What trip?'

I said, 'Oh, quite a marathon. First I'm going to Leeds, of all places, for a weekend of meat and potatoes. Then I'm flying to Florida to visit my half-brother, Ripley, and meeting up with the Gleesons in Miami. We're taking a Murder Mystery cruise to the Leeward Islands and after that I'll go back with them to Horseheads for Christmas.'

'Enid!' he cried. 'I'm begging you!'

I said, 'Goodbye, Bernard.'

It was the hardest moment. If I wavered at all, it was then, but the pang soon passed. Bernard ensured that.

'Gaetano's eulogy?' he said. 'What did he say, exactly?'

I said, 'He described you as a man of many parts.'

He said, 'Was that all?'

I said, 'No. He also said it's widely known that the cure for any ill is salt water. Sometimes it takes tears, sometimes sweat, sometimes just being at sea.'